WHEN I SAID TH
TO KILL M

I didn't mean the shooting incident.

We left Aunt Eileen's with Ari at the wheel and drove down Silver Avenue to Alemany, where he cut off three drivers in fast traffic and swerved violently into the left lane. In a blare of horns we turned off onto a side street. Eventually, we reached O'Shaughnessy. This particularly long street runs along the edge of a shallow valley called, with a profound lack of imagination, O'Shaughnessy Hollow. A steep dropoff falls down to high grass studded with nasty looking rocks, on your right if you're traveling uphill, which we were.

Ari had just swerved around another car when I saw a truck barreling toward us in the wrong lane, our lane.

I screamed before I could choke it back. Between perception and rational thought lies a dangerous interval. Ari kept going at top speed and drove right through the false image.

"What did you see?" he remarked. "Something ghastly, I suppose."

"A semi in the wrong lane." My pounding heart began to slow down. "Sorry about the shrieking."

Ari laid on the horn and swung around a white sedan that was traveling too slowly for his taste. My heart sped up again, especially when I looked into the rearview mirror and saw a police car, lights flashing, trying to pull us over. I said nothing. It vanished. What would have happened, I wondered, if I'd been driving and stopped? Who might have appeared for real to work a little mayhem?

A third illusion followed later. We'd turned onto Sloat Boulevard out in the avenues when I saw flashing lights, flares, and what appeared to be a six-car pileup ahead.

"Do you see that accident?" I said to Ari.

"No. Is there one?"

"Not if you can't see it."

He drove straight on and passed right through the shadowy cars and flares.

KATHARINE KERR

LOVE ON THE RUN

A NOLA O'GRADY NOVEL

DAW BOOKS, INC.
DONALD A. WOLLHEIM, FOUNDER
375 Hudson Street, New York, NY 10014

ELIZABETH R. WOLLHEIM
SHEILA E. GILBERT
PUBLISHERS
www.dawbooks.com

First Printing, August 2012
1 2 3 4 5 6 7 8 9

For my three nieces
Rebecca, Katherine, & Rhiannon.
Amazing women, all of them!

Acknowledgments

Many thanks to all the friends who helped make this a better book! Alis, Darcy, Megan, Jo, Jan, Trevor, Madeleine, Berry, Karen, and Cliff—I very much appreciate all your feedback.

CHAPTER I

ON THE SUNDAY that my boyfriend and I announced our engagement, some unromantic soul tried to kill me.

When my aunt, Eileen O'Brien Houlihan, found out that Ari had bought me a ring, she insisted on throwing a party at her house in San Francisco's Excelsior district. In my family, a party means food, in this case a backyard barbeque and a double-length picnic table buffet. I'm one of seven kids, and so's my aunt, so you can imagine how many people showed up. By nightfall, most of the family—now overstuffed—had drifted off homeward. My older sister Maureen and I stayed to catch up on gossip. I hadn't seen her in almost two years.

By the light of a string of tasseled paper lanterns, I was giving her a close look at the gold-and-sapphire engagement ring when I heard a bang. Something whizzed past me like a very fast bee or very large mosquito. On the buffet table the crystal punch bowl exploded.

"Down!" my fiancé yelled. "Everybody!"

The female relatives screamed. I grabbed Maureen and

pulled her to the grassy ground just as a second shot whined over us. Ari dodged behind the thick, gnarled trunk of the ancient apple tree and drew his Beretta from its shoulder holster.

"Police!" he called out. "Drop your weapon and come forward!"

I heard rustling in the neighbor's shrubbery. A light went on in their window. Ari fired a shot into the ground. A man yelped in fear. The neighbor woman shrieked. More rustling, then running footsteps—at the sound Ari left shelter and raced down the length of the fence, yelling, "Police! Stop!" all the way until he fetched up against the locked gate in the tall safety fence.

Ari swore in Hebrew and tried to shove the gate open. Whoever it was kept running. A motorcycle revved up and sped away. I ran a fast Search Mode: Danger.

"He's gone," I called out.

There are times when being a psychic in a family of psychics has its rewards. Everyone believed me. They all began talking at once, more outraged than frightened. Ari strode over to join me.

"Nola," Ari said, "take everyone into the house. The sodding bastard might come back." He learned his English in London, and he sounds middle-class British. In case you haven't guessed, he's also a police officer—with Interpol to be precise. I got up and helped a trembling Maureen to her feet. Maureen's two children, Brennan and Caitlin, rushed over. She gathered them into her maternal grasp. Brennan, just turned seven, squirmed out of it again.

"Aunt Nola?" Brennan said. "Were those real bullets?"

"Sure were," I said.

"I bet it was Chuck," Caitlin, the nine-year-old, said. "He's a creep."

Chuck was Maureen's ex-boyfriend, a drug dealer, and, I'm glad to say, not the children's father.

"We don't know it was him," Maureen's voice shook. "I hope not."

"Let's all go inside." I spoke as firmly and calmly as I could. "Everyone, stay away from the windows."

Between us, Ari and I managed to herd the relatives inside. Uncle Jim had already called 911 on his cell phone, but Ari put in a separate call to the police in his official capacity. After Aunt Eileen closed all the drapes in the living room, Maureen distracted the kids by turning on the TV. The teenagers who lived with the Houlihans—their son Brian, my brother Michael, and his girlfriend, Sophie—joined them. Maureen stayed with the kids while the remaining adults— Ari, Aunt Eileen, Uncle Jim, and I—huddled in the kitchen. Uncle Jim went straight to the counter by the sink and poured himself a juice glass full of whiskey. The rest of us sat down at the round maple table.

"I suppose this has something to do with that lousy job of yours." Uncle Jim saluted me with his glass.

"Probably," I said. "Being a federal agent does have a few drawbacks."

My name is Nola O'Grady. I work for a government agency so secret that you won't find it listed on any Web site or Washington directory. Two State Department officials act as our liaison to the security apparatus as a whole. The CIA, the FBI—they'd never accept as real the threats we agents battle with our various psychic talents. The forces of unbridled Chaos threaten our civilization, just as the masters of Chaos threaten civilizations throughout the multiverse. My agency's job: stop them wherever we find them.

I'm the head of the San Francisco bureau, the Apocalypse Squad, as they refer to us back in DC. Ari Nathan, my fiancé, is technically my bodyguard and officially an Interpol officer, but he's also an Israeli national who works for a mysterious agency of his own. This makes him a seconded officer, as Interpol calls them. Besides Ari, I have several full-time operatives on staff and one part-timer, my younger brother Michael. For complex reasons, my entire family carries the genes for a variety of psychic talent. Most know how to use them. The Agency would love to hire more of my relatives, but I'd prefer that they stayed away from danger. Obviously, considering the end of my engagement party, danger often comes to us.

Uncle Jim had barely sipped from his glass of whiskey when we heard sirens blaring up the hill. As the squad cars squealed to a stop out on the street, Ari got up and ran into the living room to open the front door. I hurried down the long, oddly angled hallway after him. Ari stepped out onto the front porch to meet the officers. The crowd in front of the TV looked up.

"That had better go off," I said. "Sorry, kids. How about going upstairs?"

My brother Michael stood up. "Come on," he said to the children. "You can play a game on my computer."

The kids made a rush for the staircase. The three teens followed more slowly. Maureen turned off the TV and gave Michael a grin of thanks as he walked by. She and I stayed downstairs to talk with the police. I could hear Ari explaining the situation out on the front porch. Eventually, he came back inside, followed by two beefy officers. They paused just inside the door and looked around the long white living room. I noticed that the Hispanic guy had a quick smile for the portrait that hung on the wall down at one end of the room: my uncle, Father Keith O'Brien, in his Franciscan robes. The white guy was more interested in sizing up me and Maureen.

"The second pair of officers are going next door," Ari told me. "And Sanchez is on his way. The department called him at home."

"Poor guy!" I turned to Maureen. "Detective-Lieutenant Sanchez of Homicide. We've worked with him before."

The two cops followed Ari back down the hall and outside to look over "the scene," as they called it. I heard Uncle
Jim's voice bellowing, then fading—I could guess that he
went out with them. Aunt Eileen came into the living room
to join us. She'd taken off her party shoes and put on her
favorite pink bunny slippers. Somehow, they went with her
black toreador capris and vintage Fifties pink blouse.

As usual, the family gathered at the end of the room that
housed some comfortable chairs, the TV, and scatter rugs to
keep snacks off the white carpet. At the other end, an
orangey-gold brocade sectional sofa stood under the portrait of Father Keith. I'd never seen anyone sit on its shiny-
clean upholstery.

"I'm so glad no one was hurt." Aunt Eileen paused to
tuck a lock of her gray hair behind one ear. "It's a good
thing we'd already cleared off most of the food. There were
bits of glass flying everywhere, and I'll have to throw the
rest of the fruit salad out, just in case some of the splinters
ended up there. Once the police are done, of course."

"Yeah," Maureen put in. "They won't want anything
touched."

Aunt Eileen nodded her agreement. "I'll admit to being
sick about losing that Waterford punch bowl. I was planning
on giving it to you, Nola, when the wedding comes round."

I arranged a solemn expression. I had no intention of
ever marrying Ari or anyone else, for that matter. In my
line of work, it's best to avoid legal entanglements, especially with foreign nationals. Ari knew how I felt. We'd
staged our so-called engagement to keep the unlapsed
Catholic members of my family from nagging us about our
living together. At least, I hoped that Ari wasn't secretly
plotting marriage. I glanced at my left hand and the ring, a
simple gold band set with a marquise-cut sapphire that
must have cost him several thousand bucks, judging from
its size.

"It's such a deep blue," Maureen said wistfully. "Really lovely."

"Have you thought about the date yet?" Eileen said. "For the wedding, I mean."

I was saved from answering by my cellphone, which rang in my shirt pocket.

"That'll be Dad." I took the phone out.

"Yeah," Maureen said. "It's him."

I clicked the phone on and answered.

"What's going on over there?" Dad said. "I picked up something dangerous."

We call this "mental overlap" in the family.

"Someone took a shot at either me or Maureen," I said. "Out in the backyard."

"That bastard ex-boyfriend of hers, I bet. I'll be right over."

"You don't want to. The house is crawling with cops."

I heard him sigh. Since he'd gotten out of prison only a few weeks previously, being around police officers other than Ari gave him the creeps.

"But if you need me," Dad went on, "I can manage."

"No, it's okay, really. Ari's got everything under control."

Dad snorted, but it was a pleasant snort. "He usually does. All right, then, darling. But call me later and let your mother and me know what happened. I'll want to know that you're all safe."

Dad's comment about Maureen's unpleasant ex reinforced what Caitlin had said earlier. The problem was that Maureen and I look a lot alike. Pretty much everyone in my family shares a look: black hair with a slight wave, dark blue eyes, the typical tilted Irish nose, thin lips, and decent cheekbones. I'm something of an exception in that my eyes are hazel; witch eyes, we call them. While none of us are particularly short, none of us are particularly tall, either. Maureen and I had been standing together under a Japanese lantern lit by a white Christmas tree bulb, that is, in poor light. As far as I could tell, the bullets had passed between us. The shooter could have been aiming at either of us.

Ari had reached the same conclusion, it turned out, when he and the two patrol officers returned to the living room. I got a good look at their name tags when they walked over to study the family group.

"You're right," Officer Ruiz said to Ari. "They do look like twins, not just sisters."

Officer Owens nodded his agreement. "Miss O'Grady," he said to Maureen. "Your current companion is named Chuck Trasker. Correct?"

"No," she snapped. "That's his name, but I don't have anything to do with him anymore. I broke up with him two weeks ago now."

"That's what Inspector Nathan told us. Just confirming it," Owens said. "And you and your children are living with your parents?"

"Until I find a new job, yes. It's too far to commute to the old one."

If you've watched them on TV, you'll think that police investigations are interesting, maybe even thrilling. Well, no. The two patrol officers asked me and Maureen questions. The cops from the second squad car finished with the neighbors and came inside to stand around and listen. Aunt Eileen went into the kitchen, then returned. The Forensics team arrived, and everyone official, including Ari, trooped out back again. Maureen took the chance to run upstairs and check on the kids.

"Where's Uncle Jim?" I asked Aunt Eileen.

"In his study. There's a baseball game on TV."

"Good. Keeps him out of trouble." I paused, listening. "Someone's coming up the front steps."

The someone turned out to be Lieutenant Sanchez of the Homicide squad. A tall man, with dark eyes that reminded me of birds of prey, he had a bristling mustache and thick black hair. He was wearing his trademark navy blue suit.

"No one's been killed," I said. "I'm surprised they bothered you at home."

"Let's not play games, O'Grady," Sanchez said. "You know why I'm here."

I did. Sanchez knew I worked for a government agency. He merely didn't know which one. I have ID from a well-known bureau that I can show around as necessary. While I don't belong to them, the ID's not exactly fake, because they know I have it. Sanchez disliked the idea of seeing a federal agent murdered in his territory. It would definitely have made the San Francisco police look bad.

"Where's Nathan?" Sanchez continued.

"Out in back with Forensics. Come on, I'll show you."

I took Sanchez out back to the scene. Someone, probably Aunt Eileen, had turned on the back porch light to supplement the Japanese lanterns. A member of the Forensics team stood on the far side of the picnic table and directed the beam of a powerful police-issue flashlight onto the shards of the crystal punch bowl while an investigator picked through the ruins. Sanchez trotted over to talk with the team leader. Ari left the group and came over to stand next to me.

"They find anything?" I said.

"The bullets. The second shot lodged in the fence. They're photographing everything to get some idea of the angle of incidence."

"What about the neighbor? The one who turned on the light and screamed. Did she have anything to add?"

"Quite a lot of hysterical outburst. Nothing I'd call useful." He smiled with a little twist of his mouth. "Forensics will be going over to her yard next to take more pictures. It's fairly obvious where the fellow got in, and where he crouched in the shrubbery. She really should get a safety gate between her and the street."

"I bet she does after this. She'll probably call a contractor first thing in the morning."

"Good. By the way, the first officers here put out an all-points for that motorcycle. I don't suppose they'll bring him in, but they'll try."

I returned to the living room to wait some more. Finally, after an hour or so, all the police left but Sanchez. He lingered for a moment on the front porch to fill Ari and me in.

"We're putting out a warrant for this Trasker guy. O'Grady, your sister is pretty sure he was dealing drugs. Meth, probably. They were living out in Livermore, and the suburbs are full of housewives snorting crystal meth to lose weight." Sanchez rolled his eyes in disgust. "He's threatened her life and threatened the children, so she needs to get a lawyer, come to court, and get a restraining order put on the SOB."

"How seriously does your department take those?" Ari said.

Sanchez shrugged. "I don't know anything about domestic violence cases. I can find out for you."

"I'd appreciate it," Ari said. "She is my sister-in-law, or will be shortly."

My stomach clenched in sheer terror. Restraining orders only work when someone respects the law. Chuck didn't. Maureen had told me that he used his own illegal substances, and methedrine does not a level head make.

"You think the shooter was Trasker?" I said.

"He's a likely suspect," Sanchez said. "Who do you think the intended victim was?"

"I don't know. He was such a bad shot that we were both in danger."

Sanchez laughed with one wry bark. "Be glad he was. If he was a sure shot like Nathan here, you'd both be dead."

On that happy note he left.

If the shooter had been aiming for me, I had a list of possible suspects, but how could I have given it to Sanchez? The possibilities included: 1) a member of an alien species evolved from leopards who lived on a deviant level of the multiverse; 2) the human ally of a gang of criminal psychic squid from an alternate Venus; 3) a minion of the Chaos masters that my agency's sworn to oppose—species to be determined later. Better that the police blamed Chuck the Scum, who needed to be taken off the streets whether he'd fired the shots or not.

Ari went to talk with Uncle Jim while I returned to the living room and Maureen. I sat down in the chair next to hers just as Sophie came downstairs. She told us that she was going to help Aunt Eileen clean up the kitchen.

"That's good of you," Maureen said. "I should help, too."

"No, it's okay. I like helping." Sophie glanced my way. "You've all done so much for me."

I merely smiled for an answer. Maureen didn't need to know that Aunt Eileen and Michael had rescued Sophie from a life on the streets as a prostitute—not that Michael's motives were pure. You can't expect purity from a seventeen-year-old boy.

"The kids are okay," Sophie continued. "They're playing some game where you collect jewels."

"Sounds good," Maureen said. "I'll stay here, then. I want to talk to Nola."

Sophie trotted off toward the kitchen. I waited until she'd gotten out of earshot.

"Mo," I said, "did you really tell the cops about Chuck's dealing?"

"You bet I did. I figured they'll arrest him and keep him away from us."

"They will if they can find him. But in the meantime, if he finds you, you've just put yourself in a lot of danger."

"I'm already in a lot of danger." Her voice dropped to a frightened whisper. "Nola, he said he'd kill me for leaving him, and I believe him. He wasn't just bluffing." She paused to gulp for breath. "Besides, how's he going to find out? That I was the informer, I mean."

"Who else?"

"His damned druggie partners, maybe. He owes them a lot of money."

"Oh, good! Maybe they'll off him and get rid of him for us."

"As long as they don't come after me for the cash."

"Crud! Mo, look, we may have to get you into a witness protection program."

"Maybe so." Her voice squeaked as it ran into tears. "I don't know what I ever saw in him. I didn't know he was so into drugs when we got together. Really I didn't." She fished a Kleenex out of her skirt pocket and wiped her eyes. "Those protection programs—I'd have to move somewhere away from here, away from all of you guys. I want to be close to the family."

"Well, as our Aunt Rose says, we'll burn that bridge when we're crossing it."

Maureen managed to smile.

"Let's get you and the kids home for tonight, anyway," I said. "In the morning Mom will find you a lawyer, and you can get that restraining order on the record."

I phoned my father and gave him the all clear. At that time he and my mother were living in a big flat up on Diamond Heights, a neighborhood of condos and apartment blocks on the southeast flank of Twin Peaks, maybe fifteen minutes away from Aunt Eileen's by car. Dad arrived a bare couple of minutes after I called him, because he's what we call a "fast walker," that is, he can shorten any journey by what amounts to teleportation. He can also bring others with him on these jaunts. Although he's not precisely sure how the process works, he's been told that he can "generate a field" that does the carrying.

"I thought I'd best take Maureen and the kids home the direct way," he told me. "That bastard Chuck might be laying for her somewhere near the flat. He must know what her car looks like. I don't want to drive up and have him fill the thing full of bullets."

"Good thought," I said. "She can pick it up tomorrow."

"No, I'll pick it up tomorrow. When it's light, and Chuck can see who's driving."

Maureen called up the staircase to the children. When they refused to leave their game, she had to go up to fetch them. Michael solved the problem by turning off his computer, and everyone trooped down again. The August night had turned chilly with the usual summer fog. Maureen got the kids into jackets and accepted a sack of leftovers from Aunt Eileen.

"Is Ben going to shoot at the car?" Caitlin asked.

"No," Dad answered. "We're not going by car."

Brennan wrinkled his nose. "The bus?" he said.

"No," Maureen said. "Granddad is magic. You'll see." She glanced my way. "They've gotten the family lecture, of course, the one about keeping secrets."

"Lots of times." Caitlin laid her hand over her heart. "What's family stays in the family."

"We saw that on TV," Brennan put in. "About some dumb city somewhere. Granddad, are you really magic?"

"Yes." Dad winked at Maureen. "And I'm about to show you a trick, so you'll know it's true."

"I'll call you tomorrow, Mo," I said. "Hang in there!"

As they left the house, the kids each took one of Dad's hands, and Maureen followed close behind him. About halfway down the front steps to the street, they all disappeared in a shimmer of pale blue light, that mysterious field, I supposed, that he generated.

"It really is useful to have Flann back," Aunt Eileen said

as she shut the front door. "And your mother's certainly much more pleasant to have around now that he's home."

"That's for sure. I've seen her twice in two weeks, and we haven't had a fight yet."

There remained the problem of getting me home safely. Ari and I lived on the opposite side of San Francisco, out in the fog belt of the Sunset district close to the ocean. We had a heavily modified car that his mysterious agency had supplied. It looked like an ordinary Saturn, but it carried armor under its plastic shell and had a few other distinctive features as well. It could outrun and outmaneuver any assassin on a motorcycle.

The difficulty came down to the driver. Ari is Israeli. He drives like an Israeli—no, that's not fair to most Israelis. Make that "like the macho Israeli guy he is." Until recently, I'd done all the driving rather than risk death from friendly fire every time we got into the car. Unfortunately, a few weeks earlier someone had thrown an illusion into the path of the car. Had we been in traffic at the time, I would have swerved into a nasty accident. Ari does not see psychic illusions. Ari, in fact, can be absolutely dense about psychic anythings, which in this case proved to be a definite plus.

When I said that someone tried to kill me that night, I didn't mean the shooting incident.

We left Aunt Eileen's with him at the wheel and drove down Silver Avenue to Alemany, where he cut off three drivers in fast traffic and swerved violently into the left lane. In a blare of horns we turned off onto a side street. Eventually, we reached O'Shaughnessy, which would take us across Twin Peaks and out to the western edge of the city where we lived. This particularly long street runs along the edge of a shallow valley called, with a profound lack of imagination, O'Shaughnessy Hollow. A steep drop-off falls down to high grass studded with nasty looking rocks, on your right if you're traveling uphill, which we were.

Ari had just swerved around another car when I saw a truck barreling toward us in the wrong lane, our lane. I screamed before I could choke it back. Between perception and rational thought lies a dangerous interval. Ari kept going at top speed and drove right through the false image.

"What did you see?" he remarked. "Something ghastly, I suppose."

"A semi in the wrong lane." My pounding heart began to slow down. "Sorry about the shrieking."

Ari laid on the horn and swung around a white sedan that was traveling too slowly for his taste. My heart sped up again, especially when I looked into the rearview mirror and saw a police car, lights flashing, trying to pull us over. I said nothing. It vanished. What would have happened, I wondered, if I'd been driving and stopped? Who might have appeared for real to work a little mayhem?

A third illusion followed later. We'd turned onto Sloat Boulevard out in the avenues when I saw flashing lights, flares, and what appeared to be a six-car pileup ahead.

"Do you see that accident?" I said to Ari.

"No. Is there one?"

"Not if you can't see it."

He drove straight on and passed right through the shadowy cars and flares. I turned to look back and saw nothing but empty street.

Despite the excitement we reached home safely. When we'd been looking for a place to live, we'd had two requirements, a location close to the ocean and a building that we could occupy without putting other people in danger. Since most houses and apartment buildings out near the beach stand cheek by jowl in solid rows, we'd been lucky to find an anomaly: a building with a wide driveway on either side and an even wider empty space around back. It housed a pair of flats over a garage, which meant our front door stood at the top of a stairwell and thus was more secure than one opening onto the street. The building was an ugly example of local architecture—a stucco shoebox stuck on end would sum it up—but we could live in the top flat and leave the bottom one empty as a buffer zone between us and whoever might want to break and enter. If someone did firebomb or shoot up the place, the neighbors would remain reasonably safe.

As a further precaution, Ari had installed a high-tech security system with the help of an old friend of his, a guy named Itzak Stein. We parked across the street from the building and sat in the car for a few minutes while we each ran a security check in our own way. He used his special smartphone to get a report on the technical system, and I ran a psychic Search Mode: Location. Both readings came up clear.

"No more illusions, I should hope?" Ari said.

"None so far."

"That illusion of a lorry you saw on the way home. If you'd been at the wheel, you might have pulled right off the road and over the edge of that drop-off. Should we bundle it with the first attempt on your life, or do you think it's a separate occurrence?"

"I'd vote for a separate attempt. That shooter probably was Maureen's Unpleasant Ex. The attacks on me tend to be subtle. Chuck's a basic type. A club would probably be his weapon of choice, but in the modern world a gun will do."

"Good point. Of course, you might have two different enemies trying to kill you."

"What a lovely thought! But you're right. Let's hope not."

"Hope's not enough. I don't intend to take any chances. We'll just put the security system on high alert tonight."

"Good idea." I considered possibilities. "I don't suppose whoever sent the illusion wanted to kill you, and I was just incidental to the plan."

"Anyone who wanted to kill me would use a gun, not this

psychic—" He hesitated. "Let's just say, these overcompli-
cated methods."

"Psychic bullshit, you mean."

Rather than answer, Ari started the car and turned into
the driveway. As he did so, the headlights swept across the
front wall of the flats, a large pale blue stucco surface beloved
by the local graffiti artists. Someone had spray-painted a couple of four-letter words while we'd been gone, but the wall
was otherwise clear.

We put the car into the garage and went upstairs to our
typical San Francisco railroad flat: a living room with oblig-
atory bay window at the front, and at the rear, a long hallway with the other rooms opening directly off it. We had a
mismatched collection of furniture: an old blue couch, a
couple of overly modern wooden armchairs with burgundy
leather seats and back cushions, and a coffee table, all set
around a beat-up Persian carpet. Opposite the couch stood
a bookcase and a stand for the TV. In one corner I kept my
computer, linked to a specially scrambled DSL line.

Ari turned on the floor lamp that stood at the end of the
couch. He took off his jacket and tossed it onto the coffee
table, then lifted his arms over his head and stretched out his
back. I admired the display. He's not movie-star handsome,
but he's macho gorgeous, to my way of thinking anyway. He
has dark, curly hair and deep, dark eyes that remind me of a
Byzantine icon. He also works out a lot, and it shows. I
glanced at the clock: a little early to go to bed, maybe.

"I really should see if there's any e-mail from the
Agency," I said. "I hope Seymour's gotten his butt in gear.
That vision I had keeps nagging at me, and I need him to
interpret it."

"Which vision? You have so many."

"The one about the possible end of a world. The one
with the corpses."

"Oh. That vision."

"Not a happy one."

"Do you ever have happy visions?"

"No. Sorry."

Ari sighed and strode out of the room. I heard him heading down the hall toward the bathroom. I sat down at my computer desk. Before I could boot up the desktop, an image began to form on the monitor screen. Occasionally I received psychic communications from an entity who lived in a parallel world, or a deviant world level as the Agency termed them. This particular sending followed the standard procedure. First the familiar black circle appeared with its seven arrows, four protruding from the top half, three from the bottom. Once it was fully formed, the circle turned into the image of the shaved head and stern-eyed face of the man I called Cryptic Creep. For some months now he'd been contacting me at random intervals, and always for a few brief moments at a time.

"You again, huh?" I spoke aloud. "What is it now?"

He answered psychically. "We must discuss this business of the Yaldaboathian heresy."

Even in psychic communication, he had a strange voice—high and fluting.

"Why?" I said. "I don't believe in Yaldaboath."

"That is a great relief. I was afraid that you were backsliding." He smiled, and at that moment he reminded me strongly of my priestly uncle, Father Keith. "Then why did you tell me that it created the universe?"

It took me a couple of moments to remember our last conversation, in which he'd quizzed me about various religious beliefs.

"What is this," I said. "Catechism?"

"Of course. Who—"

"Oh, okay!" I made my answer up on the spur of the

moment. "The Peacock Angel under the direction of the Invisible Highest."

His grin broadened. I could have sworn he was smiling upon me with deep affection, just as Father Keith would have—except that I would have trusted Father Keith.

"Good enough," he said. "I can stop worrying, then. I was afraid you'd gone over to our enemies."

"Our enemies?" I said. "Are you telling me we're on the same side?"

"Side? I wouldn't put things in those terms. There are a great many more than two sides to these questions. Nola, come back home! You need to speak with me face-to-face."

"Rather than indistinctly through a mirror, huh?"

He frowned, puzzled.

"Okay," I said, "maybe you know that in the other translation: now we see as through a glass darkly."

His eyes widened, his mouth slacked, and he snorted.

"From one heresy to another," he said. "I take it fragments of that drivel survive there."

"Fragments? No, four canonical gospels and a lot of Paul's letters, plus history books and some deviant gospels. It's one of the dominant religions where I live."

"Worse and worse! Nola, you absolutely must join me. Your soul is in grave danger of damnation."

"Oh, come off it! You're a fine one to talk. Why are you using an unbalanced Chaos symbol to contact me?"

His grin vanished. "What?"

"The circle with seven arrows. Or doesn't it mean unbalanced force?"

"It certainly doesn't! It represents the inherent dynamism of the universe, the striving toward consciousness of all matter."

This revelation left me speechless. I remembered just how complicated inter-world communication could be. Take nothing for granted, O'Grady, I told myself. Nothing, nada, zip. From the circle on my monitor he watched me, narrow-eyed.

"You really should have known that," he said finally. "About our circle, that is."

"Look, I just realized something. I'm not the Nola you think I am."

He stared at me openmouthed. "What do you—ai! Wretched power circuit!"

His voice faded, and his image disappeared. The black circle slowly vanished after him.

"Crud!" I said. "I wanted to ask him about the illusions."

He might have known something about the attempts on my life, I figured, since he'd referred to "our enemies." I sat for a moment staring at the blank computer screen. Out of our entire conversation, I focused on one phrase as the key to a good many riddles: "Nola, come back home." When I told Ari about the exchange, he agreed.

"As for the rest of it," Ari said, "it's a lot of sodding nonsense, religion. His strikes me as particularly odd."

"What counts isn't the religion itself," I said, "it's his faith in it."

"Why?"

"Because the Peacock Angel construct looks to be the dominant religion of his world. Or I should say, one version of that construct. I'll bet he's a churchman. They're always sniffing out heresies."

"I take it he's found some."

"Yep. The Valentinians for one. The Yaldaboath believers are still around, even though they died out in our world level a long time ago. He also knows about some form of Christianity. Huh, I wonder if the Peacock Angel church persecutes Christians? That would be a nifty example of karma in action."

Ari laughed his real laugh, the one he usually reserved for Roadrunner cartoons. When I considered how my coreligionists had treated his over the centuries, I couldn't begrudge it to him.

"So," I continued, "I know now why I wanted to study all that material about the Gnostics. Cryptic Creep is one."

"Yes, and a member of that Peacock Angel cult. Nothing but trouble, that lot."

"Maybe. There could be more than one interpretation of the angel figure. More than one cult, I mean. I get the feeling that old C. C. here is a man who follows the Order principle, not Chaos."

I'd given Cryptic Creep his name because I had believed him to be a member of a dark Chaos cult. Now I was having doubts. His catechism, his horror at the thought that his version of me might be sliding into sin, his explanation of the arrow and circle symbol—they didn't fit a member of some Chaotic nightmare mob.

"Well, you'd know better than I would," Ari said. "I can't even see him when he contacts you. Very rude of him, I must say."

I had to smile at that. "I suspect that Cryptic Creep could tell us a lot of things we need to know." A gloomy thought occurred. "Of course, I may have blown it by blurting the truth. He's probably decided I'm not worth contacting again. The wrong Nola, that's me. Somewhere there's one of my doppelgängers who's related to this funny uncle. Lucky old her."

Ari sighed and sat down on the couch. He reached for the remote control.

"Going to watch TV?" I said.

"If you're going to do e-mail, yes."

"I don't have to do the e-mail now."

"Well, it's a little early to go to bed." He looked my way and grinned. "Unless, of course."

"Unless what?"

The grin deepened.

"It's not that early," I said. "Let's."

I got up, he got up. We met in the middle of the room for a long kiss. But before we went to our bedroom, Ari checked out the entire security system and put all the alarms on high. I sealed the doors with Chaos wards as well. As I told Uncle Jim, being a secret agent has its drawbacks.

CHAPTER 2

ON MONDAY MORNING, I woke early from a nightmare. Since I see visions, at times it's hard to tell what's an ordinary dream and what isn't. Even if you're pretty sure that what you're experiencing isn't a dream, it can be difficult to find its source. In this particular dream-incident a chunk of fallen masonry pinned me to the floor as flames crept toward me. I could see nothing but smoke and hear nothing but women screaming. I knew that in a minute or two I'd be burned alive. I tried to pull free of whatever had trapped my legs, but my hands slipped on a floor slick with blood. The agonizing pain of my crushed legs made me scream aloud.

I sat up in bed with a yelp. Ari had already gotten up. Around me, the sunny bedroom had never looked so good. I even liked the sight of his dirty clothes lying on the floor. I got out of bed and washed the emotional dregs of the nightmare away in the shower, but its content stayed with me. The big question: was it a vision of something that might happen to me in the future? Or something that had happened or was happening to someone else? Or a symbolic presentation of arcane information from the Collective Data Stream?

Ambiguity is a way of life when you're psychic. I knew that. It annoyed me, anyway. I mean, if you're going to face the possibility of being burned alive, you'd like a clear message on the subject. It would also be nice if you could see a way to avoid it. I wrote up the dream or vision or warning, whatever it was, in my private journal, but I decided that I'd wait and see if it proved important enough to send to the Agency.

I did file my report on the shooting. I added the illusions I'd seen the night before. The Agency runs a site on the Internet for e-mail and a bulletin board, TranceWeb as we call it. Not only is the location secret and the material heavily encrypted, anyone accessing it has to go into trance to read it, a requirement that keeps the vast majority of hackers out. As usual, I found a long list of official e-mail waiting for me. As the head of the San Francisco bureau, I had administrative details to handle, mostly concerning things like health insurance premiums and official changes to the reporting format.

As the day went on, I learned nothing about the dream but far more than I ever wanted to know about rivalry between various law-enforcement agencies. I could have directed a movie called, "When Bureaucracies Collide!" It began when Ari in his official capacity as my bodyguard filed a report with Interpol about the shooting. Ari also phoned his mentor, who was part of a top-secret unit attached to Interpol. They call it TWIXT—Transworld Interpol X Team—though they added the X only to prevent the acronym from spelling "twit." As the name implies, TWIXT handles cases that cross world lines, that is, they're responsible for tracking down criminals who operate on more than one deviant level.

Although Ari had applied to join TWIXT, he had an

important bureaucratic step left to take. That morning his mentor, Austin Spare14, gave him the news he'd been waiting for.

"My qualifying examination's finally been scheduled," Ari told me. "Tomorrow. They certainly don't give you time to worry over these things, do they? There's a difficulty. It's being held on a different world level, not here on ours."

"Which?"

"Terra One, Spare's own home world. It should be quite interesting to see. When I told him that you'd been attacked, he said he'd get clearance for you to accompany me. I'm not leaving you unguarded."

"Thank you! I'll tell the Agency."

That's when the trouble started. About ten minutes after I'd sent the e-mail, my handler's secretary called to set up a trance appointment. Immediately, she said, if at all possible, which meant that the situation was serious. I told her yes, then hung up the landline.

"I don't like this," I told Ari. "We know that the higher-ups want the liaison with TWIXT to go through. But Y really hates the idea."

Even though I've worked with this handler for years, I only know him as Y.

"If he sees it as a threat to his authority," Ari said, "you'll have to be very careful in what you say."

"You bet. Walking on eggs is in order."

I grabbed a notebook and a ballpoint pen from my desk to record any automatic writing I received while in trance. For privacy's sake, I went into the bedroom because at times I speak aloud during trance. I knew that Y would resent it if he thought Ari could overhear. I lay down on the bed and let myself drift into the proper frame of mind.

During these sessions I seem to be sitting in a chair in the middle of a gray mist. Another chair appears in front of me, and Y walks out of the mist to sit down in it. His image mirrors his physical self, he tells me, a middle-aged Japanese-American man, very distinguished, with silver streaks in his black hair. Since I've never actually seen him in the flesh, I have to take his word for that, but I tend to believe him. That particular morning I could tell that he was angry the minute his image walked into view. He sat down in the chair and crossed his arms over his chest.

"Let me guess," I said. "You don't want me to go to a deviant world level in the company of a couple of TWIXT agents."

"Damn right, I don't!" Y glared at me. "The higher-ups may be taken with these people, but I think we should be more cautious. This offer of liaison sounds good, but we haven't properly researched them yet."

"Caution is always good, yeah, but I've worked with Spare14 now, and I know he's trustworthy. Honorable, even, in his way."

Y's expression turned sour. "Why do you always refer to him as Spare14? That strikes me as suspicious. Is he one man or a team?"

"Just one man. He's a clone, actually, grown from cells of the British artist, Austin Osman Spare. The fourteenth guy in that clone cluster."

Y's image froze for a long moment. Finally it moved, and he sighed. "I should have known," he said, "that it would be something outré like that. The advanced tech level of their society—that's what's intrigued our higher-ups. They think they can get some futuristic gadgets from these people."

"They probably can. I've seen some amazing communication devices, like I've told you in my reports."

Y made a snarling sound, and his image froze again. I waited until it moved.

"I've already had one series of attempts made on my life," I said. "Maybe two if that shooter was after me, not Maureen."

"Yes, I've read the reports. I'll admit, they worry me."

"If I remove myself to a different world level, it's bound to throw the assassin off my trail, at least for a while."

"That's a good point." Y drummed his fingers on his knee while he considered. "We certainly can't have you left on your own without a bodyguard, and it would take too long to find a temporary replacement for Nathan. We'd have to go through TWIXT for that anyway, I suppose."

"We couldn't even be sure that the replacement was completely trustworthy. We know that Nathan is."

"Yes, that's true. Congratulations on your engagement, by the way. Just never marry him. He's not an American citizen."

"I have no intention of doing that, don't worry."

"Good." He continued thinking and drumming. Finally he shrugged. "I can't give you an answer now. I have to conference with the higher-ups. I don't want you going in any official capacity. You work for the Agency, not their outfit!"

"I know that, you know that, but best of all, they know that."

Y scowled again and disappeared. I shut down, woke up, and sat up to see what kind of automatic writing my hand had scribbled while I'd been in trance. Not much—only the word "careful" in big letters. Perhaps my hand had written that word because there was a giant squid in the bedroom. To be precise, a large silvery cephalopod was hovering over the dresser about six feet away. It stared at me with one yellow eye and made a gurgling noise.

It looked so solid, with its clustered tentacles and long, torpedo-shaped body, that I figured it had to be a Chaos creature rather than a mere projected image. I sketched a Chaos ward in the air with one hand and sailed it straight for the beast. It scooted to one side but too slowly. The ward smacked it right in the eye. It shattered into a cluster of squid chips, which dissolved and vanished.

Chaotic, all right. Yuck! I got up and shuddered.

When I returned to the living room, I found Ari standing by the bay window, Beretta in hand. Not to shoot anyone, I'm glad to say, but to study the street. He usually wore his shoulder holster even at home. Every hour or so he'd make the rounds of the windows in our flat and peer out, looking for any sign of anything unusual that might presage trouble.

"How was the session?" Ari said.

"Sticky. Y does not want to agree to let me go."

Ari sighed and holstered the Beretta. "I'll just give Spare14 a ring, then."

Ari went into the bedroom to talk in private. When he got off the phone, though, he immediately passed intel on to me.

"Y may be doubly suspicious because of the situation with Michael," Ari said. "Spare14 admitted that TWIXT would very much like to recruit him. So, of course, would the Agency."

"Has Spare actually done anything like contact my aunt?" Eileen was Michael's legal guardian for a variety of complex reasons.

"Yes, I'm afraid so. He admitted that it was a mistake. Apparently, she told the Agency representative about it, honest soul that she is."

"Honest like hell! I bet she's playing one against the other to get the best deal she can for Michael's college fund. You've never seen her bargaining for vintage clothes at a flea market. I have. It can be scary."

"I see." Ari pondered this for a moment. "It's rather a moot point, though. Will Michael even be able to go to college? He's not done well at all in his secondary school."

"That's putting it mildly. Eileen's taken him out of school altogether. He'll have to get his diploma by examination. California has that program, the GED." I grinned at him. "Father Keith has volunteered to do home schooling for

Mike and Sophie. Mike will end up working his butt off, and it couldn't happen to a nicer little brother."

"Serve him right, yes." He paused to reach up and finger the minimally longish hair above his collar. "You know I really need a haircut."

"I like it that length."

"It's too shaggy. I don't want to look like a hippie."

"Ari, darling, you could never look like a hippie no matter how hard you tried."

He glowered. I sighed.

"Okay, I'll call Maureen," I said. "That's how she's been earning her living. Cutting hair."

When I phoned her, Maureen had nothing better to do than earn twenty-five bucks. I insisted that we'd pay her for the trim. We drove over to Diamond Heights and my mother's apartment in a fairly new, nicely designed complex right across the street from a small park. She had a two-bedroom place in a pleasant wood-shingled building with plenty of windows and a view from the living room of eastern San Francisco. Dad let us in, then went back to playing Chinese Checkers with Cattie and Bren. I took a good look around. Thanks to the unpleasantness between us, I'd never seen my mother's apartment before. Her taste ran to severe Scandinavian furniture in muted yellows and browns, but she compensated by scattering framed family photos and silver knickknacks on every available surface.

"The kids are going stir crazy," Maureen said. "But I'm terrified to let them go outside. They can see those swings and the jungle gym from the window, but I won't let them go over there to play."

"Good," Ari said. "It's a common form of revenge, in these cases, for the man to kidnap the woman's children."

"Yeah, so I've heard." Maureen turned pale, but her voice stayed steady. "Come into the kitchen. I've set up in there."

Maureen gave Ari a really good haircut—the one he

wanted, shorter than I thought it needed to be. She was just sweeping up when her cell phone rang. She took it out of her shirt pocket but waited till the caller ID displayed before she answered.

"Hi, Mom!" she said. "What's up?" She paused. "Today? Okay, I'll get ready to go. A suit would be best, huh? Yeah, thought so. See you soon." She clicked off. "Mom's found a lawyer already. We're going to go and get the restraining order."

"From what I've heard, you really need a lawyer," I said.

Ari nodded his agreement.

"You bet," Maureen continued. "I checked it out online last night. The worst part is you're supposed to tell the guy that you're asking for the order."

"What? You mean you tell him so he can come beat you up and stop you from doing it. Who wrote that law?"

"A man, obviously." Maureen hesitated, considering me. "I guess you don't want to be here when Mom arrives. She's on her way."

I reached for my shoulder bag and stood up. Ari joined me.

"Anyway," Maureen went on. "I'll leave the kids with Dad. They should be safe enough inside."

Ari and I were just leaving when I saw my mother drive up in her little blue sedan and park in front of the building. I froze in the doorway, then decided it would be better to face her in the open air. If something unpleasant happened, I didn't want the kids upset. We stepped outside and walked down the short concrete path to the sidewalk. Mom finished locking up the car, turned, and saw me. She's a tiny woman, about five feet two and slender, with an auburn wash over her hair to hide the gray. That morning she was wearing a navy blue skirt and a frilly white blouse. She paused to look me over with her usual piercing glare and little twist of a smile. Cataloging all my flaws, I figured. It's kind of a hobby with her.

"Hi," I said. "Mo was just cutting Ari's hair."

"It needed it, yeah," Mom said. "Did you pay her?"

"Of course," Ari snapped.

They scowled at each other while I felt a strong danger warning—not from them, but from close by.

"Uh-oh," I said. "Chuck's around here somewhere."

Ari reached under his jacket for the Beretta. I'd expected Mom to argue, to tell me that I was being stupid, that I couldn't possibly know. I'd misjudged her. She knew that her grandchildren's safety was at stake.

"Where?" she said. "What direction?"

"Behind you across the street. In those trees by the children's play area."

Mom turned around and stared at the trees in question. I heard a cracking sound, then a bang like an explosion. Distantly among the trees someone yelped. Crashes, booms—leaves flew into the air—the sand under the swing set rose in a dust devil and swept into the foliage. A man's voice screamed in rage. Dad came running out of the apartment. I saw Maureen hauling the kids away from the open front door. Ari drew the Beretta and jogged across the street, but before he reached the play area, we heard a motorcycle start up and drive off with a roar. Ari returned, and we all listened to the sound dying away downhill.

"I wonder what caused all that?" Mom said. "I sometimes think this place is haunted."

"Deirdre, for the love of God!" Dad snarled. "When will you admit that you—"

"Oh, don't be ridiculous!" Mom turned on him. "Besides, it doesn't matter. He's gone." She scrutinized me one last time. "That jacket's too big for you. I wish you'd get some clothes that fit."

With a toss of her head she marched past us all into the building. Dad sighed, shrugged, and followed her. Ari muttered something under his breath in Hebrew. I didn't ask for a translation.

We returned to our flat and work. Ari had his usual mysterious online research, and I had a case that I'd been working on for months, ever since I'd returned to San Francisco at the beginning of the year. I'd picked up the trail of the Chaos masters in the form of a would-be coven, a small group led by worshipers of the Peacock Angel, who were pretending to be practicing ritual magic to cover their drug dealing. They'd come from the deviant world level known as Terra Three, or as I called it for convenience, Interchange, because it contained a plethora of gates to other levels of the multiverse. Unnatural gates, that is—they'd been created by a disaster that had turned Terra Three into a radioactive hellhole.

I'd seen the disaster in a vision where I stood on some kind of height and looked down at a city. An enormous spray of energy, colored like the rainbow, fell into view from high above the Earth. When the rainbow lights finally disappeared, the buildings on the skyline glowed with an evil violet glare. As the sunlight faded into night, I smelled rotting meat, the overwhelming, gagging stench of corpses.

Not a happy vision, no. At first, the vision and the Chaos master case had seemed to have nothing to do with one another, but I'd found the link in the nature of the deviant Peacock Angel cult. Islamic clerics believed that this cult identified the Peacock Angel with Satan or Ahriman, both symbols of the principle of Chaos Unbound. Could their worshipers be good candidates for the authors of that terrible disaster? The hypothesis seemed plausible.

What on our world level was a small, weak cult might well have been a powerful force toward evil on some other world, capable of the destruction I'd seen. Another possibility was that the dark cult had found a home on Interchange after the gate creation, when the survivors reacted to the disaster with despair and cynicism. At the very least, the cult could be profiting from that despair. The society I'd seen there lived and breathed Chaos.

I'd reported the vision to the Agency weeks ago, but so far Seymour, our interpretation expert, had made no comment. I sent him a follow-up e-mail and learned the problem: he had yet to find a high-level astrophysicist who could be trusted to keep his or her mouth shut about the interpretation.

"No one in the Agency's qualified," Seymour told me. "I'm sure not!"

Bureaucracy again! I could understand and sympathize while still feeling frustrated. Annoyed, even—I'll admit it. I did, however, realize that I had a possible way to run a cross-check on my own.

Another piece of the puzzle: I'd recently investigated a self-taught visionary named Reb Ezekiel, who had a direct connection to Ari's family. He had psychic talents, and significant gifts at that, but he'd never learned how to check his internal perceptions against the outer world. He sincerely believed aliens who looked like cherubim were going to invade the Earth in a swarm of spaceships shaped like the Ark of the Covenant. Crazy? So you'd think, but I could see a different explanation. Maybe Reb Zeke had stumbled onto some real—though symbolically presented—threat to the cosmic Balance between Chaos and Order, like, for instance, whatever force had destroyed Interchange. Ambiguity again—the psychic's curse.

Although he'd died of pneumonia a couple of months earlier, at one point in his career Reb Zeke had published a set of books about his visions. I spent two hours hunting around the Internet for copies but found none available anywhere, not on specialized sites, not on the big British rare booksellers, not even a pirate copy in a murky scan. On various book blog sites, several collectors of occult material commented on the lack. One person repeated a rumor that the publisher had been bribed to take them out of print.

Could I be seeing another feather from the Peacock Angel's wings?

I included these theories in my daily report to the Agency. My failure to find Reb Ezekiel's books left me with only secondhand versions of his prophecies. Fortunately, I had another source, if I could access it.

My contact for this source had gone downstairs to perform the horrendous series of exercises he did to keep in shape. I did my best to remain ignorant about Ari's workout routine. In an hour or so, Ari came back upstairs and put his stinky gym clothes in the washer. He took a quick shower, started the washer, and grabbed a bottle of his favorite storm-gray sports drink from the fridge. With smiles and wiles I let him get comfortable on the sofa, but when he picked up his cram book, I struck.

"Before you immerse yourself in trans-world law codes," I said, "there's something we need to discuss."

"Oh?" He raised one eyebrow.

"I really need to contact your mother."

He dropped the book. Swearing in several languages at once, he fished around on the floor till he found it again. He clutched it in both hands and scowled at me.

"Why does that make you so uptight?" I said. "Do you think she's going to hate me or something?"

"Quite the opposite. I'm afraid you'll get along famously."

"And?"

"You'll hear all the ghastly stories of things I did when I was a child, the sort of things every man wishes his mother would forget."

"I take it she told them to a previous girlfriend of yours."

The scowl deepened.

"And I take it that means yes," I went on. "But, look, I don't want to ask her about you. I want to ask her about

Armageddon and Reb Ezekiel. Itzak Stein told us that she was part of the inner circle on the kibbutz. She must know the details of the visions. I can't ask Zeke, after all."

"Right. Being as he's dead."

"If it'll make you feel better, I won't mention our relationship. I'll use my cross-agency identity, and so I'll just be yet another government agent asking for a debriefing about the rebbe and his weird retro kibbutz. She should be used to it by now."

Ari sighed and contemplated the ceiling. "Too late for that."

My turn for the "oh?" and I put some force behind it.

"Well," Ari went on, "I do occasionally send her an e-mail. It's the least I can do, keeping in touch. She is my mother. She appreciates hearing from me."

"Yeah, and I applaud you as a dutiful son and all that, but what do you mean, too late?"

"I told her I'd met the woman I was going to marry. It's the sort of thing mothers want to hear, isn't it? And we are engaged."

"Yeah, but I am not going to marry you. I'm not going to marry anyone."

"I know that. I didn't know it when I sent the e-mail."

I decided against kicking him. After all, I did want something out of him.

"Okay," I continued, "I get it now. When I contact your mother, she's going to treat me like your intended. And you figured I'd be furious when she gushed about it."

"Something like that, yes. She's not really one for gushing." He hesitated briefly. "Are you furious?"

I sighed and consulted my mental state. "Annoyed, but not furious."

"Aha! A step in the right direction."

I ignored that comment. "But look," I said, "speaking logically and all, I really need to know more about Reb Ze-

ke's visions. There's a possibility that he picked up on something real unpleasant coming our way. She can probably tell
me what I need to know. I told you about the vision, right?"

"Yes."

"Okay, so suppose Reb Ezekiel was correct about an
interstellar invasion force heading for Megiddo. Wouldn't
Israel have need to know?"

Ari stared stone-faced. "Do you really think—" he began.

"I don't know what I think. That's why I need to consult
with your mother."

The stone face transformed into droop-eyed martyrdom.
"Oh, very well," he said. "I suppose you want her e-mail
address."

"Yeah, exactly that. Do you know if she has video conferencing capability?"

"I don't, no, but you can ask her. I doubt if she has a
scrambler or an encryption system at her end, though. Itzak
might be able to figure out how to rig something up here
that will protect the data there."

Ari wrote the e-mail address of his mother, Shira Flowertree, on a sticky note and handed it to me. She'd been
married twice since leaving Ari's father. When I asked Ari
about the current husband, him of the unusual moniker, he
responded with an inarticulate growl.

"Er," I said, "I take it you don't like him."

"You're quite right. He's a vegan."

"They can sometimes be annoying, yeah, but—"

"It's not the only thing. Look at his sodding name. What
was wrong, I ask you, with Blumbaum? Not good enough
for him, so he had it legally changed. Besides, he wears
clothes made from handwoven fabrics."

"Sounds like he belongs in Berkeley."

"That's not a recco in my book." Ari made a sour face.
"Berkeley or Glastonbury. Hard to say which is worse."

"I've only been there once, but I liked Glastonbury."

"You would! But as for Lev, I dislike the way he wormed his way into my mother's life. Popped up out of nowhere, and the next thing I knew, he'd moved in with her."

"Where did she meet this guy?"

"At an astrology class." Ari looked more sour than ever. "In Hampstead." He ostentatiously opened the cram book and glared at a page. I figured the subject of Mr. Flowertree had been closed.

I had an e-mail account separate from the Agency site, though it was heavily encrypted in its own way. When it came to writing the e-mail, I decided that I could humor Ari a little or at least refrain from embarrassing him. I opened by telling Shira how happy I was to have her son as a partner, then got down to business. I figured I was safe in assuming that she had some psychic talents of her own and would thus understand about the ambiguity inherent in Reb Ezekiel's vision of Armageddon.

"I'm afraid that he might have seen some real trouble ahead," I told her. "Not flying saucer people, but trouble nonetheless. I'm hoping you can tell me what sort of images and narratives he received."

I'd just sent the e-mail when Spare14 called Ari. His higher-ups in TWIXT "would prefer," as he put it, that I have official clearance before I'd be allowed to accompany Ari. We had an awkward three-way conversation on the subject that boiled down to protocol and procedures and Spare14's supervisor's justified fear that Y would cut up rough if provoked any further. Best I stay home, according to this mysterious higher-up, and TWIXT would provide a new bodyguard.

"No," Ari snapped. "I'm her bodyguard. No one else need apply."

"They're being unreasonable, I know," Spare14 said in a soothing tone of voice.

"So is my handler," I said.

"We simply must know by tonight. Do you think you possibly can get him to act that quickly?"

"I'll try."

"I suppose that's all any of us can do." Spare14 paused for a sigh. "I'll continue pursuing the matter on my end. Do let me know as soon as you learn anything further."

I promised I would, and we ended the call. I returned to the computer and checked the time: not quite eleven, which meant two PM in Washington. I didn't have a lot of time left for changing Y's mind.

Ari drew the Beretta and wandered down the hall to look out of the windows in our bedroom, which gave a clear view of the garages out in back of the building. I thought he was just making his usual rounds, but I felt a danger warning when I heard him talking on his smartphone. He was calling the police. I took a few steps down the hall only to have him yell at me.

"Stay in the front of the building, but get away from the window!"

"Okay," I yelled back. "But are you at risk?"

"Never mind that now! Just follow orders!"

"Yes, sir!" I added a sauce of sarcasm to the words. "On the double."

He ignored it.

I went to the head of the stairs that led down to our front door and sat down on the top step. That way, I figured, I could always run outside if trouble came up the back steps. I could feel my pulse racing busily along while I wondered what in hell was happening. Not hearing gunshots was a good sign, but I would have preferred more information than that. I ran a couple of scans, including a Search Mode for danger. Nothing. I got up and went back to the hallway.

"Ari!" I called out. "I'm not picking up any threats."

"I don't care. Stay in the front of the building!"

I returned to the living room and heard sirens wailing. I placed them as coming down Moraga. The wailing grew louder, and I heard them turn onto our street with a screech of tires. A squad car and a small fire engine pulled up in front of our building. Ari came running down the hall, gun in hand.

"What—" I began.

"Suspicious vehicle, potential car bomb." He barked out the words and pushed past me. "Follow me out. If someone shoots at me, duck back inside."

Ari clattered down the stairs. He opened the door partway, showed himself, ducked back behind the door. No one shot at him. He flung the door open and raced out to join the police on the sidewalk. Since I could pick up absolutely no danger from anywhere, my pulse had steadied itself. I proceeded more slowly. The front door opened directly onto a small porch, the landing at the head of the stairs—these open to the sky—that led down to the street. I leaned over the stucco wall to listen.

The uniformed officers were taking the potential threat seriously. They drew their guns and followed Ari around the side of the building. Just across the driveway stood a big apartment house. When I looked up, I could see the people in the corner apartment on the second floor staring out their window. The crew from the fire department stayed on board their vehicle and waited out in the street. I did another scan: still no hint of physical danger, though I picked up danger of another kind with my normal senses.

I heard voices—angry voices—out in the driveway. One of them was Ari's, and the other belonged to a woman who was practically screeching with rage. Curiosity drove me down to the bottom step.

"My sister's car!" The woman bellowed. "Why can't she park there?"

"I told you," Ari snapped. "Restricted area."

"There's been nothing but noise and trouble since you people moved in! I don't care if you are a damn cop."

Time to intervene! I ran around the side of the building and saw what I'd feared to see. The woman, short, stout, blonde, and as furious as a banty hen when her chicks are threatened, was standing much too close to Ari. Her hands were on her hips and her face was scarlet with rage. So was Ari's. The two uniformed officers stood uselessly nearby and merely stared at the pair of them.

"Ari!" I called out in a nonthreatening singsong. "Anger management!"

Ari took a couple of steps back. I rushed in between them. The woman finally realized that the situation had taken a dangerous turn. She moved back and clamped a hand over her mouth. From where I stood I could see the offending vehicle, a small white sedan, parked parallel to and only a few feet from our wooden back steps and the plastic recycling and garbage bins.

"I'm sorry," I said to her. "But don't you realize that all these men are armed?"

"Oh, God!" she spoke through muffling fingers.

I ran a quick Subliminal Psychological Profile on her. Terror had replaced rage.

"Does that car belong to your sister?" I asked.

She nodded a yes. Her SPP revealed that she was telling the truth.

"I'm so sorry for the trouble," I continued. "There have been death threats. Could your sister move her car around to your side of the back lot?"

She nodded, then turned and bolted for the open side door of her building. One of the cops snickered, then stifled it. Ari pointed at the white sedan.

"If that had been a car bomb," Ari said to me, "the building would have caught fire."

"Yeah," I said. "Sure would have."

"It was the way it's parked," he went on. "Very suspicious."

"Maybe, except we're not in Israel at the moment."

Ari blinked at me, glowered, and let out his breath in a sharp sigh. I could feel that he had his rage back under control. The police holstered their weapons, and in a few seconds, so did Ari.

"I'll let you finish up here," I said, as cheerfully as I could manage.

I left before he could object. He'd called out the troops, I figured, and he could deal with them. When I reached the front steps, I did wave to the firefighters and yell, "All clear! Thanks!" before I hurried upstairs again. My hands were shaking from the close call—not from any hypothetical firebomb, but from Ari's temper. I understood why his mysterious deep cover agency and Interpol both were letting him move over to TWIXT. He was one of their best officers in many ways but, in others, the proverbial loose cannon.

Even though the incident had been a false alarm, I could use it to my advantage. Before Ari came back upstairs, I called Y's secretary and asked for another trance conference.

"There's been an incident here," I said. "A possible IED planted in a parked car."

I heard her speaking to someone elsewhere in the room. She returned to our call.

"Just go inside," she said. "He'll be there immediately."

"Inside," of course meant "inside your own mind." I returned to the bedroom and did so. I'd barely sat down in the image of a chair when Y joined me. This time Y looked martyred rather than angry.

"Oh, very well," he said. "This latest threat has tipped the balance. I'll withdraw my veto, which means you can go with Nathan."

"Ah. The higher-ups had already approved the move, I take it?"

"Yes, but only if you go as an observer. I don't want you to be an official part of the TWIXT team, and the higher-ups agreed with that. We need research into TWIXT methods. This will be a good chance for you to observe them firsthand."

I received an icy-cold touch of psychic insight: he was speaking truer than he could know.

"If there's trouble," I said, "I may not be able to stay neutral."

"Do your best. Get out of trouble's way. You have a license to ensorcell. Do what you need to do to protect yourself, and leave the scene as soon as possible. That's a direct order. I do not want you entangled in some TWIXT-related debacle."

I was about to point out that leaving a deviant world level might not be as easy as taking a bus home, but the truth might have led to him revoking permission.

"I'll do my best," I said instead.

"Good. I'm still making an official protest, by the way. It will go into my file, not yours, so don't worry about repercussions."

With that, he disappeared. I woke up and found Ari standing in the door of the bedroom, watching me.

"Y's allowing me to go," I said, "but only as an observer."

"I'll ring Spare14 and tell him. I've settled everything with the police, just by the way."

"Oh, good." I sat up and swung my legs over the side of the bed. "Y'know, I didn't feel the slightest trace of danger. I would have if that car had really been rigged with a bomb."

"Admittedly I may have overreacted. But I'm not being paid to take chances with your life."

That was as much an admission as he'd ever make, I figured, that he'd been wrong.

"I know," I said. "And I appreciate that. But—"

"Yes, of course, and the next time I'll listen to you."

He turned around and stalked off down the hall. I got up and went to use the bathroom. By the time I joined him in the living room, he was sitting on the couch with his cram book in his lap. He looked up at me and smiled, a perfectly normal, calm smile.

"I'll be glad to have this exam behind me," he said.

"Yeah, I bet! What did Spare have to say?"

"We're to be at his office at nine o'clock tomorrow morning. The world-walker will meet us there. You know, I can understand Y's feelings in the matter. I'd be angry, too, if my superiors had overridden my better judgment. Especially if they were doing it to further some sort of arrangement that I disliked. But I'm certainly glad that everything's a go."

"Not quite everything." I smiled to take any urgency out of the words. "I've got to call Annie and tell her she'll have to hold down the fort here for the day we're gone. By the way, did Spare14 say anything about what we should wear?"

"No. How like you to ask! Something respectable, I should think. That means a suit and tie for me."

"And something besides jeans for me. The glen plaid pants suit, I think. Or maybe the plain gray with the blue silk blouse."

Ari sighed and opened the cram book. I took the hint and shut up.

CHAPTER 3

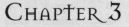

Spare14 KEPT A SHABBY LITTLE OFFICE down near the Hall of Justice, on an alley just off Bryant Street. Next morning, we took a cab down, but we paid off the driver and got out two blocks away in order to keep our destination reasonably secret. As we walked along Bryant, an ambulance went screaming past. In that brutal neighborhood, I thought little of it until the ambulance turned down the right alley, at which point its siren fell silent. Ari muttered something in Hebrew.

"We'd best hurry," he said in English.

We did. At the mouth of the alley we saw that the ambulance had stopped right in front of the building that housed Spare14's office. Just down the block a patrolman was getting out of his squad car. He glanced around, yelled something at the ambulance driver, and ran upstairs. The bail bondsman who had the office on the ground floor had come out to watch, but he seemed only curious, not involved. We jogged down to join him.

"Do you know what's happened?" Ari said. "We had an appointment upstairs."

"I don't," the bail bondsman said. "Everything was nice and quiet until—bam!—this ambulance pulled up, and the medical guys went running up the stairs."

Ari and I walked over to the open door that led to the stairwell. The patrolman stepped out and held up his hand for us to stop.

"Interpol." Ari pulled his ID out of the inner pocket of his suit jacket.

The patrolman looked at it and nodded. "Okay, Inspector," he said. "She with you?"

"My assistant, yes."

Although I wanted to kick him, it would have been unwise. I merely flashed a small smile and followed Ari up the stairs. Toward the top I noticed drops of fresh blood dotting the gray carpet. Not a good sign.

A pasty-pale Spare14, alive and unwounded, met us at the door and ushered us into the office, a small white-painted room with a white pressboard desk and filing cabinet sitting on moldy turquoise carpet. Dusty venetian blinds hung at the two narrow windows. An inner door gave us a view of the second room, equally plain, dusty, and sparsely furnished. Two emergency medical techs knelt on either side of a white woman lying sprawled on a stretcher on the floor. As far as I could tell she was still alive, but I could see blood soaking her blue flowered shirt. The med techs were working hard with bandages and devices.

"The world-walker," Spare14 murmured. "Two women waylaid her about a block from here. One stabbed her. They grabbed her bag. You know what that means."

Ari let fly with a muttered string of Hebrew words. I was too shocked to say anything. In that bag she would have carried her focus orbs, the devices that allowed a world-walker to travel precisely where she wanted to go. It took me a moment to realize that one detail stood out. Two female assailants? My back brain twitched and delivered a wild guess—maybe a coincidence, maybe not.

"Your cover's broken," Ari said, also sotto voce.

Spare14 nodded. At the moment I was more worried about the woman on the floor than the cover story, but rationally I knew the situation sucked all around.

One of the techs sat back on his heels and smiled at the victim. "You'll be okay," he said. "Bleeding's stopped. We're going to get you to a hospital now."

She whispered something too faint for me to hear. I did however get a clear look at her face, pale, sweaty, and distorted by pain though it was—black hair with a hint of a wave, hazel eyes, and fine features, though her nose was straight, not tip-tilted like mine.

"Ari," I said, "she looks kind of like me. Maybe it wasn't the bag they wanted. That could have been a prop to make the attack look like a robbery."

Ari reflexively laid a hand on his shoulder holster. I took that as meaning he agreed. My wild guess seemed slightly less wild. The woman criminal I was thinking of had reason to hate me, which might explain the stabbing. During our original encounter she'd only seen me from a distance. She could have made the easy mistake of thinking the world-walker was me.

The EMTs began strapping the world-walker—Evelyn Murphy was her name—to the stretcher. Since Spare14 needed to accompany Murphy to the hospital, he designated Ari a temporary admin assistant and gave him the day's passwords. As the EMTs carried Murphy out of the office, Spare14 grabbed his sports coat from a chair and hurried after them. We heard him speak to the police officer. The ambulance siren started wailing, and the engine roar followed. Slowly the sound died away.

"I hope she'll be okay," I said.

"So do I." Ari sat down in the chair behind Spare14's desk. "I'd best check in with HQ. At times I wonder why I have to sit the sodding exam. In some ways I'm already part of TWIXT."

I ran an assortment of scans but felt no danger or threat close at hand. Ari used the trans-world router in Spare14's desk to report in to TWIXT HQ and call for backup on a four-oh-one request—their highest emergency code. I went downstairs to speak to the officer at the door. When I handed him my cross-agency ID, his eyes widened, and he made a small deferential coughing noise.

"The victim was robbed," I said, "of a courier bag containing important material. Spare gave us the description, a pale tan leather shoulder bag, about two feet by eighteen inches. Is it possible to get a search underway? The thieves will probably grab what they want and dump the rest."

"Right. We can do that for you. I'll just call in from the car."

"Thanks. I appreciate it." I made a point of checking his name and badge number. "I'll mention your help in my report."

He smiled and hurried off to the squad car. I returned upstairs.

Our backup arrived some fifteen minutes later. TWIXT could move fast when it needed to. I heard a familiar voice in the inner office room, saying, "All that blood on the floor. Looks real bad to me."

"Willa!" I called out. "Yeah, it is real bad."

Willa Danvers-Jones walked out of the room, followed by Jan Hendriks, a TWIXT officer we'd worked with before. Hendriks was a white man, on the portly side, with brown hair and eyes. He was wearing a pair of blue slacks with a gray blazer, which hung slightly open to give him access to an automatic in a shoulder holster. Willa, a tall Black woman, was wearing her usual work clothes, disguised as someone too poor to rob in many layers of torn, faded tops over a skirt over a pair of bike shorts. She carried a beat-up mesh shopping bag that appeared to be full of cloth scraps. Hidden inside, I knew, lay her focus orbs.

"I can only stay a minute," Willa told me. "But what happened? HQ told me that Murphy was seriously injured."

"She was stabbed by thieves," I said. "Spare14's with her at the hospital."

"I'm here to replace him," Jan said. "She'll have a twenty-four-hour guard, and I'm the first shift."

"Excellent," Ari joined in. "Willa, are you going out into the streets here on Four?"

"Nope. I'll be going back the way I came in."

"Good," I said. "Why didn't Murphy arrive inside like you just did?"

"She's new," Willa said. "She doesn't have the pinpoint control yet. I'm assuming she landed at the overlap point with One. It's about six blocks south of here. She must have walked to Bryant and met up with the creeps nearby. Damn good thing she managed to make it to the office."

"Yeah." I turned to Ari. "Did they take her to San Francisco General? That's usual."

"I don't know which hospital." Ari looked vexed. "Spare14 didn't say."

The landline rang. Mental overlap kicked in. "That's him now," I said. "You can ask him."

Ari picked up the phone and answered with a set of numbers: TWIXT code, I assumed. For some minutes he and Spare14 conversed mostly in numbers with a few scraps of English thrown in. Occasionally Ari made a note on a pad of paper on Spare14's desk He hung up the phone and turned to me.

"Yes, General Hospital at the Trauma Center," he said. "Hendriks, I'm to lock up here, and O'Grady and I will escort you."

"Nathan," I said, "what about your exam?"

"It'll have to be rescheduled," Willa broke in. "The boss mentioned that to me when I was leaving. Which I need to do. Gotta take a couple of agents elsewhere. Very elsewhere."

Willa walked into the other room. Through the open door I saw her take a couple of steps and vanish in a flicker of pale light. Hendriks shuddered.

"One never quite gets used to it," Jan said. "Nathan, do you have the keys to the office?"

"No." Ari patted his pants pocket. "But I have my lockpicks. They do work in reverse."

Ari secured the doors, and we left. We'd just reached the street when a black sedan pulled up at the curb, an unmarked police car, in fact—you can always tell one when you see one. Detective Lieutenant Sanchez got out of the driver's side.

"Just in time," he called out. "I need to talk with you, Nathan."

"And we need a lift," Ari said. "Could you take us to S.F. General? I suspect you'll need to go there yourself eventually."

"Yeah, sure thing." He shook his head. "Sometimes I gotta wonder if you two are psychic or something."

We smiled and got in the car, me in the front, the two guys in back. Ari introduced Jan as another Interpol officer and informed Sanchez that the stabbing victim was a courier for that agency. Needless to say, he never mentioned TWIXT.

"Okay," Sanchez said. "I've put out a search team for that bag. The officer who called in mentioned your affiliation, O'Grady. I hope that's okay. It made it real clear that this is a serious business."

"It is," I said. "You never know who might be behind incidents like this. Foreign nationals of the worst sort is my guess. Let's just say that Tehran might be interested. I can't tell you more at this point, but I'll try to get clearance to let you have more intel."

"Thanks. I know you can't say much, but I'd appreciate knowing what in hell's going on."

In the rearview mirror I could see Jan smiling at me in admiration. Hey, when you grow up in a family like mine, lying comes easily. It's a survival technique. Besides, for all I knew, Tehran might well have been interested—assuming they ever heard about it.

By the time we reached S.F. General, Murphy had been stitched up, transfused, and transferred from the Trauma Center to a private room in a part of the hospital set up for police cases—a locked ward, in essence. The point, of course, was not keeping her in but rather keeping her assailants out. When we arrived, she was more-or-less awake, lying propped up and groggy with pain meds on her hospital bed. They'd hooked her up to an IV and an assortment of monitors. Gray fog light filtered in through the bars over the narrow window. Spare14 got out of his chair and walked over to usher us in.

"Not the most cheerful place to recover," I remarked.

"We'll be transferring her as soon as possible." Spare14 glanced at Sanchez. "With police permission, of course."

"Since she's the victim, that shouldn't be a problem," Sanchez said. "Is she up to answering questions? You're another Interpol man, right?"

"Quite. Sorry." Spare14 took his wallet out of his pants pocket. "I should have offered you my ID before this."

"That's okay," Sanchez said. "Nathan and Hendriks here vouched for you in the car."

"Very well." Spare14 put the wallet back. "About those questions, perhaps I can answer them. She's given me what report she could, and I do think she'd best rest."

Spare14 gave me a glance of significance before he led Sanchez out into the hall to talk. I walked over to the bed and introduced myself to Murphy. She smiled and seemed reasonably aware.

"I'm the local psychic talent," I told her. "Hendriks can vouch for that."

"Fine." She spoke in an exhausted whisper. "Have they found my bag?"

"No, not yet. They're looking. Did you have orbs?"

"Three of them, yeah. From the general stock."

"Does that mean the thieves can use them?"

"Only if the little cunts are world-walkers. But, yeah, they're not tuned orbs."

"These girls." I decided to test my earlier wild guess. "Was one of them blonde?"

"Yeah. Slender, tall, pretty. Vicious." Her mouth twitched in a smile. "Bruised. I got one good chop on her lousy little face. She squeaked real loud. I hope I broke a tooth."

"I've got a theory about her. Look, I don't want to wear you out. But can you see EIs? Extruded Images, that is."

"Yeah, if you can put a little extra Qi behind them."

"Not a problem."

I summoned Qi, then extruded my memory image of Ash, a hardened young criminal type from Interchange. I shrank it down to about three feet high so that it hovered over the bed. Murphy caught her breath with a little gasp and moved uneasily against the pillows.

"That's her, all right. She did the stabbing. A Japanese girl grabbed the bag." Murphy frowned as she tried to reclaim her drug-scattered memories. "One of them yelled, 'I've got it.' Not sure which."

I retracted the image rather than distress her further. "Sometimes hunches pay off," I said. "The blonde's name is Ash, and she called me a bitch once. She's going to have some reasons to call me that again, I promise you."

"Good. Kick her in the guts for me if you catch her." Her voice faded away. "I think I've got to go to sleep."

"You do that. Best thing for you."

When I moved out of the way, Jan pulled a chair up to her bedside and sat down. He opened his jacket to reassure Murphy that he was armed. She smiled, sank back into the pillows, and fell straight asleep. When Sanchez and Spare14 came back in, I huddled with them in a corner and lowered my voice.

"Robbery," I said. "They wanted the courier bag. Murphy confirmed it."

"All right," Sanchez said. "Should I keep my men looking for it?"

Spare14 sucked his lower lip and considered the question. "Doubtless a waste of their time," he said at last. "I very much doubt if it was merely an ordinary robbery."

"Yeah, with O'Grady involved, I doubt it, too." Sanchez smiled briefly in my direction. "Okay. You can get in touch with me through Nathan if you need to."

Sanchez left, as Ari, I, and Spare14 did a few minutes later. We caught a cab and returned to Spare14's office. By then the patrolman had gone, and the drops of Murphy's blood had dried on the stairwell carpet. So had the pool of blood on the carpet of the inner room of the office. Spare14 looked at it, winced, and shut the door to hide the sight.

"I'll call one of those housekeeping services," he remarked. "The kind that specializes in crime scene cleanup."

"You're going to keep this office?" Ari said.

Spare14 shrugged. "Moving may not do the slightest bit of good," he said, "if my suspicions are correct. O'Grady, I got the impression that Murphy identified the assailant."

"She responded to an EI, yeah. Ash. The Axeman's assistant in the Interchange kidnapping case. They escaped to Terra Six just as we moved in on them."

"I remember it all too well. Ash, was it? Another confirmation of my suspicions." Spare14 sat down behind his desk and waved in the direction of other chairs. "Do sit down. I'll brief you on my own authority. Nathan, my apologies for your interrupted examination, but frankly, at this rate it's only going to be a formality. Your active duty credit tally must be rather high by now."

"I have the feeling it's about to go higher," Ari said.

"You may well be right about that. O'Grady, did Murphy tell you how many orbs she was carrying?"

"Three." I held up three fingers. "One to get her here to Terra Four. The second to get us to Terra One. As for the third, I don't know. Do you?"

"It would have been for Terra Six." Spare14 gave me a thin smile. "That's where Murphy's based. She'd need it to get home."

Ari muttered a sound something like "aha!"

"Yeah, and that's where Ash is based, too," I said. "Coincidence? I don't think so. Here's my wild guess. Someone tipped Ash off. She knew that a world-walker was coming here with orbs worth stealing."

"Not so very wild a guess," Spare14 said. "There's something wrong at the TWIXT office on Terra Six. The last time I visited there, I felt some sort of imbalance, I suppose we might call it. To use your Agency's terms, TWIXT stands on the side of Cosmic Order. The TWIXT office smelled of Chaos to me." He paused for a frown into empty air. "O'Grady, you know that my own talents are weak. They're not organic, not a part of me. I had to learn them. I was too uncertain to file a formal report. Those reports are serious matters. The entire staff would have been placed on administrative leave, and a full-scale investigation would have followed. The process is nothing to invoke lightly."

I didn't need to be psychic to see what was coming.

"So you want us to go take a look?" I said.

"Yes, very much. I have a legitimate reason to send you. The Axeman, Ash's old confederate, was last seen heading for Six. TWIXT has a warrant out on him."

"I get it," I said. "I can recognize him. I've seen him in trance."

"Exactly. You'll need clearance from your agency, of course. I understand that."

I considered what Y was going to say about the idea of my taking off for Terra Six. I also considered how much I disliked Ash. In our previous encounter, Ash had set up an attempt to murder someone I admired. If I'd not been on the scene, the intended victim would have been stabbed to death. Now the little bitch had nearly killed someone else. It occurred to me that Ash was entirely too fond of knives.

"Er," Spare14 said. "Do you think you can get clearance?"

"No." I saw no reason to lie. "I think Y will veto my participation, assuming, of course, that he knows about it."

"Damn!" Spare14 frowned at his desktop. "What a pity."

Ari chuckled. I suppose you can call the repressed morbid snort he makes a chuckle.

"What is it, Nathan?" Spare14 looked up, annoyed.

"Assuming he knows," Ari said. "I doubt very much that O'Grady's planning on telling him."

I smiled. Ari smiled. Spare14 smiled and reached for the trans-world router.

"Let me just see how soon I can get another world-walker," Spare14 said. "And you'll need official clearance and a briefing on the situation on Six. It's quite vexing. Tomorrow, I should think, would be the earliest you might go, but we'd best not get our hopes up. Nathan, I'll send you a background file over our network. O'Grady, you'll have access to it as well."

"Okay," I said. "I'll file a report with the Agency, telling them that Ari's examination has been postponed and moved. Which is, after all, perfectly true."

"Quite so," Spare14 continued. "I should warn you both

about something now. TWIXT may be dedicated to fighting Chaos, but working for them becomes utterly haphazard at times. We're always short-staffed and underfunded. It usually seems that we live on the run. Situations change so very fast when one is dealing with a multiverse."

"I can believe that," I said. "It's the same with the Agency, though of course we've only got one messed-up planet to deal with."

Spare14 smiled at that. "As for this mission, it shouldn't take you long to get a reading on the office. If I could sense something with my paltry talents, the aura field there must be extremely disturbed."

We returned home just after noon. While I called Annie to tell her that we'd be leaving some other day, Ari rooted around in our refrigerator for lunch. Since I was still battling a serious eating disorder, I viewed the rooting with trepidation. Ari could and would eat anything when he was hungry. I had trouble getting good food down, much less the things he served. But then, even a normal gorge would have risen when faced with toaster waffles crowned with tuna fish straight from the can, oil and all, or maple bars topped with crumbled chicken sausage.

"I'd better go, Annie," I told my second-in-command. "Ari's starting to cook something."

"You do have smoke alarms, don't you?" Annie said.

"God, you're optimistic today! Yeah, don't worry. I made sure of that."

Ari managed to make grilled cheese sandwiches without causing a disaster, and I managed to eat one of them, a successful meal all round by our standards. When he doused some leftover potato salad with catsup, right in the cardboard carton, I retreated into the living room and picked up my e-mail.

At my non-Agency address, Shira Flowertree had replied. When Ari had told me that his mother wasn't one for maternal gushing, he hadn't been kidding.

"I'm glad you and my Ari are happy," Shira said. "I'm doubly glad that you work in law enforcement yourself. No doubt you two understand each other. And I do hope you have some self-defense training. You'll need it. If he ever becomes truly angry with you, and he doubtless will at some point, never ever turn your back on him. He can be quite dangerous. I blame his experiences in the Israeli army. He had a temper as a child, but it never got out of hand."

I knew exactly what she meant. I was merely surprised that his mother would see it and admit it. She went on to say that she had a good friend who had a video conferencing setup she could use, provided I didn't want to talk early in the morning. I told her not to worry, that early mornings there meant the middle of the night in my time zone.

I was about to switch over to TranceWeb when I felt something watching me. I swiveled around in my chair and found a small silver cephalopod sitting on the coffee table. I banished it with a Chaos ward and got back to work.

Filing my weaseling update to the Agency brought me a crisis of conscience. In the psychic universe there are two main principles, Chaos and Order. Too much Order means social stagnation and the death of every creative process. Too much Chaos means social violence and suffering, usually physical. Eventually, each situation turns into its opposite in an eternal ugly dance of extremes—unless the two merge in the right proportions, and Harmony results. Each conscious individual, whether human or alien, shares the nature of both principles and has the capacity to choose to work for Harmony. Unfortunately, few make that choice.

I knew that my essential nature held an excess of Chaos, but I'd chosen to strive toward Harmony by embracing Order. So what was I doing lying to my superior at the Agency?

I put the question to Ari when he returned to the living room after glutting himself on leftovers.

"If you want to call off the trip," he said, "I'll just ring Spare14 and tell him so. He's asking you for a tremendous favor, after all."

"I don't want to call it off. That's the problem. Something's pushing me to go along. Or pulling me, I guess I should say. There's something there I ought to see."

"If it's some sort of corrupt individual, and if that individual's connected to the Axeman and Ash, then you'll certainly be serving Harmony by helping root them out."

"That's true, isn't it? But—"

"The problem lies with Y, not you," Ari continued unabated. "From what you've told me, he's being entirely too rigid. Too Orderly, I suppose you'd say. His position, his authority, the regulations, fear of change—all of that rot is what's motivating him."

"You have a touch of Chaos yourself, don't you?"

"No. I simply have too much respect for the Order principle to see it misused. He's overdoing it, rather, and for the wrong reasons."

Every now and then Ari surprised me with his insight.

"You know," I said. "You've just given me a good idea."

I sent Y an e-mail over TranceWeb, stating that Ari's higher-ups had rescheduled his examination, and that I'd be going with him to Terra Six rather than Terra One when the time came. I admitted that there were possible complications that might keep me there longer than either the Agency or I wanted.

"The intel Spare14 shared with me," I wrote in the e-mail, "indicates that the Chaos masters may have established a base of sorts on the deviant level of Terra Six. At the very least, they have introduced a spy or corrupted a local. We should explore this possibility in case it leads back to the Peacock Angel cult, and I have reason to suspect it will. Their main method does seem to be infiltration. I understand your reservations about TWIXT, but in this case, their concerns may have dovetailed with ours. Since you expressedly asked me to investigate the Peacock Angel phenomenon, I feel duty-bound to follow this lead."

The "duty-bound" line of thought came from Ari's insight. Y had indeed asked me to find out if Chaos masters controlled the Peacock Angel bunch—some months before, but he'd asked. The phrasing worked. Permission came back in twenty minutes.

"But be very careful," Y finished up. "Remember that you have observer status only."

I assured him that I would and thanked him as well.

All that remained was waiting until Spare14 could get a TWIXT world-walker to transport us. I briefly thought of suggesting my brother Michael, who could use my father's orbs, but I ruled that out. He'd already displayed too much of a taste for Chaotic venturing around the multiverse to encourage him. And my father would never have agreed to work with the police in general and with TWIXT in particular, because he'd spent thirteen years in prison after being arrested by the self-same Spare14. His crime? Transporting fellow IRA members across world lines to escape from a deeply oppressive imperial Britain on Terra Five. Know who Oswald Mosley was? The leader of the Black Shirts, a violent Fascist group in the 1930s. On Five, he'd won.

Later that day Ari received the background file on Terra Six that Spare14 had promised us. He printed it out and brought me the copy rather than risk forwarding it to me digitally. I suppose that if I had had his skill with computers, I might have been able to obtain routing information or some such thing from an e-mail. I didn't and couldn't, but Ari liked to keep his paranoia well-fed and exercised. I appreciated getting the file in whatever shape or form. Ari handed me the stack of paper in a cold silence. Each page had a header announcing that the information was restricted material.

"Jeez, do you look sour!" I said. "What's wrong?"

"Nothing."

"Yeah, sure! You don't really want to give me this, do you?"

"Since Spare14 authorized your access, there's nothing I can do about it."

"Wait a minute! I know why you look so sullen. I don't have to offer you some kind of weird bondage sex just to get a look at it."

He blushed scarlet. I'd hit it in one. I smiled. He continued blushing.

"Oh, very well," he said eventually. "I'll admit to being disappointed." Slowly his color returned to normal. "But of course, should you feel like rewarding me for being so honest . . ."

"I'll read the file first, and then I'll see what I feel like."

"I'll be in working with my laptop if you should want to seduce me."

"Okay, I'll keep that in mind."

"At the kitchen table."

"Yeah, okay."

"With the handcuffs ready. Just in case you're in the mood for those."

I felt the level of my Qi rising. He was watching me with an innocent smile.

"Or if you're not," Ari continued, "I'm sure I can think of something else you might like. A silk scarf around your wrists? Kinder than the cuffs. Just as—" he paused and smiled. "Controlling."

I began to perceive the Qi as heat, a spread of warmth through my body. I certainly enjoyed making love with Ari in all the ordinary ways, but whenever he took control of me in bed, I felt safe from the Chaotic side of my nature. It gave me tremendous freedom to let go and revel in what he was doing to me. He knew it, too, damn him! I laid the stack of papers down on the coffee table.

"I could put on those black stockings," I said.

"Please do," he said. "I'll fetch the scarf and meet you in the bedroom."

When I stood up, he caught me by the shoulders and kissed me. The Qi blazed into sheer unadulterated lust.

CHAPTER 4

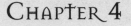

EVENTUALLY, SOME WHILE AND a short nap later, we got out of bed. While Ari ordered pizza for dinner, I started reading the file. The information made me glad we'd had our fun before I saw the grim situation ahead of us. I might have been depressed into abstinence.

Terra Six is a member of our local cluster of deviant levels, but one where the vast majority of its inhabitants have no idea that the universe is really a multiverse—the same situation, in other words, as here on our own Terra Four. By the way, the numbers of the levels mean very little, a naming convenience only, not a hierarchy, not even an expression of closeness or distance. Our entire local cluster within the multiverse had deviated around 1919, our time, during one of the great fractal generation events that produces gates and worlds.[1]

On Terra Six, among many other events, the United States fell apart during the Great Depression. When Wall

---

[1] TWIXT has graciously allowed a release of information on this process for those interested. See the Appendices.

Street-backed Fascists assassinated President Roosevelt, no one else emerged to unify the country. California and Oregon formed a new California Republic. Washington state joined Canada. The New England and Atlantic states put together the Republic of America, and the Deep South returned to the Confederacy—without Texas, which became a republic and a member of OPEC. The vast middle of the country now belonged to the Fundamentalist-dominated Kingdom of Christ.

The Kingdom hated California, that bastion of ecology and devilish ideas like the equality of women, and their preacher-leaders did more than give sermons against it. The TWIXT report concluded with a discussion of various acts of terrorism against the Republic. Every Californian assumed the Kingdom lay behind them all. Evidence existed to back up this belief. Most recently, the terrorists had attacked San Francisco. They'd tried to bomb General Hospital and its women's health clinic—preying on those they saw as weak, as terrorists always do. On a tip, the police were waiting and arrested four operatives.

Some days prior to the issuance of the report I was reading, the terrorists—in revenge—had set off a number of bombs in the Emporium, a huge department store on Market Street. A lot of people, mostly women, had died in the explosions and fires.

"These people are crazy," I said to Ari. "Why blow up a department store?"

"It's not as well guarded as a bank or civic building, I should think. We've had bombings in shopping areas and restaurants at home. Anywhere the terrorists can cause pain and chaos will do them nicely."

When Ari talked about "we" or "home" in this way, he invariably meant Israel.

"Well, yeah," I said. "I guess that's what terrorism is all about, pain and chaos. Bastards!"

I could remember the Terra Four version of the Emporium, which had changed hands and no longer existed as such here. I'd gone there often as a child with my mother or Aunt Eileen. In the basement the store carried merchandise that seemed to my child-self to date from the Dark Ages, things like boxes of little white cotton gloves or stays for mending corsets. When the terrorists bombed the building on Terra Six, the upper floors would have collapsed into that basement and the store's beautiful baroque dome come crashing down on top of the ruins. The thought made me shiver.

We'd just finished eating when I had a reason to shiver again. Maureen called me, and she sounded exhausted.

"I've been meaning to call you," I said. "I was wondering how the lawyer's appointment went."

"Lousy. That's why I didn't call you last night. I needed to think things through."

"What's wrong?"

"He told us not to get the restraining order. He says they make the situation worse."

"What?"

"He says they put you in more danger. The police don't really do much, and then the guy just gets angrier and more determined to hurt you. Some of them take it as a challenge, he says. Or a way to rebel against authority. He had loads of cases to tell us about. The police really won't act until he tries to beat you up or kill you, and then it's usually too late."

I felt sick-cold. "That's awful," I said. "Mo!"

"Yeah, real awful." Her voice slid toward tears. "Not the worst, though. We saw him, Chuck, I mean. He must have been trailing us. We got out of the lawyer's office, and I looked across the street, and there he was. Hiding in a doorway, but I know it was him."

I could hear my father's voice in the background. Although I couldn't distinguish the words, I could tell he was furious. I must have looked upset, because Ari got up and came over. I gave him a quick summary.

"The lawyer may be right," Ari said. "He knows the situation in California better than I do. She'd best take his advice."

"Mo," I said. "Did you hear that?"

"Yeah."

I held the phone away from my ear so Ari could hear her answer.

"I think," Maureen continued, "we're going to do what the lawyer suggested, which is to try to get me into the witness protection program because I can testify about Chuck's dealing. It's creepy, isn't it? They'll maybe protect me as a witness, but death threats to some ordinary woman—they won't do anything about those."

Ari winced. "I'm afraid so," he said. "It's obvious that Chuck knows where you're living. You need to move somewhere else."

"Yeah," Maureen said. "Kathleen offered to take us in. I'm going to call her."

"Good idea," I put in. "She's got that big house."

"With an eighteen-foot fence around it." Maureen's voice got a little stronger. "And all those dogs."

"And a husband who's an ex-Marine. Jack owns even more guns than Ari does."

She managed a weak little laugh at that. Although I tried to think of soothing things to tell Maureen, and we chatted for a while more, she stayed on the edge of tears the entire time. Not that I blamed her, mind. Not at all. Ari hovered by the phone, looking grim, until I clicked off so Maureen could call Kathleen. He sat down on the couch and continued looking grim. I swiveled my desk chair around to face him.

"I'm really scared," I said.

"I don't care for the situation myself," Ari said. "If Trasker's using methedrine, and Maureen's quite convinced he is, then he'll behave erratically. Men in this situation tend to be determined to get their revenge no matter what the risk to themselves. Being irrational will make that tendency worse. However, if he stops worrying about his own survival, he'll be easier to find and arrest. Irrationality works both ways."

"What if he kills Maureen? Having him arrested then isn't going to do us any good."

"True. I'll call Sanchez in the morning to see if he can do anything. I've been afraid of this all along. The situation with the restraining orders..." Ari shook his head and scowled. "The laws in these situations do more to protect the man's rights than the woman's life."

My stomach clenched so hard that I felt like vomiting. An evil thought made things worse.

"What if he hires someone to kill her?" I said. "We won't even know who to look for."

"Very unlikely. He'll want to do it himself for the satisfaction."

I felt too sick to comment.

"If Chuck causes trouble at Jack and Kathleen's, she may have to leave the area entirely," Ari went on. "Go to a place where he won't think to look for her."

"Oh, great! Take the kids away from everyone they know, disrupt her whole life, and here he's the goddamn criminal, not her."

"Unfortunately, that's the way it works. I'm worried about what will happen once the children return to school. He may try to get at her through them. They can't stay shut up in Kathleen's house forever, though I suppose the family can get them a tutor until the situation calms down. Eventually, these men give up. It usually takes a year, perhaps less if the woman's lucky."

Lucky. For a minute or two I couldn't speak, thanks to a

combination of terror and fury. I got myself under control. "I wonder if we could lure him onto a deviant level and then leave him there." I wasn't joking. "He'd fit right in on Interchange."

Ari came out with his sort-of-laugh, sort-of-snarl chuckle. For some minutes we sat and stared at each other. My sister was one of the lucky ones. What would happen to a woman on her own or one with only minimal family to help? I shivered again.

"There's nothing we can do till morning," Ari said. "I'll call Sanchez then."

"Okay. Thanks."

"I might as well look over the trans-world codes again." Ari opened his cram book. "Some of the details are irritatingly hard to remember."

"I believe it. I guess I could get some work done. I really wish Cryptic Creep would get back in touch with me. I never thought I'd say that, but that's the way things go sometimes."

"Have you ever tried getting in touch with him? Initiating the process?"

"There are times when you're positively brilliant."

"Of course." Ari smiled at me. "I'm glad you recognize it."

I refrained from throwing something at him. He stood up from the couch.

"I'll be in the kitchen studying," Ari said. "I know you need privacy to work."

I thanked him and swiveled around in my chair. Since Cryptic Creep had often appeared on the blank flat screen of my computer, staring at it seemed a logical place to start. Nothing happened until I realized I'd have to do more than just stare. I formed a memory image of him in my mind and tried projecting that out onto the screen. Again, nothing, though I did eventually see the image as if it truly did exist. Sound—that's what I was missing!

I spoke aloud, softly, "In the name of the Peacock Angel, let me see him."

The black circle with the seven arrows began to form on the screen. When I repeated, "In the name of the Peacock Angel," it snapped into focus. Cryptic Creep, however, did not appear other than in my memory. As I contemplated that memory image, it finally occurred to me that I knew his name because I knew his doppelgänger here on Terra Four.

"Keith," I said. "Father Keith, priest of the Peacock Angel. In that name I would see you."

For a moment, nothing—then the familiar face swept into view, surrounded by the black arrows like a halo or crown of thorns. The familiar fluting voice, higher than ever out of sheer surprise, sounded in my mind.

"Nola!" he said. "Which . . .?"

"Not the one you know," I said aloud. "Do you know what a doppelgänger is?"

"Yes. I owe you a profound apology. I can only contact you for a few brief moments, you see, before the power supply overloads, and so I jumped to conclusions when I saw you."

"You use some kind of machine for this?"

"Yes, of course. Don't you?"

"No, but don't worry about that now. The other Nola, is she missing?"

"Yes. My niece."

No surprise there.

"Are you a churchman? Of the Peacock Angel, I guess it'd be."

"Yes, a bissop."

Their version of bishop, I figured, both adapted from the Greek *episcopos*.

"I take it," I continued, "that your church aligns itself with the principles of Order, decency, and other such virtues."

"Most assuredly." He sounded amused by my question, but as he spoke, his voice became more and more urgent. "We all must serve the Eternal Light, each in our own way, and fight against the darkness in our souls. This world was created perfect. It's our sins that have soiled and torn it. The Peacock Angel can only repair his handiwork with our help, sinners though we are."

This moral structure sounded even grimmer than the Catholicism of my childhood, but on the whole I felt relieved. I could tell that he was speaking the truth as he saw it, which made him very unlikely to be an enemy.

"Is there also a heretic cult of the angel?" I said. "Worshipers of Chaos."

"Yes! Which is why I worried, why I . . ." The image began to fade.

"Quick!" I snapped. "I've been approached by one of your doppelgängers. He seems to be a threat."

The image flickered out. The arrow circle vanished. I could only hope that he'd heard me. Restoring contact immediately was out of the question if his power supply had just overloaded. I needed time to think, anyway. I was pleased that he'd confirmed my theory about the existence of two forms of Peacock Angel worship, but a complicated situation had just become worse, especially since we'd be leaving home soon. I doubted that Bissop Keith could find us once we'd reached another world level.

Spare14 called later to confirm that very trip.

"Willa will be free tomorrow, thank heavens," Spare14 said. "She's the best world-walker on the team. Nathan, I've made arrangements with our TWIXT linkman in the Republic of America. New York City will be your alleged home office while you're on Six. I've finalized your cover story. You're bringing an important witness—that's O'Grady, of course—to make a deposition. The Axeman's been put on the trans-world Most Wanted list, and TWIXT have good reason to believe he's hiding out on Six. O'Grady can recognize him and Murphy's assailant as well."

"How is Murphy?" I asked.

"Recovering on One. I decided she'd be safer in a new location."

"Probably wise, yeah. Uh, what happens when Nathan and I need to leave Six?"

"Oh, you'll have transport orbs, don't worry!"

"Good," Ari said. "Will we eventually go after the Axeman?"

"Yes, of course. Reconnaissance first, however. We need to understand the situation on Six before we proceed."

As the call progressed, Ari had a lot of questions about procedure as well as possibilities. Once we'd gone through them all, Spare14 ended the conversation with a cheery, "All should go well. It's only a very short stay."

I went to bed in a less than optimistic frame of mind. Although Ari went right to sleep, I lay awake for some time, worrying about Maureen and the kids and brooding over the scraps of information that Bissop Keith had given me. As soon as I got back from our short jaunt to Terra Six, I promised myself, I'd contact the bissop again.

Maureen at least would be safe over at Kathleen's. For a while, anyway. I tossed and turned, trying to forget that the fence, though tall, was chain-link. Someone—Chuck—could shoot through the holes. Was he a good shot? Did he have a sniper's rifle with a long range? I didn't know. I was reminded all over again of how much I hated guns. He knew where Kathleen lived. He'd been there. The family had tried to welcome him when Maureen first brought him round. He'd responded by moving her to the edge of the Bay Area, all the way out to Livermore, where we couldn't see what was going on with them.

Ari turned over onto his back and began to snore loudly enough to make my brain quiver. I relieved my feelings by poking him viciously in the ribs. He woke up and muttered something in Hebrew.

"You're snoring," I said.

He muttered something else and turned over onto his side. The snores shrank to a tolerable level. I'd just managed to fall asleep when one of the security alarms by the bed went off with a soft but insistent chirping. I woke and sat up. Ari was already out of bed and pulling on his jeans.

"Qi alert," he said. "Someone's trying to scan the flat."

"Should I turn on the light?"

"Yes. This alarm registers energy beams only. No one's physically breached our perimeter."

I took this to mean that no one had broken into the flat. I leaned over and turned on the bedside lamp. Ari touched the alarm unit to silence its chirp. His laptop sat on top of the dresser by the bedroom window. When he flipped up the lid, the screen lit and Hebrew letters lined up in tidy columns. I scooted over to his side of the bed to watch.

"Could you put that into English?" I said.

"Certainly." He tapped a few keys,

The text changed to tidy columns of incomprehensible abbreviations in the Roman alphabet. No, I don't know why I bothered to ask. For a few minutes Ari stared at numbers scrolling across the top of the display.

"Attack's repelled," he said eventually. "It came from dead west at a distance of maybe two kilometers, maybe less. From out to sea, in other words. From a boat, I suppose."

"Or a psychic Venusian squid."

Ari wrinkled his nose, started to snarl, hesitated, and blinked at me. "Sorry," he said, "I keep forgetting that those are real."

"Very real, and they can gather Qi from seawater. Like, to blast at someone."

Ari frowned and sat down on the edge of the bed. "More projections like Belial?"

Belial was a squiddish Chaos master that my team had managed to corner and arrest.

"Maybe. Their species doesn't produce world-walkers."

"But consider the transport orbs. This time they might be physically here."

"Huh, I wonder if this is why Ash wanted Murphy's orbs, for transporting squid clients. She and the Axeman might be playing their old game—trans-world coyotes."

"Why would the squid want to come here? Our oceans are filthy."

"I dunno. Maybe they're running from the law on their own world. We know the cephalopods have a justice system."

"Criminal psychic squid on the run." Ari's voice faded toward hopelessness. "I should have been an insurance adjustor. My father was right."

I glanced at the clock: three fifteen, way too early to get up. Ari reset the alarm, then stood up to take off his jeans. I lay back down and admired the view.

"I'm having trouble sleeping," I said.

He grinned at me. "Just leave the light on," he said. "I can do something about that."

And he did. Afterward, we both slept till the conventional clock alarm went off at seven.

For our trip to Terra Six, Ari wore what he always called his "police clothing," a navy blue pinstriped suit with a white shirt and yellow-and-red-striped tie. Since I was going as a witness, not in some official capacity, I wore jeans but with a proper blouse, the flowered red-and-white one, and a gray suit jacket. I brought a shoulder bag, too, to carry transport orbs, some of Ari's little electronic devices, and an extra clip for the Beretta.

I also decided to leave my engagement ring in the wall safe in our bedroom. It was too beautiful to risk damaging or losing. In my job, the chance of damage and loss tends to run high. Ari opened the safe and brought out a blue velvet jeweler's box. I noticed that it contained three small drawers. When I held out my hand for the box, he didn't give it to me.

"Um, Ari," I said, "is there something wrong with that box? Like, it's going to explode if I touch it?"

"What? Nothing of the sort! Just being helpful. If you'll hand me the ring, I'll put it away."

"Ari!"

With a sigh he handed the box over. I put the engagement ring into the top drawer, then checked. As I suspected, the other two drawers held wedding rings. I glared.

"I got a much better price on the set," Ari said, "by buying them all at once."

"I am not marrying you!" My voice may have gotten a trifle loud.

"No need to shout! I thought, well, you might change your mind. Once we're both older, perhaps. Menopause sometimes does odd things to women's minds." He stepped back out of range.

Had he not done so, I would have kicked him in the shin.

Before we left, we had important phone calls to make. I called my second-in-command Annie again, and Ari got in touch with Lieutenant Sanchez. Sanchez waffled about getting Maureen into the witness protection program, but he did have important news, which Ari relayed when he finished the call.

"Someone tried to get in to see Evelyn Murphy," Ari told me. "She claimed to be Murphy's sister, but oddly enough, she didn't know that Murphy had been transferred to another hospital."

"Was she blonde?"

"Oh, yes. And when the nurse at the desk asked for ID, she turned and ran out of the lobby."

"It's a good thing that Spare14 got Murphy out of there."

"Yes, I'd say so. Ready to go?"

I was. We took a cab down to our arranged meeting place, South Park, an oval of greenery some blocks south of Market Street. Willa, we were told, would be arriving there from Terra Three around ten in the morning. We arrived early, but we had only a short wait before Willa, dressed in her disguise of scraps and cast-offs, stepped out of a small grove of trees. She carried her shopping bag, crammed with junk. I was expecting her to bring out a focus orb, but instead she hurried over to us.

"We're going to Spare14's office," Willa said. "Not to Six. Something real bad has happened, but I don't want to explain it twice."

"Is Murphy okay?" I said.

"Yes. That's not the problem, and thank God for that!"

Since Willa had already contacted Spare14 with one of TWIXT's high-level communicators, he was waiting for us at the office. As we came upstairs, I noticed that the blood-stained carpet had been removed. He'd brought chairs into the outer room, the one that held his desk and files. We all sat down and looked at Willa. She spent a moment or two rummaging through the clumps of stuff in her shopping bag. Eventually, she brought out a small leather card case.

"Here, Nathan." She handed it to Ari. "Your new ID, compliments of HQ."

Ari flipped open the case and showed me an Interpol ID different from the one he usually carried. Under his picture it listed his home office as New York City, Republic of America. He slipped it into the inside pocket of his jacket. Willa set her bag on the floor and considered the three of us in turn.

"The problem I'm having," she said, "is knowing that none of you understand math. It would be real easy to explain if you did. It'd still be a bitch and a half of a problem to solve, mind, but at least you'd know why."

"I shall be perfectly happy," Spare14 said, "to trust your opinions on the matter."

Ari and I both nodded. Although I had no idea how much math Ari knew, I myself had studied only two years of high school algebra—and that, my teacher had told us, wasn't even real math.

"Okay," Willa said. "Basically, we're in danger of losing touch with Terra Six. It's always floated, and these days it seems to be floating farther and farther away. It's getting harder and harder to exchange information with it."

"The trans-world router's not working there, you mean?" Spare14 broke in.

"Not what I meant, no, although their routers are probably the next thing that's going to go blooey. I'm talking about something different, a concept from that old-fashioned quantum physics. We—world-walkers—are the information that gets exchanged when we go from world level to world level. Think of us all, you, me, all of us, as packets of information that vibrate at a given frequency. Each world has a distinct frequency, which is why the orbs have different colors. When someone vibrates at a new frequency, their information travels to that new world level."

"Oh," I said. "Like the transporter in *Star Trek*?"

Willa coughed. "No, honey," she said in a soothing tone of voice. "Kind of different from that. Don't worry about it."

"Um," Spare14 put in. "Perhaps we shouldn't spend time on the background briefing. What are the practical consequences?"

Although he spoke firmly, I realized that he felt as I did—as dumb as a bucket of mud.

"Good idea," Willa said. "The consequence is that it's damn hard to get in to Terra Six these days. The head of my team and I ran a check this morning from Three. It has the most gates, and so we figured it was the best world level for the tests. The overlaps to Six are floating. Some may close right down. We don't know yet."

We stared. She sighed.

"This means," Willa continued, "that a world-walker can't travel back and forth with a focus orb alone. We'll need a proper gate or transport orbs to help boost the frequencies. It's the damage to Interchange that's made Six so unstable. They were linked, and those links were broken. Three should have been anchor point for Six." She paused to look at us each in turn, perhaps to judge if any of us understood what she was telling us. "Anyway, Six moves, the whole world level, not just Terra Six. The stars, the galaxies, the whole shebang from the big bang on. It's swinging in an irrational arc through the quantum foam." She paused again and sighed. "Okay, I'll spare you the details."

"Please do," Ari said. "So the upshot—are we going today or not?"

"Ever direct, that's you, Agent Nathan." Willa grinned at him. "I'm pretty sure I can get you there. I've got a transport orb for Six with me. I'll be able to leave without one. Whether or not I could ever get there again—I don't know. Murphy was born on Six. She shares its substance. Its frequency is bred into her, as it were. If she were well enough to travel, things would be easier. But she isn't. The knife wound in her side just missed a lung, they tell me."

"How many times was she stabbed?" I said.

"Three, but one was just a scratch, and the other hit her upper arm when she tried to defend herself. She's damn lucky she didn't bleed to death."

I remembered Murphy's pale, nearly bloodless face—shock and pain, I'd thought at the time. Near-death experience was more like it. More and more I realized that Ash needed to be locked away from knives.

"Last night I checked various databases," Spare14 said. "I found a good many reports of orb theft."

"Way too many and just lately, too," Willa said. "Orbs have gone missing from vaults and from world-walkers getting mugged just like Murphy did. What evidence we've found always leads back to Terra Three and SanFran as the destination for the stolen orbs."

"The Axeman's original location," Ari murmured.

"So," Willa said. "Time's a-wasting. Sneak, are we going or not?"

"First a question," Spare14 said, "Without you, can the team leave Six again?"

"Probably." Willa shrugged. "I brought a couple of orbs for Four to get them back. I'm assuming they'll work. So is our research team. We're not guaranteeing anything."

"After all the lousy trouble I went through to get permission for this trip," I said, "we had damn well better go!"

"The situation does seem to warrant the risk." Spare14 rubbed his chin in thought. "The question is, do I have the power to authorize without a formal risk assessment?"

Willa rolled her eyes heavenward. I could smell bureaucracy in the air. In case you're wondering, bureaucracy smells like sour grapes and spilt milk.

"O'Grady," Ari said, "please don't scream."

"Okay, Nathan," I said. "For you, I won't."

In the end, screaming proved unnecessary. Spare14 fired up his trans-world router and checked in with his HQ. For some while they conversed as usual, in numbers interlarded with English words. Ari and Willa both seemed to understand what he was saying. I waited to be enlightened. Finally, Spare14 smiled and logged off.

"Permission granted," he said. "On the condition that the world-walker agrees."

"She does," Willa said.

"Good!" Spare14 continued. "One last thing. Nathan, you can trust the liaison captain in San Francisco Six. I know him well, JaMarcus Spivey. We were at the Police Academy together. They assigned roommates alphabetically, and so we ended up sharing quarters. We've been friends for thirty years."

If this were a *Star Trek* episode, I thought, Spivey would have turned traitor or been killed. Both Picard and Kirk's old friends always seemed to do one or the other. I refrained from saying so, of course. Ari and Spare14 were strangely ignorant about such important cultural matters, and—let's face it—the thought was weird even for me.

"Yes, Spivey's a good man," Willa said. "Now can we get on the road? We've wasted a couple of hours as it is."

"Back to South Park?" I asked.

"Nope. The closest overlap with Terra Six is in McLaren Park. When HQ linked with Six, they put the TWIXT office near it on purpose. Real convenient."

CHAPTER 5

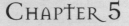

IN BOTH WORLDS, ours and Terra Six, McLaren Park lies in the southeast corner of San Francisco. It sprawls across the crest of the hill still known as University Mound, even though the college that once stood there is long gone. The hill rises above the Excelsior district to the west and the Portola district to the north. To the east on our world level, you can look down to the bay and the Hunter's Point shipyards. These are not locations known for famous landmarks unless you count the big blue water reserve tower up in the park, which I suspect you don't.

Just as in our world, the park on Terra Six featured mostly grass and trees, dotted with a structure or two: a children's playground, a tiny Greek theater, a small lake rimmed in concrete, a public golf course. The deviant world overlap area lay across a bulge on top of the hill, Bernt's Knoll, it's called in both worlds, though on Six it rises from a street called Redwood Drive instead of Shelley. Willa brought us through successfully to a big square of decaying concrete surrounded by trees and shrubs. Weeds poked up through the slab here and there.

"This is the overlap area," Willa said. "Don't try to use the transport orb anywhere else if you can help it. If someone's chasing you with a gun, sure, use one of the orbs, but I suggest you pray while you're doing it. You'll only have about thirty seconds to get into the cloud, remember, so don't take any time to kiss your boyfriend here."

"Very funny," I said. "Ha ha."

"I take it," Ari said, "that one needs to throw them onto something hard enough to shatter the glass or whatever that material is."

"They're made of frequency-wave-stabilized ice. Think of it as lasers for water molecules. That's why the shards melt away once you destabilize the stuff—they turn back into ordinary ice. So, yes, bouncing them on the lawn isn't going to get you squat." She paused to rummage in her bag. Eventually she brought out two blue-green orbs, each about the size of a large orange. "Here you go, O'Grady. These'll get you back to Terra Four. Put them in that bag of yours. I'll show you the path down to the office, and then I'm getting out of here. I can feel the float, and it's making me dizzy."

I took the orbs. "They don't feel cold," I said.

"That's because they're stabilized. The stuff won't absorb heat energy from their surroundings until you violate the sphere's integrity." She grinned. "That means breaking them."

Willa led us east on a narrow path. When we came clear of the trees, we had a good view down to the city streets below and the bay beyond, a view that shocked me. In our world I would have seen far below the big cranes and docks of the Naval Shipyard. On Six I saw only houses and what appeared to be small business districts stretching out to a bayside green belt.

"There wasn't any war with Japan here," Willa told us. "Didn't need the ships."

"Fascinating," I said. "Where's the TWIXT office?"

"See that concrete building down there?" Willa pointed to a flat-roofed, three-story, grim gray structure just across a street from the grassy lawn marking the edge of the park. "That's it. Second floor. They should be expecting you. I don't know if that's good or bad."

"Neither do I," Ari said. "The briefing was more than a bit ambiguous."

Briefing? I thought. *What briefing*?

"I bet!" Willa said. "Well, good luck. I've got to get out of here before I throw up."

She turned around and trotted back west to disappear among the trees.

"Shall we go?" Ari said.

"Sure, but what briefing?"

He looked vaguely guilty. "It came this morning in e-mail. You weren't cleared for it."

"Bastard!"

I strode off on the path downhill. Ari swore under his breath and caught up with me.

"I'm sorry," he said, "but Spare14 had already authorized one release of classified information. A second one would have been a bit much."

"You had better hope that I don't need the information in that briefing. That's all I can say, Agent Nathan!"

I set off downhill through the trees. He shoved his hands in his pants pockets and followed sullenly along.

In two more strides we came clear of the overlap area. As soon as I stepped out of it, I felt the pull. A psychic sensation grabbed me as palpably as the clutch of a hand. Something close by belonged to me or needed me and wanted me with a desperate longing. If I gave in, the Pull, as I called it to myself, would drag me downhill in the wrong direction. I stopped walking and caught my breath in a gasp.

"What's wrong?" Ari slipped a hand into his jacket and reached for the Beretta.

"You don't need that," I said. "I think I must have family on this level."

"Not precisely family." He took his hand away from the gun. "They may have genetic similarities, but they've been raised in a different environment and culture."

"Yeah, yeah, but I overlap with them. I can feel it."

Ari snorted and scowled.

"And what's so wrong with that?" I set my hands on my hips.

"I don't want you brooding about your father and mother's situation."

"Oh. Well, okay. You've got a point. We've got work to do, and I need to keep my mind on it."

I also needed to shield myself against the Pull. If I had put up a full psychic shield, I would have insulated myself from the entire aura field. My talents would have vanished and left me confused and helpless. Instead I tried a different technique. I visualized a flaming torch and swung it— mentally only—around and around me at the edge of my personal aura. The Pull gave up and faded away.

"We're heading into a difficult situation," I said. "Let me run more scans."

Ari waited patiently while I did a Search Mode: Location on the gray office building. I registered a few psychic talents, all minor, but SM: Danger brought more dramatic results. At least one person, a male, in that building was panicking over something. He was furious, brooding violence, frightened that he was about to be caught out, and trying to hide all of those feelings from the world.

"Okay," I said to Ari. "Be on alert the whole time we're

in there. Someone knows we're coming, and he's not happy about it."

As we made our way downhill, I stayed in contact with Mr. Panic. In a few moments his fear spiked, to be replaced by the smooth surface of a psychic shield. I stopped and held up one hand to tell Ari to do the same.

"He knows I know," I said.

Ari nodded to show he understood. I could follow the track left by Mr. Panic's shield like following a lump in gravy with a spoon. Get too close, and it would dissolve. I felt him travel away from me, leave the building, head downhill. Another mind, unshielded, joined his, a woman though not Ash. Her, I could follow easily. They got into a vehicle and drove away toward the west and the city. She must have been driving because he had the leisure to extend his shield and cover her.

"Damn!" I said. "I've lost them."

We continued on to the gray building and discovered that it housed three different agencies. First floor was a credit union, second floor the Interpol offices, and at the top, a security guard firm. Smooth pale marble coated the ground-floor lobby and made our footsteps echo as we walked in. On the far wall I saw a pair of elevators with bronze doors. According to the indicator panels above them, each car waited at the second floor.

"I don't like this situation," Ari said. "It's too quiet."

"I'm picking up danger. It's emanating from above and in the direction of the far wall."

Ari sniffed the air. He walked over to the elevators and sniffed again, just like a dog hunting for a scent.

"Do you smell that?" he said.

"What? No."

He started to answer just as the street doors swung open. A pair of young men walked in, very ordinary looking citizens in jeans and T-shirts. In one hand the red-haired guy held an old-fashioned bank book clutched around a pile of paper checks. I scanned. Nothing wrong with either of them. They were talking about baseball as they headed for an elevator. As soon as one of them reached toward the call button between the elevators, the warning hit me hard.

"Don't!" I yelled. "Don't touch it!"

"Police!" Ari drew the Beretta. "Everyone outside! Now! Move!"

The young man spun around to face us. I got a clear look at his terrified face: pale, thin dark hair cut short, a scraggly mustache under a beaky nose. The two men ran, and so did we. Once we'd gotten to the sidewalk, Ari holstered the gun and took out his small black TWIXT communicator. He pressed a couple of buttons while the two young men gawked at him.

"Agent Nathan here," he said. "We have a terrorist emergency. Clear the building, but do not, I repeat, do not use the elevators. Come down on the fire stairs only. I repeat, on the stairs only."

The dark-haired young man sat down quite suddenly on the ground. His friend knelt beside him and trembled. Ari went on speaking into the communicator. I heard a distant wail from down the hillside toward the west and the city. From inside the building a deep-throated horn began hooting an alarm in short bursts. I felt as if I'd been stretched very, very thin, turned into mist, maybe, a cold foggy mist. The sunlight brightened to a white glare. When I grabbed my terror and suppressed it, the sunlight returned to normal, as did my body-consciousness. Other wails broke out down below, more sirens, these from police cars. Fire trucks screamed up the hill and squealed to stops out in the street. The two young men got up again. The dark-haired guy looked at me.

"I nearly set it off, didn't I?" His voice shook and swooped like a terrified child's. "Ohmigawd!"

"Yeah," I said, "but you didn't. It's okay."

He turned and ran off downhill. His friend gave me a sick little smile and followed.

The front doors burst open and the first evacuees raced out, all of them dead silent, white-faced, and grim. They pushed past me and ran across the street in a well-rehearsed troop, not a mob. They'd practiced this drill, I realized: terrorist alert! Run but carefully. Don't get in each other's way. Stick with your office mates. I turned to watch as they organized themselves into little groups on the distant sidewalk. For each group one person walked back and forth, counting his charges. I studied them and ran scans. Here and there I picked up a trace of talents, but nothing as strong as those of the man I'd spotted earlier, the one who'd driven away just in time.

Yeah, he sure had, hadn't he? Just in time.

A bright red car and a sleek black one arrived in a scream of sirens. The men who got out of each wore uniforms dripping with gold braid. They ran to huddle with Ari. The hooting of the warning horn stopped abruptly. One last person walked out of the lobby, a tall, lean Cal-African man in a gray business suit that matched the gray in his close-cropped hair. His eyes narrowed as he looked over the crowd. He glanced around and started to join Ari and the others, then noticed me. When he waved me over, I went. He wasn't the kind of man whose orders you disregarded.

"I'm JaMarcus Spivey." He had a dark voice worthy of a Russian basso. "Are you O'Grady?"

I ran a discreet Subliminal Psychological Profile. He was exactly as Spare14 had described, honest and trustworthy.

"Yes, sir," I said. "Did Spare14 —"

"He's just 'Spare' here." Spivey's mouth flicked in a brief grin. "But, yes, he did. Let's get across the street. I need to check with the group leaders, and then move everyone farther away. If this thing blows, the rubble's going to rain down like hellfire."

I walked with him across the street to the edge of the park. By then the danger warnings were pounding on me like fists. My body wanted to turn and run away as fast and as far as possible. My mind kept me where I was. Uniformed police were trotting up and down the row of small businesses on either side of the office building, pounding on doors, ordering the inhabitants to evacuate. Just in case, they said. Situation under control, but just in case. Once Spivey determined that everyone who worked in the building had been accounted for, he barked crisp orders.

"Move down the street, two hundred yards away. That's past the next corner. If you see smoke from the building, run. The bomb squad's on its way."

The white-faced crowd moved, and fast. I lingered behind. I refused to leave until Ari got farther away from that hidden IED. Two men in suits and a young woman in a skirt suit stayed where they were as well. They huddled together, talking in low voices. When I ran a quick SPP, I picked up nothing but fear and outrage. I heard someone say, "The fucking Kingdom again!"

"Interpol people," Spivey remarked. "They're staying to get HQ on the line and keep them informed."

"Okay. I'll stay here, too. You might need my—uh—insights."

Spivey nodded and trotted back across the street to confer with the fire and police chiefs. I noticed a black truck, about the size of a delivery van, pulling up in front of the building. Four men got out, dressed in black clothes that appeared to be made of padded Kevlar and wearing plastic helmets with the clear faceplates raised. They began unloading a robotic unit from the back of the truck. I noticed that the unit looked crude, a gangly arm topped by a claw, a lot of machinery and motor at the base—a prototype, maybe. Spivey and the other chiefs came hurrying across the street to get out of their way. Ari, thank Whomever, came with them.

Squads of firemen moved into position close to the building and began unreeling hoses. Just in case, I thought. Ari walked over and stood next to me. A skinny, middle-aged white man with a shaved head but bushy salt-and-pepper eyebrows joined us. He introduced himself as Agent de Vere. We shook hands. The other two agents kept their distance. They were both speaking into communicators.

"We're short-staffed today," de Vere told us. "Two of our agents are giving evidence in a trial downtown. They left just in time to miss all the excitement, the lucky dogs!"

I managed to smile. Ari's eyebrows quirked. I figured he was thinking along the same lines as I was. Had they left because they were lucky or because they—or one of them— had planned this all out in advance?

"I'm sorry about this, Miss O'Grady," Ari said. "It appears we picked the wrong day to take your deposition."

"The right day is more like it," de Vere said. "What made you sound the alarm?"

"The smell." Ari smiled briefly. "Old-fashioned cordite, some kind of nitrogen fertilizer, and something else I couldn't quite identify."

"I see." De Vere turned to watch the bomb squad. "Damn good thing you didn't have a cold!"

Ari caught my attention and mouthed "your warning." I nodded to show that I understood he wasn't taking all the credit. Two of the men from the bomb squad lowered their faceplates and opened the building's doors. They headed inside and dragged their jerry-built robot platform after them. The remaining two stayed on the sidewalk and worked on what appeared to be tablet computers—I was too far away to be sure. I assumed they were providing some kind of information backup to the men and robot inside.

I took a couple of deep, gasping breaths. Ari raised a questioning eyebrow.

"Sorry," I said. "I'm just scared."

"With good reason," Ari said. "De Vere, tell me something. The lifts—was one of them supposedly out of order?"

"You bet," de Vere said. "Someone had put a sign up outside our offices. I told the fire chief which elevator it was." His mouth twisted in a caricature of a smile. "But during the evacuation, I noticed that no one had posted a sign down on the ground floor."

"Right," Ari said. "I'm fairly sure the IED is armed through the call button."

In the upper windows of the buildings fluorescent lights shone. All at once they went dark.

"They've cut the power to the entire building," Ari told me. "That should kill the trigger in the call button. One hopes."

Spivey walked over and suggested that we all move down the street. The other agents followed as we walked about halfway down to the corner, but the firemen stayed at their posts. My back brain twitched. I was missing something. I stared at the building and ran every scan I could think of. No one remained inside but the bomb squad. The man with the psychic shield—where was he? On his way downtown to give evidence? Or was he perhaps a religious fanatic from the Kingdom?

The question revolved around another question: why destroy this particular building? Blowing up a credit union would have had little effect on the Republic's finances. The security firm appeared to be small and local. That left TWIXT as the primary target unless the goal was some kind of personal revenge on an individual. Unless we were dealing with a madman, killing everyone in the building to get back at one or two people seemed unlikely. The man I'd sensed seemed sane enough, merely frightened and upset for some large reason.

The firemen had hooked up hoses to hydrants and stood in a ring, ready to move in if necessary. Minutes crawled by. No one spoke. Ari kept looking at his watch. I took the chance to run thorough SPPs on the staff members of the various offices. Everyone seemed decent and dedicated. De Vere and Spivey took turns contacting their headquarters in southern California over their sleek black communicators, or so they said. I assumed that one of them had a link to TWIXT HQ on Terra One

"The other liaison post's in L.A.," Spivey told us. "We're the only two in the Republic. The CBI's a bit touchy about Interpol's presence. That's the California Bureau of Investigation. Territorial instincts. Protocol and hierarchy, you know."

"Yeah," I said. "I certainly do."

The firemen closest to the building suddenly cheered. The building doors swung open, and the bomb squad emerged. As one man wheeled out the platform, I could see that the robot's claws held a cluster of black metal pieces wound with wires. The second officer came out more slowly because he was lugging a wooden box, about two feet on a side. The cheers spread through the neighborhood.

"The trigger mechanism," Ari said, "and the first charges. I'm assuming that there's more material still in the lift, but it's harmless now. That wooden box would have caught fire when the explosive in the trigger went, you see, and set off its contents. They, in turn —"

"Yeah," I said. "I can guess. Like Jericho, the walls come tumbling down."

Ari gave me a wry smile and nodded.

Squads of police moved into the building for a thorough search. The evacuees began straggling back uphill. I assumed that it would take several hours before they'd be allowed inside to shut up the offices and reclaim their purses and jackets and the like. In the confusion I had the chance to give Ari privately some questions that I needed answered. He drifted away to ask them of de Vere and Spivey. I stood at the edge of the crowd and ran some SM: Personnel scans for Ash and the Axeman. Neither of them was close enough for me to pick them up. Ari came back with the answers to my questions.

"The trial date's been set for several weeks now. The two agents won't return here after the trial ends for the day. One of them's a woman. The other is a bloke named Scott Trotter. I received the impression that neither de Vere nor Spivey care much for Trotter personally, though both assure me that he's competent enough. He was in his office all morning until it was time to leave for downtown. The woman officer, Lupe Parra y Cruz, was working in her office as well. I heard nothing but praise about her."

"Huh," I said. "So neither of them could have built that bomb in the elevator."

"Actually, I don't see how anyone could have done it. It's not like the McVeigh case, where he and his confederates packed their IED in a closed van and then drove it up to the Federal Building. You can't just fill a lift full of explosive material in broad daylight without someone noticing."

"So you'd think. Who would have been in charge if Spivey had been killed?"

"Trotter." Ari smiled, tigerlike. "Interesting, I thought."

"You bet. Very interesting."

"Your last question." Ari dropped his voice and glanced around to make sure that no one was eavesdropping. "Yes, they do keep orbs on the premises. In a locked safe."

I tried to consider the problem of planting the IED, but the crowd of people around us radiated so much raw emotion—fear, relief, anger, exhaustion, residual terror, downright rage—that the sheer massive output from other people's minds kept mine addled. I could also feel the Pull, the family overlap, nibbling at my defenses.

"Ari, I need to get away from here. Where can we go?"

"Home, I should think. I'll have to give a detailed report, and there's the matter of your deposition, but no one will have the time to take those today. Spivey's already given me leave to go. He'll contact Spare when they need us to come back."

"Oh, joy. I can't wait."

"Well, it's better than Interchange, isn't it?"

"Very true. I'll take comfort in that."

As we hiked back to the overlap area, I stayed on alert. I alternated running scans with allowing my mind to open up to the aura field. Ari kept his right hand close to the Beretta under his jacket. We crossed back into the park, found the path, and made our way uphill through the trees. I had just seen the concrete slab through the obscuring shrubbery when I felt someone watching us. I stopped, and so did Ari.

"I've picked up a spy," I said.

Ari turned in a slow circle and studied the area around us while I ran an SM: Danger. I registered no one close by, but distantly I felt a presence out on the aura field. As soon as I focused on it, the presence vanished.

"All clear," I said.

"Good. I don't see any threat either. Let's get out of here."

We walked out onto the concrete slab. Ari opened my shoulder bag and took out one of the orbs.

"I'll throw it onto that stain over there," he said. "Then we dash into the cloud."

"Okay." I swallowed and took a deep breath. "Should be easy."

He grinned at me and tossed the orb. It cracked in a burst

of blue-green smoke that billowed in a near-perfect sphere rather than pluming like normal smoke. We raced into it. I expected it to sting my eyes and make me cough, but as soon as our bodies touched the smoke, it disappeared.

We nearly ran out into the traffic on Shelley Drive before we realized we'd returned to Terra Four. When I looked back downhill through the trees, I saw the familiar view. The gray building, the fire engines, the crowded street had all vanished. Ari let out his breath in a puff of a sigh.

"Very good," he said. "A walk in the park."

I laughed, he laughed, and he caught me by the shoulders and kissed me. Only then did I realize that he'd been as scared as I was—not about the near-miss bombing, but about throwing the orb.

"We need to report to Spare14," Ari said. "Let's hope we can find a cab."

"Out here? Very funny. Ha ha."

"I'll just call one." Ari started to take his phone out of his shirt pocket.

"Don't bother. We could wait for hours. The cabs stay close to downtown and the tourist areas."

We left the park and walked a good distance before we reached Bacon Street and the nearest bus line, the 54. Since we had to transfer several times, Ari groused the entire way about waiting for buses, riding buses, and buses that stopped every block or so. Fortunately, we reached Spare14's office before I strangled Agent-Recruit Nathan and ruined TWIXT's hopes.

"Next time," Ari announced, "we will figure out somewhere to leave the car."

"Aunt Eileen's isn't all that far from the park. We could take the bus from there."

Ari snarled but mercifully said nothing more.

When we sat down with Spare14 in his office, we learned that messages over the trans-world router had preceded us.

Spare14 leaned back in his chair and smiled at both of us impartially.

"Well done," he said. "Thank God you were there, in fact. I shudder to think."

He didn't need to tell us what he was shuddering about.

"Yeah," I said. "Let me give you my opinion straight out. You were right in your suspicions about that office. I could feel Chaos all around me, and I don't think it's only because of the bomb threat."

"Very well. Could you zero in on any of the personnel?"

"I'd trust Spivey with my life. De Vere and the other agents I got a chance to vet are okay. Two agents had left the office just before the attempted bombing, so I didn't get a chance to vet them. I might have picked up their departure, however. Notice I say 'might have.' I could have registered some other pair of sapients. The male has strong talents, and he used them to hide from me."

Spare14 made a thoughtful sort of mumbling noise. "Parra y Cruz and Scott Trotter would have been the agents," he said. "I had quite a long talk with her the day I was there on routine inspection. She struck me as quite a good agent. Reliable and steady, I'd say. Trotter, oddly enough, was home ill that day."

"Oddly and conveniently?"

"Um, yes. I begin to wonder. Since I missed meeting him, I can't say if he has talents or not. Could you possibly write up your observer's opinion for me?"

"Not a problem. I'll do it tonight."

"Thank you, O'Grady. I very much appreciate this." Spare14 glanced at Ari. "You must have a rather acute sense of smell."

"It comes from being Israeli," Ari said.

"Quite. I understand." Spare14 drummed his fingers on his desk while he thought something through. "I hate to do this, but I really do think I have to file that formal report. Just before you arrived, Spivey contacted me. He told me that he thought it was time for some official oversight, as he put it. He said little more than that, though. It wouldn't have been fair of him to name names at this point. Still, his comment was telling. And now, O'Grady, I have your report." He sighed and looked away at nothing in particular. "Yes, I'm afraid I really shall have to contact HQ."

"I understand that this is a major step," Ari said.

"Most definitely. The procedure will take a while to implement. Everything has to be done precisely in the correct way with the proper legal safeguards."

"Will everyone in the TWIXT office be put on leave?"

"Not immediately, no. There are preliminaries to get out of the way first."

"I ask," Ari went on, "because of the Axeman case. I'd like to be assigned to that. I failed to apprehend him. It gripes me. Without a home office, won't the case be in abeyance?"

"Not necessarily. You could operate out of Los Angeles." Spare14 looked my way. "O'Grady, is there a chance that the Axeman and Ash might be linked to the terrorists?"

"There's always that chance," I said. "Scum tends to clump together at the top of the soup pot. I'm fairly certain that Ash is what we call a fast walker. Her talent would be useful when it came to smuggling operatives—" I stopped with my mouth half open. The insight I'd failed to receive in the midst of the terrified crowd on Six finally worked its way to the surface of my mind. "She'd also be able to walk into small spaces so quickly that she'd be hard to see. Like the elevator in the building. Like, carrying explosives. If she couldn't rig the device herself, she could bring someone with her who could."

Spare14 smiled, a grim twitch of his mouth that reminded me of Ari's tiger smile. "Quite so," he said. "A suspicion only at this point, but a valid one."

"And what about the orbs?" I continued. "We know she

obtains orbs by theft. What if she also obtains them from someone with access to that safe in the TWIXT office? Could she have used the orbs to gain access without anyone seeing her?"

"Not as I understand it. The transport orbs are not that precise, and she'd have to be coming from some other level to use them at all."

"Okay. What if Ash and/or the Axeman are buying them for reasons of their own? A TWIXT officer would be in a good position to deal in contraband orbs."

Spare nodded and grabbed a pen. For a few moments he wrote notes on a pad of paper. "Thank you, O'Grady." He looked up. "Very helpful, very important. Nathan, we really must get that examination out of the way. Once you're sworn in, you could be sent back to investigate the possible linkage O'Grady has just postulated."

"Thank you," Ari said. "I realize that things are difficult at the moment."

Spare14 nodded. Difficult, I thought. What a word for it!

We left Spare14 to his grim job of whistle-blowing. Luckily, cabs abound in that neighborhood, so I was spared Ari's grousing on the way home and his driving as well. There's something about nearly being exploded into microscopic shreds that makes you long for peace and quiet.

CHAPTER 6

WE SPENT THE REST of the afternoon writing reports, sending them off to our various agencies, and answering e-mail. After the day we'd had, routine business had its attractions. I was trying to put the morning's events behind me, and I thought I was doing pretty well. When I finished with TranceWeb, I found e-mail waiting for me on my other account. I saw an unfamiliar address in my queue and started to delete the message. I realized in time, however, that the subject line read "Actually from Shira Flowertree." First I ran a security check; then I opened it.

"I'm sorry to tell you that it will be a few days before we can conference," the message said. "Lev is being difficult about my willingness to be interviewed. He says I should be putting the kibbutz behind me, not wallowing in its memory. We had rather a nasty argument about it over breakfast. I shall have to let him calm down. You may reach me here at this address, which belongs to Barbara, my friend with the conferencing equipment. Shira."

I called Ari over to the computer. "Does this look like your mother's prose?" I said.

He read the e-mail. "Yes," he said. "It also sounds like something that idiot Flowertree would do."

"Interesting. I wonder about the guy. Could you find any dirt on him?"

"What makes you think I tried to?" But Ari grinned at me. "None, actually. I'll confess to being disappointed."

"Is it possible that he was provided with a new identity somewhere along the line?"

"I couldn't find any trace of that, either. What makes you think it might be the case?"

"I'm not sure." I paused to focus on my mental processes. "But I'm feeling that I should take an interest in him. I'm just not sure why. Do you have the dossier you put together on him?"

"Somewhere. I don't remember if it's on this machine or not. They married some years ago now, and I've upgraded since then. I'll look."

While he did, I ran a Web search on Lev Flowertree and found that he'd written a book—a self-published book, but a book nonetheless. It contained his research into one of the crazier occult preoccupations, the lost continent of Mu, the supposed Pacific Ocean counterpart of Atlantis. I brought up Flowertree's web page. It featured a black-and-white portrait photo of the guy, a decent-looking man in his 50s with dark hair, streaked with gray, and a gray beard about a quarter-inch longer than stubble. His grin and crinkly eyes said "out-doorsman" to me. He was wearing an open-throated pullover shirt decorated with a geometric design, possibly handwoven, possibly embroidered, Bohemian in either case.

I read on and learned that unlike so many writers about the imaginary continent, he'd actually gone to the South Pacific to do research. He'd lived in Tonga for two years,

Samoa for two more, and visited Easter Island and the Galapagos group as well. He also was an accomplished SCUBA diver, or so he said, and had some formal training in oceanography.

At that point the alarm rang in my brain. I logged off and went to talk with Ari, who was working with his laptop at the kitchen table.

"No dossier, unfortunately." Ari looked up from the screen. "I must have archived it in offsite storage from another machine."

"Too bad," I said. "You told me that Flowertree wormed his way into your mother's life. For real, or do you just think he's a worm?"

"Both. He met her at that sodding astrology class, but later he admitted he'd taken the class to get to know her."

"She doesn't have money, does she?"

"No, if you mean an independent income. He's the one with money. When she met him, she was working as an editor for a British occult publisher. She was grossly underpaid, if you ask me. Flowertree wined and dined her. At first, he was trying to sell her his book, as you might expect."

"Did she buy it?"

"No. She thought he'd go away at that point, but instead, he began to court her, I suppose you'd call it." Ari paused for a scowl. "He does actually seem to care for her. That had best be the case, or I'll—" He slammed his right fist into the palm of his left hand.

Flowertree had certainly hit the stepson jackpot. I felt a deep sympathy for Shira, caught in between those two, but I kept that thought to myself. "Did he ever mention Reb Ezekiel?"

"Oh, yes, or so she told me later." Ari paused for a couple of deep anger-management breaths. When he spoke again, he sounded reasonably calm. "He was quite curious about the kibbutz back then. Odd that he wants her to forget it now."

The alarm sounded again, louder.

"What?" Ari said. "You've got that peculiar expression on your face. It usually means something equally peculiar is going on in your brain."

I muttered something rude and sat down at the table.

"I'm thinking three things," I said. "First, Flowertree's an occult author with contacts in that scene. I bet he's read Reb Zeke's books, which means he knows about the visions. Second, he's spent a fair amount of time underwater. Third, he doesn't want your mother to talk with me."

"He's got one of three right, then."

I ignored this last remark. "Four things, actually," I went on. "He's also a vegan."

"That last bit —"

"It means the psychic cephalopods from Venus might trust him."

Ari sat back in his chair and stared at me, just stared with an expression so appalled that I felt sorry for him.

"Well," I said, "they don't trust us because our species eats squids and octopi. So if they find someone who doesn't, they might approach him."

"I won't eat them, either. Nasty foreign muck, and tref at that. They've never approached me."

"They probably don't like being called 'unclean.' They're natural psychics, y'know."

Ari made a snorting sound.

"What I'm saying," I finished up, "is that your mother's husband may be a secret agent for the squid. A kind of underwater mole."

"Do you honestly think they'd have agents here?"

"Consider the late, unlamented Caleb. He was, for sure, one of their dupes. Reb Zeke mentioned agents, too,

before he died. It makes me think their tentacles are
everywhere, and we're the suckers."

Ari stared at me.

"Sorry," I said. "I just couldn't resist the joke."

Ari rubbed his forehead with one hand.

"Headache?" I said.

"Now, yes." He lowered his hand and looked at me with
deep sorrow in his dark eyes.

"The question is, what do the psychic cephalopods have
to do with the destruction of Interchange?"

"What makes you think they have one sodding thing to
do with it?"

"Proximity of occurrence and karmic gravity."

He stared again.

"I explained karmic gravity to you months ago," I said.

"Yes, and I didn't believe it then, either."

I sighed. "Both the psychic squid and Interchange came
into my life and work at roughly the same time. So did you,
and you bring your mother, the kibbutz, and now Flowertree with you. It may look like coincidences, Ari, but it
adds up to critical mass."

Ari crossed his arms over his chest and leaned back in
his chair. I knew I had a hard sell ahead of me. I needed to
think up a new metaphor, I figured, and looked away. A
large squidlike creature was hovering in the air over the
sink. It flapped its mouthful of tentacles at me and darted a
few feet forward in an attempt to gain dominance.

"Oh, stop it!" I said. "I am so sick and tired of you!"

"What?" Ari said. "What did I do now?"

"Not you!" I got up so fast that I knocked my chair over.
"Go away, you filthy piece of squid shit! I am sick and tired
of you guys bothering me!" I strode over to the counter and
grabbed my big German steel carving knife. "Do you hear
me? Get out!"

The squid-shape retreated back against the wall. I thrust

the knife in its direction and screamed. "I said get out! I'll turn you into calamari salad! Deep-fried! Cut off your tentacles!"

It flapped its tentacles again to reveal its circular mouth, fringed with triangular teeth. I drew a Chaos ward in the air. The ward hovered gleaming on the point of the knife. I flicked it forward like a tennis ball from a racquet. "OUT!"

The squid popped like a balloon and disappeared. One writhing tentacle fell onto the floor near me. When I raised a foot to stomp on it, the slimy thing curled and vanished. I lowered the knife and stood panting for breath.

"I take it," Ari said calmly, "that you saw one of those Chaos creatures again."

"A big one, yeah. Squiddish, this time. They're driving me crazy."

"Well, it's only a short drive."

I spun and glared at him. He stopped grinning.

"Darling," Ari said, "do put that knife down. Please?"

Because I really did love him, I laid the knife on the counter. Ari sighed in relief.

"I was afraid I might hurt you," he said, "if I had to take it away from you."

I nearly picked the knife up again to use on him. Instead, I set my chair upright and sat down. I ran my hands through my hair to push it back from my face. My hands, I realized, were shaking.

"You're really quite nervous tonight," Ari went on. "What's wrong?"

"What's wrong? We were nearly killed, that's what! If that guy had punched the elevator button—" I shuddered.

"Oh. That."

"Are you putting on an act or something? I can't believe how macho you're being about what happened on Six."

"It's not macho." He spoke softly, slowly. "Nola, I've spent my entire life ready to die. When I was a boy, we lived in fear of an Arab invasion, to say nothing of the PLO. Then I went into the army, and we were there to fight and die. I was military police, worse yet, a walking target for the terrorists. I could have been killed at any minute. I knew it, I lived with it, I accepted it. Don't you understand that?"

All at once I did, partly because of my talents, but mostly because of the way he was looking at me—so openly, so seriously, his eyes perhaps a little puzzled at my failure to see what it meant to be a man like him from a place like Israel.

"Okay," I said. "I do get it now."

He smiled. I couldn't.

"I need to call Itzak," Ari continued as if we'd just been discussing the weather. "These Chaos creatures don't set off the alarm system when they appear. They should."

Although he was an American citizen, Itzak Stein was Ari's long-time buddy and something of a technical genius. He'd been working as an IT expert at one of the big banks when I'd first met him, but as a favor to us, he'd designed and installed the security system that Ari and I relied on. He'd done such a good job that a colleague of mine, LaDonna Williams, had recently recruited him for the Agency. Keeping TranceWeb up and running took a lot of skill and hard work.

I did wonder, now that Ari had pointed it out, why the appearance of Chaos creatures failed to trigger the alarms. When Ari called him, Itzak had a theory ready. Ari asked him to hold on a moment while he relayed the information to me.

"He says that the creatures don't breach any perimeter. They arrive inside from some other dimension. This means that they're not crossing any of the boundaries that the security system has set up."

"Crud," I said. "Does that mean a fast walker could just plop herself down here?"

Ari returned to his phone and asked.

"He says he doesn't know," Ari told me. "It depends on

where she came from, I should think." He paused to listen further. "Itzak wonders if you could ask your father."

"Sure. I'll do it right now."

Ari switched to Hebrew, which he and Itzak tended to speak when they were talking about their shared boyhood on Reb Zeke's retro kibbutz. I got out my cell phone and called Dad. Although he answered promptly, he sounded vague and distracted. I could hear my mother's voice in the background, but I couldn't make out her words. She sounded annoyed, but then, she usually did.

"Are you busy, Dad?" I said. "I can call back later."

"No, no, you've called at a good time. Your mother says she's got something important to tell me, but we've not started discussing whatever it is yet."

Danger ahead! I sensed a SAWM, an ASTA, and a general uh-oh. Whatever bomb Mother was planning to drop did not concern me—that I could tell—but I knew it was going to cause trouble. I decided that hanging up would be cowardly.

"I just have a quick question about fast walking," I said. "And alarm systems."

While I explained the problem, Dad listened carefully.

"It depends," he said when I finished. "Someone who's also a world-walker could drop in from elsewhere. They wouldn't set off the alarm."

"Okay," I said, "what about someone who's only a fast walker?"

"Now they would set it off. It's not like you're changing dimensions when you're fast walking. The process—" He paused to think. "In a way you're streaming yourself along, but you don't leave the world you're on at the time. You're still physical, just fluid rather than solid. You dissolve and re-form a fair bit. It's a hard thing to be putting into words."

"That's okay. I think I get it. Thanks, Dad! I'll let you go."

I caught Ari's attention and relayed Dad's information.

He switched to English and repeated it all to Itzak, almost word for word. Ari has an amazing memory for language in all its forms. They talked for another couple of minutes before they ended the call. Ari laid his phone down on the table, and I slipped mine back into my shirt pocket.

"Itzak says we should be safe enough on that score," Ari said. "Judging from what your father said, a fast walker would breach the perimeter and thus set off the alarms."

"That makes sense. It's also a relief. Ash can't be a world-walker. If she was, her gang wouldn't have needed to kidnap Michael the way they did."

"True." Ari stood up. "We should have some dinner. There's leftover pizza. I could even heat it up."

"Okay. For you, I could even eat some of it."

I managed to eat an entire large slice and some chocolate ice cream as well. If you've never suffered from borderline anorexia, you won't understand what a victory this was. On days when I felt happy and relaxed, I could eat more and do it more easily, but that night every bite cost me real effort. Ari had learned by then to say nothing when I was having trouble eating. He occasionally looked my way with an encouraging smile. We'd just finished when my phone chimed in my shirt pocket. I answered it: Aunt Eileen.

"Nola," she said. "Did you hear the explosion?"

"What?" I came close to panicking. "Where?"

"I'm sorry, darling. Not a real explosion. I was trying to be funny."

"I guess I'm just on edge tonight." I decided against explaining why I'd never find jokes about explosions funny again. "What—"

"Your mother's told him. Your father, I mean. About Sean."

"Oh, God help us!" I was glad that I was sitting down. "I take it Dad's views on gay people haven't changed any."

"Yes and no," Aunt Eileen said. "He's gotten to the point where he can tolerate it in someone else, but not in his son. Your mother's awfully upset. She actually cried on the phone."

"Well, Sean's always been her favorite."

"I know, which is why she decided to tell your father herself rather than letting Sean do it. I guess Flann went storming out of the apartment. The question is, where are they all going to end up? Here or at your flat?"

Normally, troubles in the family meant a general invasion of Aunt Eileen's living room. For years, she'd acted as referee, peacemaker, and the psychological equivalent of a traffic cop.

"Why would they come to my place?" I said.

"Well, now that you know, too. I've always thought that whoever knows the secret ends up having to take care of a lot of details." She sighed. "I suppose 'details' is the word I want."

I nearly choked.

"I always wanted a big family," Aunt Eileen went on, "but I suppose God knew I'd have to help take care of Deirdre's, so Jim and I only had the three. It's not the fault of you children, of course."

"Ah, er." I managed to spit out a few noises to clear my throat. "I take it you had one of your dreams. About me finding out the family secret, I mean."

"Of course." She laughed in a titter of suppressed hysteria. "Are you surprised?"

"I shouldn't be, no. Okay, so I guess I've joined the club. They who know about my mom and dad."

"It's just the two of us, I think. Though your Aunt Rose might know in her own weird way. I'm not sure, and I'm afraid to ask her. If she even would understand the question."

The doorbell rang. Overlap rang in my brain as well.

"He's here," I said. "Ari, would you let my father in? And you don't need to greet him with the damned gun."

"I'll hang up," Aunt Eileen said. "I suppose the rest of the family's going to poke their noses in. I'll admit to being relieved that someone else knows. Things will be easier now that we share it. Good luck!"

Easier for you, maybe! I thought. But aloud I said, "Thanks. I'll call you tomorrow."

I left my phone on the kitchen table before I went into the living room. Now that I'd been appointed Traffic Cop Number Two, I knew that more family calls lay ahead, and I didn't need it ringing right under my chin. Dad came marching upstairs lugging two six-packs of dark beer. We were in for a long night of it.

"What's all this crap, Noodles?" he said. "Why didn't Sean tell me himself?"

"Because he knew you'd act like you're acting now," I said. "Enraged. Irrational."

Dad snorted. He closed his eyes and hissed from between closed jaws, a sure sign of a tirade coming. Ari walked up behind him and laid a filial hand on his shoulder.

"Do sit down, Flann," Ari said. "Shall I put the beer in the refrigerator for you?"

The tirade stalled. Dad opened his eyes, set the six-packs on the coffee table, and sat down on the couch. "No," he said. "Unless you'd like to chill some of these bottles for yourself."

"I learned to drink beer in Britain. Room temperature's fine with me."

"I'll get you men some glasses." I managed not to simper.

I ran for the kitchen to compose myself before I screamed. Fortunately, the room had stayed free of giant squid. I brought the four tall glasses I owned and set them down on the coffee table. Dad looked them over.

"Are you joining us, Noodles?" he said.

"No, but someone else will. Probably Sean at least. You can bet on that."

"And how will he know we're discussing him?"

"Dad!"

"Oh, very well." He rolled his eyes. "Your mother doubtless called him the minute I left."

"After she called Eileen. Eileen told me that Mom was in tears on the phone."

That gave Dad pause. He and my mother loved each other without reservation, intensely, passionately, and illegally, because even though he'd been born on a different world level, he was genetically her brother. Their parents had been exact doppelgängers. Incest—that was the secret in our family and of our family. Inbreeding had reinforced our tendency to wild talents. He picked up a bottle, twisted off the cap as if he were strangling a small animal, and glowered as he poured the beer into the glass.

"I didn't mean to upset her," he said. "I'm sorry about that."

Ari sighed and reached for a bottle of beer. He would probably nurse one all evening, I figured, knowing him the way I did. He was just pouring some of it into his glass when the doorbell rang.

"That's Sean now," I said. "And probably Al with him."

Dad growled and drank about a third of his glass off in one gulp. Ari got up, drew the Beretta, and headed for the stairs.

"Do you have to wave that gun around?" I said.

"I never wave a gun around," Ari said. "It might not be Sean."

"Nonsense!" Dad put in. "As if Nola wouldn't know that her own brother was at the door!"

Ari ignored us both and hurried down to open the front door. I stood up and wished I'd never laid aside my teenage desire to become a nun. In a minute or two I heard Sean's voice on the stairs, saying, "I know he's here. That's why I came over."

Sean led the way. His partner, Al Wong, followed more slowly, and Ari brought up the rear. All of us O'Gradys are decent looking, but Sean is gorgeous—perfect features, wavy black hair, big dark blue eyes, lean but muscled. He was wearing jeans, a black leather jacket, and a long-sleeved 49ers T-shirt that night, perhaps for the macho implication, more likely because the clear red flattered his tanned complexion. Because Sean looks so perfect, people tend not to notice Al, who's a good-looking guy himself, as handsome as any Hong Kong movie star.

Sean charged into the living room. Dad set his beer down on the coffee table and got up to face him.

"Why the hell," Dad said, "didn't you tell me yourself?"

"I was going to," Sean said. "Mom jumped the gun. I've got too much respect for you to let you hear it secondhand."

Nicely played, I thought. For a blessed minute Dad stayed silent, staring at him.

"All I want is for you to accept me like I am," Sean said. "I love you, Dad. I wish you could love me."

"Of course I love you," Dad glared at him with narrowed eyes. "Why else would I be concerned about your immortal soul?"

"What a load of crap!" Sean said. "Can't we leave the damned church out of it?"

"No, we can't! Of all the stupid things to say!"

Ari opened a bottle of beer and handed it to Sean. Al and I exchanged a glance and retreated into the kitchen. Ari could play referee, I figured. The Beretta he was wearing in its shoulder holster would lend him a certain authority. We could hear Dad and Sean yelling at each other about Saint Paul.

"Anyone who thinks men choose to be gay," Al remarked, "should have to listen to this."

"I wish Dad had left religion out of it," I said. "It's a Catholic thing, I guess, to drag it in."

"I suppose so. Sean's tried to explain all that to me. I don't get it."

"Is your family Buddhist?"

"No. Presbyterian. I'm not sure if that's worse than Catholic or not."

"Well, I know your dad has problems with you being with Sean."

"That's because of the grandchildren. I'm the oldest son. I'm supposed to procreate whether I want to or not."

We shared a moment of gloom. The yelling continued in the living room. Occasionally, I could hear Ari's voice. He was trying to stay calm and logical, which was having zero effect on Sean and Dad. No, I was not surprised.

"Well, anyway," Al said. "When are you guys going to get married?"

"Never, if I have my way. We got engaged to keep Dad off our backs. I don't want to marry anyone. Ever."

"Weird, isn't it? Everyone's pushing on you to get married. Sean and I want to, and we can't."

"Weird, and kind of sad."

Al sighed and nodded his agreement. I would have said more, but my cell phone rang.

"Kathleen," I told Al and picked up the phone to answer it.

"Nola!" Kathleen said. "What is going on over there? Mom just called me, but she didn't make any sense at all."

"She rarely does," I said. "But she told Dad about Sean."

"Ohmigawd! Look, we'd come over, but Jack doesn't want to leave Maureen and the kids here without us on guard."

"That's fine!" I thanked Whomever for small favors. "There's nothing anyone can do. We've just got to let them thrash it out."

The doorbell rang.

"Mike's here," I said. "He must have walked over."

Since Ari was busy preventing a riot in the living room, Al got up and trotted off to answer the door.

"I'd better let you go," Kathleen said. "I hope they don't get to the throwing things stage. I'll call you tomorrow when we can have a normal conversation."

"Okay, great." If, I thought, you can call any conversation about my family normal.

I walked to the living room doorway and stood watching. Mike's arrival brought a moment of silence. Sean and Dad had taken off their jackets, but they were still on their feet, glaring at each other. Ari sat down and had a swallow of beer right out of the bottle. Mike took off his black Giants logo jacket, dropped it on the floor, and helped himself to beer.

"By the way, young man," Dad said, "the drinking age in this country is twenty-one."

"What if I say please?" Mike gave him a smile calculated to charm. "It's not like I'm driving, Dad."

Dad sighed. "Oh, very well, but don't tell your mother."

"Promise." Mike twisted off the cap with a practiced hand. He'd learned how to drink on a recent jaunt to Terra Three. Beer was better than the marijuana he used to smoke, I figured, so I said nothing against it. I would have drawn the line at whiskey.

Al and I returned to the kitchen. I heard Sean say, "Mom accepts me like I am, y'know." Dad squalled. I shut the swinging kitchen door to blunt the voices.

"Did you want a beer?" I said to Al. "I'll go get you one."

"Brave woman! But no, thanks. I may have to drive Sean home any minute now."

Distantly I heard the landline phone ringing. Since I felt

no overlap, I stayed where I was. In a few minutes Ari opened the kitchen door and stuck his head in.

"It's the realtor," he said. "Mr. Singh. The neighbors have complained about the incident over the neighbor's parked car."

"You talk to him," I said. "I've had all I can take for one night."

Ari retreated and shut the door behind him.

I'm not sure how long Al and I cowered in the kitchen, listening to raised and muffled voices, waiting for the sound of thrown things hitting the walls. My supply of knickknacks had been depleted in a burglary about five months earlier, but the thought of all those beer bottles haunted me. Fortunately, I never heard a crash. I did hear Ari finally crack. He raised his voice and joined the shouting match.

The landline rang again. I heard Ari bellow, "It's Deirdre! She's weeping. If you might be quiet for ten seconds altogether . . ."

The shouting match stopped. Michael darted into the kitchen with a half-empty bottle of beer in one hand.

"If I try to talk to her," Michael said, "it'll only make things worse."

"Yep," I said, "you're right about that."

He had a slug of beer from the bottle. My little brother was growing up into a man just like his father and brothers. How heartwarming. I suppose.

I got up and opened the kitchen door just wide enough to peer into the living room. Dad was talking on the phone. Ari stood near him, and Sean was opening another bottle of beer. A cluster of empties stood on the coffee table. Dad turned and held out the receiver in Sean's direction. I held my breath.

"She wants to talk to you," he said. "Son."

I let out my breath in a puff of sheer relief. Al managed a smile. Together we crept into the living room and stood un-

noticed by the door, ready to run for the kitchen again like
the cowards we were. Sean said a few words now and then,
but as was usual with my mother's phone calls, he mostly
listened to her. She tended to deliver a nonstop verbal
downpour with the occasional high-pitched tornado thrown
in. Eventually, he held out the receiver again. Dad took over
the job of listening to her.

"What was that?" he said at one point. "One of your
eruptions . . . that crash and splatter I heard in the
background . . . no, it's not the neighbors, it's you . . . listen to
you, and you the wife of a man in the building trades! . . .
why do you keep denying . . . oh, very well, have it your way!
I'll be home soon anyway." Dad hung up the landline with a
slam of the receiver and turned to Sean. "Now, as I was
saying—"

"Don't say it!" I snapped. "Haven't you guys argued
enough for one night?"

Dad stepped back as fast as if I'd threatened to bite him.
I'd grown up in the time that he'd been gone, and he was
finally realizing it.

"Judge not lest ye be judged!" I went on. "That's what
the gospel says, isn't it? Since you want to drag in religion."

Dad set his hands on his hips and scowled. All I'd done
was draw his fire. It's time, I thought, to bring out the nuclear bomb.

"Besides," I said in as calm a voice as I could manage.
"Being gay is pretty much a matter of *genetics*, isn't it? It's
not like Sean can help it."

I knew he understood the reference to The Secret by the
way his face went utterly expressionless. He cleared his
throat twice and turned to Sean.

"There's no use in upsetting your mother any more tonight. Or your sister, either." He glanced my way. "You look
tired, Noodles."

"You finally noticed?" I said. "Yeah, I'm exhausted,

wiped out, worn out, wrung out, brought down, and anything else you want to add to that list." For a brief moment everyone in the room looked like a squid to me. Phantom tentacles reached out to claim my attention. "Out!" I snapped. "I have had enough!"

Ari got to his feet and glowered impartially at everyone except me. Dad opened his mouth and shut it again. Al stepped forward and grabbed Sean's arm before he could drink from the newly-opened beer.

"Let's go home," Al said. "Mike, need a ride?"

"Nah," Michael said. "I'll just walk home. Y'know, like Dad does."

"Oh, God," Al muttered. "Another O'Grady mutant!"

Sean put the full bottle down and grabbed his jacket from the couch. He waved good-bye as Al propelled him in the direction of the stairs. Mike and Dad finished their last swallows of beer and left soon after. They took the remains of the six-packs with them. I turned off my phone and put the landline on the answering machine.

"Enough," I said. "Enough, enough, enough!"

"Quite," Ari said.

"This is only Round One, y'know. Dad's not going to let this go that easily."

"Yes, I assumed that. Unfortunately."

I took one step toward the couch, but the long day bitch-slapped me. All my suppressed terror and stress rose to the surface in the form of tears. I hated myself for it, couldn't stop, stood there in the middle of the room like an idiot and sniveled. Ari put his arms around me and pulled me close. I buried my face against his shirt and finally managed to stop crying. When I looked up, he kissed my face twice, one gentle kiss under each eye. He picked me up before I could even say thank you. I slipped my arms around his neck.

"I know what will make you feel better," he said.

He carried me into our bedroom. He was right. It did.

CHAPTER 7

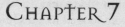

AFTER A GOOD NIGHT'S SLEEP, things looked better in the morning, at least, that is, until I logged onto TranceWeb and found an e-mail cluster from Seymour about the end of the world. Well, okay, about the end of Interchange, but there were further implications that I disliked. A lot.

Seymour had found a top-flight astrophysicist, Dr. Amanda Weinstein, to comment on my vision. Not only was she good, but she was open-minded, a necessity in our line of work, as well as willing to keep certain things secret. To interpret my vision, Seymour also consulted NumbersGrrl, that is, LaDonna Williams, PhD, our mathematical expert. The team's analysis provided a perfect example of how—and why—visions need interpretation. Taking them literally gets you nowhere. I read their entire exchange of ideas before replying.

They'd come to the conclusion that I'd seen the results of an enormous thermonuclear reaction near Interchange's version of Earth. Such a catastrophe would have had two results. First, it would have stripped off most of the ozone layer, which my vision symbolized as the blue sky drawing back to reveal the naked black of night. Such depletion would have resulted in the high level of X-rays that Ari had previously detected on Interchange.

Second, and worse, it would have produced an electromagnetic pulse that ionized the lower atmosphere—the evil rainbow waves of my vision. The pulse would have produced enormous lightning bolts, erratic magnetic fields, and other ill effects until all the electrons finally got back to where they belonged. Since a nuclear war would also produce a pulse, this effect probably lay behind the belief of the survivors living on Interchange that they'd suffered such a war.

The rainbow colors I'd seen might well have corresponded to the colors that the world-walkers used as symbols of the various deviant levels, or so Seymour thought. LaDonna Williams agreed, citing studies of psychic access to the Collective Data Stream.

"O'Grady has a very high success rate when it comes to the accuracy of her visions," LaDonna wrote. "The colored radiation beams would then correspond to the gates the aliens were trying to open with their overload of destructive force."

Since all this talk of gates was news to her, Dr. Weinstein considered the explosion itself. A possible suspect was a supernova within ten light-years of the planet, but it seemed unlikely to her that a natural astronomical phenomenon would be confined to one deviant world level. Yet it had certainly never happened in our part of the multiverse.

"Logically speaking," she wrote, "that means it must have been artificially produced. Someone or some alien race made a star, probably a white dwarf, go nova on purpose, maybe to open those inter-world gates Agent O'Grady saw as holes in the Swiss cheese. If so, their tech level was extremely high."

Seymour disagreed about the supernova but agreed about the tech level. "If they had fusion bombs at their disposal, or something worse," he wrote, "they wouldn't have had to trigger a star."

All three of them found one question particularly urgent: were the aliens, whoever they were, going to do it all again? Like, on our world level?

"The tech level of the city Agent O'Grady saw," LaDonna wrote, "was low. I read it as early twentieth century, pre-WWI most likely. If they'd been coming, they would have been here by now. The splashback from that kind of event would have been enormous. I bet they bit off more than they could chew, and it was lights out for them, too. Could have been an accident, even, like an interstellar antimatter drive blowing up. You know, like the *Enterprise*."

Mixed metaphors and a *Star Trek* reference did provide some mental comfort, but I would have preferred hard data. Dr. Weinstein would have preferred it as well.

"It would have taken a massive amount of antimatter to produce such an explosion," she remarked. "If they'd collected that much fuel, they must have been deliberately intending to use it."

This made sense. Unfortunately.

"But you must remember that I'm merely speculating," Dr. Weinstein continued. "I'd need more data before I could reach anything we could call a conclusion. Seymour tells me that he might be able to arrange for me to read a paper from elsewhere in the multiverse. Dr. Williams and I are also trying to set up a meeting to exchange ideas and confer. Science gets done by teams these days. The lone genius is pretty much a myth."

I thanked all three, then logged off. Reading their e-mails had left me with a question none of them could answer: why would the aliens have opened all those gates unless they were planning on using them?

I brooded about this question all morning without finding an answer until, around noon, Spare14 called. He had news of a victory for common sense. The TWIXT higher-ups had agreed that Ari could be sworn in prior to fulfilling the exam requirement. Apparently, Ari had earned so many active duty credits, to say nothing of his long résumé of police work, that he only needed to get forty-five per cent of the answers correct to pass. I got the impression that TWIXT tended to run short of qualified candidates and thus grabbed any they found by any means possible.

"There certainly aren't any other candidates here on Four," Spare14 told us during the conference call. "They're doing this as a favor to me, actually. They know I'll need Nathan fully qualified thanks to the cock-up on Six."

I shuddered when I realized that TWIXT had every intention of sending us back to that terrorist-plagued version of San Francisco. I reminded myself that I had Agency business there. A city plagued by terrorism would provide an ideal location for the Peacock Angel cult to work its own mischief. Ash and the Axeman would doubtless find scope for their talents as well.

"How's the investigation going?" I said. "Well—if you can say. I don't want to intrude on your protocols."

"It's quite all right, O'Grady. You are involved."

"True," Ari put in. "More than I want her to be, speaking as her bodyguard."

How cheery of him! I thought to myself. Spare14 made a few dodge-and-hedge noises.

"Standard procedure is proceeding," Spare14 continued, "I've submitted my report to HQ along with O'Grady's opinion as an addendum. HQ is sending a special investigator to the other liaison office in Los Angeles. Neutral ground, you know. I can't be that investigator because Ja-Marcus and I are friends. He'll be flying to Los Angeles to meet the S.I., who will then place everyone in the office on

administrative leave if he—the S.I—thinks it warranted.
O'Grady will still have to make a deposition about the Axeman connection."

"She can't just make that here?" Ari said.

"I asked. The answer was no. I think HQ want to have
her go to the office for a further look around, as it were, but
they couldn't quite come out and admit that. At any rate,
they'd like it done as soon as possible. We should be able to
get Danvers-Jones if you can travel today. How soon can
you reach my office?"

"In an hour," Ari said. "Let's get it done."

Since we were anticipating a quick trip into Six and then
out again, we took our car down to the office. We picked up
Willa, drove to McLaren Park, and found a safe place to
leave the car on a side street. As we hiked up the hill to the
overlap area, we received our first sign of trouble coming.
Willa abruptly stopped dead on the sidewalk and stared
across Shelley Drive.

"Uh-oh," she said. "I'm not feeling the overlap yet."

"Isn't it right over there?" I pointed to the slope of the
knoll.

"It should be. O'Grady, run a couple of scans, will you?
See if there's someone waiting for us who shouldn't be
there."

I did and picked up no trace of danger whatsoever.

"Damn," Willa said. "That's worse. If no one's suppressing the overlap, it could be fading on its own. Bad news."

Willa left the sidewalk and jogged across the street with
the two of us trailing after. When we reached the other side,
she led us at a quick march into the trees where we'd found
the overlap before. All at once she smiled.

"Here it is!" Willa said. "Having a world-walker step on
them is good for overlaps now and then. Still, I don't like
this much. O'Grady, you've got a transport orb to get you
back home, right?"

"Two of them." I patted my shoulder bag. "Spare14 handed me another one this morning."

"Good." She paused to rummage in her mesh bag of cloth scraps. "Let's see if my focus orb here will take us. Without any extra help, I mean."

It didn't. I was so used to seeing Willa hold up an orb and shift us into another world without any seeming effort that it took me a minute to realize what had happened: nothing, that's what. We were still on Terra Four.

"Not good at all," she said. "Okay, I've got a transporter for Six." She paused to fish a second bright yellow-green sphere, somewhat larger than the focus version, out of her bag. She handed it to Ari. "Now let me see . . . ah, there's a nice flat rock. Nathan, you throw this one onto the rock and break it while I concentrate on the permanent version here in my hand. Then we run into the smoke. Got that? Good. On the count of one, two, three!"

Ari threw, we all dashed, and sure enough, we stumbled out of the cloud to find ourselves standing on the weed-cracked concrete slab that marked the overlap on Terra Six. Willa made a slight retching sound.

"God in heaven," she said. "This place is spinning and tilting. Good luck. I'm going home."

She buried the yellow-green focus orb in her bag and brought out a violet replacement. While we watched, she took one step forward and disappeared. Ari shuddered.

"I have to admit," he said, "that I find this business of orbs a bit unnerving."

"Only a bit? I find it unnerving as all hell. Especially the transport kind."

We shared an ironic smile and headed downhill. I could feel the Pull, the overlap from members of a family that had to be doppelgängers to my own. I managed to cut them off and block the Pull by wielding the mental image of the flaming torch to seal my aura.

When we walked into the dour gray building that housed the TWIXT office, we found a security checkpoint, manned by two guards from the third floor firm, in front of the elevators. For all anyone knew, the terrorists might try again. Ari showed them his ID and vouched for me. One of the guards made quite a show of looking down a list of persons approved for entry. He had us initial the spaces beside our names.

As we took the elevator up to the second floor, I ran scans. Being inside a metal box made them difficult to read, but I received a couple of muddled warnings.

"Ari," I said, "something's really wrong."

He reached under his jacket and loosened the Beretta in its holster. As soon as we stepped out of the elevator, I knew that an important person had died. I had just time to say as much to Ari before we walked through a pair of swinging doors into the office. Under fluorescent lights I saw a spread of six desks and a bank of blue computer boxes wired to CRT monitors. Beyond them two doors led into smaller rooms. A skinny young man with sandy-brown hair stood at the computer station, but he turned when we arrived and walked down an aisle toward us. Agent de Vere got up from his desk and acknowledged our presence with a nod and a raised hand.

A twenty-something woman in a dark gray business-cut skirt suit hurried over to greet us. She had short black hair, a tan complexion, and dark eyes narrow with worry. For some odd reason I noticed that she wore silver-and-turquoise earrings. Although she didn't bother to smile, I could tell that she meant us no harm.

"Agent Nathan?" she said. "I'm Lupe Parra y Cruz. I'm in charge here today. Temporarily, I hope."

"How do you do?" Ari said. "I take it that Spivey's in Los Angeles."

"Yes, he left on a morning flight." She hesitated, glancing

my way. "Perhaps de Vere can fill you in while I take Miss O'Grady's deposition."

I remembered that I had a cover story. So, apparently, did Ari. He looked around the office for a moment, then said, "You can be open in front of O'Grady. She's actually another agent, an observer from a government bureau on Four."

"Oh." Parra y Cruz allowed herself a tight smile. "I wish someone had told me that."

"There were reasons," Ari said. "Can you contact Austin Spare on Four? He'll explain."

"Yes, and I will. Thank you."

I took out my cross-agency ID and handed it her. Although the name of the agency meant nothing to her, it looked so official that she smiled, reassured, as she handed it back.

"If you're in charge," I said, "Trotter isn't here."

"No, he's not, and no one knows why. We've called his home and his mobile. We've sent him e-mail. No answer to any of it."

I felt a stab of cold dread coupled with a profound surprise. I'd guarded myself against Trotter out of sheer suspicion, sure that he was a danger, not that he was in danger himself.

"What is it, O'Grady?" Ari said. "You've gone quite pale."

"Trotter's dead." I turned to Parra y Cruz. "I'm a certified police psychic on my home world. Spare will vouch for that. You need to send someone to Trotter's address. I should go with them to see if I can pick up traces."

Parra y Cruz laid a quick hand to her throat. The two men in the office both swore. No one doubted me. Under their very real shock I picked up an undertone of puzzlement but none of guilt. If someone in that room was the murderer, his or her psychic talents far outweighed mine.

De Vere, he of the bald dome and the bushy eyebrows, volunteered to do the driving while Parra y Cruz made all the necessary communications to Spare14, Spivey, and HQ. The young clerk would hold down the front desk. Ari and I walked with de Vere out to his car, a small gray sedan with an "official business only" seal on the side. If, indeed, we found Trotter dead, de Vere told us, he'd call in the local police to handle the actual case.

"Though, of course, Interpol would follow it closely," de Vere said, "and give them full cooperation and access."

"I take it they know nothing about TWIXT," Ari said.

"Not a thing. They wouldn't believe it anyway, even if we did tell them."

Trotter, who was single, lived in an apartment on Alemany Avenue, a very different street than the broad thoroughfare in our world. This Alemany ran as a mere two lanes, bordered on both sides by houses with decent-sized lawns planted with shade trees. Trotter's building, a white stucco two-story, sat on a corner. The front door of the building was kept locked, which meant we'd need a key to get into the lobby, or so de Vere thought. Ari pulled a piece of wire out of his pants pocket and opened the door while de Vere was still trying to remember how to call the building manager. De Vere's bushy eyebrows shot up in surprise.

"He's a handy sort of man to have around," I said.

"Apparently so," de Vere said.

Ari merely smiled and pocketed the wire.

We walked into a tiny lobby, floored in black-and-white tile. Stairs carpeted in dark brown led up to the second floor. Trotter's apartment stood on the right side of a narrow hall, which smelled moldy and doggy. As an undertone, though, I registered the scent of sour blood like an old meat package. Although the door was locked, Ari waited to open it.

"Should we call the police directly if no one answers?" Ari said.

"Probably," de Vere said.

"No one's going to answer." I could feel death like sea fog seeping under the door.

Inside the apartment someone moaned as if they felt it, too.

"He might still be alive," Ari said. "Emergency procedure."

Without a word, De Vere stepped back and let him pick the lock. As Ari opened the door, a dog barked and staggered up to stand on three feet. It limped forward, a big golden Lab with one front paw slashed open. Blood clotted its neck fur because someone had cut off one of its ears. Behind it, we could see a male body stretched out on the floor, a man in his thirties, dark hair, not very tall but thickly built. He wore only a pair of unbelted khaki slacks. He looked oddly familiar from what I could see of him. The closed-up room stank of old blood.

"Jesus God!" de Vere muttered. "The poor critter! He's what moaned. His name's Rodeo."

"Quite so," Ari said. "You'd best call the police right now."

"Uh, hey," I put in. "Is that Trotter?"

"Sorry." De Vere laughed with much too high and brittle a sound. "I forgot you wouldn't know. Yeah, it is, all right, poor bastard!"

The dog barked once more, then flopped back down by its master's corpse. Trotter's throat had been slashed almost from ear to ear, so deeply that I could see a knobbly neck bone. His hands and bare arms bore knife cuts, too, where he'd tried to shield himself from the knife-wielding attacker. And the blood, clotted everywhere—I turned away fast.

"I bet they find a long blonde hair or two on the body somewhere," I said to Ari. "Make sure Forensics knows it's important."

The police in San Francisco Six wore dark green uniforms,

which made them look like park rangers to me. They were efficient and fast, however, professional toward the two Interpol officers, tolerant of me in my guise of Ari's assistant. As soon as the first two officers on the scene saw the corpse, they called in Homicide and Forensics. The team arrived with film cameras and flashbulbs, which reinforced my belief that the tech on this deviant level lagged behind even my own Terra Four, to say nothing of One. Their unit leader, a skinny Cal-African guy, got right to work.

I stayed out of everyone's way but took a good look around the sparsely furnished front room of the apartment. Although a pleasant green-and-blue carpet covered the floor, the white walls were utterly bare of pictures. A struggle had upended a couple of chairs and smashed a floor lamp. On a desk at one end of the room a bright blue computer lay in pieces—CRT monitor, keyboard, speakers, and on the floor, the opened-up box itself. Ari walked over to take a look.

"Someone's removed the hard drive," he said to de Vere. "I suppose there was evidence of some sort on it."

"Good guess," de Vere said. "Maybe he backed up on flex disks. They probably took those, too, though."

"If they had any brains at all, they did. I don't suppose he had off-site storage?"

"What?" de Vere blinked at him. "Somewhere else to keep the flexies?"

"Maybe at the office. Or at a friend's house?"

"We'll follow up on that. Good idea."

Although Parra y Cruz had mentioned e-mail, their version of the Internet apparently lacked some of the features of ours. Since de Vere knew we came from another world level, I asked him outright as soon as I could be sure that none of the cops could overhear.

"Internet?" de Vere grinned at me. "I only wish! Lupe's told me about it. Sounds great. Here, if you know where the right lists are, you can find stuff online, yeah, but there's none of those links and hyper thingies."

As soon as the Forensics team had finished photographing the scene, de Vere fetched water for the wounded dog. He knelt down and put the bowl on the floor, then helped the dog stand and drink.

"He's got a bad contusion on his head behind his right ear or where the ear was," de Vere said. "They must have hit him with something. He would have attacked to defend Trotter."

"I was wondering about that," Ari said. "But why take the ear?"

"I have no idea." De Vere shuddered. "Fucking creepy!"

When he offered to take the dog to the same vet who tended his own dogs, the police allowed him to do so. Although Rodeo knew and seemed to trust him, de Vere prudently wrapped its head in a towel before he picked it up to carry it out to the car. The dog whined and struggled, but it was so weak from losing blood that it went limp before they even reached the stairs.

"We'll phone-fax our report to your office," the Forensics team leader told Ari. "I'll get right on that when we get back to the morgue. There was no sign of forced entry. Must have been someone he knew well enough to let in."

"Interesting," Ari said. "Rigor?"

"Well advanced. I can't say more than this, but I'd bet he died sometime in the middle of the night. Two AM. Something like that."

"Did you happen to find any blonde hair on the body?"

"You bet, just like you suggested. Caught around the fingers of the right hand. He must have grabbed the assailant's hair at one point during the fight." Forensics paused to look around the apartment. "It must have been a hell of a tussle. There's blood splashed around, some on the wall, even."

"Surely the other tenants in the building heard something."

"Probably. That's up to Homicide to find out."

"Quite so. I'll be looking forward to your report."

Two uniformed officers brought up a stretcher and a shroud. They wrapped up Trotter's corpse under Forensics' direction and took it away. The cameraman stepped forward to snap photos of the blood on the floor. The homicide detective, a skinny little white guy named Edwards, allowed Ari to accompany him when he examined the apartment. I trailed along behind as they went into the bedroom—a double bed, a cheap wood dresser, no pictures on the wall, nothing else. The smell of urine hit me as soon as we walked in, a real stench. Empty beer cans sat by the left side of the bed.

The blankets had been thrown to the floor at the foot of the bed to reveal a rubber sheet and a drying pool of the smelly substance in question. On the left pillow lay a couple of long black hairs. Edwards yelled for Forensics, who came trotting in with tweezers and a manila envelope.

Forensics tweezed up the hairs and studied them for a moment. "I'll have to put these under the scope," he said, "but I'd guess they were from someone ethnically Asian."

I remembered Murphy saying, a Japanese girl grabbed the bag. I was only guessing, of course, that Ash had committed the murder, even though I registered dim traces of her presence throughout the apartment. She might have been present but not been the assailant. I reminded myself of that, even as I doubted that she was innocent. I'd never seen the other girl and thus could pick up nothing concerning her. I nearly gagged. Ari caught my elbow to steady me.

"You might want to wait out in the hall," he said. "I realize this must be hard on you."

"It's not the smell," I said, "it's the vibes."

He quirked an eyebrow as if to ask what I meant, but Edwards turned to speak to him. As I left the apartment, I passed the open door to a small bathroom—bare walls, a dirty white bathtub, a mirrored medicine cabinet above a filthy sink. On the closed toilet lid lay a peacock feather. A decoration gone awry? Not in that place!

I went to the lobby and sat down on one of the lower steps. The police had propped open the front door, and the air smelled clean and fresh. Through the open door I could see squad cars parked outside. Across the narrow street a cluster of gawkers had gathered on a lawn in front of a pale green house—neighbors, wondering no doubt what in hell was going on, all the terrorist attacks and now a murder right in their own neighborhood.

I ran a quick SAF, a scan of the aura field, then a Search Mode: Personnel. Both returned traces of Ash. I decided against zeroing in on the traces in case her talents could warn her about scans focused in her direction. I did receive a clear indication that she existed in this world level's version of San Francisco. When I scanned for the Axeman, however, I picked up nothing. Wherever he was, he was out of my range. I wanted to do a Long Distance Remote Sensing, but I needed the proper equipment for it, my crayons and drawing paper, which I'd left behind.

When I heard footsteps behind me on the stairs, I got up and moved out of the way into the lobby. The Forensics team came clattering down, laden with their equipment, and left the building. Ari followed more slowly.

"Did you see the peacock feather?" I said.

"Oh, yes. I pointed it out to Edwards, too."

"Good. What about the other tenants?"

"The apartment directly under Trotter is empty. Edwards is interviewing the tenant across the hall right now."

"Will he send a report?"

"Yes. When de Vere comes back, we'll return to the office. I want them to open the safe and see if it still contains orbs."

"Trotter had the combination?"

"Trotter was in charge of them. He requisitioned orbs from HQ as needed and dispensed them to agents who had to travel."

"Isn't that interesting?"

"Very, but he wasn't the only one with access to the safe. They keep other crucial supplies in it. Everyone had the combination." Ari shrugged in annoyance. "Well, not the clerk, but all the agents. If the orbs are gone, that will make finding the thief more difficult, of course. Too many suspects, though Trotter's the most likely."

"Trotter was the most likely suspect for a lot of things, but now he's dead. When thieves fall out, maybe?"

"Again, likely, but we don't know." Ari thought for a moment. "If he was the man behind the IED attempt in the lift, then he failed. He may belong to a group that dislikes failure enough to punish it."

Like the Peacock Angel cult, I thought. While we waited, Ari phoned in the news of the murder to Parra y Cruz, who promised to relay the message to Spare14 over the transworld router. De Vere drove up just as Ari was putting the communicator away. When we got into the car, de Vere announced that the dog would recover.

"I'll adopt him, of course," de Vere said. "One good thing I'll say about Trotter, he loved poor old Rodeo. Least I can do is take care of his dog."

"Quite," Ari said. "I take it that Trotter wasn't the most popular man in the group."

De Vere snorted at the thought and started the car. We drove straight back to the office building and parked nearby. We checked in with the security people in the lobby, then took the elevator back up to the second floor. The first thing Parra y Cruz asked about was the health of the dog. She never mentioned Trotter. No, Trotter had not been a popular man with his coworkers. Nice dog, though, apparently.

"About the orbs," Ari said. "I suggest we open the safe

and see if any are missing. I think Trotter's murder may be related to thefts that have happened on other world levels."

"Good idea," de Vere said and glanced at Parra y Cruz.

"Yes, I agree," she said. "By the way, I did manage to reach JaMarcus and give him a report. He can't get away today, but he'll be coming back as soon as possible. The S.I. may come with him. Unless he's already here."

Everyone turned to look at Ari, who smiled with a twitch of his mouth. "Not me, I assure you," he said. "I'm too new to know the proper procedures."

Everyone relaxed. I could understand why Parra y Cruz had pushed the point. She was still smarting from finding out that I was an agent, not some innocent witness.

One of the doors at the rear of the long room led to a storage area and the wall safe. Parra y Cruz confirmed that all of the agents knew the combination. When she opened it, I saw a large, deep space, about five feet on a side, divided by three shelves. One held weapons and ammunition; another, flat boxes of official forms and the paper currency of various deviant world levels. The third was empty.

"Suspicion confirmed, Nathan," Parra y Cruz said. "We should have had an array of twelve transport orbs here."

"Were any for Terra Three?" Ari said.

"Not that I remember." She frowned in thought. "No, we had orbs for One, Two, and Five, and then Six, of course, so we could get back again if need be. Our unit rarely sees linkage with cases on Three."

"That may be about to change," I said. "The suspect that Nathan and I are tracking has ties there."

"HQ is going to have to give us a restock," Parra y Cruz said. "I'll put in a requisition."

"Yeah, good idea," de Vere put in, "since we're flat out of all of them. This is quite an expensive loss."

Ari's communicator beeped. He took the square of shiny black plastic out of his pocket and flicked it on. "Nathan here." He walked out of the room while he listened to Spare14—I could pick up that overlap. Apparently their trans-world router could service the entire office.

De Vere, Parra y Cruz, and I stayed where we were and all stared at each other. I ran a tentative SPP on Parra y Cruz. When she gave no sign of feeling it, I ran a stronger version of my profiling talent and found her honest, as Spare14 had told me, bewildered, a little frightened at the responsibility that had fallen on her as lead agent. Nowhere did I pick up a trace of grief for the dead Trotter.

"A question," I said. "Is long hair a popular style for men on this world level?"

"Not in San Francisco," de Vere said. "You see it in New York City, though. Especially during the winter. Keeps their necks warm, I guess."

"Another question. Does the name Peacock Angel mean anything to you?"

It didn't. Their SPPs made that amply clear.

"I'm investigating a peculiar secret cult back home," I said. "I was wondering if it had turned up here."

"Send me a report with cross-agency authorization," Parra y Cruz said. "And I'll double-check our records."

"Thank you! That would be a great help. And I'll send you my information on the Axeman rather than doing a deposition here."

Ari returned. "Spare wants us back on Four, O'Grady," he said. "Parra, you'll be receiving a call from HQ shortly. They're quite concerned for your safety. Do you have family here?"

"No," she said. "This is my first trans-world posting."

"Good. De Vere, I take it you're established?"

"Yes. I'm new to TWIXT, but I was born here on Six. I'm married. And of course, I've got dogs to worry about."

"HQ will be calling you, too." Ari glanced around the room. "Since I'm an outsider, I may be coming back to continue the investigation. No one knows anything definite at the moment. Trotter is the first TWIXT agent lost in twelve years. His murder's caused something of an uproar at HQ, Spare tells me."

"Well," Parra y Cruz said, "we all knew that the job had its dangers when we signed up. But I'll be glad to get that call."

Ari and I used one of our transport orbs to return to our home world and McLaren Park. The Saturn was waiting where we'd parked it. Ari pointed out at some length how much more convenient driving was than taking the bus. I agreed and ignored most of his tirade against the local public transportation. My mind kept circling around the evidence but always returned to Ash and the Axeman.

"After you check in with Spare14," I said, "I want to go over to Aunt Eileen's and talk with Michael. He's the one who knew our suspects. Entirely too well, in the case of Ash."

"Brilliant," Ari said. "Let's. And I wouldn't mind finding lunch somewhere, as well. I'm quite hungry."

I gagged again. The image of Trotter and his dog, lying in a mixture of their own blood, rose in my mind.

"Sorry," Ari said. "I can wait to eat until you don't have to watch."

"Thanks. I'm sure Aunt Eileen will feed you if you ask."

We arrived at the TWIXT office without incident. Spare14 mostly wanted Ari to sign the recruitment papers. Although they did discuss the case, I had a hard time listening to Ari's rehash of the details. An insight nagged at me, just out of reach in my memory, until I heard Spare14 say the words "black market in orbs."

"Wagner's bookstore in SanFran," I said. "He told us that he didn't know where the guy who sold him orbs came from. Think it might have been Trotter?"

"Possibly," Ari said. "We really should go back and ask.

We might be able to pick up more information about the Axeman as well."

"I can get you a picture of Trotter," Spare14 said, "the one from his ID file if nothing else. If you get a positive ident, it would be very helpful. Let me see what I can arrange."

I nearly groaned aloud. Me and my big mouth! SanFran on Terra Three was the last place in the multiverse that I ever wanted to see again.

As I'd predicted, when we reached Aunt Eileen's house, and Ari mentioned that he'd not had time to eat lunch, she immediately took him into the kitchen where she could, as she put it, "scrounge up something halfway decent," a feast by most people's standards, I assumed. I went upstairs to Michael's room, where he was supposedly studying his Latin homework. Through the door I could hear sounds of a baseball game. Our local Giants' announcers aren't known for broadcasting in Latin. I knocked. The sounds disappeared. When Michael opened the door, I could see his computer screen, which displayed a passage from Cicero and various translation aids.

"Funny," I said. "I thought I heard a radio."

"I don't have a radio," Michael said, all innocence.

"Then you've set it up so you can get the Giants' games over the Internet."

He winced. I walked into the room which, as usual, sported wall-to-wall litter as its main decoration. His little blue Chaos critter, Or-Something, was lying on his unmade bed and chewing on an empty soda bottle. It looked up at me and wagged its scaly, skinny tail, then returned to trying to gnaw through plastic. I tossed a couple of stinky T-shirts off a wooden chair and sat down.

"Never mind," I said. "I need to talk to you about Ash and the Axeman. Professional business."

"Okay, yeah. I'll turn the other stuff off." Michael kicked a pair of dirty jeans out of the way and returned to his computer. He fiddled with it for a moment or two, then put it on standby.

"Where's Sophie, by the way?"

"Off with her wolf pack. It'll be the full moon soon, and they're having a prelim meeting." He hesitated. "Larry, the alpha guy, he came to pick her up. I sure don't like the way he looks at her."

"He doesn't like her, or he likes her too much?"

"Too much. Way too much. I guess from what she said, they don't have an alpha female in their pack. So I bet he's on the prowl."

"You sound so indignant, bro. After you and Ash—"

He winced again. "That was dumb of me, okay?" he said. "I'm sorry I ever screwed her."

"Well, it wasn't fair to Sophie."

"Yeah, I know. I'm sorry about that. Seriously. Besides, Ash is kind of a dangerous girl."

"Kind of? She may have just slit someone's throat. That's why I need the information."

His eyes went wide. "I wouldn't put it past her," he said after a moment or two. "Yeah, I really wouldn't." He sat down on the edge of his bed.

For a week or so Michael had been somewhere between a prisoner and a member of the Axeman's gang on Interchange. As a world-walker he'd been a crucial part of the Axeman's grandiose plans. The gang wanted to charge big money to take desperate inhabitants of that deviant level to worlds like Terra Six, which despite the terrorists was better than Three. A real world-walker who could use focus orbs would spare them the expense of buying the transport version on the black market.

"I've never understood," I said, "what these refugees were going to do once they got to Terra Six. I mean, there they'd be, no ID, no money, no family to go to."

"Yeah, you'd think." Michael said. "But the Axeman did

change the money for people. He took a big commission, of course. He talked about getting them fake IDs once they'd made the run. And some of them had jewelry and stuff to sell once they got there. I dunno where they went, though. The Axe talked about some kind of village he wanted to build or take over. Up in the Sierra, like around Tahoe, y'know?"

"What were these people going to do once they got there? Open a ski resort?"

Michael shrugged. "I wasn't there long enough to learn everything. The Axeman never really trusted me. He isn't stupid. Maybe if I'd, like, stayed there longer and kept up my act he'd have trusted me, but thank God you guys rescued me. I thought maybe you'd just leave me there. I mean, it was hella dumb of me to go through the gate. Especially with Sean along."

"I was afraid you'd develop a taste for the life of crime."

Michael grinned at that. "Ash thought I was hot, and she worked on her dad to let me be a regular gang member, but he kept telling her it was too soon."

"Who was her dad?"

"The Axeman. You didn't know that?"

"No." My voice may have squeaked. "Somehow he didn't strike me as the paternal type."

"Huh? Yeah, he is. He really thinks Ash is special and way cool. That's why he wouldn't let her work the streets."

"How sweet. Touching, even. Did she have a friend who looks Japanese or Japanese-American?"

"Yeah, Izumi. She was the number two girl in the gang, and she went through the gate with Ash. The one I opened, I mean. Is that, like, important?"

"You bet. This Izumi, did she work the streets?"

"No. She had a few special customers, though, but only a few."

"Special? What did she do?"

Michael turned a bright red and squirmed in his chair. I took that as meaning she'd offered him a free sample.

"Uh, well," he said, "you don't want to know."

"Something really kinky?"

He nodded.

A thought occurred to me. "Let me take a wild guess," I said. "She liked to pee during the um well, the process, let's just say. A golden shower queen."

The red turned darker, dangerously close to purple. Michael managed a strangled "Yeah." He stared firmly at the floor. "I thought that was real gross. She offered, and I said no. Seriously."

"I believe you. I would never have done it, either."

" 'Course not." Briefly his facial expression reminded me of Dad. "Not my sister!"

I smiled and waited until his color had faded to pink.

"It's gross, yeah," I said, "but it's also an important clue. That's why I'm here. I need to know everything you know, even if it's embarrassing as hell."

"Okay." Michael took a deep breath and looked at me again. "I've still got to get debriefed by TWIXT. I guess that hearing's going to happen soon, so I'd better figure out what I'm going to say, anyway. Spare14 told me that the higher-ups weren't real pleased that so many bad guys got killed."

His voice dropped, and he looked away. He'd shot one of the dead criminals himself. I held it to his credit that the act grieved him. Guilt has its place.

"Wait a minute," I said. "You've been in contact with Spare14?"

"Yeah. Didn't he tell you?"

"Nope. From now on, buster, I'd appreciate it if you'd pass this kind of news along to me right away."

"Sure. No one told me to keep quiet. I just thought you already knew." He looked at me again. "What do you need to know?"

I spent a profitable half hour picking my brother's brains about the Axeman, his setup, his customers, and his lovely daughter, Ash the Knife. At times Michael could be a flake, particularly about schoolwork, but he was a lot smarter than he acted. He'd noticed all kinds of pertinent details. I took notes rather than risk forgetting any of it. We'd just returned to the subject of what all these refugees were supposed to do once they made it to their new world level when Ari came upstairs and joined us.

"I just spoke to Spare14 again," Ari told me. "He's received the homicide reports on Scott Trotter's murder from Six and sent copies to my laptop. You're authorized for access."

"Oh, goodie," I said.

The sarcasm went zipping right by Ari, who blinked at me, then shrugged.

"Trotter?" Michael said. "Who?"

"A guy who was just murdered, possibly by your old girlfriend," I said. "On another world level, that is."

"Trotter," Michael said, "was Scorch the Torch's real name. Scott Trotter. The guy I shot on Three. Y'know?"

"Whoa!" I said. "That's why the corpse looked familiar. Doppelgängers. Déjà vu all over again."

"Déjà vu means 'already seen,'" Ari put in. "You're being redundant."

"Yeah, I know, Mr. Helpful. It's a joke."

"Oh." He digested this for a moment. "If you say so."

I stood up. "Thanks, Mike," I said. "I really appreciate all this information. If you think of anything else, call me, okay? We need to get back to Ari's laptop."

"I will for sure." Michael sighed in deep melancholy. "And I really gotta get back to the homework. Father Keith's coming over tonight, and I bet he gives me a quiz."

CHAPTER 8

A S SOON AS WE GOT HOME, Ari brought his laptop out of our wall safe. He found the data from Spare14 and printed out a copy of the homicide reports for me. I always get printout from Ari rather than letting him transfer information to my laptop or desktop, because I'm always afraid he'll transfer a Trojan horse along with it. I know he loves me, but he loves Israel more, and I don't want him browsing my machines for tidbits to send home. Printout is sanitary.

The homicide reports contained interesting details but no revelations. The person who lived across the hall from Trotter's apartment had spent the night with her boyfriend and so had heard nothing. Like everyone else who'd known him, she was much more concerned about the dog than about Trotter. The boyfriend had confirmed her story, and he, too, was glad to learn that Rodeo would recover. They both agreed that Trotter had made several "really crude" passes at the young woman during the six months she'd lived in the building.

"Those crude passes," I said, "I wonder if they involved urine?"

"Quite possibly." Ari hesitated. "I take it you know what Trotter's particular tastes in sex involved."

"It was kind of obvious from the scene in that bedroom. You look shocked."

"I'm merely surprised that you're not."

"I really don't care what consenting adults do with each other. Well, just so long as they don't want to do it with me." I grinned at him. "Or with you."

He returned the smile. "What I'm wondering is if he was paying Izumi or if she shared his tastes."

"According to Michael's evidence, she got off on it."

"Then I suppose they had a relationship of sorts. Interesting. She must have seen something in him that no one else did."

I refrained from stating the smutty obvious and returned to the report. The Forensics team had found and captured a good many fingerprints from various locations in the apartment. Most could have been made at any time, not necessarily at the time of the murder, except for one set. They'd found four bloody fingerprints on the refrigerator door. The blood type matched the victim's, but the prints, which were all from the same individual, did not. Someone who had Trotter's blood on their hands had opened the fridge, taken out a piece of chocolate cake, and eaten most of it before leaving the remains on the kitchen counter.

"God!" I said. "That's horrible."

"Sociopathic," Ari said. "And arrogant. You'd think they would have wiped the prints off. That's hard evidence of presence if not of the murder itself. Whoever it is really doesn't think she can be caught, which is another indication she's sociopathic."

"I notice you say 'she.' I'm only guessing that Ash did the killing."

"I do need to remember that. But since world-walker Murphy identified her, and a member of her gang may well have been servicing Trotter, Ash is the best lead we have. Your brother doesn't have very good taste in women, I must say. Werewolves. Sociopaths."

"Sophie is a perfectly nice girl except for once a month."

Ari started to grin, wiped it away, and set his lips tight together.

"Don't you dare say it," I said.

Ari's survival instincts did their job. He cleared his throat, coughed once, and returned to studying his laptop screen.

In the morning, we headed back out across the multiverse yet once again. I began to see Spare14's point about living on the run.

The California of Terra Three, or Interchange as I'd termed it before I learned the official naming system, qualifies as a hellhole—low tech, poverty-stricken, essentially Chaotic, though here and there one could find a few pockets of Order and decency. What makes it hell on its earth is the high radiation level. Huge clouds of yellow dust sweep through the atmosphere, scattering radioactivity wherever they drift. Birth defects and a short life expectancy keep the low population desperate.

In this pinchbeck version of the Golden State, a San Francisco of sorts exists. SanFran, the inhabitants call it, a town rather than a city and one that lacks both bridges and charm. Gangs rule territories within it, and werewolves run the police force. If you are Catholic, you root for the Giants and join an Orange gang. If you're Protestant, you root for the Sackamenna Dodgers and pledge your loyalty to Blue. You can guess that the beery fights at the ballpark have a certain intensity that they lack on more civilized world levels.

It was no wonder, I thought, that the Axeman found

plenty of customers in SanFran for his trans-world coyote scheme. It was also no wonder that I hated returning there. Since I had no choice in the matter, Ari and I dressed in jeans and shabby shirts so we'd fit in with the locals. He carried the Beretta, of course, somewhat hidden between a T-shirt and a loose denim work shirt, worn open. In San-Fran, it pays to let everyone know you're armed. We also brought a suitcase of necessary items with us down to Spare14's office. Willa had already arrived and waited for us on a chair in the front room. She asked about the encumbering suitcase.

"Professional clothes for Six," Ari said. "There's a gate in SanFran that leads there. After we've interviewed Wagner, we'd like to go through to join up with the TWIXT team there."

"If we can," I put in.

"Depends on that gate," Willa said. "The one in Sutro Gardens?"

"That's it, yeah," I said. "You must have read Ari's report."

Willa smiled. "The Guild gets all the news about gates, honey. Don't you worry about that! Your dad told us about the Diana statue."

"My dad?"

"Once a Guildsman, always a Guildsman. Soon as he got out of slam, he reported in and got his status back. That was over on Five, when he was first paroled."

I gaped. Willa chuckled at my surprise.

"Even when he was hiding out here on Four, he was in touch with us now and then," Willa continued. "Now of course he's hoping to get his son into the Guild, and I don't see why not. Michael, one of your brothers. You must know he's—"

"A world-walker. Oh, yeah," I said. "He isn't real good at hiding it."

The suitcase might have been a nuisance, but Spare14 took charge of it. One of his desk drawers had a limited trans-world capacity. Although it couldn't transfer items to every deviant level, he'd had an office with another such desk on Three for years. The connection remained alive even though he himself no longer worked there. He put our suitcase, which was a lot bigger than the drawer, into the drawer and closed it, even though it shouldn't have closed with that large a suitcase in it.

"There," he said. "You can pick it up at my old office in SanFran. The new operative has the place."

"Who is it?" Ari said.

"Hendriks, poor fellow." Spare14 sighed in sincere pity. "The liaison captain there—Anna Kerenskya, if you remember—wants to keep an eye on him, so she got him the post. She thinks he's too prone to hasty action and needs seasoning." He shook his head. "Poor fellow."

Spare14 gave Ari things we'd need, like wads of different kinds of cash for SanFran and San Francisco Six, and little badges of pink gel that would monitor our radiation exposure in SanFran. He also handed me an old-fashioned photograph of Scott Trotter—an alive Trotter, that is—which I put in my shoulder bag. We left the office and took a cab down to South Park, the overlap area with Terra Three. Unlike the situation with Six, Willa brought us through without the slightest difficulty, although we found a problem waiting for us in SanFran.

The run-down oval of green space teemed with Dodger fans holding a rally. They'd assembled a platform of sorts out of wooden produce crates, where a guy with a bullhorn was leading anti-Giants cheers. Occasionally, he made an obscene reference to the Pope, as well. We found a quiet corner among two trees and an overgrown shrub.

"I've got another job," Willa said. "But I'll meet you at Hendriks' office late in the day. Around four PM. Okay?"

"That will be fine," Ari said.

Loud cheers drifted over from the rally as an actual Dodger player stepped up on the platform to speak. Willa fished a violet focus orb out of her bag, held it up, and vanished. Ari and I headed for the street that curved around the park. A couple of thugs dressed in blue Dodger paraphernalia shoved their way in front of us. They reeked of beer and cheap dope.

"You!" one of them snarled at Ari. "Are you Orange or Blue?"

"Purple," Ari said calmly. "I'm Jewish."

I've never seen anyone look so utterly confused as the Dodger Dude did at that moment. We smiled, stepped around him, and hurried on our way.

Ari had to guide me through the maze of shabby streets, all of them paved with brick, not asphalt, that led to Market, the main downtown street in SanFran as it was at home. Terra Three in general, and SanFran in particular, teems with other psychic minds. I was registering such an overload of warnings, intuitions, images, and fragments of visions that I had trouble remembering why we were there. Fortunately, I'd learned some ways of dealing with the babble during our last trip there. I pulled free of the mob a few minds at a time, shutting off one psychic healer here, a pair of tarot readers there, a couple of raw untrained intuitives in the distance, a few honed talents nearer by, on and on until at last I'd cleared a free space around me on the aura field.

"Feel better?" Ari said.

"Yeah," I said. "I can think again."

By then we'd reached Market Street, lined with four- and five-story soot-stained buildings instead of skyscrapers and fancy stores. On this deviant level it runs to six lanes, just like at home, but unlike at home, the traffic's sparse. Only occasionally did we see a boxy, 1920s-style automobile, cobbled together out of disparate parts, go chugging past on the brick pavement. Down the middle of the street ran battered yellow streetcars. We took one out, that is, away from the Ferry Building, to the corner of Turk, a few blocks away from *Wagner and Son, Used Books*.

The shop occupied the ground floor of a grubby stone building. Behind a layer of orange cellophane, the front window displayed heaps and piles of books and magazines. We went inside to the jingle of bells attached to the door. Books were stacked everywhere in the long, dimly lit room. Dusty shelves lined the walls and divided the middle of the room into narrow aisles. In between the rows, cardboard boxes held stacks of books. Between the boxes, heaps sat right on the floor. We picked our way through the aisles to the long wooden counter in back. The proprietor himself stood waiting for us in the pool of light cast by a tarnished gooseneck lamp—an ordinary looking guy, neither tall nor short, dressed in a dirty white T-shirt and a pair of much-mended gray slacks. At the sight of us, his dark eyes narrowed behind his wire frame glasses.

"Oh, Jesus," Mitch said. "It's my dear old Jamaican friend again. What is it now?"

"Mind your manners, Wagner," Ari said. "You must know who I really am. No doubt it's all over town."

"That you're a CBI agent?" Mitch said. "Yeah, it is. What do you think I've done, and what will it cost me to get out of it?"

"Nothing new and nothing. I need an ident, that's all. O'Grady, you've got the photo."

I took the picture of Scott Trotter out of my bag and handed it to Mitch. His SPP screamed surprise, and his face mirrored the feeling.

"It's not Scorch," Ari said. "But this bloke is equally dead. You don't have to be afraid of him."

"You're sure about that?"

"Yes. I've seen the stiff. Someone slit his throat for him."

"Good. I like whoever it was already. Yeah, I know this guy."

"Is he the one who sold you the transport orbs?"

"You got it, yeah. I take it I won't be getting any more of them."

"Not from him," I put in. "Unless you can wake the walking dead."

"Very funny." Mitch gave me the photo back. "I'll miss the money the damn things brought in, but I can't say I'll miss the guy. Not one little bit. He scared the shit out of me."

"The Axeman will have to find another source for orbs, too, won't he?"

"Jeez!" Mitch took a step back from the counter. "You guys have been busy digging up dirt."

"It's our job." Ari reached into his jeans pocket and took out a twenty dollar bill of SanFran money. "Do you know what the Axe does with the people he takes off this level?"

Twenty bucks bought a lot in California Three. Mitch looked bitterly and honestly disappointed. "No," he said. "I don't."

"Do you know where they contact him?"

Mitch brightened again. "Yeah. Over in Cow Hollow. A cathouse called Peri's."

"What is this?" I said. "A men-only scam?"

"No," Mitch said. "During the day it's safe for a dame to go into the front room and leave a message with the madam. Peri's is a high-class place."

Ari laid the bill down on the counter. Mitch snatched it and slipped it into his shirt pocket.

"What about you, Mitch?" I said. "Have you ever thought about leaving SanFran?"

"No." He looked honestly shocked. "I couldn't take my books with me. What good would that be?"

"The Axe doesn't let his clients bring a lot of luggage, then?" Ari said.

"Nah. They've got to be ready to run in case there's cops waiting for them. You never know when someone's going to rat you out in an operation like his. And he's got to have help, if you know what I mean, on the other side of wherever."

"True. Some advice. Keep your nose clean. I might have to come back and ask you more questions." Ari flipped open the shirt to reveal the Beretta. "Get it?"

Mitch groaned. "All too well, yeah. I hope you have real good luck—somewhere else."

We left the bookstore and walked to Powell to catch the cable car up and over Nob Hill. We got off at Broadway, a quiet, narrow street lined with houses and trees for the first part of our trip. When we reached Stockton, I was appalled to realize that the easy-access tunnel I was expecting did not exist. We were faced with one of the city's steepest hills, the kind where the sidewalks have stairs built right in.

"Just as well," Ari said. "I wouldn't have trusted the tunnel anyway. Too dangerous if someone was waiting for us inside."

I moaned piteously, but there was no hope for it—up and over we went. As we climbed, Ari strode right up the stairs while I panted along behind. At the top I stopped and refused to go on without a rest.

"If you'd only work out," Ari said, "you wouldn't have these difficulties."

I had just enough energy left to kick him. He laughed.

The view from the top of the hill looked eastward across the bay to Berkeley and Oakland, small clusters of houses and other buildings set against mostly open hillsides. I could pick out the campanile on the university campus—assuming it was indeed the campus, of course, and not some other institution with a bell tower. No bridge spanned the water to Yerba Buena Island and beyond. A few fishing boats bobbed in the bay, and I saw a ferry churning along toward Berkeley. The city below sounded oddly quiet, eerie without the mutter of the traffic that I would have heard at home.

Overhead, the yellow sky swirled with clouds of radioactive dust. In them I saw faces, angry women's faces, their mouths contorted in rage, their long hair streaming out behind them as they flew, darting back and forth, swooping low only to climb again on huge wings that flashed with sparks of yellow fire. Their long tunics billowed around them. Their claws lashed at the air. In the wind I heard their voices shrieking in a strange language. I heard one of them cry out, "*Oi moi! Peplegmai!*" and realized that it was Greek, very old Greek.

"Nola!" Ari caught me by the shoulders. "What is it?"

The women disappeared. I saw only the yellow dust of Interchange and heard only the wind.

"Nola, please?" Ari shook me, but gently. "Talk to me."

"Okay. I, uh . . ." I felt the earth moving beneath my feet and forgot what I wanted to say.

Ari caught and steadied me. "What did you see?"

"The Furies. Come for Agamemnon, I guess. For someone."

"Do you need to sit and rest? I can't carry you down. It's too steep."

"I'll be all right in a minute. Just one of my visions. Or an omen, this time. I guess. I don't know."

He put an arm around me and supported me while I trembled. It only took a few moments for the fit to pass off. I filed the vision away in my memory and concentrated on breathing. As my breath calmed, the earth stopped moving. I could see the daily world again.

Once I felt normal, or as normal as I ever do, we climbed

down more stairs to the flat or at least flatter sidewalk below. Broadway continued narrow and quiet, unlike the gaudy strip mall of vice that existed on our own world level. We hiked all the way down to Columbus. In the alley behind La Venezia Bookstore we arrived at the front door of a shabby little building. It housed a defunct nightclub on the ground floor and the TWIXT observer's office above. Ari took a lockpick out of his jeans pocket and opened the security door to reveal the stairs up. Distantly I heard an alarm ring.

"It's just us, Hendriks!" Ari called up.

We stepped in and shut the door behind us. At the top of the smelly, narrow stairs Jan stood waiting, Beretta in hand, but he kept the gun pointing down at the floor. Unlike his usual sober clothes, he was wearing tight white slacks and a red, magenta, and gold flowered shirt that just about glowed in the dark. I averted my eyes as we climbed the stairs.

"That shirt!" Ari said.

"If I'm a numbers runner, I should have poor taste," Jan said. "I have inherited Sneak Spare's business, you see. His clients expect a lowlife, and a lowlife I have become."

"They should call you Flash Hendriks," I said, "if you're going to dress like that."

He grinned. "I like that. I'll use it." He stroked the shirt. "I got this in The Hague on Four. There's a big flea market on the Malieveld. You can get all sorts of things there."

"Legal or not, I suppose," Ari said.

"They are legal in the Netherlands." Hendriks thought for a moment. "At least, they are on Four."

At first sight, the office had changed little since last I'd seen it: the same dirty white walls, beat-up gray-and-green carpet, and sagging green couch. Spare14's old desk sat by the window with its rotary dial landline phone upon it. Our suitcase stood next to it. After our long walk, I had to use the bathroom off the tiny kitchen. In both rooms, the cream-

and-black tiles and the appliances had been scrubbed, a very welcome change.

I came back out to the office to find Ari reading printout from TWIXT. When I sat down on the couch, he handed it to me, a report on the Kingdom of Christ over on Terra Six. It took only a couple of sentences to make my stomach clench. They were Reconstructionists, allegedly Christian but Dominionists of the worst stripe, those who believed in theocracy and the rule of Biblical law—according to their own interpretation of the Bible, of course.

If ever the multiverse needs yet another example of the evil that results when the Order principle gets taken to extremes, I've found one on Terra Six. The Kingdomites were determined, according to the TWIXT report, to spread their doctrines until their leaders ruled North America. I was willing to bet that if by some weird fluke they succeeded, they wouldn't stop at North America.

I'm a totally lapsed Catholic, but some remnant of my childhood rose to the surface of my indignant mind. "These people," I said, as calmly as I could manage, "are not real Christians."

"Don't ever say that to them," Jan said. "It could prove fatal."

While I finished reading, Ari told Jan what we'd learned from Wagner down at the bookstore. I was too angry at what I was reading to listen. Women as property and baby-producing machines, gays punished by death, Morality Police everywhere, preachers in every government post, other religions strictly prohibited—the Kingdom of Christ had so little to do with Jesus' actual words that I was surprised they hadn't banned the gospels. They'd certainly banned enough other books that disagreed with them. At the very end of the report came the kicker. They'd reinstituted slavery because it existed in the Old Testament. Poor people ended up owned if they couldn't pay their debts. Children born in slavery stayed in slavery. The theocracy's big upgrade—slaves could be any color or race. Why limit the field when there was profit to be made?

Slavery. Profit. The words floated up from my subconscious and refused to leave. During a previous visit to SanFran, I'd come to suspect the Axeman's criminal gang of abducting children to sell on some sort of black market here on Terra Three. What if he sold them elsewhere? I leaned back on the couch, put down the report, and Scanned the aura field. What did happen to those people that the Axeman took from SanFran in particular and California Three in general? A village up in the Sierra, huh? That would be on or near the border with the Kingdom, which had taken over the old state of Nevada. The mountains of the Sierra are high and wild, full of rocky little passes and hidden valleys, too long a border for the California National Guard to patrol.

I don't know what emotion was showing on my face, but I realized that both men had started watching me.

"What is it, O'Grady?" Jan said.

"A line of speculation," I said. "A pretty high probability, but still, speculation at this stage. Ari, don't the materials for IEDs cost money?"

"Yes," Ari said. "High nitrogen fertilizer like McVeigh used on Four is cheap, but the equipment to set off the device can be expensive."

"And the terrorists who infiltrate California have to have expenses, travel money, and so on. Fake IDs, too." I thought for a moment. "The government of the Kingdom keeps denying that they finance these people."

"The people who finance terrorism always deny it," Ari said. "They usually disguise their contributions as charity."

"Or else they run drugs and stuff to get the money," I continued, "like the CIA in Nicaragua."

"True. That does happen."

"Slavery's profitable in the Kingdom. What if the terrorists buy slaves cheap from the Axeman and then resell them to finance their little adventures?"

They both gaped at me but not in disbelief.

"The trans-world crime of the century," Jan said at last. "Several centuries, actually, assuming it's true."

"Talk about cutting bread from both ends of the loaf!" I said. "He takes money for getting the people to Six, steals whatever jewelry, currency, and other goods they've brought with them, and then sells the people themselves for a nice wholesale price. If, of course, my speculation's correct. It just came floating in from the aura field."

"I wonder how Trotter's murder might figure into this?" Ari was gazing into the distance as he thought things through. "The stolen orbs play a role, certainly. The attack on the TWIXT building on Six—he could have been an accessory and then have known too much once the attack failed. Or he might even have been getting cold feet at the scale of the violence."

"Accessory to the Axeman or to the terrorists?" Jan asked.

"Why not both?" I said.

"No reason," Jan said. "If, as you say, this is all true."

"Quite," Ari said. "We need evidence. This madam down at Peri's. She must have some information as to the supposed terms of the Axeman's offer. How much, what he'll do for that amount, and so on. We also need to know if anyone's ever returned from one of these jaunts or sent for a family member. If no one ever has, that's another reason to suspect the slavery angle."

"You're already involved with the cases on Terra Six." Jan sighed with great drama. "I suppose that leaves me to go down to this top-flight whorehouse in the line of duty."

"Be careful of what Kerenskya says about that," I said.

This time his sigh was genuine. "I do need to be careful," Jan said. "She thinks I need seasoning."

"So Spare14 told us, "Ari said. "Too prone to hasty action. I've got a problem that way myself, I'm afraid."

"Oddly enough, there's a Dutch idiom about that." Jan paused for a grin. "But it means the opposite of what Kerenskya has in mind. Too much seasoning—*peper in iemands reet stoppen*. Pepper up his arse, I think we could translate it."

While we waited for Willa, reports and messages flew back and forth over the trans-world router from Ari and Jan on one end and Spare14 and HQ on the others. Since I was sitting only a few feet away, they were forced to share the intel with me, or at least, some of it. I suspected them of transferring classified information directly to Ari's laptop back in our safe on Terra Four, but I decided that I could get it out of him later in private rather than making a fuss right there and then. I was beginning to chafe at my "observer only" status—seriously, as Michael would have said. To use my psychic talents accurately, I need anchors in the real world of evidence and fact.

"HQ are quite interested in your theory." Ari did tell me that much. "It jibes with some observations JaMarcus Spivey had made earlier about the terrorist attacks on Six. The perpetrators seem quite well funded, for one thing. Besides that, the California National Guard have captured several cells of the alleged terrorists. Often they have weapons which shouldn't be available on Terra Six, some advanced night scope rifles from Five, for example."

"So orbs and level-hopping are factors," I said.

"Most definitely. Which points in the direction of the Axeman's gang." Ari considered for a moment. "The slavery hypothesis strikes me as correct, but we badly want another source of information."

"What about Major Grace?" I said. "Y'know, at the

Mission House. She knows us as CBI agents. We can be honest with her."

"Not terribly honest. There's the question of deviant world levels."

"Ari, half the people in SanFran know the multiverse exists. Besides, she has to come from another level herself. Don't you remember the poster in the hall? Jesus' sister Sophia, the light of the world? That's not standard Christian doctrine here any more than it is on Four."

"Right." Ari glanced at his watch. "We have time to go see if we can speak with her. Willa won't be here for several hours."

We walked downhill under a swirling yellow sky. Major Grace's mission stood at the corner of Sackamenna Street and Joice Alley, a grim, cubical building painted fortress-gray. Wrought iron grates covered its ground-floor windows. A beefy young man in a black-and-maroon military-style uniform stood in front of the closed door, but when he saw me and Ari, he smiled and stepped aside. I recognized him from an earlier visit to SanFran on Three, during which Ari and I had saved Major Grace's life.

"Good to see you again, Agent Nathan," the guy said. "We're being more careful these days."

"Good," Ari said. "We'd all hate to lose the Major."

The guard opened the door and bowed us inside to the pleasant, rose-pink foyer. We walked on down the long hall-way, decorated with various religious-themed posters in the usual brightly-colored, overly glossy style. Right beside a stairway hung the framed poster of Sophia that I remem-bered, a woman in Middle Eastern dress with a strong, handsome face. An aureole of light streamed around her.

Major Grace, the leader of this mission to the poor, had an office near the head of the stairs. When we knocked on the door, she opened it herself, a tall, square-shouldered woman dressed in a severely cut black-and-maroon dress.

Her gray hair was escaping in wisps from the black heads-carf she wore like a medieval wimple.

"Well!" she said and smiled. "Eric and Rose, or should I say, our two CBI agents! I'm afraid I'll always think of you two as Eric and Rose. You really did fool me, you know. Come in. It's good to see you again."

"Thanks," I said. "It's good to see you, too."

We followed her into her office, a yellow room with a big oak desk, an old-fashioned swiveling office chair behind it, a filing cabinet, and two plain chairs for guests. She waved at us to sit down and returned to her own chair.

"What brings you here?" Major Grace asked.

"We're looking for information," Ari said, "concerning a criminal case. I believe I remember that you keep a red ledger with notes on people who've disappeared in odd circumstances. We have a theory about what might have happened to them."

"I do, yes." Major Grace opened a desk drawer and brought out the leather-bound book. "I'd certainly like to get to the bottom of this."

"What we're wondering," I put in, "is how many of the disappearances can be related to the gang run by the Axeman."

"The Storm Blue gang? You know, it's odd. For a long time most of the missing persons I heard about did seem to have some connection with them, but just recently—not long after you arrested the men who tried to kill me, in fact—that changed. Almost no one has disappeared, and those that have tend to be eventually found floating in the Bay."

Ari and I exchanged a glance, which Major Grace acknowledged with a wry smile. "Here." She slid the red ledger across the desk. "I'll want that back, but there's no reason why you can't have it for a day or two."

"Thank you very much." Ari picked up the book. "There could be a pattern here that might prove useful."

"I hope so. I'd very much like to see a permanent stop put to that sort of thing. May I ask what exactly you think happened to them?"

"We think," I said, "that the Axeman took money from these people to get them to a different world level, off of this one, that is, and then sold them into slavery on a world where one of the governments is trying to reinstate the laws of the Old Testament."

Major Grace stared at me, her mouth slack. Her SPP registered surprise but not skepticism.

"Yes," I said, "we do know about the multiverse. We didn't originate on Three. I guess you didn't, either, huh?"

Major Grace smiled, took a deep breath, and said, "What makes you think we come from elsewhere?"

"The Sophia poster in the hallway," I said. "On my home world level and on this one, Jesus doesn't have a sister. Or so the doctrines say. For all I know, he does, and the doctrines are wrong."

"I'd say they're wrong. I didn't realize how glaring the difference would be. She's my favorite figure in the gospels, and I just couldn't bear to leave her behind."

If those gospels featured Sophia, then her religion had a different set of books than my church did. Curiosity ate at me. I wanted to ask her for details—where they came from, who they were, what they were doing on Interchange—but she was too valuable an ally to risk alienating. Besides, their mission was giving a chance at life and health to the poorest of the poor in SanFran. I couldn't risk driving them away by prying into their secrets.

"We're certainly not going to report this to anyone," I said. "Besides, the CBI doesn't know where we come from, either. I doubt if they care."

"That's reassuring. Thank you." Major Grace leaned back in her chair and frowned in thought. "Sold into slavery," she said eventually. "How horrible! You know, this might explain something. One very sad case. Excuse me a moment."

Major Grace got up and walked out into the hallway. I heard her calling down to someone on the floor below to ask if they'd bring Sarah up to her office. She came back and sat down.

"Someone I think you should talk with," she said.

In a few minutes a very pregnant young woman, blonde, blue-eyed, who would have been pretty if her eyes hadn't looked out so starkly on the world, walked into the office. She held her hands just under her swollen belly to support it. I guessed her age as about twenty even though she had deep lines on either side of her mouth, the sort of thing you expect to see on a much older woman. Ari stood up and helped her into the chair. She neither smiled nor said thank you, just looked straight ahead. Ari leaned against the nearest wall next to a poster of the Ten Commandments.

"Sarah," the Major said. "These are two law officers from Sackamenna. The California Bureau of Investigation. They might know something about your missing husband."

Sarah turned her head very slowly and looked at me. "Is he dead?" she said.

"We don't know," I said. "We're hoping to find out. Did he make some kind of a deal with the Axeman?"

She nodded and turned her sad eyes back to Major Grace.

"Would you like me to tell them?" the Major said.

Sarah nodded again.

"The Axeman promised to take Sarah and her husband to another world, a better one than this," Major Grace said. "They didn't have enough money for his fees, even after they sold everything they owned. So Joshua went first, because the Axeman promised that after a couple of months of work, he'd come back for Sarah. He never did. It was right after he left that she realized she was pregnant, so that would have been seven months ago. Then the Axeman disappeared. Sarah went to the police, who thought she was crazy. She lived on the streets for a while, but fortunately, one of our members found her and brought her here. I assured her that she wasn't crazy, that there were indeed other worlds."

"Abandoned," Sarah whispered. "Bad enough."

"Do you think Joshua meant to abandon you?" I asked. She nodded. "Unless he's dead."

"I doubt if either's true." Ari peeled himself off the wall and came around so that Sarah could see him. "We think the Axeman sold him into slavery on this supposedly better world. I'm sure he'd come back for you if he could."

She looked at him. Two tears ran down her cheeks, that was all, just two. She was too depressed to even cry, I figured.

"He was all I had," she whispered. "And they took him."

"We'll do our best to find him," I said. "But it would be cruel to hold out a lot of hope."

She nodded, got up from the chair, and turned and walked out of the office without a word.

"I am having very bad thoughts," Major Grace said, "about the Axeman, that is, at this moment. May God forgive me, but I really wish him ill."

"You're not alone," I said. "You can trust me on that."

We returned to the TWIXT office and gave Jan the red ledger to study. He promised to send us any information he gleaned from it. He also agreed that Sarah's story sounded like just the sort of evidence we needed.

"The Axeman is a thorough bastard," Jan remarked. "Let's hope we track him down."

"Just so," Ari said. "And by the way, that ledger should go back to the Major when you're done."

Willa arrived shortly after. While she sat down and rested for "a few minutes, and God knows I deserve it," as she put it, Ari and I took our suitcase into the apartment's narrow bedroom and changed our clothes for Six. He had his navy blue pinstriped suit, and I'd brought my glen plaid pants and jacket. As I zipped up the trousers, I remarked that they were getting tight.

"Not tight," Ari said. "They're beginning to fit you. You're too used to wearing clothes that hang on you."

"I didn't think they were that bad."

"That's part of the eating disorder, isn't it? Wearing everything much too large so people can't see how thin you are?"

He was right, damn him! He smiled, caught me by the shoulders, and kissed me.

"I can't see your ribs anymore," he said. "It's much sexier that way."

"Okay. So there are compensations."

And, I figured, I wouldn't have to buy new clothes for another ten pounds. On my salary, this was good news. We returned the suitcase with our old clothes to Spare14's office via the desk drawer. Here in Jan's office I had a better look at the process than I'd gotten before. Jan opened the drawer, which appeared to have an ordinary wooden bottom like any other desk drawer. He turned the suitcase to insert the narrow end first, then slowly pushed it in—and through. I couldn't quite see any part of it disappear, but at the same time, I couldn't see the whole suitcase, either. Watching the process left me feeling so disoriented that I was sorry I'd peeked.

I'd also been wondering how we'd get out to the beach and the trans-world gate to Terra Six. It turned out that Jan had a car of sorts in the former nightclub downstairs, very much of sorts as was usual in SanFran, a patchwork of parts from a WWI Packard and pieces of a Duesenberg that had survived the disaster on Interchange. The Axeman and his gang had trashed the place when the nightclub's owners had refused to pay protection money, and they'd done it so thoroughly that the landlord couldn't afford to make the repairs. Since no one wanted to rent the mess left on the ground floor of the building, Jan had persuaded the landlord to let him park the car inside for a small monthly fee. It had double entrance doors large enough to drive through.

The car started with a crank, but it started. We all piled in and headed out down to Geary, which would take us on reasonably level terrain all the way out to Ocean Beach. The Richmond district on Terra Three is a dismal, half-populated place of squatters' cottages and tumbledown houses. Only on Geary do you find shops and decent-looking homes. Just a few blocks to the south the sand dunes and weeds still rule between dirt tracks named as streets in a misbegotten hope of better days.

We were aiming for the area known back home as Sutro Heights. In SanFran, people just called it "the old Sutro place," the remains of a millionaire's once luxurious mansion and gardens. In our world the gardens have been turned into a tidy little park just off 48th Avenue, but in SanFran on Interchange they exist as a jumble of weeds, trees, briars, and broken statuary that covers twice the area the park does at home. When we reached the edge of this miniature wilderness, Jan let us out of the car, but before he drove away, I received a full-strength ASTA, an automatic warning of a threat to our survival.

"Could you wait here for a few minutes?" I said. "I'm picking up danger loud and clear."

"Of course!" Jan said. "Nathan, you might need your agent's best friend."

Ari smiled and brought out the Beretta.

"I've got my communicator," Ari said. "I'll call you when we're about to leave."

"Or if you're not leaving, I'll be here." Jan drew his own gun. "Just in case."

Ari led the way on a narrow dirt path into the trees. We put Willa in the middle, and I took the rear guard. As we walked, I began to gather Qi. I wrapped it into a loose skein, but I stayed ready to tighten it into a sphere in case I had to ensorcell someone—or something. The path led us through a pair of stone lions, half-broken and covered with graffiti and a pair of rusty iron gates. Overhead, the remains of an iron arch dangled like a threat. We walked through into waist-high weeds and scraggly second-growth saplings. For the first twenty yards or so, I heard birds chirping and calling, but just as we were about to come clear of the trees, they fell silent. I could hear the nearby ocean muttering on the beach at high tide. Ari held up one hand to signal a halt.

Ahead, on the other side of a long stretch of low-growing grass, I could see our goal, a marble statue of the goddess Diana, beautifully caught as she pulled an arrow from the quiver on her back. Beside her, a marble hunting dog leaped up in anticipation of the chase ahead. All around the grassy strip stood trees and banks of weeds. Nothing moved; nothing made a sound. Overhead, the yellow dust clouds glowed orange and magenta in the lowering sun. The ASTA turned me cold enough to shiver.

"We don't want to go much farther," I murmured.

"Very well." Ari spoke just as softly. "Do you know why?"

I was about to answer that I didn't when a second statue materialized about ten feet away. To be precise, I only perceived him as a statue, carved from the same white marble. He actually was an angel, St. Maurice in his after-death translation, a tall slender figure with huge wings. He wore a Roman tunic and armor, and at his side he carried a short sword. The ASTA ceased as soon as I identified him. When he beckoned to me, I started forward. Ari caught my arm and stopped me.

"What are you doing?" he snapped.

"St. Maurice is here," I said. "I forgot you can't see him. It's safe now."

"Neither can I," Willa said. "Who? What?"

"Nathan can explain," I said.

When Ari let me go, I trotted out onto the grass to meet the angel. Maurice greeted me in the Roman manner, one hand up, palm outward.

"Salve, filia," he said.

"Salve, magister," I said. *"Si vales, valeo."*

"Valeo, sed obstat periculum vobis, periculum magnum." He pointed at the statue. *"Fractus est. Ponte nolite uti! Ducet vos a nihil—nihil per aeternitate."*

"Crud! I mean, *gratias tibias magnas*."

He smiled and disappeared. I turned around and jogged back to the others.

"He says the bridge is broken. If we use it, it'll lead us into nothingness. Permanent nothingness."

"Oh kay!" Willa drawled the "okay" into two words. "Always good to know! I'll be glad to take your invisible friend's warning, but I'd also like a look at the gate. I guess that's what he meant by bridge."

"I think so, yes."

"Makes sense. The names are only metaphors anyway."

"It's safe to cross the lawn now. I don't see any sign of the old tunnel collapse." I glanced at Ari. "The grass is a lot shorter than it was the last time we were here. Do you think someone's mowed it?"

"Goats," Ari said. "It's been grazed. I recognize the cropping pattern. The little people who live out here must have acquired some livestock."

"I keep forgetting that you started life as a farm boy," I said. "Let's go."

As we walked across the lawn, I was intent on avoiding what the goats had left behind, but Ari kept looking around him. Although he carried the Beretta with the business end pointing down, he never holstered it. When we reached the statue, we found tribute laid on the base at Diana's feet: a chipped white bowl of red wine, an orange, peeled and splayed on a little plate. Willa rummaged through her mesh bag and brought out a small black orb.

"I've never seen a black one before," I said.

"It's just a diagnostic," Willa said. "Won't take you anywhere."

She held the orb chest high and began to walk around the statue. Every now and then the orb beeped, but it was a plaintive little sound. She'd gotten around to the other side when she called out to us.

"Come look at this!" she said.

I hurried around to join her. Ari followed more slowly, Beretta raised, his head turning as he scanned for possible enemies. On the statue's base but behind the goddess, someone had left another offering—an unsealed white envelope, about six inches square, decorated with three Japanese characters in brushstrokes of black ink. My hands itched, as they always did when I saw or heard information I needed. When I picked up the envelope, something metal slithered around inside. I looked in and saw six coins and a thin detached braid of black hair.

"Something fell out." Willa pointed at the ground.

I retrieved the narrow slip of rice paper. It had been inscribed—and misspelled—in the Roman alphabet: sayanara Scotty yer sakura.

"Whoa!" I snapped. "This could be raw coincidence, but Ash and Co. know about this gate. It's how they got away from us, and I'm willing to bet they've used it since then."

"Um," Ari said, "what—"

"Six coins to cross the rivers in the land of the dead," I said, "and a farewell note to someone named Scott. In a white envelope. White's the color of mourning in Japan. An ironic gesture, maybe, if our arrogant murderer left it here to sneer at him and us. Maybe not ironic at all, if Izumi actually loved Trotter or, at least, liked him."

"If so," Ari said, "she's the only person in the multiverse who did."

"What I wonder," I continued, "is why she'd leave it here instead of on Six."

"So Ash wouldn't find it, perhaps?" Ari said.

"Very good point. I bet it's unhealthy to show any sympathy for one of Ash's victims."

"I'd expect so, yes." He turned to our world-walker. "Danvers-Jones, what's your diagnosis of the gate?"

"Dead as a doornail," Willa said. "O'Grady's invisible friend was right. I wonder if your suspect spiked it as she left?"

"That would be a logical move on her part," Ari said. "Keep us from following."

"It was unstable the last time we were here," I put in. "My father said he wouldn't trust it. The suspects must have been desperate enough to try with TWIXT moving in on them."

"Then they got real lucky." Willa paused for a shudder. "I don't even want to think about where a broken gate would dump you. Permanent nothing, yeah. The big question is, would your wave packet spread fast enough so you'd never know what was hitting you? Let's hope so."

Ari holstered the Beretta. He pulled the silk handkerchief out of his suit coat's breast pocket and handed it to me. "If you'll wrap that envelope up without getting any more of your grubby fingerprints on it, we'll take it with us. If it's not relevant to the case, then my apologies to the spirits of the dead and all that, but it's too interesting to leave behind." He took out his communicator. "I'll tell Hendriks we're coming back."

Jan drove the three of us back to the office. Willa used

the trans-world router to contact the Guild about other possible gates or overlap areas to Six only to be told there were none in SanFran. The nearest lay several hundred miles to the north.

"Our best bet," she told us, "would be to go back to Four and the overlap area there. Assuming it's still open. I don't like this, gates up and closing on us for no good reason."

"A good many people have been using stolen orbs," Ari said. "Would that be having an effect?"

"Possibly, if they were using all of them at the same gate. Otherwise, no. I'm going to consult with the head of the Guild about this." Willa turned to Jan. "How about a ride down to the overlap?"

"That's why I left the car out." Jan stood up. "We'd better leave before someone steals it, or parts of it, anyway."

We returned to South Park on world level Three. The Dodger rally had ended some time before, though a drift of trash marked where the fans had gathered. An old woman, wearing three different calico housedresses, was searching through the trash and gathering the beer and soda bottles left in the litter. She could probably return them to a store for a few pennies each, I figured. When we walked past, she looked up and scowled at Willa as if she feared a possible rival.

Instead of fighting over the bottles, Willa took us straight back to world level Four and the clean, well-kept version of South Park. Before we left the overlap area, Ari decided to phone Spare14, and a good thing he did. The orders from TWIXT HQ had changed. Thanks to Willa's report of the dead gate, Ari and I were being instructed to stay on our own world level until further notice.

"I'm to check with Spare14 first thing tomorrow," Ari told us. "Danvers-Jones, the Guild wants you back at your HQ."

"Tell Sneak to tell them I'm on my way."

While Ari did so, Willa brought out her violet orb. She took a few steps away from us. I never saw her fade or vanish in a pool of light. All at once she simply wasn't there.

CHAPTER 9

W E STARTED TO WALK the couple of blocks to the exorbitantly priced parking lot where we'd left the Saturn. We were passing through a neighborhood of warehouses and semi-industrial businesses. Large, faceless buildings, most white or gray, sprawled on either side of the wide streets. Loading docks and trucks filled the alleys that crossed the middle of the blocks. By then, rush hour had clogged the approach to the Bay Bridge which, in that location, around Third and Brannan, ran over the street on huge concrete pylons. I could smell the traffic jam in the drift of exhaust from the trapped cars above us. A good many drivers had given up and managed to return to ground level at the last exits. Honking, snarling traffic crawled along beside us.

We'd just turned off Brannan onto Third—I could see the baseball park looming in the distance ahead—when I heard an animal growl directly behind us. It sounded like a mix of lion and bear, loud and threatening. I glanced at Ari, who smiled at me. He'd heard nothing.

"I need to look behind us," I said. "Let's stop for a minute."

He obliged. I swirled around and saw a monster. A large green reptile, red eyes, slavering mouth, huge teeth, and about the size of an SUV, crouched ready to spring. With another roar, it raised a nasty-looking clawed paw. I drew a Chaos ward and threw. It exploded in a rain of green crystals.

"Was anything there?" Ari said.

"Yes and no. An illusion or a Chaos critter. I don't know which, but it's gone now. Y'know, if I weren't used to crud like this, I might have screamed and run right into the traffic." I looked at the street, where large metal machines streamed by us at about fifteen miles an hour. "Squashed Nola all over the street would have been the result."

"I do wish you wouldn't joke about it." Ari fixed me with a mournful stare. "And I also wish these apparitions were something I could shoot."

"That's one reason why I love you." I slipped my arm through his. "Let's go redeem the car from bondage. I want to go home."

As we drove back to our flat, I tried to apply some logic to these illusions that kept threatening my life in their oddly indirect manner. Thinking helped me ignore Ari's driving, which threatened my life directly. I finally decided that of my list of suspects, the psychic squid criminals from the alternate Venus were the most likely candidates. Ash and the Axeman would have come right after me with a knife. The Maculate leopard-woman from Terra Two had good reason to hate me but great difficulty in traveling in our world. She had three pairs of breasts, skin marked with rosettes like leopard spots, and ears at the top of her head. Other than at science fiction conventions, she would stand out too much in any crowd to be an effective assassin.

Could she have hired the cephalopods, that evolved mixed race of squid and cuttlefish, to take me out? An ugly possibility, but a real one. Worse yet, would she have put this hypothetical contract out on Ari instead of me? He'd shot and killed her lover. An even uglier possibility, but one that I needed to keep in mind, assuming that she knew what had happened to Claw, the mate in question. He'd died on a different world level than hers only a few weeks previous to this barrage of squid. It was possible that she still had no idea he was dead.

The cephalopods hated me because I'd broken up their ring of human allies and then arrested Belial, the leader of their advance squad. Belial had controlled enough power to try to murder me in a tentacles-on way, but apparently the current lot lacked his talent. Until they managed to find new human allies, their aquatic nature kept them from simply shooting me or running me over with a truck. They did have the means to act through images and illusions, because they possessed a machine, a form of trans-world router that allowed them to send psychic projections from their world to mine. I could assume that Bissop Keith had access to similar technology, though I doubted if he were in league with the cephalopods.

Add to this the Chaos critters in the form of squid—spies, probably, trying to pin down my exact location so their operators could focus their trans-world apparatus. It was possible that through these spies, their controllers had learned enough about our world to choose suitably frightening images to send. The recent reptile, for example, looked like something from a bad movie about cavemen and dinosaurs.

Once I started thinking about the squiddish critters that had appeared in our flat, it occurred to me to wonder how they knew where to find me. A red light had just forced Ari to stop his mad career through the traffic.

"Ari," I said, "does your mother know our mailing address?"

"Yes. I assumed it was safe to send it to her. After all, she is my mother."

"I wonder if Flowertree has it, too, now."

Ari swore in Hebrew. The light changed, and he laid on the horn in order to intimidate a large delivery van. The Saturn sprang ahead. I tried not to panic. When no crash occurred, I opened my eyes again.

"Sorry," Ari said, "I never should have sent it to her. Actually, I did tell her—" He paused to swerve into the right lane in a blare of other people's horns. "—not to give it to the husband. But I wouldn't put it past him to go through her things when she's out shopping or some such."

"If we live to see home and my computer, I'll ask her about it."

"Of course we'll live. Don't be silly!"

I restrained myself from saying unladylike things in a loud voice. I murmured them to myself instead.

"Why are you worried about the address?" Ari said.

"Because Flowertree could be an ally of the psychic squid from the alternate Venus."

When Ari made no reply, I glanced his way and ran a quick SPP. He was concentrating on his driving to suppress his memory that such cephalopods existed. I said nothing more rather than break the spell.

We stopped and had dinner on the way, but we did live to get home. Like the normal modern couple we pretended to be, we both went straight to our respective e-mail accounts as soon as we'd changed out of our business clothes. Ari retrieved his laptop and took it into the kitchen to work at the table there. Since my desktop was running its security routines, I joined him.

"Ari, darling, my beloved," I said. "If you've received

more information on Ash and the Axeman, please remember that I have need to know."

"I will. The question is, will HQ allow me to share the intel?"

I set my hands on my hips. He squirmed in his chair, a good sign. I glanced at the laptop screen—filled with Hebrew letters.

"Ari, come off it!" I said. "You're willing enough to pipeline everything you think they'll want to your deep cover agency in Israel. Why not give me what I need?"

He actually blushed. "Oh, very well!" he said, and while he sounded surly, at least he was talking about the problem. "I've pointed out to Spare14 as well as to HQ that, without you, we'd have precious few leads in the Agent Trotter murder case."

"You've got a handler at HQ already? Huh. Interesting. They really want you onboard."

He snarled at his slipup. I grinned. In a moment he sighed and smiled himself, albeit sheepishly.

"The real problem," Ari continued, "is the Agency. As long as they keep you on observer only status, HQ will wonder why and not trust you. You very much need to convince Y that you absolutely must have full freedom to act during this case."

"I'll send him a stiff e-mail tonight."

Before I did so, I checked my non-Agency e-mail because I knew there would be less of it than the official business. In that queue I found only two messages: some pictures of her infant son from my old buddy Mira Rosen and a letter from Ari's mother. Shira Flowertree was planning on visiting her friend Barbara, the woman who owned the videoconferencing equipment, the next afternoon. Afternoon, that is, London time. Her suggested hour worked out to seven AM in San Francisco. Since Ari had to be up early, anyway, to see what Spare14 and HQ had decided for our next move, I agreed.

I switched over to TranceWeb. I found a long queue of routine Agency mail to work through after I sent off my blistering missive to Y. As I answered bureaucratic queries, I found it harder and harder to concentrate. I kept turning around in my desk chair, expecting to see Chaotic squid images or critters floating around the living room. None were. Slowly my unease crystallized into a Semi-Automatic Warning Mechanism, as the Agency terms them. I logged out and left the computer to walk into the hall. I could see through the kitchen door that Ari was still working with the laptop. I noticed he'd changed over to English.

I went on down to the bathroom. No squid, no apparitions of any sort lurked in there, and the bedroom was cephalopod-free as well. The SAWM kept growing stronger. I was picking up Ari's scattered clothes from the floor when the truth dawned on me: I wasn't in any danger. Someone in my family was, and the most likely person was Maureen. I let his shirt lie where he'd dropped it and grabbed my cell phone from my shoulder bag. Fortunately, I had Kathleen's number on speed dial.

Kathleen answered right away. "Oh, hi, Nola," she said. "I was just thinking about you, wondering when the wedding's going to be."

"We can worry about that later," I said. "Where's Maureen?"

"Right here. Why? I—uh-oh!"

In the background I could hear the dogs start barking, howling, yapping, growling in alarm. Kathleen moved her phone away from her mouth and called out, "Jack! Something's wrong!"

Distantly I heard Jack answer. Kathleen returned to the phone.

"Someone's prowling around outside," she said. "Jack's

got his rifle, and he's going to flip on all the outside lights.
We've kind of been expecting this. Chuck's been too quiet
lately."

"Gathering steam, huh? Where are the kids?"

"Upstairs asleep. Well, they were asleep, but with all the
dogs . . ." She paused briefly. "Maureen's gone up to check
on them. The kids, I mean, not the dogs."

"I figured that. Tell her to stay away from the windows!"

Kathleen relayed the order; then there was silence, a
minute or two of it, maybe, while I felt my heart pounding
much too fast. I sat down on the edge of the bed and waited
some more. I was just about to scream at her to say something when she did.

"Did you hear that?"

"No," I said. "What was it?"

"A couple of shots. Jack just fired them. I could see him
through the front window."

"You shouldn't be by the window either."

"Oh. Yeah, I guess you're right. I'm moving."

"Well, for God's sake, Kath! Did he hit him? I mean, did
Jack shoot anyone?"

"No. He was firing into the ground. Oh, yeah, I should've
told you that."

Kathleen is not the most intelligent O'Grady, in case you
haven't guessed by now. Ari, meanwhile, had heard my side
of the conversation and come into the bedroom. He stood
listening with his arms crossed over his chest while I gave
him a quick report.

"I'd like to talk with Jack," he said and took his phone
out of his jeans pocket.

Jack, it turned out, wanted to talk with Ari. Ari sat down
next to me on the bed. We had a peculiar four-person, two-
phone-calls conversation, the upshot of which boiled down
to this. Chuck had been prowling around the fence. The
dogs started throwing themselves against said fence and

scared him off even before Jack fired, which he'd done to let Chuck know that he was armed and serious. Jack had heard Chuck's Harley racing away a few moments after the second shot

"I don't want Chuck shooting one of my dogs," was Kathleen's final comment. "Maybe we can get them little Kevlar thingies to wear."

"Oh for God's sake, honey!" Jack said.

They both clicked off, probably to have a fight about Kevlar vests for dogs. I put my phone down on the bedside table. Ari pocketed his.

"What counts," I said, "is that Maureen and the kids are okay."

"Quite," Ari said. "I suspect that Trasker's a coward. Men who prey on women generally are. He'll keep away for a while, at least."

"But we can't know for how long."

"True. It's going to be hard on Maureen, wondering."

"She should be able to go out during the day, shouldn't she? I know she wants to look for a job. She kind of needs to. I mean, Jack'll be willing to support her and the kids, but that'll gripe Maureen. She's always been the independent type."

"It could be too dangerous. It depends." Ari shrugged. "On how angry Chuck is, that is to say. If he's willing to risk death to get at her . . ." He let his voice trail away.

I desperately wanted to cry. I squelched the impulse as not helpful. Ari put his arm around my shoulders and gave me a comforting squeeze.

"Mike's not the only O'Grady who's got lousy taste in partners," I said. "Maureen's husband was a wild kind of guy, too, but he never would have hurt her or the kids."

"What happened to him?"

"She divorced him. He had another woman on the side. Maureen kind of knew, but she could ignore it until the other woman turned up pregnant. They had the DNA test, and yeah, the baby was JD's."

Ari muttered something in Hebrew. "JD?" he said. "That was his name?"

"Yep. He was from Kentucky originally. Another wild Irish-American guy. O'Connor is the kids' last name. Maureen took O'Grady back."

Ari rolled his eyes and repeated whatever it was in Hebrew. I stretched out my arms, so tense by then that they ached.

"I want a long hot shower," I said.

"Good idea." He smiled at me. "I could use one myself."

One of the good features of our flat was the walk-in shower, roomy enough for two, nicely tiled in blue and green. So we had our shower, and the inevitable activity after being so close and warm and wet together. We went to bed early, and a good thing, too, considering that we had to be up by six-thirty.

The dawn was just breaking through the ocean fog when I staggered out of bed and went into the kitchen to start some coffee. Another damn squid was floating over the sink. It scuttled away into the multiverse before I could pop it with a ward. Its prudence indicated that it was no illusion. It was either the projection of an actual sapient squid's mind or a full-blown Chaos critter that had some capacity to think or at least to react.

Once I'd drunk my first mug of coffee, I set up my laptop for secure video conferencing. I wanted no one to have any contact with my desktop, especially not other persons with psychic talents, not even Ari's mother, if indeed I'd guessed correctly and she did have talents. Since Shira would be able to see me, I put on the dark blue silk blouse and accented it with the gold brooch Ari had given me. I took my laptop into the kitchen, plugged it into the DSL line there, and sat at the table.

Shira called right on time. She'd dressed for the occasion, too, in a pale green shirt and an amber necklace. Her hair was as dark and softly curly as Ari's, though she wore hers long, pulled back into a gold clip. Anyone who saw them together would have had no trouble realizing that they were mother and son. Her eyes were as dark and large as his, and there was a touch of chiseled strength to her face that marked her not as masculine, but as handsome rather than beautiful.

After the usual polite greetings, Shira got right down to the business in hand.

"I've written out everything I can remember about Ezekiel's visions," she told me. "I've sent this material to you as an e-mail attachment. You're quite right to suspect him of seeing his visions as the literal truth. His dreams, as well. He insisted upon that, no matter who tried to explain about symbolism and the like."

"That must have been irritating," I said. "Arguing about it, I mean."

"It certainly irritated him." She flashed me a smile that reminded me of Ari's rare open grins. "But it's not the reason I left the kibbutz. One thing that every official interviewer has asked is what drove me away. They all seem to think that it must have been a sexual proposition, but it was nothing of the sort. Since you're female, you're more likely to believe the truth."

"From what I've been told about the kibbutz," I said, "I got the impression that women existed mostly to cook, clean, and produce babies."

"Unfortunately, that's accurate, but at the beginning at least we were allowed to study Torah. The Orthodox, like my family, would never have countenanced that. It's the main reason I was willing to join Ezekiel's movement."

"I see. You said 'at the beginning.' Did that change?"

"Eventually, yes. The last straw was his declaration that

women were absolutely forbidden from studying any of the Merkabah material. After several days of arguing, I realized that the situation was hopeless."

I had only the most general idea of the mystical system she called "the Merkabah material," but I did know its importance.

"I can see how that would have driven you away," I said.

"Thank you," Shira said. "I did try to explain it to some awful little man from MI5, but he simply could not see why I'd reacted the way I had."

"I can't say I'm surprised."

"To make things worse, my husband insisted that I follow our rebbe's declaration. I left them both behind. I wanted to take Ari with me, but his father would have fought me tooth and nail in court over the divorce if I had. I did insist on joint custody."

"That's why Ari spent so much time in the U.K.?"

"Yes, exactly. Not enough time, to my way of thinking, but there you are. It was the best I could do. I wept every time I put him on the plane to go back."

Her voice shook, remembering. I paused to give her a chance to compose herself.

"Now, about the Messiah," I said next. "Did Reb Ezekiel think he was the Messiah himself?"

"No, not at all. He wasn't that daft." She paused, thinking. "Ezekiel hated to be wrong, you know. Being ignorant was even worse. He had absolutely no idea who the Messiah might be, so he preferred not to speak of him at all."

"The prudent course, huh? I tried to find copies of his books. But I couldn't, not even on the Internet."

"Not even for ready money," Shira said with a faint smile. "They went 'oh pee'—that means out of print—a very long time ago. For a while one could find them on the occult collectors' markets, but about ten or twelve years ago, someone bought up all the remaining copies. It was very odd. Rumor had it that an Orthodox religious fanatic in Japan wanted to destroy them. He must have been fabulously rich, because his agent bought copies from individuals for very high prices."

"I've never heard of any fabulously rich Orthodox Jewish Japanese people."

"Neither have I. I have no idea what the truth behind all that was."

"Did you sell your copies of the books?"

"Unfortunately, I'd already burned them in a fit of pique when I left the kibbutz, or I'd send them to you." She sighed and looked away from the camera. "I was still so young then. I hope I never feel so bitterly disappointed again."

"You'd invested a lot of yourself into that kibbutz."

"Yes, too much. Well, things like that do happen." She shrugged with a little shake of her shoulders. "One must go on. Do you have any other questions?"

"Well, speaking of books, your husband's written one, hasn't he? About the lost continent of Mu."

"Oh, yes." Her look of long-suffering reminded me strikingly of Ari's expression when he felt martyred by something I'd done. "At least he has an original thesis."

"What's that?"

"That Mu never existed above the water. He thinks the legends, such as they are, refer to an underwater civilization of—" She sighed and braced herself. "—of psychic squid."

I gaped and stared. She misinterpreted.

"I know it's mad," Shira said. "I love him anyway."

"I understand." I hesitated until I'd found just the right words. "Are copies available? I love to read science fiction and fantasy, you see, and actually that sounds like a good story."

"You know, you have a point. Huh. I wonder if he'd care to rewrite it from that angle?" Her eyes gleamed, and I saw the editor in her soul. "That really might sell, you know, as

a novel. But, at any rate, about copies. We have twelve cartons of them sitting in the upstairs bedroom. Please allow
me to send you one. A single copy, of course, not a carton,
much as I'd love to unload one. Even the Oxfam bookshops
have taken to refusing them."

We shared a laugh.

"That would be lovely," I said. "Do you have our mailing
address?"

"Oh, yes, Ari sent it to me. I hope that's acceptable?"

"Yes, that's fine, though please don't spread it around.
After I read the vision material, can I contact you again?"

"Oh, yes, please do. But at this e-mail address. I don't
know what's wrong with Lev. He's being so grumpy about
my talking with you. Of course, knowing you want to read
his book might improve his mood."

We shared another laugh, mine forced, because I suspected that he'd be less than pleased.

"Tell you what," I said. "Don't tell him, and I'll write him
a fan letter as if I'd found it for myself."

"He'll love that. Thank you!"

"In the meantime, can't you tell him that you mostly
want to get to know your son's live-in girlfriend?"

"That might work." She considered me for a moment.
"Do you really want to marry Ari? You seem so intelligent."

"No, I don't," I said, "but that's not because of him. I
don't want to marry anyone."

"Wise of you, my dear. Very wise. He won't listen, of
course."

"Very true. We have the occasional argument about it."

"Well, as long as they're only occasional." She paused,
and her eyes went slightly out of focus, and her mouth,
slightly slack. "I don't know why," she said in a soft voice,
"but this is important. You really should read the Book of
Enoch. It's online, I believe. Read about the Beni Elohim."
On the last sentence her voice rang.

"I will, then," I said. "For sure."

Shira shook her head and shrugged with a little off-center twitch. She had psychic talents, all right. She looked at me with a puzzled frown that told me she didn't quite remember what she'd just done.

"You delivered a message," I said, "about the Book of Enoch."

"Ah." Shira reached up and fussed with the collar of her shirt while she recovered herself. "Oh, yes, Ezekiel was quite taken with that, and with the Apocalypse of Abraham, too. Noncanonical, both of them, and really rather odd." She smiled briefly. "At times I wonder why it took me so long to realize that he was quite mad."

"Lack of experience?"

"Quite possibly. Youth! I was just eighteen when I married Ari's father. He was much older. I think he turned twenty-nine that year. My family approved of him, you see, and my father was quite keen on the marriage." She smiled again. "But Yosh Nathan did have gifts, in his own way. I think that's what finally convinced me to accept him."

"Psychic gifts, you mean?"

"No, artistic. He was a very talented musician, a pianist, but working on the kibbutz ruined his hands. The calluses, and then he lost a finger in a tractor accident."

Even though I'd never met the man, I felt as if this information had punched me in the guts. A talented pianist, doing grunt farm work, ending up working in the insurance business—I shook my head to throw off the feeling it gave me. I may even have uttered a small moan.

"Yes," Shira said. "I felt so bad for him. Once the kibbutz collapsed, he'd given up everything for nothing." She sighed. "Yosh has his good points, and he did give me Ari. Only the one child, but considering what a handful he was, one was probably enough. Speaking of whom—"

"I'll fetch him. I'll bet he'd like to talk with you, too."

I left them having a mother-son chat on my laptop in the kitchen. I returned to my desktop computer and picked up her e-mail concerning the visions. When I downloaded the attachment, I realized she'd sent me over thirty pages of single-spaced material. Although I'd need to study it in detail later, I gave it a quick scan. Most of it concerned figures from the Tanakh, fellow prophets as Zeke called them, but toward the end I found a piece of crucial information.

In a rainbow-colored sea of light, metal bubbles moved through the stars, each of them a gleaming silver sphere. When Reb Ezekiel called upon an angel to reveal their secret, one of the spheres became transparent.

Concerning the spheres, Shira had written, "I wish I could remember his exact wording, but it's been too many years. I do remember that he saw beings inside the transparent one, strange beings floating in water. They had tentacles. I mentioned this to Lev, who told me that Ezekiel must have been receiving sendings from the last giant squid mages of the Muvian civilization. I rather doubt that."

So did I. The question remained: what were the wretched Venusian squid up to? And why had Reb Ekeziel seen them in vision? They certainly posed no threat to Israel. Why would aquatic creatures want to invade the Negev Desert? They also didn't match the rebbe's other visions about aliens who looked like cherubim invading in ships built like the Ark of the Covenant. I decided that later, once I had more time, I'd do some concerted meditations and aura fieldwork on the images.

There remained a possible threat to other parts of our planet, Terra Four. Could the cephalopods actually present one? Spare14 had mentioned once that the cephalopods had well-developed psychic powers that did make them a threat to other species through, most likely, their ability to influence the other sapients' actions. I made a note to pry more information out of him.

While I waited for Ari to finish chatting with his mother, I printed out the material she'd sent so he could have a copy for himself. This way he'd know what lay behind his memories of the rebbe's ideas, which were as muddled as childhood memories always are. A few minutes later he carried two steaming coffee mugs into the living room to join me. He handed me mine, for which I thanked him profoundly.

"I've logged off and shut down," he said. "Mother said you might have printout for me."

"I do, and here it is." I made another note to run security programs on my laptop, in case Ari had loaded something on to it. "She's got very strong talents, by the way."

He winced and scowled. "Oh, I suppose so!" he said eventually. "I've always preferred to ignore them, but doubtless you're right."

"She told me some very interesting things. Say, do you know anything about the Beni Elohim?"

"I've heard the name. They appear in the Tanakh, don't they?"

"In Genesis, yeah, but she suggested I look in one of the apocryphal books for more information. All Genesis says is that they were angels who mated with the daughters of men. My girlfriends and I giggled about it when we came across it in religion class. We wondered what it would have felt like, if we'd been some of the women, I mean, all those feathery wings and stuff. Sister Peter Mary gave us all demerits."

"I should think so!" Ari paused for a sip of coffee. "Don't you ever think of anything besides sex?"

"It's your own fault. You're the one who's so good in bed."

He blushed scarlet.

"Have a nice talk with your mom?" I mentally chalked up a point for me and changed the subject.

"Yes, quite. She approves of you, by the way. She even

promised she'd fly over for the wedding. Well, if we ever do marry. Eventually."

I screamed. Ari muttered his grim chuckle. Point to him!

"I'm going to call Spare14," he said. "I hope he'll have some concrete information for us about today."

"So do I. I'd better see if Y's answered the e-mail I sent him last night."

Ari took his coffee back into the kitchen to make his phone call. I logged back onto TranceWeb and found no answer from Y. As far as the e-mail program knew, he hadn't even read my missive of the night before. I considered deleting the original and substituting a milder version, but in the end I left it the way I'd written it. I wanted to be forceful. Somewhere in my back brain I had the feeling that getting official status could be extremely important. I decided to call the office, in fact, and see if I could get a trance appointment, only to have the secretary tell me that Y had taken a "personal leave" day thanks to "stress."

"Does this have something to do with the liaison question?" I said.

"You guessed it, honey," she said. "Gosh, you must be psychic."

She laughed. I didn't. I thanked her and hung up. The situation wasn't serious enough for me to use our psychic emergency frequency. My one hope: Y sometimes worked through holidays, though if he was stressed because of the TWIXT offer, I doubted if he'd read e-mail from me on his day off. I was scowling at the computer monitor when Ari returned.

"They want us back on Six," he announced. "HQ are shutting down the TWIXT office there, and the S.I. wants that memorial envelope shipped down to L.A. We also need to take your fingerprints in front of witnesses, so they can be eliminated in the dust-out." He glared. "Why did you pick it up like that?"

I should have used a tissue or handkerchief. I knew that.

"I'm afraid," I said eventually, "that's how my talents work sometimes. When I come across important information, my hands itch. I grabbed that envelope because I knew it was relevant."

"If it's relevant. That's what the S.I. needs to find out."

"Okay." I decided against arguing the point. "I wonder if Izumi has a police record, maybe under her real name."

"Um, real name?"

"Well, it could be Izumi, I guess, but do you know what that name means in Japanese?"

"No. I'm afraid I'm utterly ignorant about Asian languages."

"It's the word for fountain." I smiled. "I think it might be her working name, not what her parents gave her." Saying the word "parents" made my mind twitch. "We know that the Axeman is Ash's dad, which explains why Ash is in the gang. I wonder what Izumi's story is?"

"Any girl raised on Interchange is at risk for criminal behavior, I should think. They probably run an even higher risk of being a victim of it."

"Unfortunately, yeah. When is the world-walker due at Spare 14's?"

"Soon." He glanced at his watch. "Around nine-thirty, he told me."

"I should get dressed." I paused to yawn. "God, I'm sick of all this level-hopping. I feel like one of those electrons, y'know, bouncing around from atomic orbit to orbit."

"More or less, we are. That's one of the analogies the study guides give. The world levels are called levels because they have a certain similarity to atomic orbits. World-walkers can transfer their wave packets up or down the levels as needed. Their home level, the one they were born on, functions like the most stable orbit, the innermost."

He'd just shared TWIXT intel with me. I smiled at him fondly and said, "Thank you."

"Not at all," Ari said. "You need to try to eat before we leave. And let's take one of those power bar things along with us. You've skipped lunch too many days in a row now."

"Yeah, you're right. I'll need the energy. Sometimes I feel like we're the ones on the run, not the perps."

Before we left, I checked my e-mail. Still nothing from Y. I also sent Annie a note, telling her that we were off and running again, and to contact the head office if anything Chaotic happened while I was gone.

We arrived at Spare14's office just as Willa did. She and her shopping bag both were filled with gloom over the prospects of getting us back to Terra Six. The shopping bag held extra orbs. Her mind held new information about the gates. The Guild had spent the previous evening running arcane diagnostics.

"Something's real wrong with Six," Willa said. "We tried going in from a good strong gate on One. Very difficult. We did make it, and we made it back, but the president's just declared that gate off limits till further notice. It used to lead into New York City, but who knows where it'll go in a day or two?"

"Good God!" Spare14 said. "Is there a chance it'll repair itself?"

"There's always a chance. A real small one, in this case." Willa turned to me. "It's probably about as big as the chance your father will agree to work with the TWIXT division."

I held up my thumb and forefinger with about a quarter inch between them.

Willa nodded her agreement. "We hope he'll join the other Guild projects, anyway. We've got a research division."

"I don't understand," Ari said. "I thought your Guild was part of TWIXT."

"TWIXT would sure like to think so." Willa's voice drawled with irony.

Spare14 pushed out a weak smile and glanced out a nearby window. Another damn layer of bureaucratic infighting! I kept that thought to myself.

"I'm hoping we can at least get O'Brien—I mean O'Grady—Flann, that is—to do some research with the Guild," Willa continued. "He'll have to recover from being inside for so long first."

Spare14 began examining his striped tie for nonexistent gravy spots.

"Dad's tough," I said. "He'll recover sooner than later. I think getting back to Guild work could be the best thing for him."

"Good." Willa smiled at me. "You know him better than any of us do. Can I pass that opinion along?"

"Sure, as long as they know it's just an opinion."

"They will. I'll see to it." Willa stood up. "Let's get out to the Six overlap site. I want to get this over with. I warn you, though. If it's not safe to go through, we're not going. Let me give you the extra orbs now in case we can get through. Getting out again—you might have to throw two at once. Try using just one first. If that doesn't work, throw two and pray."

I could feel Ari's twinge of fear, quickly stifled, at what failure might mean. I was terrified myself. I put the extra orbs in my shoulder bag, which was filling up fast. I'd brought my crayons along as well as the packet of evidence we were delivering. That day, I wore a plain blue shirt and gray jacket, along with a pair of gray slacks that really were getting tight, so I took my sharp-cornered ID out of my pants pocket and put that in an inside pocket of the bag.

We drove over to McLaren Park and left the Saturn, locked and alarmed, on a side street just outside. A grim-faced Willa led us up the hill to the overlap site. Despite her fears, thanks to a transport orb as well as her focus, we did get through to Six successfully. As she was leaving, though, she warned us not to stay too long.

"I can't guarantee what this overlap's going to do," she said. "Or if any of the gates to Six will still be stable in a couple of days. I keep wondering if the terrorists on this level are doing something to disrupt them, but that may be too simple an answer. We don't really understand how the multiverse works sometimes."

"How reassuring," Ari said, "but yes, so I've noticed."

Willa held up her violet orb and vanished.

Before we left the overlap site, I ran scans. Immediately I felt the Pull, that deep close tie to persons who had to be doppelgängers of my family members. I sealed it off before proceeding to the various types of Search Mode. I ran them all, Personnel, Danger, Location.

"Nothing in the immediate vicinity that concerns us," I told Ari.

We'd walked maybe five yards when I ran into a scar on the time stream, a ripple of horror across the sunny day. I stopped and held up one hand to warn Ari. Fresh danger? No, it had happened, it had ended, but yes, the consequences surged and throbbed all around us. Danger—distant but overwhelming—fire, screaming, smoke—and—oh, God— the noise, the screaming, the sound of flames, and the booming crash of slabs of concrete falling, shattering— I let out a moan.

"Nola!" Ari grabbed me by the shoulders. "What—"

"Another bombing." I could barely speak. "We've got to get down to the others. Fast!"

CHAPTER 10

ALTHOUGH A PLACARD in the lobby announced that the TWIXT office had closed, the security guards recognized us and let us through to the elevators. We stepped off on the second floor to find the door to the office locked. Ari took out his black TWIXT communicator and beeped a few buttons. In a minute or two de Vere opened up. I could feel his anger and grief like hot sparks on my skin, an impartial rage at others, not at me.

"Have you heard the news?" he snapped.

"About the bombing?" I said. "Where was it?"

"At the airport. It happened about ten minutes after JaMarcus got off the plane. I was talking to him when—" De Vere stopped and brushed tears from his eyes. "I heard the explosion. His communicator went out. I haven't been able to raise him since."

I knew, then. We all knew. Any explosion or falling debris that would have destroyed Spivey's communicator would have been close enough to kill him along with it.

"Shit," Ari said. That he'd used English showed how upset he was. "I'm so sorry to hear it."

"Yeah," de Vere said. "Well, come in. We've got to carry on. The truck's going to be here real soon. We're packing up files and flexies to go down to L.A."

Big white-and-green cardboard cartons from some shipper called Republic Express littered half the office floor. At one desk the brown-haired clerk was putting handfuls of low-priority papers through a shredder. He was a skinny guy in his early twenties, with a long face and a circular birthmark of some sort on his high forehead. When I realized that I'd never heard his name, I asked him for it.

"Dave Rasmussen." His voice shook as he fought with pure grief.

Lupe Parra y Cruz came out of the room that held the safe. Mascara mixed with tears streaked her face. She carried an armload of bundled currencies, which she dumped into the nearest carton.

"That's the last of it," she said to Rasmussen. "Tape that up when you get a chance."

Since neither Ari nor I knew which papers went to L.A. and which to the shredder, we couldn't help sort. Ari did grab a roll of cello tape and begin closing up full cartons. I took the memorial envelope, still wrapped in Ari's blue-and-white silk handkerchief, out of my shoulder bag and held it aimlessly in de Vere's direction.

"What should I do with this?" I said. "The evidence we found on Three."

"I'll take that. I've got a special priority carton for it."

"Is this stuff going to be safe?" I handed him the bundle. "From the terrorists, I mean."

"We're shipping everything by armored truck. With a security guard escort. They're closing down their office upstairs, too. The credit union'll be moving next. Their downtown office is safer."

"I see. What about your people?"

"My wife and kids are already in America. Her sister Megan's in upstate New York. Thank God they flew out last night, not this morning." His voice choked, sweat beaded his face, and for a long moment he shook. He'd not quite realized the implications of their departure time until that moment. With a gasp he pulled himself back under control. "The dogs are at my brother's over in Marin. He'll pick up Rodeo for me, too."

"I'm supposedly heading home for One," Lupe put in. "I'll take Dave with me. If the gate still works. HQ's very concerned."

"If nothing else you can come with us to Four," I said. "It's easy access to One from there. De Vere, I don't know how you'll get to New York now."

He thought briefly. "I'll go to L.A. with the shipment and get a plane out of the airport there. It'll be good to have another gun along, and I hope to God they try to give us trouble. It would do me good to take a few of them out."

Lupe started to speak, then stifled it.

"Well, for God's sake!" de Vere snapped. "He was one of the best men I've ever met, and now those warped stinking bastards have—" He stopped, gulped, and looked away. "And everyone else caught in the slaughter. My God! Women with kids!"

"I know." Her voice sounded steady out of sheer force of will. "I feel the same way, but we're not here to add to the evil and the chaos."

I ran a quick SPP, but she'd used the word only as a word, not as signal to me. I could continue to assume that no one here knew about the Agency.

"A question," I said. "How many people work for the security firm and the credit union?"

"Six office personnel for the security firm," Parra y Cruz said. "Most of their employees worked elsewhere, of course. Twenty-seven in the credit union."

"So the terrorists would have killed thirty-three people," I said, "to cover up the theft of the orbs? I'm assuming that's why they wanted to bomb this building."

"It's the only motive I can think of," Parra y Cruz said. "And I'm assuming this is why HQ is shutting us down. How can you reason with people like this? Or even logically predict what they'll do?"

"You can't. They think God's on their side."

"The world's most dangerous bullshit, yeah." De Vere turned to me. "Let me take your fingerprints. We'll enclose one sheet with the evidence package so they can sort things out. Or I will, since I'm going with it."

I sat down in a chair at the side of his desk. He opened a desk drawer, rummaged around, and brought out an ink pad and the heavy paper forms with their little boxes for each finger's print. He filled in my name and the date with a pen. I held out my hand and let him ink each finger and roll them, one at a time, onto the paper. I'd had my prints taken before, when I went to work for the Agency, so I knew what was coming.

"Jeez!" de Vere said. "You've got the strangest damn prints I've ever seen."

Sean and Michael had them, too, not that I was going to tell De Vere that. For all I knew, the rest of my family members bore the same mark. Except for Dad, no one else had ever had theirs taken. In the middle of each finger pad, the print showed a tiny, squashed oval. Straight lines, three on each side, radiated out of the oval for just over an eighth of an inch, then began to curve around like a more normal print. Ari leaned over my shoulder for a look.

"I've seen something similar," Ari said. "Not that I can remember where at the moment."

"Squished bugs," I said. "That's what the guy who took mine for my ID called them."

No one smiled. De Vere wrote a brief note on the paper sheet and tucked it into the special carton with the memorial evidence. Back home, they would have digitally scanned the sheet. De Vere handed me a jar of lotion and a handful of tissues to clean off the ink, then got up and returned to his packing. I had a couple of tissues left over and shoved them in my jacket pocket without thinking.

The landline on Parra y Cruz's desk rang. Everyone yelped except Ari. Lupe answered in English, then switched to Spanish. She paused and put a hand over the mouthpiece of the phone.

"It's the security people in the lobby," she said. "There's a girl who's desperate to reach us. She says her name's Izumi Hakura. She says she wants to turn herself in. Do you think she's legit?"

"I'll go see." I got up from my chair. "Tell them to hold her, but keep watch on the front door. Someone may try to shut her up with a bullet."

"If you're going down there," Ari said, "I'm coming with you."

"Of course. I sure as hell wasn't going alone."

In the bronze box of the elevator car I found it impossible to run definitive scans, but I picked up no trace of nearby danger. When the doors opened at the lobby, I felt nothing but a distant threat that encompassed the entire city. At the security desk the two guards were standing in front of a young woman, maybe twenty at the most, with long black hair and ethnic Japanese features. She wore a pair of tight jeans, a discordantly pretty flowered blouse, and a black leather jacket. Her SPP radiated honest terror and a deep, gut-level disgust but not even a whisper of treachery. When she saw Ari and me, she began to tremble.

"Quick!" Ari said. "Into the elevator."

She darted forward. He caught her arm and pulled her inside. I punched the buttons. While we rode up to the second floor, Izumi said nothing. She merely continued trembling. When we got into the office, she sank into the nearest chair and covered her face with both hands.

"You're safe now," Ari said. "And we'll endeavor to keep you that way."

"Thanks." She had a pleasant voice, low with a California accent. "I just can't take anymore, dealing with those creeps." She lowered her hands and looked at me.

"Creeps?" I said. "Ash and the gang?"

"No, the Soldiers of the Risen Lord. Ash is a sweetie compared to them. Although, y'know—" She hesitated, trembled again, and began to cry. "I wish she hadn't offed Scotty."

Ari grabbed the box of tissues from De Vere's desk and handed it to her. He mouthed "girl to girl" to me, then went to help Rasmussen drag packed boxes over to the door. I pulled up a chair opposite Izumi and sat down. In a couple of minutes she snuffled back her tears and wiped her face.

"You were fond of Trotter," I said.

She shrugged and tossed the damp tissue into a nearby wastebasket. "I dunno if fond is it," she said. "But I like, understood him. He came from the Kingdom, y'know."

"I didn't know, no."

"A lot of the old guys in the Kingdom have a bunch of wives, and that means some of the young guys are kind of in the way, because they'll never get a wife. So the old guys give them a train ticket and a visa to California or Texas and run them out. Scotty was one of those young guys. That's why he was so arrogant and stubborn and weird." She snuffled back a few more tears. "Goddamn Ash anyway!"

"Why did she kill Scotty?" I said.

"Same reason she'll try to kill me. He was ready to go to Spivey and tell him everything. It's the bombings. Okay, yeah, the Axeman must look like a creep to you, but he took me off the street when I was a little kid. He gave me a home, him and his lady. The gang, they don't hurt anyone without a reason, y'know? But these Kingdom people—" She leaned forward and held out one urgent hand. "They're crazy. They're really crazy. They don't care how many people they kill. They just don't."

"I got that impression, yeah."

"I don't want to deal with them no more. I can't. Scotty couldn't either. When they ordered him to help bomb this place, he panicked. When you guys stopped it, he was glad. And he slipped up and showed he was glad."

"So they killed him."

She nodded. "Ash came for him with three of the goons. We couldn't do nothing. At least she didn't make me watch. She let me get dressed and get out first."

"After you left, he put up one hell of a fight. He must have gotten loose for a couple of minutes anyway."

"Did he?" Her eyes grew wide. "He didn't do nothing while I was there. Just stood there and let them hold him against the wall. He told me to just go, get out."

"He didn't want them to hurt you, I'd say. Once you were safe, he could try to get a little of his own back."

Two tears ran down her cheeks. She nodded her agreement, then wiped her face on her sleeve.

"Tell me something," I said. "Why has the Axeman joined up with this bunch of murderous loonies? Does he believe in their version of Jesus?"

"Oh, hell, no! It's the money. They pay us for the people we bring, and then they sell them back in the Kingdom."

So I'd been right about that. Sometimes you'd rather be wrong.

"These soldiers, they must know about TWIXT," I said. "I know the Axeman does."

"I guess. No one told me nothing. I was never in real

tight with Ash, y'know. She was the boss' daughter, and she made sure everyone knew it."

De Vere's phone rang again. Izumi turned so tense that she stopped breathing for several moments. De Vere answered, listened, and said, "The truck's here. We've got to get this stuff down to the lobby with as little confusion as possible."

"No," Ari said. "With as much confusion as possible. That will let O'Grady and me get Izumi and the refugees out of the side door while everyone's busy at the front. De Vere, is there any body armor in this office?"

" 'Fraid not. No one thought we'd need any when we set this all up."

"Then we'll have to move fast. Across the street and into the park at the trot, up the hill as fast as you all can walk. Izumi, you and Parra y Cruz will travel in the middle of the squad. Rasmussen, travel behind them and keep everyone moving fast. O'Grady, you go in the middle, too."

"No," I said. "I've got to be a few steps behind to run scans."

"You've got the gifts, don't you?" Izumi said to me. "I figured someone here did."

"Just about all of us do, in one way or another," I said. "Do you know where Ash is?"

"On her way, and I bet some of the goons come with her. They'll kill me if they can."

"Yeah. We know."

Men from the shipping company brought wheeled dollies up to the office for the heaviest cartons. Men from the security guard firm came down to carry the rest. Although the security firm had body armor, they lacked enough to share or even sell us. I couldn't blame them. We needed speed, anyway, not encumbrance. While Ari gave the men a few quick orders, I tucked Izumi's long hair into her jacket and handed her a small carton to carry so that it would obscure her face.

Once everyone had the freight under control, we hit both elevators. Our group of refugees huddled together behind a row of men with loaded dollies. Down we went. The door sprang open, and everyone hurried out. The shipping people and the security guards followed orders and milled around the lobby to hide us from the glass front doors. Izumi set her carton down. Ari, the two women, and Rasmussen scuttled for the side door while I brought up the rear.

As soon as I stepped outside, I felt danger, as strong as smoke in the air, as frightening as a drawn gun. "They're nearly here!" I called out.

Everyone broke into a fast jog. We jogged across the street, made it into the park, and ran across the flat strip of lawn toward the path that led up to the overlap area. The steep hill slowed everyone down. I found myself panting by the time we climbed it. The danger behind us had lessened, but I sensed a threat in front of us. Two more steps and I saw it.

One of the gang members must have been sent on ahead. A thickset guy in gray slacks and a filthy green sweatshirt appeared out of a grove of trees. He was carrying a plastic thing that looked like half a shoebox with an antenna stuck on top. I tossed Ari my shoulder bag with the orbs as we hurried the last few yards to the overlap area. I needed my hands free.

"Get one out!" I said. "Wait to throw it till I tell you."

I started to gather Qi. When the goon held up the thing he carried, I realized that it was a mobile phone of sorts. "I see them!" he yelled into it.

The clunky phone in his hand hampered the goon just enough. I managed to wind the Qi into a sphere before the goon ditched the phone and pulled a gun out of his leather jacket.

"Overlap just ahead!" Ari called out. "I'll activate the orb."

"No, wait!" I yelled as loudly as I could.

The goon was raising his gun to shoot. I flung the sphere of Qi straight for him. It hit. He screamed as light like fire detonated on his chest and swept over him. I heard a bang like firecrackers behind me. Ari had thrown the orb. Too much Qi—between the ensorcellment and the gate device, Qi floated in the air as thick as gunpowder. The Qi from the ensorcellment rebounded and plunged into the gravity waves blasting out of the gate. Blinding glare, a triumphant yell from Ari, a crash that turned me deaf—the exploding force slammed me facedown onto the ground.

By the time I struggled to a kneeling position, the smoke had thinned enough for me to look around. My talents confirmed what my eyes saw. Ari had gotten the others safely through, but I'd been left behind, alone on the wrong side of the vanished gate.

The only things I wanted to do were panic and howl. I squelched those impulses and staggered to my feet. My head ached like thunder from the outpouring of Qi, or so I assumed, combined with the backlash from the explosion. The goon I'd ensorcelled lay on his back nearby, smiling to himself and scratching his balls. Occasionally he giggled. He'd be unable to remember what had happened once the ensorcellment wore off. His gun and the broken mobile phone lay on the grass nearby.

The long lawn of the park stretched out around me in the afternoon sun, which shone entirely too brightly on the green. I stood in plain sight. I needed to get away before Ash herself arrived. I thought about returning to the building and joining up with de Vere, but a scan showed me that the truck had already sped away. The same scan pinpointed Ash. She and her little friends had reached the office building and stopped to reconnoiter. Since I'd drained so much Qi, moving fast was out of the question. As I lurched uphill through the trees and obscuring underbrush, I tried to think things through, but the pain in my forehead made thinking difficult.

I was too frightened to be more than distantly furious with Ari. He'd never looked back, not once to see if I could follow him. Maybe he hadn't heard me telling him to wait. Maybe he was sick of following my orders. Did it matter when I might never see him again? I remembered Willa telling us to hurry and get out of there, that she couldn't guarantee that the overlap would work much longer. The thought hit me so hard that I nearly vomited. Beyond that, even if a rescue team got through, TWIXT might never be able to find wherever it was that I was going to end up. My position could perhaps be best expressed by the square root of minus two—an awful joke. Somehow I couldn't bring myself to laugh.

I might never see my family again, either. My family. Sean. My brother the finder, the guy whose talent allowed him to place anything or anybody he'd seen at least once. He knew me really well. If I could contact him, or if he could somehow get through to Six, he could find me. The realization allowed my mind to settle. I gathered Qi, calmed myself, and kept walking.

Eventually I reached a pair of stone gates, the exit from the park, at the place where in my own world Mansell Avenue begins its run downhill. On Six, they'd named it Roosevelt Drive, in homage to the assassinated president, most likely. I stopped to breathe and take a quick inventory. I owned about five bucks' worth of the currency of this world level, my clothes, a couple of crumpled-up tissues, and a chocolate energy bar. That was it, not even a comb, no ID, no nothing. The shoulder bag I'd tossed to Ari contained everything else.

I ran an SM:D and felt danger all around me, though most of it lay at a distance in time. Nightfall, I felt, would bring the threats close. I had no idea if this version of San

Francisco had homeless shelters. If it did, I needed to come up with a story for the aid workers. I tried another Search Mode while I fought to focus my aching brain on safety and finding a place to hide. At last I remembered the Pull I'd felt, the sense that my family's dopplegängers lived nearby. I opened myself to the Pull and did a scan. The Houlihan house. Refuge lay in the place where the Houlihan house stood in my world.

I was already standing in the equivalent of the Excelsior district. Since the house's approximate location lay downhill and reasonably close at hand, I figured I had the energy to reach it. When I came free of the trees, I saw the blue water tower just uphill and south of me, exactly where it should have been. Its existence encouraged me enough that I kept on walking through the tract of houses below.

Mansell may have been missing, but the other streets I crossed had the same or similar names to those on my home world level. When I finally found the correct cross street, I turned down it. Walking had become torture, but the pain in my head receded when I recognized the hillside lot, planted with a rock garden far more elegant than Uncle Jim had ever managed to grow. I stood at the base of the brick steps and stared up at the building at the top.

The house looked something like the Houlihan house, in that it had three stories at one end, one in the middle, and two at the other end. Someone had put a lot of work into it, though, judging by the pearl-gray siding, the elegant multipane windows, and a new brick chimney that indicated a fireplace in the living room. A sleek blue car sat at the top of the driveway instead of Uncle Jim's old truck.

Well, O'Grady, I said to myself, you've found it, your one and only goal. I could go up and knock, I suppose, see if anyone recognized me, try to explain who I was. It all seemed hopeless; a waste of effort, a cruel joke to think anyone would welcome me.

The front door of the house opened. I heard a high-pitched shriek, followed by a somewhat lower-pitched shriek. Two kids, a girl of about six and a boy of maybe nine, burst out and came racing down the steps toward me. I stepped away toward the street, but the dark-haired girl flung herself at me and threw her arms around my waist.

"Mama, Mama!" she was weeping and gulping for air between words. "I knew you weren't dead. I knew it knew it knew it."

The boy began screaming, "Dad, Dad, come out!" at the top of his lungs. The girl looked up at me, her dark blue eyes full of tears, her nose running green snot. I fished a tissue out of my pocket and wiped her nose before I spoke. She grabbed the tissue and held it as tight as a holy relic.

"I'm not her, I'm sorry," I said. "I must look like your mom, but I'm not her."

"You've got to be," the boy said. "You just don't remember. They told us you might not remember if you hit your head."

"I called you," the girl said. "I called and called, and so you heard me."

I'd found the origin of the Pull. "I did hear you," I said. "But I'm not your mom. I just look like her."

The girl stared up at me—and believed me. She let go and sat down on the sidewalk, where she covered her face with both hands and wept even harder. Exhausted as I was, I could think of nothing comforting to say. The boy stood looking back and forth between us.

"She's Beth," he said, "and I'm Donnie. Do you remember now?"

"No," I said. "I'm sorry, but I'm not your mother."

He knelt down and put a skinny arm around his sister's shoulders. She buried her face in his shirt and wept as she clung to him.

A man came out onto the porch. As he hurried down the steps, his auburn hair caught the sun. Silver touches gleamed at his temples. He was tall, a little paunchy, with blue eyes and the freckles I remembered, a dusting across his nose and cheeks, because at that point, I recognized him. That is, I knew who his doppelgänger in my own world had to be, even though this man had aged, heading toward forty. So, I reminded myself, had his doppelgänger by now.

"Cam," I said. "Cameron Douglas."

"Nola?" He started to say more, but his voice caught, and he merely stared at me. Slowly, like a robot, he held out his hand. I took a step back. He took one forward and held out both hands.

"I'm not your wife," I said. "That's why Beth's crying. She thought I was."

"You just don't remember." His face went slack, as if he might laugh hysterically or weep or both. "Oh, my God, it's a miracle. You're home. Thank God, you're home."

"I'm not who you think I am!"

"Honey, come on, who else would you be?" He was trembling and smiling both.

I had nothing to fall back on but the honest truth. "Another Nola O'Grady entirely who got pregnant by another version of you. Who didn't marry that other you when he honorably offered. A long time ago and far far away." I glanced at the boy, then back to Cam. I chose my words carefully so Donnie wouldn't understand exactly what I'd done. "I never had your child. My mother refused to let me just put him out for adoption. So I went to the right kind of clinic, and she never forgave me."

"I—" His voice cracked and stuck.

By this time Beth had stopped crying. Donnie was trying to wipe her face with the mangled remains of the tissue I'd used on her nose. I fished the second one out of my pocket and gave it to him, then turned my attention back to Cam.

"I guess this Nola did marry you," I said. "Was she only seventeen, like I was?"

He winced, nodded a yes, and stared at the sidewalk. His mouth had twisted into a knot of old pain. "You're not a ghost, are you? Come back to remind me?"

"Of your early sins?" Somehow I managed to smile. "No. Ghosts don't carry tissues in their pockets. Cam, I'm sorry you lost her."

I turned on my heel and walked off, heading toward the cross street.

"Wait!" Cam called out. "Nola, wait, don't go."

I stopped and looked back, but I stayed where I was. He said a few words to the children, then trotted after me. I glanced around and saw that several neighbor women had come out onto their porches and front steps. When Cam caught up with me, he said nothing at first, merely stared with narrowed eyes. I ran an SPP and picked up a flood of utter bewilderment, but in the flood bobbed an aching concern like an unmoored boat.

"Where are you going?" he said.

"I don't know," I said. "I've got no idea at all."

"That's what I thought. I've never seen anyone look so lost."

I remembered that he'd always been a decent man, a kind one, really, and a good teacher, too, until his one unfortunate affair with a seventeen-year-old student. Or at least, I reminded myself, the Cam I'd known had been decent, and this one seemed to follow the pattern.

"Please?" he said. "Come back to the house? Maybe you're not my Nola. Okay, for the sake of argument, you don't have to be." He forced out a smile. The tone of his voice changed, the soft wheedle a person might use to coax a frightened pet out from under a sofa. "Come home—I mean, come back to the house anyway. Maybe you're not her. Or maybe you've just been wandering around going crazy after what happened. I don't know which. But I can't stand seeing you with blood over half your face and acting so lost."

"Blood?" I raised my hand and touched my cheek.

Something sticky covered it. I looked at my fingertips: dark red. "No wonder you thought I might be a ghost."

"It looks like someone cut you with a knife. Or was it the shrapnel? Do you remember the department store and the explosion?"

"Was that where she died?"

"You didn't die. It must feel like that if you don't remember anything. But, yeah, you left me a note. I'm going downtown, you said, to the sale in the Emporium basement. You saw one of our neighbors at the bus stop. She almost went with you, but she decided against it, and you went on alone. And you never came home until just now, so we thought you were dead."

He spoke so calmly, with such certainty, that I almost believed I was the other Nola. Almost, and only for a couple of seconds.

"You've been hurt," he said. "It's killed your memory."

"I took a bad fall. I must have hit my head."

I started shaking. If I'd let myself go, I would have fainted at his feet, but I steadied myself.

"The town's full of soldiers and terrorists," Cam went on. "What's going to happen to you if you're wandering around like this?"

"Nothing good," I said.

"Exactly. Come back to the house. Please?"

I considered saying no. I also considered what would happen to an exhausted woman alone on the streets in a panicked town.

"Thanks," I said. "I will. But I'm not your Nola. You've got to believe me. I don't want your children heartbroken a second time."

"Neither do I." He hesitated, staring at my face, then winced. "You need to see a doctor."

"It's just a shallow cut. Cam, you don't believe me, do you, when I say I'm not your wife?"

"Well, for crying out loud! You have her name. You know my name. You know why we got married. And you come staggering back home—" His voice choked.

He wiped tears from his eyes on his shirtsleeve. I looked down the street and saw a middle-aged Hispanic woman shepherding the children up the steps. One of the neighbors, I figured, helping out.

"Please?" Cam said. "Please come back."

"All right," I said. "Maybe I can think of some way to explain."

We stared at each other for a moment more. When he held out his hand, I took one step toward him and felt the world drop away from under my feet. He caught me before I hit the pavement.

CHAPTER II

I WOKE UP ON A COUCH in a living room that was both familiar and ridiculously strange. The long white room belonged in the Houlihan house, but the furniture didn't match: tidy armchairs with checked blue-and-white slipcovers, plant stands complete with potted begonias, little maple end tables holding lamps with frilly shades, a pair of maple hutches filled with knickknacks. A pile of towels lay under my throbbing head. Cam knelt on the floor beside me. He was wiping the blood off my face with a washcloth that he kept dipping in a basin of warm water.

"It's not a deep cut," he said. "But it looks like it bled a lot. Honey, just rest. I'm going to call a doctor."

"Don't call me that," I said. "I'm not your wife. I do not have amnesia."

He put the washcloth into the basin of red water, then sat back on his heels and surveyed me with a sad little smile. Exhausted though I was, inspiration managed to strike.

"Did she have Donnie by Caesarean?" I said. "They told

me I'd have to have one if I carried the baby to full term. Narrow hips."

"Yeah, that's right. Both kids."

I unzipped my gray slacks, pulled them down an inch or two, and opened the fly wide.

"No scar," I said.

He stared, then looked away. His shoulders slumped, and his eyes filled with tears again. I could tell from his SPP that he believed me, and that the belief hurt, a terrible bitter hurt of hope destroyed. I zipped up the slacks. When I tried to sit up, he put a gentle hand on my collarbone and pushed me back down.

"Don't try to move just yet," he said. "I don't want that cut to reopen."

"Thanks," I said, "but I need to get out of here. I don't want to make things worse for you and the kids."

"I appreciate the concern, but I can't turn someone away when things are so bad out there, not even a stranger." He sounded half-sick with disappointment. "I'll talk to the kids."

"Can you tell them I'm just their mother's cousin or something? Coming to visit you all, but I got hurt in the explosion, the one at the airport this morning, and my suitcase went up with it."

"Yeah, I can do that. The story'll pass muster. She did visit her cousins. We'll need a name."

"Rose. That's my middle name."

"Okay, Rose it is." He hesitated, thinking. "The offer of shelter still stands, as long as you need it. I don't care who you are. You need help. And you can't go out there. There's a curfew tonight, and the National Guard's on patrol. You could get shot on sight."

So could Ari, if he came back to hunt for me. The room shimmered as I panicked, then steadied when I got control of myself.

"Thanks." My voice sounded like a stranger's to me, very weak and thin. "I didn't know that."

"It's horrible, isn't it? I never thought things would get so bad. It's like some kind of lousy movie. Fascists attacking our republic. Christ!"

Cam got up, then picked up the basin of bloodstained water and carried it out of the room. I heard children's voices in the hall, and his voice murmur in answer, but the sound faded as they walked on to what I assumed was the kitchen. My head hurt, a slice of hot pain along the cut, a dull ache from what was probably a mild concussion, but I could think again thanks to the safety and the silence.

Sean. I sent my mind out like a beacon of agony. *Sean. Please find me. Soon. Sean, find me and tell Ari Sean, you're my only hope. Sean, help!*

I never felt an answer, but then the mental overlap had never returned anything like a clear response. It wasn't as good as a cell phone. When that idea made me giggle, I realized that I had a bad concussion, not a mild one. Calling a doctor began to seem like a good idea.

Cam returned with gauze and adhesive tape. The children trailed behind him. Tears had streaked their faces and dried. Cam stepped back and let them come up to the couch to talk with me.

"I'm sorry," I said to them. "I tried to tell you the truth."

"Yeah," Donnie said. "I didn't want it to be true."

"I can understand that."

Beth took a few steps closer and stared at my face. "The blood's gone," she said. "You look kind of different. Real thin."

"Thinner than your mom?"

"Yeah. But will you stay and be our mom?"

"Beth, please don't." Cam and Donnie spoke together. Their weary tone of voice told me Beth usually said the wrong thing at the wrong time.

"No," I said. "I'll stay for a little while, but no one else can ever really be your mom."

Beth turned and ran weeping from the room. Cam dumped the first aid supplies onto the couch next to me and took off after her. He was a good father. I'd always figured he would be. Donnie sighed and sat down on the floor. He picked up the roll of adhesive tape in its plastic box for something to hold.

"I'm so scared," he said.

"So am I," I said. "So's everybody."

"Will they come blow up our house?"

I considered this possibility. It wasn't the terrorists who wanted me dead, of course, but the Axeman's gang. They'd find their ensorcelled goon in the park and assume that we'd all made it through to some other world level. I scanned to make doubly sure and picked up a distant trace of Ash, furious with disappointment.

"No, the terrorists won't hurt us," I said to Donnie. "We're not important enough. They only want to blow up big things and get on TV."

Donnie smiled at that. "Will the army make everything okay again?"

"Sure." I did my best to sound confident. "They'll catch the people who are blowing things up, sooner or later."

Or the TWIXT team will—I grabbed a second chance at hope. Ari and our informant knew I'd been left behind. Izumi could tell them where the Axeman was hiding. Surely they'd send a team to clean things up, and Ari would demand to be on it. I could count on him for that.

If, of course, they could get through. I stared at the ceiling and wished I still believed in God. It would have been nice to pray.

"There's blood all over your shirt," Donnie said.

I looked down and saw the spatters, dried to rust. "Yeah. There sure is."

He nodded at the flowered wall-to-wall carpet, Donald
Douglas, who maybe was the child I never had. The boy I'd
refused to let into my world sat on the floor and made car
noises as he ran the roll of adhesive around one of the pale
blue flowers on the rug. I remembered my mother's tears
and sullen rage, the things she'd said to me, the worst things
she could think of to say.

If he was that boy, I wasn't a murderess after all, I supposed, because there he was, alive, healthy. With his auburn
hair and dusting of freckles, he was as handsome as his father had been, back when I was in high school. All of the
girls had a crush on Mr. Douglas. Mr. Douglas, it turned out,
had a crush on me.

Cam came back to the living room and managed to smile
at Donnie. "Your sister's watching cartoons in the family
room," he said. "You can go watch, too, if you want."

Donnie beamed at him and put the roll of tape back
onto the couch. He got up, then tilted his head to one side
and considered me.

"Aunt Rose," he said. "You're not going to die, too, are
you?"

"Not right now, no," I said. "Long time from now. Way,
way after you're grown up."

"Okay." He turned and trotted off, heading down the
long hallway.

Cam watched him go. "I told them they could call you
aunt. Is that okay?"

"Sure. Good idea."

"I did talk to the doctor, or I should say, I talked to the
nurse in his office. Every doctor in town is down at the airport. The casualties are bad, she told me. A couple thousand
of them. How many of those are deaths—she didn't know."

"Oh, my God."

The room lurched around me. I shut my eyes to steady
things. Cam waited to speak until I opened them again.

"First aid will have to do, she told me," Cam said. "We'll see how you feel in a couple of days. If you're feeling okay, then we'd better not take up his time."

He knelt down and opened the box of gauze pads. "We keep stuff like this in the house," he said, "for the kids, y'know. Donnie had a hard time learning to ride a bike."

Would I have watched and worried if my Donnie had been wobbling down the street on a treacherous two-wheeler? I could remember being terrified at first when Michael learned to ride a bike, but balance came easy to him. What if I'd had two children to raise, my little brother and a baby boy, and me only eighteen by then, by the time Donnie had been born and I'd recovered from the Caesarean?

"Cam," I said, "was Nola happy with you and the kids?"

He concentrated on opening the plastic pack around the tape. "No," he said eventually, "not at first, anyway. She was too young to marry and have a family, but—Christ forgive me—I didn't know what else to do but marry her."

"It was decent of you."

"I suppose. I felt like such a—" He paused, his mouth framing soundless words. "Such a bastard, total scum, seducing a young girl, one of my students. I knew it was wrong even in the middle of it. I still don't know what hit me. I couldn't think of anything but her." He glanced at me with honest anguish. "I never wanted anything in my life the way I wanted her. I'd had relationships with women my age, sure, but nothing like that. Sexual obsession, I guess you'd call it."

"I'm willing to bet she felt it, too."

"Yeah, but I was the adult. I should have said no."

"That's true." I groped for words and found none readily available, since my headache was pounding and my world lay scrambled around me. Lies I could invent. Truth lay beyond me.

Cam picked up a gauze pad and placed it carefully over the cut on my forehead. "Don't move," he said. "I'll get some tape on that."

I lay still and let him secure the pad. The tape itched, but itching beat bleeding all over. He sat back and looked at the patch, then nodded in satisfaction.

"There were times," Cam said abruptly, "when Nola ran off somewhere and left me with Donnie. For a couple of months once. When she came back, she wouldn't tell me where she'd been. I was always too afraid to demand an answer. I didn't want her running off again."

"She was visiting her cousin Rose," I said. "A first cousin. They were so close as girls, almost sisters."

"Of course." He smiled with a brief twitch of his mouth. "When she came back the last time, she was glad to be home. She told me she loved me. That's when we had Beth. She never ran off again."

What had kept her here, I wondered, in this house that dreamed of suburbia? Love or a sense of defeat, of talents squandered because never trained? Was she settling for safety because she couldn't find anything better? Unlike her, I'd known upfront that marrying my Cam Douglas meant misery, but again, Michael was a factor in the decision I'd made. I wondered if she'd been raising her baby brother, too.

"What about my family?" I said. "How many of them are there on this world?"

"What?" He gave me a tentative smile. "Uh, what do you mean by that?"

Metaphorically I slapped my own wrist for the slip. "It's kind of hard to explain. Let's start with this house. Did you buy it from a family member?"

"Yeah, your aunt and uncle practically gave it to us—to me and my Nola—when they moved back to Ireland. We paid twenty-five thousand, dirt cheap."

Moved back to Ireland—a major deviance.

"What about her mother?"

"Deirdre? She was a saint about the whole thing." He paused for another twisted smile. "At least once I mentioned the magic word."

"Marriage, that is."

"Yeah. But your dad—that night we told them, when he slapped you like that." He shuddered in retrospect. "I knew then I had to marry you. I had to make it right. But nothing was really going to make it right, not for you. I mean, her."

"Cam!" I raised myself up on one elbow. "You've absolutely got to believe me. I'm not your wife. No scars, remember?"

"I remember. I'm sorry. This is just so hard."

I reached out and patted him on the shoulder. The effort made the room dance. I lay back down and let the furniture stop moving.

"Her folks," I said. "Do they live nearby?"

"No. Deirdre died two years ago. Breast cancer."

"I'm so sorry."

"Yeah, it was hard on my Nola. Flann went back to Ireland after it was all over. I wrote him about—" His voice caught. "I couldn't bring myself to talk on the phone about it. He's probably gotten the letter by now."

"Brothers?" I said. "Did Nola have some?"

"Well, one. Pat, the one who became a priest. And she had two sisters, Caitlin and Eilas."

"That was all?"

"Yeah. I take it you have more."

"Oh, yes. Seven of us, all told."

Cam mugged shock. He stood up, gathering the tape and the box of gauze, and walked away. At the entrance to the hall, he glanced back.

"I've got to check on the kids," he said. "They keep trying to creep down the hall and hear what we're saying."

Very carefully and slowly, I sat up. Blood stained the towel that he'd put underneath my head to protect the sofa. I folded it up and set it down on the floor away from the crisp blue-and-white checks.

Her father had slapped the other Nola when he'd learned she was pregnant. He was there to do the slapping, unlike mine. And her mother had been a saint about it, a very different Deirdre, for sure, though I could imagine my father slapping me if he'd ever known about the other Donnie.

From where I sat, I could see out the front window of the room. The sunlight was fading, though gold still gleamed in the stripe of sky dead west of the house. The view outside looked so familiar that for a moment, with the concussion throbbing in my brain, I thought I was home, and that Aunt Eileen would come bustling in to tell me that dinner was ready.

I heard footsteps on the porch. Someone knocked. Without thinking, I got up and went to the door. When I opened it, a slender white woman with gray hair smiled at me. She carried a large flat pan covered with aluminum foil. I smelled cooked chicken.

"It's so good to see you back, Nola. We all prayed for you, but I'll be honest, I'd just about given up hope." She held out the pan. "All you have to do is shove this in the oven for half an hour. Four hundred, I'd say, to crisp up the skin and the potatoes."

I automatically took the pan. "Thank you so much," I said. "But I'm not Nola. I'm her cousin Rose."

"Oh." The smile disappeared. Her face sagged into deep lines, abruptly ten years older, as if the smile had been holding up the flesh.

"I'm the one she used to go visit," I went on. "I came up from L.A. to help Cam and the kids, but I got caught in the airport bombing."

"I see. Yes, I think I remember her mentioning you, yes. Well, thank God you're safe, at least."

She turned and hurried off down the steps with a little wave. Her SPP told me that she was close to tears. I turned around and saw Cam watching me from the doorway into the hall.

"We have good neighbors," he said. "Her name's Lucy. Here, I'll take that."

"I told her I was Nola's cousin Rose from Los Angeles. Sooner or later, the story will spread around."

"Good. Sometimes we've got to lie, I guess."

When he took the pan from me, I shut the front door. I leaned against it, briefly dizzy, then returned to the couch and sat down. Cam paused at the entrance to the hallway.

"That shirt is really disgusting," he said. "The blood, I mean. I still have all her clothes if you want to change it. I kept praying she'd come back."

He left to put the chicken dish into the oven. The kids would be hungry soon. I thought about wearing some of those clothes. It was a bad idea to let him dress me up as his Nola, but blood and grass stains covered the front of my blue shirt. My slacks were almost as filthy.

I went upstairs to the master bedroom that belonged to Aunt Eileen and Uncle Jim back home. Although it sat in the same relation to the stairs up, the other Nola had decorated it with flowered chintz curtains and matching bedspread in pastel blues and greens on white. The curtains had swags and the bed, ruffles around the base. The lamps on the bedside tables had frilly shades, also matched. Aunt Eileen would have been horrified at her taste. I could imagine her sneering at the "dust catchers," as she would have called them.

Some of the clothes in the walk-in closet were big on frills and pastels, too, though I found a few low-cut dresses in stretchy fabrics, all sequins and slink. I took an honest cotton shirt in pale gray. It was a size ten, too big. Her jeans fit me so loosely that I needed a belt to cinch in the waist. She'd had two kids and spread a little.

And now she was dead. I felt like weeping for her, for her children, and for her bewildered husband, too. She'd been just my age, twenty-six, when she'd died, before she'd had any chance to spread her wings, to find out who she was and what her talents meant. I got out of the bedroom as fast as I could, before I began seeing her ghost in the corners.

They'd warned me when I joined the Agency that I'd see more misery than I could cure if I took the job. I saw the truth of that in every case I worked.

That night we ate Lucy's chicken casserole for dinner, though I felt too nauseated from the concussion to eat much more than a nibble. For dessert, I took two painkillers of a brand that didn't exist on my own world. Cam measured out dabs of ice cream for the kids, then put the dishes in the dishwasher. He got the kids to bed while I sat in the living room in a recliner chair with my feet up and felt the head ease a little. I tried to read a magazine, but my eyes refused to focus. I went to bed in the guest room early.

In the morning I woke up confused and aching, but less aching and confused than before. The guest room, a cheerful yellow, had chintz curtains in greens and blues and a pale beige rug. The narrow dresser was maple, as was the double bedstead. Maple and chintz the other Nola had consistent taste. On one wall was a big print of a painting of two small children with their arms full of flowers. It had all the style of a greeting card.

I got up and slid the closet door open. I found more of her clothes, these all size eights, which fit somewhat better. Probably she'd kept them in the hopes she'd lose some weight and get into them again. I put on another shirt that had belonged to her, a red-and-white check with long sleeves, and a pair of her trouser jeans.

The room had a half-bath attached. I washed my face and changed the gauze over the cut, which was deep enough to leave a scar once it healed—if it ever did, here on this

deviant world. I had a dark red-and-blue bruise on my
cheek, and a scrape along my chin just below it. My head
must have hit the ground at an angle when I landed facedown. The bright light in the tiny room made my eyes blink
and tear. I shut it off fast.

I went downstairs and followed the long hallway to the
kitchen with its round maple table and chairs. Cam was sitting at the table reading a newspaper, the Call-Bulletin. I
had the dim idea that in the past of my own San Francisco a
newspaper by that name had once existed. He laid the paper
down. The headline read, "Second Explosion in McLaren
Park." My handiwork and Ari's had made the papers.

"You look better this morning," he said. "Bruised, but
better. Take it easy, though, okay? Concussions need caution."

"Yeah," I said. "You're right about that."

Coffee in a glass carafe sat on the stove. I looked its way
with longing.

"Go ahead," Cam said. "Help yourself. There's cereal in
that cupboard there and fruit in the fridge."

"Thanks, but I never eat breakfast."

"You're welcome to the food." He gave me a faint smile.
"Honest."

"Thanks. When I feel better, I'll do stuff around the house.
I can't just sponge off you. Do you work during the week?"

"Yeah, for a textbook publisher. My teaching career
came to an abrupt end."

So had my Cam Douglas' career ended, when the school
authorities found out about his affair with a student. No
other district would hire him, either, not in California, anyway, where the year before he'd won awards for the quality
of his teaching. I remembered that he'd left town and gone
back east somewhere. I couldn't remember where, which
lapse struck me as sad. I'd loved him so much and then
forgotten him with the casual cruelty of the young.

Flowered mugs hung on a little rack near the stove. I got myself coffee and sat down opposite him at the table.

"Where are the kids?" I said.

"Little League. One of the neighbors took them. I don't know what I would have done without the neighbors, these last couple of weeks."

"Well, while I'm here, I'll help out. I've got a few domestic skills, though I'll warn you, I'm a lousy cook."

"Better than me, I bet."

I smiled.

"Nola—I mean, Rose," he said. "Who are you? Really, I mean, not our little fairy tale for the children and neighbors."

I sat back and wondered if I could think clearly enough to explain, if in fact I could ever explain in a way that would allow him to believe me. He waited for a few minutes, then spoke.

"You don't want to tell me, do you?" he said. "The times are making me paranoid. You're not one of the terrorists, are you? Not that you'd tell me if you were, I guess."

"No, I wouldn't, but I'm not. I'll swear that to you on any sacred name you want. Look, Cam, I'll tell you the exact honest truth, but you won't believe me. Just listen to it, okay? You can make fun of it when I'm done."

"Okay." He made a sound halfway between a laugh and a gasp for breath. "It's a deal."

"Have you ever heard of parallel worlds? Alternative histories? Deviant world levels? Science fiction stuff like that? Well, it isn't fiction. It's true, and I come from a level that deviates from yours, but not real far. If I hadn't lost my damned ID in that explosion—" I pointed at the newspaper article—"I'd show it to you. In my own strange way I'm a law officer. My partner and I came here on a murder case. We found what we needed, but in the scuffle that followed I got left behind. I'm hoping against hope that my partner—

Ari Nathan's his name—can find me and get me back where I belong."

Cam sat very still, silent, unmoving except for the occasional blink, for what seemed to be a very long time. I had a couple swallows of my coffee. He continued to say nothing.

"I told you you wouldn't believe me," I said, "but it's God's honest truth. I realize you'd prefer to think that I'm your Nola, driven amnesiac and crazy by being on the edge of the Emporium tragedy, but I'm not."

He sighed, then got up and walked over to the back door, where a pile of newspapers sat on a cane back chair. He rummaged through the pile, found one copy, and brought it back. He folded it open at an inner page and pointed to a column. By squinting my aching eyes, I managed to focus enough to read. The name jumped out.

"The bombing attempt was thwarted when Interpol agent Ari Nathan, newly arrived from the Republic of America, realized that the elevator contained explosives."

"Yeah, that's him," I said. "There are reasons why I never identified myself to the local police. Of course, you can't know for sure that I didn't read that article."

"Yeah." He sat down again. "I had that thought."

"If you're worried about me being one of the bad guys, I'll leave. I don't want to cause you any pain."

He shrugged and stared at the tabletop. "If your story's true," he said eventually, "it would explain how you knew my name and about my Nola and the baby and the rest of it. I know you didn't read that in the paper." He looked up. "You're the right age. You look exactly like her."

"Except for the scars."

"Yeah, except for that. You had an abortion? That's legal where you come from?"

"Perfectly legal. It isn't here?"

"More or less. They make it hard on the girl, but she can

get one. Do you—" He paused. "Sorry, none of my business."

"Do I regret it? Do I feel guilty? No." I considered saying, "especially not now, seeing what happened to her," but I refused to hurt someone who was sheltering me, saving my life, probably, one way or another. "I had the procedure when I was eleven weeks along. There was no soul in that lump of cells."

"I've never seen anything wrong when it's that early."

"Besides, if I'd grown that lump into a baby, he wouldn't be the son you know. He's a great kid, your Donnie, mature for his age, bright, sweet, even. Mine would have been a neurotic mess, growing up without a father in a big strange family that wished he'd never been born."

"Without a father? Would I—would he have just run off somewhere?"

"I don't know. But I'll bet my mother would have driven him away, sooner or later. She's no saint, not like your Deirdre. You see, my dad was in prison back then. Things weren't good at home."

That revelation made him wince. He began to fold the newspapers into precise oblongs, creasing each fold with his thumbnail. I finished my coffee and got up to refill my cup.

"I really shouldn't be here," I said. "I'm making things worse for you."

"Do you have anywhere else to go?"

"No." I turned around and leaned against the counter to watch him watching me. " 'Fraid not, but I'm pretty good at taking care of myself."

Inwardly I cursed the Agency's directive, TWIXT, our original cover story—everything I could think of to curse. I didn't know the liaison captain's name, much less the S.I.'s. They didn't know mine, either, and I had no ID to show them. If I'd only been an official part of Ari's team, I would have had an amazing little communicator like the one I'd been loaned on the last job we did. Maybe I could even have reached Spare14 back on Four. I certainly could have called the Los Angeles liaison captain, who could in turn have arranged shelter for me with the police. Now they'd never believe me, especially since they had a Nola O'Grady Douglas on their list of missing persons. Amnesia loomed large in Cam's explanations of me, and it probably would in the minds of the police, too, once they heard my name.

"Then you'd better stay here." Cam was smiling, but he had an odd twist to his mouth that turned the smile painful. Scar or no scar, he wanted me to be his wife, come back from the dead. His SPP told me that in a voice loud enough to be a scream of pain.

"Okay and thank you," I said, "but if I can leave, really leave, I mean, and go back to my own world, I will. Cam, you've got to understand that. This is only temporary."

"Sure. Temporary's better than never."

"Never what? Never seeing her again?"

His eyes filled with tears. I grabbed my coffee mug and carried it away to the living room to leave him alone with his grief, because comforting him would make it impossible for him to let it go. As I walked down the hall with its odd jog of an angle, I remembered that Sean had always called it the "ghostwalk," back in the Houlihan house in my own world. I paused and tried to send my mind out to his.

Sean, please! Find me! Tell Ari, tell Dad! Sean, get me out of here!

We all like to think about the road not taken. We remember some stupid mistake and wish we could go back in time and avoid it, do things right finally, mend the hurt we caused, restrain ourselves from producing a total mess of our life. Over that weekend, as I learned my way around the house and thus around the other Nola's life, I realized that I was having the reverse experience. I was seeing what would have happened had I made the mistake of marrying my Cameron Douglas. Even if we'd stayed married, even if my mother's poisonous meddling had failed to break us apart, my life would have been essentially over.

Never. The word rang like a bell through my thoughts. This world's Nola never used her talents. She'd never gone to college, never made friends her own age, never helped out on the suicide hotline, never discussed with deadly seriousness the issues raised in her classes. She'd never made contact with someone who could have trained her talents. She'd never known what she was.

She'd turned into a demon housekeeper, once she'd given up running away to Nowhere in Particular. Under every sink and in every cabinet, I found stashes of cleaning products that even Aunt Eileen would have found excessive. The furniture showed years of polishing. She'd reupholstered every piece that could possibly take upholstery, sometimes with needlepoint she did herself. Cam admitted that she compulsively washed walls once a month, floors twice a week. The kids never had a pet because of "the mess."

It passed the time, I supposed, all that cleaning and fixing, until the morning she went down to the Emporium to pass some more time and never came home. I remembered the nightmare I'd had of being caught under fallen masonry. Had that happened to my doppelgänger? As soon as I framed the question, I knew the answer. The other Nola had lain there, pinned, helpless, screaming on the floor as the huge and engulfing fire swept toward her. No wonder they'd never found her body. I could only hope that she'd gone under from the lack of oxygen before the flames reached her.

Chapter 12

C AM'S BOSS HAD TOLD HIM to take all the family
leave he needed. Now that I was in the house, and he'd
decided that I wasn't a terrorist, he returned to work on
Monday. It was the best thing for him, as I told the kids.

"But you'll be here with us?" Donnie asked me.

He looked so worried that I went down on one knee and
put an arm around his shoulders.

"You bet. I'll never leave you alone." I wondered how
much of the truth I could tell him: not much. "Now, someday I'll have to go back to L.A. But I won't leave unless
your dad is home. Okay?"

"Okay." He looked relieved, then sly. "Can we have ice
cream?"

"No," I said. "Not until after dinner."

The way he grinned told me that he'd wanted me to say
no. Following the rule indicated that some kind of normal
routine had returned. As I gave him a hug, I wondered how
it would have felt, to hug the Donnie who might have been
my child.

Over the next few days, that question recurred as my constant headache and I slipped without thinking into the housewife role. Cam went to work. I stayed home with the kids, because Cam had taken them out of school when the tragedy happened. The school year ended very early in June, so Donnie would only be missing a few weeks. Beth's first grade hardly counted as school, according to Cam. He had high standards.

We played games. We went for short walks. I tried to read to them, but my concussion refused to let my eyes focus properly. We talked about their mother and how they missed her. Often they cried, and I told them it was all right to cry, that they needed to cry. We planted some new flowers—perennial periwinkles and a rosebush—in the backyard in her memory. Donnie gathered stones and laid them in the shape of a heart around the base of the roses.

I did what cleaning I thought necessary, mostly in the bathrooms and the kitchen, though the other Nola would have judged me slovenly, I'm sure. Lucy the neighbor took us grocery shopping whenever she went, which was often. I thanked her profusely. It was hard on her, knowing that her Nola was dead while this look-alike cousin was alive in her friend's house. The other neighbors introduced themselves and believed me when I told them my story about Rose and L.A. I made sure to mention that I had a boyfriend and a job and thus couldn't stay forever.

"Cam needs to hire a housekeeper," Mrs. Sanchez told me one day. She lived across the street and knew the family well. "Once you've got to go home, that is."

"Good idea," I said. "I'll work on him to do that."

I tried, but he refused to take the idea seriously. "Later, when the kids are ready to meet a stranger," was the only answer I could get out of him. I realized that he'd stopped thinking of me as a stranger, even though he'd only known me for a handful of days.

The kids, of course, believed me to be their aunt with the easy trust of kids who know their family loves them, not that their mother had been the cuddly, indulgent type. At lunch one day, Beth spilled the end of a glass of milk, maybe a quarter cup at the most. As the puddle spread on the protective glass over the tabletop, Beth grabbed her napkin and slapped it into the puddle. Donnie gasped and jumped up. He ran for the counter and seized a roll of paper towels. The milk beat him to the edge of the table. As it dripped onto the floor, Beth began to cry.

"Hey," I said, "it's all right! It's just a little milk."

"It's mess," Beth said. "I'm sorry. I'm real sorry."

"It's all right." I put my arms around her and scooped her off her chair. "It's all right. Life is full of mess."

I hugged Beth while Donnie pulled a towel from the roll and stooped down to mop up the dribble. When I set her down, she'd stopped crying.

"Mama hated mess," she said.

"Yeah, I guess she must have." I took a tissue out of my pocket and wiped her face. "Well, it's not a crime to spill a little milk."

Beth smiled. I noticed that Donnie had done a great job of mopping up. He'd had a lot of practice, I figured. I made sure to praise him for it.

In the evenings I threw together some kind of dinner, which Cam and the kids ate without complaining, even though the other Nola had been a great cook, or so I judged by the amount of cookbooks and fancy equipment in the kitchen. Cam supervised their baths and got them into pajamas while I cleaned up. He read them stories at bedtime. I liked watching him with the kids because he so visibly loved them.

When he read aloud, he kept them involved in the story, pointing out things in the illustrations to Beth's picture books, asking Donnie questions about what they'd read in the chapter books, listening to their opinions without interrupting or correcting. Mr. Douglas had made American history come alive for his high school classes in similar ways. This Cam had the same ready grin, the same sharp wit—until he turned out the light in the kids' rooms and walked out in the hall to face his grief.

One night I happened to be cramming freshly washed towels into the hall linen closet when he came out of Donnie's room. He didn't see me, just leaned against the wall, shut his eyes, stood without moving for a long couple of minutes, then pulled himself up and turned my way. He stared, swallowed a couple of times, and walked away without saying a word. I finished the laundry and joined him in the family room off the hallway—Uncle Jim's study back in my own world. It had an old carpet on the floor and furniture with heavy terry cloth slipcovers.

In the evenings Cam and I watched the TV news, switching from channel to channel to catch every shred of information. The National Guard was making sweeps through the Bay Area, checking IDs, demanding answers from those with no local address. They managed to arrest a few drug dealers and a serial rapist who'd been on the Wanted List for some months. They never caught up with the terrorists or with the Axeman, not that they were looking for Ash and Co., of course. I'd merely hoped that they might catch the gang by accident, as it were.

The sweeps, however, did prevent any new terrorist acts. The National Guard also arrested enough looters that the looting downtown stopped. Everyone hoped that the terrorists had moved on, but no one believed it. The Kingdom of Christ kept denying responsibility. No one believed them, either.

"Is there any chance," I asked Cam, "that these terrorists aren't government backed?"

"Sure. There are degrees of fanaticism, even there."

"And so these guys might be the most extreme of the extremists?"

"Exactly. Now, officially, the Kingdom can't afford an actual war with California, not with our alliance with Japan." He paused for a wry smile. "They can't afford one with anyone, for that matter. They don't dare provoke military action. They have the smallest population of any of the nations in North America." He thought for a moment. "They're not as poor as the Confeds, of course. At least the Kingdom has grain to sell. They have government farms." He made a sour face. "Slave labor."

"No Oklahoma oil?"

"Oklahoma? That's right, it was an independent state once. It's part of Texas now. There was a referendum in Oklahoma about leaving the Kingdom and joining Texas. The vote theoretically went for Texas." He shrugged. "I doubt if it was an honest election. That nearly did come to a war between Texas and the Kingdom. Back in 1961. The Kingdom had to give in without a fight."

When the news ended, Cam got up, turned the TV off, and seemed to shrink or maybe age. Without history and politics to occupy his mind, he turned inward, curled around his grief the way a child might curl around a stomachache. He smiled vaguely in my direction and said the same thing he said every night, "Well, I've got to go to work tomorrow." He left to go up to the room he had shared with his wife.

Through this daily schedule I missed Ari, constantly, bitterly, and with a growing sense of fear. What if he could never get back? Every one of Willa's remarks and warnings insisted on returning to my mind no matter how hard I tried to squelch the memory. Thanks to the destruction inflicted upon Interchange, which should have been its anchor point, this world level moved, swinging in an irrational arc through the quantum foam—whatever that may have meant. I'd always left that kind of theory to others: Ari, Willa, and

Spare14. Now, when I was desperate to understand, I had no one to explain it to me.

Nor could I, in turn, explain it to Cam, who had the kind of mind that would have understood, could I have given him a coherent description. I did try in dribs and drabs, as I remembered things I'd been told. He listened patiently, but his SPP made it clear that he dismissed everything I said. Finally, on the second Sunday I lived in his house, I broke down and wept as we sat on the couch with news droning on the TV. Cam laid a hesitant hand on my shoulder.

"Rose, Rose," he said, "what's so wrong?"

"I just can't explain what I know to you," I said. "God, I'm so frustrated! I try to explain, and I can see you don't believe me."

"It's the concussion." He made his voice gentle. "You're not making sense, yeah, but it can take weeks for someone to get over a concussion. Things will be easier once you're well. You can tell me then."

Weeks. Would I still be in his house when weeks rolled by? No! I told myself. I will find some way out of this, no matter what it takes. First step: find the Interpol office in L.A. Maybe I could persuade them that I was the psychic whom Spare14 had mentioned in his report. If not, maybe I could find something else to persuade them. I knew about TWIXT. I realized that the knowledge, if I presented it in the right way, might be my ticket home. If I knew about them, they'd see that I had to be who I said I was.

If of course I could find their damned office. Once Cam went to work on Monday, I tried the obvious: Directory Assistance. They told me that there was no Interpol office in Los Angeles. The only listing they had was in New York, a bureau attached to the United Nations of North America. I remember Spare14's various ruses to blend in with the populations of the world levels where he operated. The L.A. office must have had a ruse of its own. I decided I'd try trawling the Internet for clues—then remembered that there was no Internet.

I spent a couple of days in despair and depression. My head hurt, the cut on my forehead still bled occasionally, and thinking challenged me as soon as I grew the least bit tired. I sank so low that I wondered if Ari had deliberately left me behind. Maybe he was sick of me and my weird family. All my other boyfriends had left me as soon as they realized that marrying me meant the O'Gradys were part of deal. I did remind myself about the beautiful engagement ring I'd left behind in the wall safe, a token that no, Ari wouldn't just desert me. I couldn't make myself believe that I'd ever see the ring or Ari again.

Or my family, either. Another thorn buried itself in my mind: worrying about Maureen and her children. Chuck had obviously figured out that she was living with Kathleen and Jack. Maybe he'd tried shooting at her through the fence, for all I knew. For all I'd ever know, maybe, but that fear I shoved away. I thought about them so much, in fact, that they made me realize that Beth may have had a Douglas for a father, but she was, in truth, an O'Grady girl.

She'd been playing in her room with her fashion dolls, a pair called Linda and Ricky. Donnie and I were walking by to hunt for a toy he'd misplaced in his room when we heard her speaking. "And Aunt Rose is here, and then there's Aunt Maureen. Two new aunts. And she's got two children. A boy and a girl and Aunt Maureen."

"Beth!" Donnie stopped and went to the doorway. "Don't make up stories. You know you're not supposed to make up those stories."

I remembered the Pull, and Beth telling me that she'd called for her mother. Things fell into place in my bruised brain. Beth had talents.

"It's not a story," I said. "It's true. Aunt Maureen and Caitlin and Brennan are real."

Beth gave me a grin of sheer relief. Donnie looked up at me with narrow eyes.

"Really?" he said.

"Really," I said. "Besides, why can't Beth make up stories if she wants? They're just stories. She's just playing dolls."

"Yeah!" Beth said. "So there!"

A thoughtful Donnie and I walked on down to his room. "Aunt Rose?" he said. "Mama didn't like it when Beth made up stories like that."

"Yeah, I just bet she didn't. It must have been scary, wondering how Beth knew those things."

"You mean the others were true, too?"

"I don't know what the other stories were. But I bet Beth knows things sometimes just because she does."

Donnie made no answer. We found his Pirate Mike action figure, and he went back downstairs without saying another word about Beth. As I walked past her room, I glanced in and saw who—or what—she'd been talking to. A little green Chaos critter was sitting on the carpet and watching her dress the dolls. When it saw me, it leaped up and disappeared. Beth just waved good-bye in its direction. I supposed she was used to seeing her friend come and go at whim.

I suspected that the other Nola had also known things "just because." Probably she'd learned to stop believing in them. She must have suppressed the raw beginnings of talents that she'd never been trained to use. Otherwise they would have driven her crazy, the whispers of things to come, the hints and suspicions about what other people might be thinking, the warning not to walk into a department store that was going to have a big sale on death that very afternoon. If she'd only listened—I shoved that thought away.

Wednesday evening on the news we learned of the first terrorist attack on Los Angeles. They'd blown up a neighborhood mosque and killed its imam as well some thirty elderly worshipers come for the third call to prayer of the day. How long, I wondered, would TWIXT keep the L.A. office open, now that the violence had swept south? If they closed it, it wouldn't exist for me to find. I kept control of myself in front of Cam, but once I went to bed in the loathsomely cheerful yellow guest room, I cried myself to sleep, thinking of Ari.

I dreamed that I pulled a cord on a kelly green parachute, which opened and wafted me home. I woke up Thursday morning thinking, "To hell with TWIXT." I'd find my own way back.

I have no world-walker talents, but thanks to my father and brother's skill in that area, plus the family overlap, I do possess a weak ability to sense gates. In the past months, thanks to working with TWIXT and Spare14, the ability had grown stronger. On Thursday evening, when Beth had fallen asleep, and Cam was reading Donnie a story to help him do the same, my brain had healed enough for me to wonder about the three small storerooms at the north end of the house. In my world's Houlihan house, they contained a gate. I wouldn't be able to use it, but if one existed in this version of the house, I might find some way to send a message through.

I switched on the light in the stairwell, then opened the door to the bottom room. It was crammed floor to ceiling with cardboard boxes, all carefully labeled in the other Nola's spiky handwriting—kids' clothes, Cam's old clothes and hers, extra dishes, Christmas wrap, out-of-style shoes, old books, and phonograph records. Her surrender to normal life had turned her into a hoarder. I shut the door fast and went upstairs.

The second room also held a goodly selection of boxes, but it offered enough space to walk in and turn around. On one box I noticed that she spelled her name in the Irish way, Nuala, which matched her sisters' names, Caitlin and Eilas, even though Cam pronounced it the American way. Their family must have emigrated from Ireland more recently than mine. I stood in the pool of ugly overhead light and let my mind range out. Not a ripple of other times, not a scent of other spaces reached me. I turned out the light and went up to the top.

When I opened the door, I could see by the light from the stairwell that this room had a floor lamp. I turned that on, and by its soft glow walked into what must have been her refuge. She'd painted the walls a soothing green and carpeted the floor in beige. She'd furnished it with a gray armchair, a hassock, and a small shelf of books in one corner. In the other, a thick pile of yoga mats and a pair of floor pillows lay next to a blue box with a monitor and a slot for some kind of disk—the yoga lessons, I assumed. A venetian blind covered the single window.

In the Houlihan house on Terra Four, the venetian blind could at times reveal a view of Interchange, produced by resonance with the gate my father had created on the ground floor. In the Douglas house on Six, I stood in the middle of the room, faced the window, and let my mind go quiet. Faintly, like the scent of roses from a neighbor's yard, I sensed a ripple in space-time. Had I been a world-walker, I could have found a gate in this room. I wasn't, and I wept a bare scatter of tears.

I went over to the window and opened the blind. I saw nothing but a view of Cam's backyard, shadowed in the night. The tears came again. I closed the blind and used the raw feeling of grief and despair to power my message. *Sean. Sean, can you sense me? Sean, I'm here, oh God, Sean, please find me.*

A footstep sounded behind me. I turned around and saw Cam, taking a cautious step into the room. He looked around him, all curiosity, as if he'd never seen the place before.

"You found her lair," he said. "That's what she called it. Her lair."

I tried to smile and failed. He crossed over to me in a couple of long strides. "Rose?" he said. "I'm so sorry. I know you don't want to be here, and at the same time, we're so glad you are. It must grate."

"Yeah, 'fraid so." I found my voice at last.

He touched the tear streaks with his fingertips, a gentle stroke to brush them away. I looked into his eyes and remembered how I'd felt at seventeen, that I could happily drown in the blue of his eyes.

"Are the kids asleep?" I said.

"Yeah. Want to watch some TV?"

"Not really."

"I'll leave you alone if you'd like."

"That's okay. I don't know what I'd like."

"I'll bet, yeah."

Yet we both knew what we both wanted at that minute. I could tell by the way his smile softened, disappeared, the way his hand trembled as he touched my cheek again. He was grieving for his dead wife. I was grieving for my lost world, for my lost love. Ari, I'm sorry, I thought, but I'm so lonely without you.

Cam bent his head and kissed me. I surrendered to the comfort of his oddly familiar arms.

We ended up on the pair of yoga mats, right there on the floor. I had the dim thought that we were far enough away from the kids' bedrooms to avoid waking them. This Cameron Douglas was the same sort of lover I remembered: gentle, considerate, eager to ensure that I felt as much pleasure as he did. He succeeded in doing just that, yet by two minutes afterward, when he cuddled me in his arms, even as he kissed my face so gently and sweetly, I was thinking about Ari.

And Sean. For the first time I felt a contact, a mere whisper, the barest touch but still a connection with my brother the finder. All that Qi, generated in the usual biological way, had gone pouring through the frequencies we call the worlds. *Sean,* I thought, *help! Tell Ari where I am! Tell Dad! He'll get me out of here!* The contact faded before I could feel any response.

I needed more Qi, and I knew how to get it from the man in my arms. I kissed him; I licked his face like a little animal. He laughed and pretended to object, then smiled at me and rubbed his hand over my sweaty stomach, as if to remind himself that it was smooth and scarless. We shared a long kiss that oozed Qi. I absorbed every shred of it.

"Rose?" Cam's voice turned soft and seductive. "Will you come sleep in my bed tonight? Please?"

I felt like scum. I was planning on using his need of me to fuel the rescue that would take me away from him. I stared at the ceiling and told him a truth, not a lie, as far as it went.

"Sleeping in that room?" I said. "I can't do it. It's hers and yours. It's not mine. I'd see her ghost in the corners."

"I can understand that." Yet he sounded profoundly sad.

"I'm sorry," I said, "but sooner or later, I'm going to leave you. I can't stay here and still be who I am."

He raised himself on one elbow and looked at me. "Whatever that is," he said. "Sometimes I still think you must be a ghost or some kind of supernatural being."

"Then think about those old stories. Ask too many questions, and the brownies never come back, Melusina disappears, Psyche finds herself abandoned."

"Sad but true." He lay back down. "Can I ask for another kiss?"

"Yeah. That I can give you. For now."

And I did, a lot of them, and more than kisses. I could tell by his gasp of surprise that he'd never expected to be aroused a second time. I gave him all the pleasure I could in payment for the flood of Qi, but the whole time we made love, I was funneling the Qi toward Sean on a tide of desperation. Afterward, I thought about Ari.

I slept in the guest room that night, and Cam in his usual bed. In the morning, the neighbors down the street called to say they were taking their kids swimming. Did Beth and Donnie want to go, too? They did, but since swimming has its dangers, I called Cam at work to get his permission. Once he gave it, I packed up their swim things and a snack and saw them off.

In the suddenly silent house I went upstairs to the gate room, as I'd started thinking of the other Nola's lair. Her taste in books ran mostly to historical fiction, a deviance from mine, which inclined more toward lurid adventures. I picked out a novel set in Elizabethan England and sat down in the recliner to read. Their version of that bit of history matched ours, as far as I could tell from that one book, logically since the fractalization had happened so much later. By then my concussion had healed. The words made sense, and they no longer danced on the page.

I'd just finished the prologue when I heard a car pull into the driveway—some kind of delivery van, I assumed. I got up and walked out onto the landing to listen. I heard the kitchen door open and the faint sound of Cam's voice, calling, "Rose?" He'd come back home. Since the kids were gone, I could guess why.

"I'm up here," I called out.

I met him at the top of the stairs with kisses, each one a lie. We spent a couple of hours up in the room that I knew was my one best hope of leaving him. I had the Qi I needed, and I used it all to blast—or so I hoped—a message through to my brother the finder.

Cam slept for most the afternoon, exhausted. I fell asleep on the couch. I'd drained both of us of every smidgen of Qi we could spare. He explained away his exhaustion by telling me that he hadn't been sleeping well, not since the bombing. When the kids came home hungry, I ordered pizza instead of struggling to cook a meal.

Late that night Cam came into my bedroom, and even though we were far from the potential gate, I couldn't bring myself to deny him. All he really wanted was to sleep next to me. He deserved some comfort after all that sex with a temporary vampire, that is, with me.

On Saturday afternoon, I was reading in the living room. Cam and the kids had gone out to the backyard to toss a baseball around. Although I could hear them laughing and calling to one another, it was quiet inside the house. Sunlight came through the front windows and lay in patches on the flowered rug. It occurred to me that if the worst happened, and Ari and Sean never found me, I could stay in Cam's house forever.

I could invent a terrible fight with that mythical boyfriend in L.A. and just stay on to care for the kids. After a decent year had passed and the other Nola had been declared legally dead, Cam and I would marry. No one would be censorious, not even surprised, that he'd fallen in love with her cousin who looked so much like her. We'd probably have another child, once my implant ran out and nature took its course.

I'd need a Caesarean. The scar would return, and Cam could pretend his Nola had never left him. Eventually, I would go stark raving nuts.

I tossed the novel aside and stood up. I was thinking that I'd go for a walk, just to get some fresh air, when I heard footsteps coming down the stairs from the storerooms. The sound seemed to jerk me out of time into a suspension of fear and joy, mingled for one brief second. I came to myself and ran straight for the corridor just as Ari walked out of the stairwell. He was wearing his jeans, his leather jacket, and the Beretta in its usual holster over a white shirt.

He grinned, a beautiful brilliant smile, and held out his arms. I rushed into his grasp. He kissed me, then kissed me again. Over his shoulder I saw Dad, halfway down the stairs and smiling. In one hand he carried an orb, the lovely blue-green orb of home.

"Sean's on the other side," Dad said. "Jeezus H, it took him long enough to find you! I'm going back upstairs. This lousy gate isn't as stable as I'd like."

He turned and hurried back up. Ari stayed with me.

"Let's get out of here fast," I said. "I can't bear to say good-bye to the family that's been sheltering me."

The back door squeaked open. Cam had heard the foot-steps, the voices. I knew he was coming down the hall and panicked. I pulled away from Ari but couldn't decide which way to run.

"What?" Ari said. "You should at least leave a note."

"I'll explain later."

Cam walked into the living room. He stopped at the edge of the rug, just behind the couch, and stared at Ari. Ari hooked his thumbs over his belt and stared back. Narrowed eyes, tense shoulders, tight jaws—both men looked only at each other in an instant male bonding of jealous rage. Explanations had just become unnecessary. I kept thinking about Ari's Beretta, so close at hand. My heart started pounding.

"I'm sorry, Cam," I said. "I'm going home." I waved vaguely in Ari's direction. "He came to fetch me. It's like I tried to tell you, I'm a cop. This is Ari Nathan, my partner, the guy from Interpol."

Feeble? Yes, incredibly feeble, but at the moment I couldn't think of anything better. Cam said nothing, merely transferred his gaze to me. I'd warned him, I'd told him re-peatedly that I'd leave, but his SPP showed that he'd never believed me till that moment.

"Tell the kids I had to go in a hurry," I said. "I'm sorry.

Tell the neighbors my boyfriend came to get me, and he was pretty angry about things." This last was true enough. I didn't need to look at Ari to know that.

"Wait." Cam sounded as if he were being strangled. "Will I ever see you again?"

Ari caught my arm and jerked his head in the direction of the stairwell. I shook free, took one step away, and froze when Donnie rushed in with Beth right behind him. I went down on one knee, and they ran to my arms. I hugged them both, then stood up. I had to pry Donnie's arms from around my waist.

"Don't go," Beth said. "Please don't go!"

"I have to," I said. "I'm sorry."

Donnie turned and raced for the hallway. I knew he was crying. I looked at Cam.

"I'm sorry," I said. "Be well. Please, all of you, be well."

Ari stepped in between us. He caught my arm, swung me around, and gave me a hard push between the shoulder blades. "Move," he said. "The gate won't stay open forever."

I moved, let him hustle me up the stairs into the other Nola's private lair, where I'd committed an odd sort of adultery with her husband. Dad was waiting by the window, open to let in the sunlight and fresh air. He held up the orb and looked into it, stayed stone-faced and utterly immobile as everything changed around us. The venetian blind came down with a clatter. The sunlight dimmed to an overhead bulb. We were standing in Aunt Eileen's storage room at the top of the Houlihan house.

Sean stood in the doorway and grinned at me. I ran to him. He laughed and hugged me while I babbled "thank you" over and over again. Finally, I let him go.

"How did you finally reach me?" Sean said. "I'd been trying ever since Ari came back without you. Let's see, I got the first hint Thursday night, and then yesterday morning— whap! The information flooded in."

"I guess I finally found the right frequency." I was afraid to look at Ari. Although he had his rage firmly under control, I could feel his hurt without even needing to run an SPP. "I was really desperate by then."

"So were we all," Dad said, grinning. "You should have seen our Ari, yelling at everybody, especially dear old Spare14."

"I'm afraid I made a fool of myself," Ari said, "several times over."

The double message made me wince. "Speaking of Ari," I said, and I managed to force out a false smile, "why don't you guys go on downstairs? We'll join you in a minute or two."

Dad laughed, Sean snickered; mercifully, they did leave. I shut the storeroom door and turned to look at Ari. Lying, I knew, would be a waste of time.

"Okay, yeah," I said. "I did sleep with that guy. That's what's wrong, isn't it?"

"Yes. Are you surprised? Do you have the sodding brazen nerve to be surprised?"

"No, but I did it because I needed the Qi to break through. I couldn't reach Sean without it. I tried from the first day onward and made no contact, nada, zip, jack. If it makes you feel any better, the sex was totally unfair to him. I never should have used him that way, but I was desperate."

"I can't imagine he suffered much during the experience."

"You don't understand. His wife was killed in a terrorist explosion, and she was one of my doppelgängers. Oh, sure, he liked it at the time, but how do you think he's feeling now? For a little while he had her back, and now she's gone again. Forever."

Ari considered this for a long couple of minutes while he looked at me with the same cold and accusing stare.

"Look," I said, "I never would have had sex with him if I hadn't realized there was a gate in that room. That's what let Sean find me, isn't it? The message I finally managed to force through. I never let him touch me until Thursday night, when I realized that the room had a gate."

"And I suppose you didn't realize sooner." Sarcasm dripped from every word.

"I had a concussion from the explosion in the park." I reached up and pulled back my bangs to reveal the scabby scar from my cut. "I could barely see straight, much less think straight."

Ari winced at the sight of the scar, but he returned his expression to the stone face. From his SPP, I could tell that he was weighing what I'd told him, back and forth in his own mind, like evidence in a deposition. All at once I was furious.

"Besides, my beloved darling." I managed to keep my voice calm, but it was a struggle. "You left me there. You never looked back, did you? You never once looked to see if I was okay and able to follow you. I was lying there bleeding on the ground, and you never looked back."

He winced again, turned halfway, turned back.

"Is that all the answer I'm going to get?" I said. "A sour face? I told you to wait before you threw the orb. Did you hear me? I yelled."

He nodded a yes. I had to admire him for admitting the truth, instead of just saying no, I didn't hear a thing. He spent a couple of minutes staring at the floor.

"Well?" I snapped. "I know you resent it, that I'm the head of the squad. Is that why you didn't wait?"

"No! I'd already tossed it and couldn't catch it." He raised his head but looked somewhat to the right of me. "I failed you. I've felt for days like living hell—I mean, that I not—that I didn't look back."

I had never heard his English glitch before. Coming from

him, it shocked me. Finally, and with a tremendous effort, he looked me in the face.

"I'm sorry," he repeated. "I was wrong. I should have checked with you first. Before I threw it, I mean."

That admission cost him. I could sense a pain that went a lot deeper than mere male ego. Living hell, all right. I'll admit to feeling a nasty little knot of satisfaction.

"I realized what I'd done the minute we got to Four. I looked back, and I knew." Ari was keeping his voice steady by sheer force of will. "Things got worse once I told the family. We were all frantic. Sean was hysterical. He thought you might be dead. Then two days ago he told us he'd picked something up. Yesterday noon the location became clear, as he told you."

"It took you a while to reach me, then," I said.

"We had to get permission to re-enter the floating level." Ari shrugged as if shedding a burden. "I finally convinced Spare14 that if he didn't let me go retrieve you, I'd quit TWIXT. I had it all worked out, not that I told him about my plan. Flann and I would go on our own. They could arrest me later, once I knew you were safe. I'd claim I'd forced Flann at gunpoint, so he wouldn't have been culpable."

"You would have done that for me?"

He nodded and turned away. He picked up a dusty book from the top of one of Aunt Eileen's storage cartons, then put it down with its edge precisely matched to the edge of the carton. Anger management? No, I decided. Guilt. His SPP reeked of it.

"I told you," he said. "I know I failed you. I would have done anything to make it right. Will you forgive me?"

I was still angry enough to make him wait. "Yes, of course," I said eventually. "I know you were thinking of getting the others to safety."

He looked at me, sighed, and held out his arms. I let him

enfold me and sensed that he'd chained his rage in its usual corner of his mind. Even his ordinary anger had faded away. The hurt remained, his, mine, and my memory of Cam's hurt. They made my soul ache. I choked back tears. And the kids!

Ari misunderstood my silence. "You do forgive me, don't you?" he said.

"Yes, I do. Can you forgive me?"

"Of course!" He sounded weary, a little sad. "It's that or live without you, and this last fortnight showed me that's out of the question. I missed you like a knife to the heart."

"And then you saw Cam and got stabbed again."

"Yes. And another thing, I'm sorry I shoved you like that. Another failure on my part. I was honestly afraid that the gate would close and trap us on Six, but that's no excuse. I was fighting with the rage from the moment he walked in."

"I saw it, yeah." I rested my head against his chest. "But you won the bigger battle. You didn't draw your gun. You didn't punch him or slap me."

"True." He hesitated. "I do know how he must feel, with you gone. You're right. You did him no favor."

"And now the kids have been deserted again." My voice broke, and much to my utter shock, I could no longer hold back my tears. "You saw how they acted when I was leaving. Those poor kids, Ari!"

He sighed again and stroked my back, murmured a few words in Hebrew, over and over until at last I could stop crying. It took some while. I found a tissue in my jeans pocket and wiped my face and runny nose.

"I love you," I said.

"Good. Remember that from now on."

"Oh, come off it, you jerk! I wouldn't have felt so deserted if I didn't love you so much."

His smile bloomed, and my face insisted on smiling in return.

"About the children," he said. "Maybe we can arrange for you to see them again, provided it's safe, of course."

"We're going back?"

"If we can. The job's not over. Ash, the Axeman, they're all still on the loose. And then there's young Rasmussen. He'd rather like to see his family and friends again. We'll need to get him back to Six."

"This time the Agency is going to have to make me official. I'm going to stick it to Y. If I'd been a recognized part of your team, I would have had a communicator. I could have just called the liaison captain in L.A. when I got left behind."

"True. Annie's already dealt with Y. Rather firmly, I gather from what she told me. He'll give you any status you'd like. I'm quite sure of that."

Rather firmly. I smiled. I figured she'd raked him over the coals, all in a quiet little voice, during a trance session or over the phone. I hoped for both.

"I'll make sure that Spare14 sets things up at our end," Ari said. "You needn't worry about that."

"Okay, and I want a word with him, myself. Are you telling me you had to argue with him about going back to get me? What was he going to do, leave me there?"

"No, of course not." Ari let me go and stepped toward the door. "The problem was the risk. Every overlap to Six has grown so weak that the World-Walkers Guild have refused to let any of their members use them. Not just the one in McLaren Park—there are gates to Six in other countries and other world levels, and none are quite right. Spare14 wanted to stockpile extra transport orbs and do a proper evaluation. This meant a consultation with HQ and another fortnight's worth of specialist examinations."

I glanced around the cluttered storeroom. "This gate worked just fine."

"Indeed, it did, but no one knew that, did they? Not until this morning. We have access to Six now, yes, but who knows for how long? If we're going after Ash and the Axeman, we have to move fast."

"Dad will know how long the gate will stay open. He's the one who made it."

"True, and it worked because he was the one operating within it. Who knows if anyone else can do what he did this morning? If there were only some way to get him to cooperate with TWIXT!"

"Yeah, and if wishes were horses, all beggars would ride. I'll talk to him, but don't hold your breath."

Ari picked something up from the floor: my shoulder bag.

"We brought this up." He handed me the bag. "Flann thought the gate might not be fully functional. It might have been possible to toss the bag through even if we couldn't transit. You would have had your ID and the second orb that way."

I took the bag and hugged it. "Yeah," I said. "I could have done something with this."

"Of course. Once you had the right tools, you would have been back the same day." He smiled. "You're quite competent, you know, in your own peculiar way."

That's when I finally, really, and truly forgave him.

We left the gate room and hurried downstairs. When we reached the hallway at the bottom, I heard voices—family voices, wonderfully familiar, my family's voices—in the living room. We walked in. Dad was talking on his cell phone while Aunt Eileen, Michael, and Sean hovered nearby. His tense voice, their frightened faces, told me that he was getting the wrong kind of news.

"Maureen?" I said.

"It's Kathleen on the phone, yes." Aunt Eileen hurried over to me and kept her voice low. "Mo's all right, but Chuck shot at her. He missed. Jack's gone to the San Anselmo police to see if there's anything they can do."

My stomach clenched. Oh, yes. I was home.

CHAPTER 13

EVERYONE HAD TO HUG ME and tell me how glad
they were to have me back. I hugged everyone in turn
and told them they couldn't be half as glad as I was. With
the ritual over, I left the family waiting for a report about
Jack's visit to the police. I went to the kitchen to call Annie
privately. When she recognized my voice, she laughed in
sheer exultant triumph.

"You're back!" she said. "They got you through."

"They sure did," I said. "Ari told me you've been in contact with Y."

"Contact? Yes, I suppose you might call it that. Once Ari
told me about the problem with your status, I was too angry
to go into trance, so I called the office. Y returned the call,
and it's a good thing, too, because we talked for an awfully
long time. It would have been so expensive! But he did finally see reason." Her voice simmered with remembered
indignation. "You need to get in touch with him first thing
Monday morning or even sooner, if you can. He's genuinely
worried as well as guilt-stricken."

"I'll do that. Have things been quiet on the Chaos front here, or have there been any eruptions?"

"Reasonably quiet. Jerry is convinced that he's being followed by giant squid. I think he takes too many drugs. That roommate of his! Who knows what he has lying around their apartment?"

"Everything available, that's what. I bet he'd sell curare if he could get it. But look, the squiddish Chaos critters are entirely too possible a phenomenon. I've seen them, too."

"Oh. Well, in that case, they probably are real. You need to call him."

I certainly did need to. Annie had given me an idea. Sean, unfortunately, had never met Maureen's Unpleasant Ex, which meant he couldn't use his talent to find him. Jerry's roommate had druggie connections all over the Bay Area. He might know where Trasker was hiding out.

I'd just clicked off when my father strolled in. He sat down next to me at the table.

"You were wanting to talk with me?" Dad said.

"Yeah. Did Ari tell you?"

"No. Why do you think he'd have to?"

We laughed, and he reached over and caught my hand.

"I've been worried sick," he said. "I thought we'd lost you for sure."

"No such luck, Dad. I knew that if I could just reach Sean, you'd come and get me."

"And you did, and we did." He patted my hand, let it go, and leaned back in his chair. "So, what's this burning question?"

I could feel his mind bounce off the subject of Sean and who or what he was. I decided to leave that painful discussion for another day.

"The gate," I said. "Is it stable? Could another Guild person use it?"

"Now that is something I can't tell you, not yet. I've put

in a call to the Guild. They'll need to send someone out, because it'll take two trained people to do the diagnosis." He paused to think with a twist of his mouth. "I'm not so sure your aunt's going to want people tromping back and forth through her house to use the damned thing, anyway."

"There is that, yeah."

"And what about the people at the other end? Who are they, anyway?"

"Relatives of ours. A widower and his two children, but the children's mother was an O'Grady. Well, actually, she was my doppelgänger. That's why they live in the house. They bought it from the Houlihan doppelgängers on Six."

"Good God!" He paused in honest shock. "Well, that makes one thing easier to understand. No wonder it spread to them while it was twisting itself around."

"Why has the gate spread? Do you know?"

"Because I wasn't here to tend it. These artificial gates are like hybrid roses. They need pruning and feeding both."

"But you built the one on the bottom floor to go through to Three, right? Michael opened the one on the top floor by accident once, but it led to Three that time, not Six."

"So he told me. Three's the only level he knows, is why. He wasn't using an orb."

"That makes sense, yeah."

We shared a companionable silence. They say that every girl's first love is her father, something that certainly was true in my case. I remembered him so well as the young and vigorous man he'd been, tanned from working outside and muscled as well, striding into the house at the end of the working day with a hug and a laugh for each of us kids. Now he was too thin from his long years as a prisoner, his hair steel gray, his eyes sad, somehow, in a web of crow's feet.

"Dad," I said, "have you thought about what you're going to do now?"

"I've thought about it, but I still don't know. I can't go

back to construction work. Everything's changed, the tools, the methods, since I've been gone. I don't have the energy I once had, either. I'll have to think of something. I can't stand to live off your mother's salary. She keeps saying that it's fine with her, but it's not fine with me."

"There's the Guild."

"I am not working with TWIXT."

"I know that. They don't own the Guild. Isn't there a research arm?"

"And what would they want with a half-trained man like me?"

"A half-trained man who happens to be a genius."

"Oh, come now! You're my darling daughter, but there's no use in idle flattery."

"You know more than anyone else in the damn Guild. Do you think an ordinary world-walker could have built the gate upstairs? They have to find them, not build them. And then there's your research, like that paper about angels. The one in Hisperic."

He gave a startled little cough. "You've got that, do you? I wondered why it wasn't in the desk when I went to look for it."

"Sorry. I'll give it back, but I used that data to induce a vision. That's how I learned about the Maculates. You made a real find when you bought that from Wagner's."

"Huh, so I did. I'd wondered what it would lead to. I wish I'd had it in prison. It would have been something to think about to pass the time."

We shared a wry smile. I found myself remembering the other Nola, her life brutally ended, her talents lost forever. He could still use his, even though the Britannic Empire had wasted thirteen years of his life.

"At least talk with the Guild." I leaned forward a little. "The world-walker who's been ferrying me and Ari around would really like to discuss things with you. She sure doesn't consider herself part of TWIXT, let me tell you."

"Well, in that case, maybe I will. I could at least hear what they want out of me. Talk's cheap enough." He stood up and looked at the clock on the kitchen wall as if it could tell him more than the time. "I've got to find something to do."

"How will they contact you? You don't have a trans-world router, do you?"

"I don't, but the man I'm in touch with here does. The Guild has members on every world we can reach, darling. We just don't tell anyone about it."

"Gotcha," I said. "I won't even tell Ari." I got up to join him. "When the Guild contacts you about the diagnostics, tell them you want to work with Willa Danvers-Jones. See what she has to say."

"Fair enough, and I will. We'd better go back to the others. Jack promised me he'd call as soon as he was done with the police."

"How long do you think that will take?"

"God only knows. An hour at least. The police will want to go out to the house, I should think, to interview Maureen. They can't act on Jack's say-so alone."

I hesitated. What I wanted to do bordered on the dangerous, but in my mind I could hear Cam's two kids, begging me to stay. Thanks to the strange ways of the multiverse and my family, they belonged to me now, I realized, not as a son and daughter, no, more like a niece and nephew, but kinfolk nonetheless.

"Dad, will you do something for me? Could you open the gate just long enough for me to leave something up there for the kids? A present, to let them know I'll see them again if I can. They're mourning their mother, and my being there helped."

For a moment he looked utterly puzzled; then he smiled. "And why not?" he said. "If nothing else, we can just slide it across like Ari was planning to do with your bag."

I took the bag with us when we went upstairs to the gate room. The dusty book that Ari had been fiddling with while we talked was an illustrated edition of Kipling's *Just So Stories*. I cleaned it off with tissues and wrote on the flyleaf, "For Donnie and Beth from Aunt Rose. Love you!" Dad produced a yellow-green orb from nowhere that I could see.

"I always keep a few nearby now," is all he would tell me. "I learned my lesson on the night they arrested me."

He opened the gate as easily as I would have opened a door. As the green-and-beige room on Terra Six solidified around us, I realized that the floor lamp in the other Nola's lair was glowing. Cam had come upstairs at some time earlier. He was sitting in the middle of the room on the floor, just sitting there, numb from his loss. He stared at us, started to speak, choked on the words. He scrambled to his feet and stared the more.

"Cam, I'm sorry I had to leave the way I did," I said. "I brought something for the kids so they'll know I'm not just deserting them." I held out the book. "Ari's got an anger management problem. I had to get him out of here before he blew."

"I could see that, yeah." He glanced at Dad and stiffened. "Flann? Flann!"

"Not the one you're thinking of," Dad said. "I don't know what wild story Nola told you, but it's doubtless all true. Other world levels, that sort of thing?"

Cam nodded and took the book from me.

"I'm this Nola's father," Dad went on. "Not your wife's. My condolences, and I mean that from the heart. It's a hard thing, losing someone you love."

"Yes. Thanks." Cam looked as stunned as if he were the

one with the concussion. He swallowed heavily, rubbed his fingers on the book as if to reassure himself that it existed, then finally found his voice. "Beth said you'd be back to give them a present. Damned if she wasn't right."

"Cam," I said, "those stories of hers aren't just stories. She's probably right about a lot of things."

Cam gave me a twisted little smile of pure disbelief.

"If she's got O'Grady blood," Dad said, "then you're going to have a fine time of it, raising her. You and I will have a talk about this, but we've got to go back now. This gate's not as stable as it might be."

"All right." Cam tried to say more, then gave it up. He hefted the book. "Thanks."

"You're welcome." Dad said it before I could. "And don't worry. You're not alone in this anymore."

Cam seemed to be about to speak, but the room began to darken. He disappeared. We'd returned to the clutter of the storage room on Terra Four.

Dad joined the family in the living room to wait for Jack's call. I decided to see if Jerry was awake and coherent, by no means a sure bet on weekends. When I went back to the kitchen, Ari followed me. I sat down at the table and took my phone out of my shoulder bag. He stood over me and shoved his hands hard into his jeans pockets, as if he needed to keep them confined. I felt the beginnings of a SAWM. Ari's not quite six feet tall, but he can loom over someone when he wants to. I had to tip my head back to look him in the face.

"What were you doing upstairs?" His voice radiated suspicion.

I considered lying, then rejected the idea as too dangerous. Dad might give the truth away. "Dad opened the gate for me," I said, "so I could leave a message and a present for the kids."

"Oh. Right, of course. The children. Did you see them?"

I disliked the way he was looking at me, a minute examination as if he were hoping for clues to feed his jealousy.

"No," I said. "I gave the book to their father."

"Their father. Right."

"Dad was there, too. We're not done talking about Cam Douglas, are we?"

"No." He hesitated, shifted his weight from one foot to the other, then finally sat down opposite me at the table. "I'm sorry. I should be able to just put it behind me."

"I have never heard a falser apology."

I'd been too blunt. He half-rose from his chair with a look so cold that I snatched handfuls of Qi in case I needed an ensorcellment. He caught himself and sat back down. I let the Qi disperse.

"Why should you be sorry?" I continued in the spirit of better hung for a sheep than a lamb. "You only found out a couple of hours ago. It must have been a shock."

"True. But I know how you work with sexual Qi. I've felt it." He tried to smile and failed. "And I know you can use that sort of energy to do things like contact your brother. I do believe you. I just—" He leaned forward in his chair and held out both hands, a little way apart as if he could trap an explanation between them. "I don't even know what I'm getting at."

"Ari, look. Sex obviously means something real different to you than it does to me. When I first met you, I figured you were the kind of guy who just chalks up scores and moves on. It's been different between us."

He shrugged again. "I wouldn't want to marry you if I was going to go around seducing other women. Do you believe me?"

"Yeah, I do. I don't want to go around seducing other guys, either. But sex is something I used to see as a tool, part of my skill set, I guess I mean. I'm not exactly detached from it, especially not with you. I don't plan on ever sleeping with any other guy ever again, but I sure didn't plan on falling into bed with Cam, either. It really was a desperate measure."

"I know that. Which is why I'm annoyed with my own reaction."

I could hear the anger management class in that statement. Ari didn't believe what he was saying, but it was a start. Inwardly, I thanked his superior officer in the army, the one who'd made him go. I leaned across the table and touched Ari's hand.

"What counts with me is that I love you," I said. "That's something I'd never say to any other guy. That's yours alone. I promise."

"I love you, too. That's the problem, isn't it?" He winced and leaned back in his chair. "That's a crappy thing for me to say."

I waited. He squirmed in the chair, straightened up, glanced away, looked at me again.

"I don't want to talk about this anymore at the moment," he said. "Can you accept that?"

"Yes, I can. Like I said, you only found out a few hours ago."

"I do love you." He hesitated. "I'd rather show you how much, but you're too far away to kiss. Hold on a moment."

I smiled. We both got up and met in the middle for a good, long embrace. With kisses, more than one, I'm glad to say, until I felt the family overlap. I pulled away.

"Jack's about to call," I said. "I really want to hear this."

"So do I. Sanchez, by the way, hasn't been able to get Maureen into the Witness Protection program. Apparently, the head of the narcotics division thinks that Maureen may have colluded with Trasker when it came to the drug deals."

"She never would have!"

"Even if she had, she'd still be turning state's evidence. Worth protecting, I should think."

We started walking down the long hallway.

"The one thing Narcotics will do for us is put arresting Trasker for drugs on a high priority," Ari continued. "That's quite a concession, because he did his dealing over in Livermore, not in their jurisdiction. Unfortunately, it's the only one they'll make."

I said something extremely unladylike. Ari grimaced but agreed.

"Sanchez is going to see what he can do sub fusc," he went on. "Unofficially, if you take my meaning."

Since Chuck had actually shot at Maureen, the San Anselmo police were prepared to take her predicament more seriously than Sanchez did, or so Jack told Dad when he called. I figured that Jack's money and social position were helping their attitude as well. Unfortunately, they could do little for her unless she filed a restraining order in Marin County. Once again, however, she'd have to notify Chuck she was doing so, an incitement to violence if I ever heard of one.

"If she files the correct papers," Ari told us, "someone else can do the notifying for her. I'll be quite glad to do so. He won't give me much trouble, I should think. The real problem is that no one knows where he is."

"Catch twenty-two," Sean muttered. "There always is one."

I felt a brief desire to scream in frustration.

"The one thing they could come up with," Dad continued his report, "is that she should stay inside where he can't see her. And then if he comes around, call them, and they'll pick him up on illegal weapon charges. It turns out that he has a prior felony conviction."

"Like he's going to just stand there and let them," Michael said. "Dad, this sucks!"

"It sure does," I said. "Look, though, I do have one contact who might know where Trasker's hiding out. If he does, maybe we can get him arrested before anything ugly happens."

"Can you call this bloke?" Ari said.

"Sure. I'll go do it now, or rather, I'll call one of my co-workers. He'll have to do the interviewing for us. The guy I have in mind won't talk if you're there, Ari, and I'm not about to go out without a bodyguard."

"Could we get Maureen a bodyguard?" Aunt Eileen put in. "Can you just hire them?"

"Oh, yes," Ari said. "But Jack told me that Trasker has a sniper rifle. A bodyguard won't be able to prevent him from using it. It's got too long a range."

Ari tactfully stayed in the living room when I returned to the privacy of the kitchen and my phone. By then, in the late afternoon, Jerry was indeed awake and reasonably sober. When I told him the situation, he agreed to question his roommate.

"I can't lie, darling," Jerry said, "and tell you that he'll be able to help. It's not that he won't want to. It's just that his mind's been scrambled for years. We don't call him Wakko Yakko for nothing."

"What? He samples his own goods?"

"Not anymore, no, but alas for abstinence! Too late!"

Not a good sign, no, and when Jerry called me back that evening, he had no information for me. His roommate had a vague recollection of having met Chuck Trasker, but as to where Trasker might have currently been or what he might have been doing, Wakko knew nothing.

"Something might come back to him," Jerry told me. "He has occasional eruptions of brain activity."

"Okay, I'll hope for that. Thanks anyway."

By then, Ari and I had returned home after a large, noisy family dinner, although Dad had gone back to his apartment and my mother. She and I had called a truce in our long war too recently to be at ease in each other's company. Besides, seeing Dad and Sean glare at each other over the food would not have helped my shattered nerves or Aunt Eileen's, either.

I'd been dreading seeing our flat again because I was sure it'd be an awful mess. Ari had been living alone in it for ten days, during which he'd been frantic and depressed in turns. Much to my surprise, when we got home I found it nice and tidy except for a stack of pizza boxes that he'd forgotten to put into the recycling.

"Did you hire someone to come in?" I said.

"No." Ari looked down at the reasonably clean kitchen floor. "Picking things up gave me something to do in the evenings. It kept me from thinking too much about what I'd done. I suppose it was magical thinking, too. If I made the place look decent, you'd be more likely to come back to it."

"You've always done half the work around here anyway."

He nodded and studied the flowers on our worn Persian carpet.

"I'm going to put this bag away," I said.

When I headed for the bedroom, I expected him to follow me. He didn't. I slung the bag onto the dresser and paused to look in the mirror at the scar on my forehead. The scabs had begun peeling to reveal the pale, overly slick tissue underneath. The bruise on my chin had faded to a faint yellow stain. I shuddered and turned away. I changed my shirt—I'd been wearing one of the other Nola's—before I left the bedroom. I put on the v-necked green top that Ari liked so much.

Ari was sitting on the couch with the TV on but muted, flipping aimlessly through the channels. He glanced up at me with an expression that told me nothing. His SPP, on the other hand, read as a tangle of lust, love, and sheer cold anger.

"Do you really want to watch TV?" I said.

"No." He turned it off and set the remote down on the coffee table.

I considered where to sit. A chair would have been safer,

but I couldn't bear to have distance between us. When I sat next to him on the couch, he turned toward me.

"I left you there." He spat it out. "The whole thing was my own sodding fault."

"I wasn't going to say that."

"Good. Thank you." He shoved his right fist hard into the palm of his left hand. "If I'd glanced back, if I'd only glanced back, I would have seen you. The others could have gone through. I knew we had a second orb in your bag. I could have picked you up and then thrown the—"

"Stop!" I laid a hand on his arm. "You've been rehearsing this over and over, haven't you? For days."

He nodded and slumped back against the cushions. "Do you know why I threw it too soon?" he said.

"No. Do you need to tell me?"

He nodded and stared across the room. "This whole business with orbs and the like. It frightens me. If it hadn't, I would have waited to throw the sodding thing until I'd cleared it with you. I wanted to get it over with."

"That's a perfectly natural reaction, I think. I got used to the idea of world levels and orbs and all this stuff fairly quickly because of the way I was raised. You didn't grow up in a family like mine."

"Yes, I did!" He turned his head and looked me in the face. "That's what you forget. That's what I want to forget. The whole sodding kibbutz, my mother's visions, all the talk of aliens—I don't know why, but I hated it all. Once we left, I did my best to keep from thinking about it, but—" He took a deep breath. "But there it is. I can't escape it. At times it catches up with me."

I should have seen it long before, I realized. He'd been determined to pretend the entire psychic world simply didn't exist, that it was all delusions and lies. He'd blocked it out of his mind so completely for so long that I'd responded to the block, not to what I rationally knew to be true.

"This is why TWIXT was so eager to enlist you, isn't it?" I said.

"Oh, yes. I never should have gone for it. Too late now."

I could think of fifty things to say. None would have helped. Ari slumped down a little farther on the couch, stretched his legs out in front of him, and rested his head on the sofa back. Distantly, I could hear the sea muttering at high tide. The beach was only a couple of blocks from our flat. Although I knew he was waiting for me to speak, I had to think things through first. It would have been too easy to just let him go on blaming himself for everything. That way I could avoid remembering the first time I'd let Cam make love to me, when all I'd wanted was the comfort of his arms.

"You have the right to be angry with me," I said. "Yes, I did what I felt I had to do. But that still means I had sex with someone else."

His expression twisted, as sour as bitter lemons.

"Look," I said. "I would never leave you for him. If it weren't for the kids, I'd never see him again. He needs to forget me and get over his wife's death in the normal way. By grieving, that is, not by trying to pretend she's still alive."

"Rationally, I know all that."

"Feelings aren't rational."

He shrugged, but I could feel his anger fading into hurt, a raw male animal hurt.

"I look at you," Ari said, "and I feel like I can see his fingerprints all over you. I know that's stupid of me."

"Oh, stop! Don't keep running yourself down! That's making things worse."

He took another deep breath and nodded his agreement.

"If you can see the fingerprints, let's go wash them off." I got up and held out my hand. "Come on."

For a moment I was afraid he'd refuse. Then he got up and caught my hand in both of his. "A shower together?" he said.

"Yeah, but you get to scrub me down. Doesn't water purify people, out in the desert? Like at Qumran?"

"Yes. I've seen the site. They had rather a lot of stone bathtubs."

We both managed to smile at that. I kicked off my shoes and let him lead me to the bathroom. I let him undress me, too. He pulled the top over my head, then took off my bra, worked his way down and tossed each piece into the hallway to deal with later, until I stood shivering and naked. I watched him take off his clothes and throw them after mine. He got the shower started, then pushed me—gently, but it was still a push—into the comfortably hot water. When he joined me, he grabbed the bar of soap and rubbed it all over me, thoroughly, a little roughly in places.

I did the same for him. I washed my hair and then his, while he knelt on the shower floor and sputtered now and then at the water in his face. Thank Whomever, the hot water held out long enough for our improvised ritual. When we'd finished and dried off, he picked me up and carried me into the bedroom. He laid me down on the bed but stayed standing.

"Looking for fingerprints?" I said.

"Yes."

"See any?"

"No." He sat down on the edge of the bed next to me. "I'd best make sure mine are there instead."

And he did. Twice. He was rougher with me than usual, more intense, certainly, controlling me by pinning my hands to the bed with his, letting me feel his weight and muscle. You know that old euphemism, "He possessed her?" I understood it that night. I was being possessed, treated like territory, marked as his. In the heat of it, I didn't mind in the least.

Yet, although the sex was as good as ever, I knew something had changed between us—or was the change mine?

We both fell asleep, snuggled under the covers, but I woke up a few hours later to find he'd moved over to his side of the bed. I lay in the dark for a while, thinking—or perhaps brooding was a better word for it. I was worried about Cam's kids and about Maureen and her kids. Even if Chuck vanished from the face of the earth overnight, Caitlin and Brennan would carry scars from the entire experience of first living with him, then seeing their mother stalked. No matter how safe our family made their world from now on, they would know that worlds are never safe. Donnie and Beth had learned the same lesson in an even more painful way.

Beth had the first small symptoms of a talent, too, which would make things worse for her as she grew up. Her mother had tried to stifle the talent in her daughter just as she'd stifled her own. What would I have done if I'd married my Cam Douglas? The same thing, probably, if we'd had a child who showed the symptoms. My mother would have aided and abetted me in that. She'd tried so hard to kill her own gifts over the years. Sometimes your own family holds the danger in its heart. I knew that. I'd learned it the hard way, when she'd thrown me out of the house for protecting my future.

Ari had learned a hard lesson, too. I supposed that he would never believe me faithful again, no matter how hard we tried to work things out, not in the way men want to define "faithful," sheer utter devotion, no eyes for anyone but them, and a blind eye turned to their own infidelities. He'd probably start leaning even harder on me to marry him. He'd want the proof that I'd do what he asked just because he wanted it.

I slipped out of bed and padded barefoot out into the hall. Our clothes still lay where he'd thrown them. We'd left the light on in the living room, too. I got dressed and walked on down the hall. When I looked out of the bay window, I could see the late spring fog swirling down the street like smoke. I shivered and turned up the thermostat to make the heat go on.

I considered working. I probably had a huge backlog of e-mail. I needed to tell the Agency I'd returned and give them a full report of the situation on Terra Six. Ari had mentioned during our drive home that Spare14 had sent me authorized intel reports on various subjects. I still had Shira Flowertree's data to study as well. If I plunged into this ocean of words, I could stop thinking about Ari and Cam and Maureen and all the children. I could stop thinking about myself. I'd used work as a drug and a cover before, to convince myself that I wasn't lonely, that I didn't care about the men who told me they loved me and then fled the minute they realized that my family would swallow them whole.

I heard a shuffling sound in the hallway. I went tense, expecting an enemy or maybe just a Chaos critter, another damn squid. Instead, Ari walked into the living room. He paused by the doorway to finish zipping up his jeans, the only piece of clothing he had on at the moment.

"Nola?" he said. "Is something wrong?"

"I don't know." I felt impossibly tired, all of a sudden. "Is there?"

He sat down on the couch and patted the cushion next to him. I hesitated, then came over and sat.

"Of course there's still something wrong," he said, "but that doesn't mean there will be forever. You're not trying to make me leave you, are you? I did have that thought, that you might want to just get rid of me."

It had never occurred to me that he might ever feel insecure.

"What?" I could barely speak. "No!"

He held out an arm. I slid over and snuggled up to him. He sighed and pulled me even closer.

"This is rather like having a bad cold, isn't it?" Ari said.

"We know we'll get over it, but it's quite unpleasant for the duration."

"That's for sure." I rested my head on his shoulder. "We need psychological nose tissues."

He muttered his usual tormented chuckle. We sat in silence for a few minutes.

"There's one last thing I have to tell you," he said. "I apologize for taking so long to come around to it."

Dread tastes like tonic water, the bitter quinine kind. I pulled away and turned slightly so I could see his face.

"I've been reprimanded for the incident," Ari continued. "For throwing the sodding orb too soon, that is. It's in my file. It's not the first write-up I've ever had, but all the others were in the army, and they were all for my sodding temper."

"What? I don't understand. Why would they—"

"I disobeyed your direct order. I didn't wait."

What do you do when you can think of absolutely nothing to say and someone you love needs you to say something? I made an odd little choking noise. "I'm sorry," I finally came out with that.

"They'll want you to sign off on it."

First impulse: say I won't. Squelched that. "I'll have to read it first," I said. "There were circumstances they probably don't understand."

"You don't have to make excuses for me."

"I won't."

"Good."

"You mean that, don't you?"

"Yes."

"That's another reason I love you."

He started to speak, then merely sighed. We sat in silence again and watched the digital clock on my desk flash red minutes.

"It's three o'clock in the sodding morning," he said. "Come back to bed, will you?"

"Sure. Good idea."

This time I turned out the living room light. We returned to the bedroom and went back to sleep.

The first thing I did in the morning was open the wall safe, get out my engagement ring, and put it on. The second thing I did was remember the reprimand. I took the ring off and put it back into its box. Ari quirked an eyebrow.

"Aren't we engaged any longer?" he said.

I realized I'd just hurt feelings I didn't know he had. "Of course we're still engaged," I said. "I don't want to wear it while I've got housework and stuff to do."

He smiled in relief. I hurried out of the room to pick up the rest of the clothing we'd left lying in the hall. I was stuffing his shirt into the dirty clothes hamper when I remembered that Cam needed to hire a housekeeper. Someone had to be there when the kids came home from school. In my mind I could hear Beth's singsong about Aunt Maureen. Ari, who was getting dressed, turned to me.

"What?" Ari said. "You've got that look on your face again."

"I just had an idea. It depends on whether or not that gate in the Houlihan house is really stable, but if it is, I wonder if Maureen would be interested in a housekeeping job. Cam has plenty of room for her and the kids. She'd be safe from Chuck there. Dad could stay in touch through the gate. She could even visit us."

"True, but what about the terrorists?"

"Good point. Unfortunately. Although they don't know or care that she exists. If she stayed out in the Excelsior, away from the danger zones? If they stayed in L.A.?"

"Possibly." He crossed his arms over his chest and scowled. "I suppose you'd need to go talk to him about it."

"Not me. Dad will take care of it. Besides, she's beautiful, she's another O'Grady, and she's a lot closer to his age than his wife was. I bet they'd get along famously."

Ari relaxed. "It sounds like an ideal solution." He smiled his tight-lipped tiger's smile. "For everyone concerned."

"Especially the children." I decided to leave his implication alone. "They've been through hell, all four of them, though the Douglas kids have had it the worst, losing their mother. I just hope they never figure out exactly how she died."

"Bad?"

"Her legs were crushed by falling masonry, and then she burned to death."

His face lost all expression, a sign that he was deeply moved.

"Izumi's right," I said eventually. "Those terrorists, they're crazy. They don't care who they kill or how."

"Oh, yes. Which reminds me. Spare14 sent us a report on Izumi's testimony. She's in custody on One. The public solicitor there is working out a plea bargaining agreement, but I don't know how lenient they can be."

"She was an accessory to attempted murder at the least." I was thinking of Murphy, the world-walker who'd been stabbed and robbed. "God only knows what else she was involved in."

"Yes. You need to eat, by the way. Eileen sent some of those scones home with us. Can I interest you in some jam? And butter?"

"Sure. But if you want tuna fish on yours, please eat it in the other room."

He wandered off to the kitchen. I sat down at my computer. As it was booting up, I realized that Ari had been home alone with both my desktop and my laptop. Had he messed with them? I had boot passwords and encryptions, sure, but they could be cracked. The desktop security routines showed no tampering. On the other hand, Ari was good at what he did. Anything on TranceWeb would be safe, I supposed. You can't hack what you can't see.

When I logged onto the Web, I found a string of e-mails from Y among all the usual bureaucratic crud. I read the most recent of them and learned that the liaison with TWIXT was going forward. He wanted to tell me that he was reconciled to the new arrangement. He also hoped that someday I'd be "in a position" to read his e-mail, which I interpreted as meaning "still alive." Much to my shock, he admitted that he'd made a bad decision by not giving me official status. I assumed that he'd written that particular sentence after Annie had blistered his metaphoric hide.

I sent him a brief note, allowing as how I was home safe and sound, had read the e-mail about the liaison, and approved. The answer came back about one minute after I sent it. "You can't know how glad I am to hear from you. Trance meeting later in the week. Explanations to follow then. Y." He'd been keeping an eye on his e-mail on Sunday. Good, I thought. I hope he suffered!

I switched to my other e-mail address, glanced through the short queue, and found the letter I was dreading: from Spare14 concerning the reprimand. He hadn't been the one to write Ari up; he made that clear in his first sentence. The official note was brief and to the point.

"Agent Nathan acted in haste. He failed to consult his superior officer before taking action. Case pending until the final outcome is received and noted. Superior officer may be permanently lost thanks to Nathan's reckless action. If so, recommendation is full hearing for possible dismissal."

"Crud!" I muttered.

Spare14 had added a note of his own to me. "If you're reading this, O'Grady, you're not lost, and I sincerely hope that's true. Since I know certain things about your family, I insisted that the case be left on pending status. Some officers at HQ did not approve of the unusual recruitment procedure I pushed through for Nathan. I suspect that may be a factor in their eagerness to reprimand. One of them, I

fear, is my own clone-brother, Spare13. We have had fraternal difficulties before."

Fraternal difficulties. Even a batch of clones had to deal
with family politics. There's no escape, I thought, and sent
Spare14 a quick answer: I'm alive, I'm here, and no, I won't
sign off on the reprimand as it now stands.

Ari returned from the kitchen with food and coffee,
which he set down on the coffee table. I logged off and
joined him on the sofa. Being home felt so good that I ate
an entire scone and some yogurt without even thinking
about it. He smiled at me and picked a crumb off my décolletage. I was about to suggest that we go for a walk on our
day off when the phone in his shirt pocket rang. He retrieved it.

"Nathan here. Yes? Right . . . we'll get down as fast as we
can. Dress officially? No, blend with the locals. Very well. I
see . . . yes, I'll tell her."

So much for Sunday rest and recreation. I thought of a
number of unladylike remarks but kept them to myself. Ari
clicked off and stowed the phone.

"That was Spare14," he said. "Important intel's come in
from Hendriks on Three. We need to get down to the office.
Danvers-Jones will meet us in South Park after the briefing."

"On the run again! What is it that you're supposed to
tell me?"

"That the Agency contacted him just now. You're officially on loan to TWIXT for the duration of this case. He'll
have the proper ID waiting for you."

"And a communicator?"

"Definitely. I'll make sure of that." He laid a finger on
my lips and stared into my eyes. "No more of those desperate measures, thank you very much."

CHAPTER 14

THE BRIEFING WAS BRIEF, very: both Jan Hendriks
and an informant had seen the Axeman in SanFran on
Terra Three. HQ wanted us to follow up the sightings in
person. Spare14 handed over my TWIXT liaison ID and
one of their tiny but powerful black plastic communicators.
I noticed that the ID read, in part, "certified police psychic,"
which turned my earlier lie to Lupe Parra y Cruz into truth.
The leather ID case had a tidy pocket on the back for the
pink gel square that monitored radiation exposure.

Once we'd settled these details, I had a sad but necessary
duty to perform. The *Star Trek* omen had proved true.

"I was really sorry to hear about JaMarcus Spivey's
death," I said. "My condolences."

"Thank you. He will be missed."

His SPP poured out grief, but his face showed no expression at all. For a long moment we all kept silence. Eventually, Spare14 swallowed heavily and cleared his throat.

"Oh, by the way," Spare14 said. "I did receive your
e-mail, O'Grady. Very glad to see you back alive and well."

"Thanks," I said. "I figured I should respond as fast as possible."

We both compulsively glanced at Ari, then looked away again, two heads swiveling as one.

"Shall I leave the room?" Ari said.

Spare14 glanced at his watch. "Yes, if you wouldn't mind," he said. "Danvers-Jones won't reach this level for some while yet."

"There's a liquor store down at the other end of the alley." Ari got up from his chair. "I'll go see if they carry energy bars. O'Grady may need one later."

Spare14 and I waited to speak until we could no longer hear his footsteps on the stairs.

"I realize," Spare14 said, "that this reprimand produces a very dicey situation for you."

"That's putting it mildly. I've been thinking. The central issue is, am I really Nathan's superior officer? In matters concerning the Agency, yes. Concerning TWIXT—what's your opinion?"

"That you certainly were nothing of the sort on Terra Six. At that time you had observer status only."

"Exactly! Here in San Francisco Four, he's my bodyguard, and I'm in charge. But we were in San Francisco Six when the incident occurred."

Although Spare14 kept his expression strictly neutral, I could sense his relief.

"We need to clarify this issue," I went on. "The way I see it is this. He's on loan to the Agency here on Four. I'm on loan to TWIXT elsewhere. I doubt if either of us is a superior officer to the other. Partners is more like it. A functional unit."

"That's an excellent way to think of it. It's an unusual situation all round. I'm afraid that the Operations staff dislike unusual situations."

"That kind of personnel always does."

"Alas, quite true! I shall write and ask for an official statement on the matter, but I have no doubt that your opinion and mine will prevail."

"Since I'm not his superior officer, I can't sign off on the reprimand. I can't remove it from his file either, of course."

"Nor can I remove it, but I do have the power to modify it. I shall do so. There's absolutely no reason for any sort of hearing, much less a full one."

"Sure isn't. For one thing, I'm not lost."

"Quite. He was reckless, however. Although he was under no obligation to follow an order from you, it would have been wise to do as you requested. I'm afraid that note will have to remain in his file."

"Yes, I have to agree. That's just the way Nathan is."

"It's one reason I was so keen on having him join us. Not that you should tell him so. Please don't! But we require agents who can and will act quickly. Sometimes that leads to mistakes. It's merely one of the hazards of our peculiar sort of police work."

"It's the same with the Agency. There are times when caution's counterproductive."

"Just so."

"I'm glad we understand each other."

We both smiled at a job well done. Curiosity poked me about an entirely different issue.

"Please forgive me," I said, "and tell me to shut up if you'd like, but about Spare Thirteen, I guess you guys don't really get along?"

"We're too much alike." Spare14 made this remark with a perfectly straight face. "It's a common difficulty with clones. We tend to get on each other's nerves."

"I can see that. I'm not much older than my sister Kathleen. We fought all the time we were growing up."

"I can well imagine it. Thirteen and I were decanted at approximately the same time. He's an hour and seven minutes older." His expression soured. "He's always held that over me."

The buzzer from the front door sounded. Rather than picking the lock as he usually did, Ari had let us know that he'd returned. Spare14 got up from his chair.

"I'll just go down," he said. "Nathan deserves to know what we decided."

They spent some minutes talking at the bottom of the stairs. When they came back up, Ari appeared more relaxed than he had since my return. Spare14 glanced at his watch.

"You'd really best get on your way," he said. "I'll contact HQ first thing on the morrow."

Rather than distract Ari while he drove, I said nothing about the reprimand until we parked in the usual exorbitantly priced garage near South Park. As we headed out on foot, I brought the matter up.

"Do you think HQ will agree to Spare14's solution?" I said. "That we're equal partners, that is?"

"He thinks so, and his is the opinion that counts." Ari caught my hand and grinned. "Well done, O'Grady."

"Thanks, Nathan." I returned the grin. "Crud! I could have worn my ring after all."

"Just as well you didn't. It might have been seen as flaunting our relationship. Spare14 could never have overlooked that."

We hurried down the last block to the greenery of the park. Willa waited for us on her usual bench. Before we left, she told us that she'd be returning to Terra Four immediately after transporting us to Three.

"I'm meeting with your father today, Nola," Willa told me. "He mentioned that you'd talked with him about the research arm. Thanks. I appreciate it."

"You're welcome. You do know about his multi-purpose gate, don't you?"

"I sure do. The one he built." Her voice dropped into

awe. "He built it. He built a gate." She shook herself with a little shudder. "And the damn fool never told anyone about it. Well, sorry, but that was an affectionate use of damn fool."

"I figured that." I grinned at her. "He can be real stubborn."

"You probably know that better'n I do. But come on, let's get you and Nathan to Three. You've got a transport orb for Four to get you home?"

"Yep." I patted my shoulder bag. "And this time I'm not letting go of it."

Willa brought us through to South Park version 3.0, then switched focus orbs and disappeared back across the worlds. Ari used his communicator to call Jan, who said he'd come pick us up. I sat down on the bench to wait. While I carved myself out a space to operate in the overcrowded aura field of Interchange, Ari stayed standing and kept watch. I'd just managed to come to terms with the buzz and chatter of other psychic minds when I heard the rattle of the cobbled-together car and the blat blat of its horn. I noticed that the mostly black car had acquired some green fenders since I'd last seen it.

"You'd best sit in back," Ari said. "Keep your head down as much as possible."

"Are you telling me that someone could shoot at us?"

"That's always a possibility here, isn't it? But if the Axeman should see us . . ."

"Yeah, I get it. If he's still on this world level, anyway."

As I got into the back seat, Jan turned around to greet me. He was wearing another hideous shirt, this one lime-green with orange parrots on it. Big orange parrots, and one of them, stretched tight over a lump, looked as if it had swallowed a shoulder holster.

"What?" Ari pointed at the shirt. "Another one?"

"Allegedly, I'm from Aruba," Jan said. "Tropical, you

know. The Netherlands here on Three are mostly underwater."

"Very well." Ari slid into the front seat. "Where are we going?"

"Wagner's first," Jan said. "He's the one source of illegal orbs that we know. I'm wondering if he's sold any for Six lately."

With assorted rattles and a cough from the clutch, the car started off. I slid down and turned sideways in the back seat to keep my head below the rear window. Since I could see out the side window, I noticed that the streets around the park were deserted on this Sunday morning. I doubted if many of the local citizens had gone to church. Sleeping off Saturday night struck me as a more likely explanation. Market Street, too, when we jounced and bounced across the streetcar tracks, lacked any sign of traffic.

"Say," I said, "won't Wagner's be closed?"

"Theoretically." Jan had to shout over the noise that the car was making. "But he lives behind the shop. If we pound on the door hard enough, we should be able to rouse him. If not, Nathan has his little ways and his pieces of wire."

"The locks here," Ari said, "are surprisingly low tech. Well, perhaps not surprisingly."

Sure enough, when Jan pulled up in front of the bookstore, the front window was dark, and a stained cardboard sign on the door announced, "Closed." Ari got out of the car and slipped his hand inside his shirt, unbuttoned to give him easy access to the Beretta. He looked up and down the street, then beckoned to me. I uncramped myself and slid out of the back seat. As soon as I got free of the metal compartment, I sensed old danger and pain.

"Ari," I said. "Open the door. Wagner might be dead inside."

Ari pulled a lockpick from his jeans pocket and strode across the sidewalk. As soon he touched the knob, the door swung partway open. Behind me, Jan swore and killed the engine. When he joined me on the sidewalk, he had his gun in hand. Ari drew his and kicked the door wide open. No one called out or shot at him. I ran a quick scan.

"The danger's over," I said. "Whatever happened, happened early."

"Good," Jan said to me. "Move! Let's get off the street."

I dashed across the sidewalk and followed Ari inside. Jan came in after me and shut the door. A dim glow from an open door behind the counter provided the only light in the store. We picked our way through the stacks of books and the maze of shelves with the occasional bump and Hebrew expletive from Ari in the lead. Now and then I heard the slither and thump of a pile of books sliding to the floor. I stepped over each heap and forged onward.

"Wagner!" Ari called out. "CBI! Are you here?"

Someone behind the wooden counter groaned and made a scrabbling sound, as if they were trying to haul themselves to their feet.

"Just lie still," Ari said.

He kicked a last pile of books out of the way. Once he had turned on the gooseneck lamp, he glanced over the counter, swore, and holstered the Beretta.

"They did a pretty good job on you, didn't they?" Ari strode around back and knelt out of my view. "Here. I'll help you sit up. O'Grady, see if you can find some water and a towel. Hendriks, if you'll guard the door?"

"Will do," Jan said. "I need to keep an eye on the car, too."

I went through the open door on the back wall into what must have been Wagner's living quarters: a long, narrow, and surprisingly clean room. At the near end I found an easy chair and a lighted floor lamp. Books sat neatly stacked on an end table. In the middle of the room stood a narrow bed, made up with a faded blue coverlet, and down at the far end, a wooden table, two chairs, and a counter with a sink on one side and a pair of wrought iron gas rings on the other. Next to the single window, a freestanding cabinet held crockery. I found a serving bowl, filled it with cold water, and snagged a pair of reasonably clean dish towels.

By the time I came back out, Ari had gotten Wagner sitting up in a chair behind the counter. Mitch's face was so badly bruised, scraped, and swollen that it looked like a meatloaf with a broken nose. Both of his eyes had swollen shut. When he opened his bleeding lips to draw a deep breath, I saw that he'd lost a couple of teeth.

"Pistol whipped," Ari said cheerfully. "O'Grady, if you'd just get one of those towels wet and hand it to me?"

I did. Wagner mumbled a few words that might have been thank you. He squealed when Ari started to wash the blood off the wounds, but he held still for the process. I returned to his room, found a bathroom off the kitchen area, and rummaged around in an old-fashioned medicine chest, the kind that looks like a suitcase, till I found a bottle of aspirin and some iodine.

It took some while before Wagner could tell us what had happened. Even then, Ari mostly asked leading questions which he answered yes or no. The story boiled down to the Axeman and a goon wanting orbs for Six and Wagner not having orbs for Six or anywhere else, for that matter. The Axeman had flown into a rage. While the goon had held Wagner's arms pinned behind his back, the Axeman had taken his anger out on the man who was telling him things he didn't want to hear.

"Jeez," I said, "it was his daughter who killed their supplier. What did the Axeman expect?"

Wagner turned his head slowly in my direction and peered out of the one functional slit between the lids of his left eye. "Ash?" he said. "Daughter?"

"You didn't know?" I said. "Yeah, she is. She's the one who knifed Scott Trotter."

"Shit." Wagner managed to say it again. "Shit." He turned his head very slowly to scan the counter with his one working eye. He said a few words that I finally deciphered as "paper and pencil" when he made a writing motion with his right hand. The letter P gave his bruised lips a lot of trouble.

I found the requested items and gave them to him. He wrote slowly, painfully, but with less pain and more clarity than he could talk. When he handed the sheet to me, I read it aloud.

"Ash is on Six. That's why the Axe is panicked. He can't get there."

"Well, well, well," Ari said. "How very interesting! Do you know where he's staying?"

No, Wagner didn't. I got the distinct impression that if he had, he'd have been glad to tell us. The last thing he wrote, before we left him alone to heal, was, "I hope you get him. Kick him in the balls for me."

On the way out Ari locked the door with his lockpick, just in case, he said, the Axeman tried to get back in.

"Is Wagner going to be all right?" I said.

"Eventually. Well, the teeth are gone forever, and he might lose the sight in one eye, but overall, he got off lightly."

"Lightly?" Jan said.

"I once found the corpse of a man who'd been beaten to death with a pistol," Ari said. "Not a pretty sight. Back when I was in the army."

"Terrorist activity, I suppose?" Jan said.

"No. A jealous husband, a Jew, killed him, not a Muslim. That sort of thing happens in a country where men still worry about their honor."

Call me paranoid, but for a brief moment I wondered if I'd been given a message.

We returned to Jan's office, where he made us some decent coffee. He'd replaced Spare14's metal percolator with a proper filter system. He took the desk chair, and Ari and I sat down on the sofa.

"I don't suppose the Axeman's gone back to the Playland hideout," Ari said.

"Not likely," Jan said. "The City Council found the money to have the place leveled and cleaned up. The project's not finished, but the worst of the filth is gone, and there are workmen there most days."

"We can eliminate that, then." Ari thought for a moment. "We've only got one other lead, Peri's, that brothel over in Cow Hollow." He glanced my way. "Is that really the name of the district?"

"It's the old name," I said. "It used to be a dairy farm way back before the Civil War. Old names last in San Francisco, but most people in SF Four would just call it Union Street now."

"He may just be using Peri's as a convenient place to receive messages," Jan said. "I doubt if the madam of a high-class house like that would allow him to shelter there."

"He might be threatening her life," Ari said. "Blackmail would obviously be quite ineffective here in SanFran."

"Unless she did something saintly and wanted to hide it," I put in. "But yeah, after what he did to Wagner, threats are more likely."

"Surely she has bodyguards," Jan said. "I went over and cased the outside of the brothel. It's quite splendid. You can see it from Union, but it actually fronts on the street around the corner. A big old-fashioned house, built in the shape of an octagon. With a cupola on top, no less!"

"Have you been inside?" Ari said.

"Unfortunately, not. I heard enough about it from the

locals to realize that a man with my cover story could never afford its services. Rather than risk being thrown out, I never went in."

"Pity." Ari was suppressing a smile. "We could have used the intel."

Jan started to speak, glanced my way, then gave me a sheepish smile. I did my best to ignore his embarrassment. I knew the building, or rather its respectable sister in San Francisco Four, a semi-public museum now with lots of open space inside. Before the conversion, it must have been a warren of small rooms and narrow hallways like all Victorian homes. The one here on Three probably still was.

"Raiding it is going to be a bitch," I said.

"Whorehouse raids always are," Ari said. "When I was military police, we ran a number of those, looking for men who'd gone AWOL. Not an easy job. We need to find out if he's actually present before we risk it."

"Can we work with the local police on this?" I said. "Chief Hafner knows you as a CBI agent, Nathan, and he owes you a big favor."

"True. He also has every reason to hold a grudge against the Axeman." Ari turned to Jan. "Opinions?"

"We'll have to wait if we want the Chief's help," Jan said. "The moon will be full on Tuesday."

Ari swore in a mash-up of several languages.

"Hafner's starting the changeover to wolf form about now, probably," I said. "And he won't be ready for action for a couple of days after the waning, either."

"And of course," Jan said. "We don't even know if the Axeman's hiding out in Peri's."

"I may be able to find out," I said. "I brought my crayons."

"Good." Jan opened one of the desk drawers. "I happen to have some large-sized paper. An LDRS is exactly what we need."

A Long Distance Remote Sensing, that is, one of the first talents that an intelligence agency ever tried to use, way back during the Cold War on Four between the United States and the Soviet Union. I'm particularly gifted at this operation. I took Jan's spot at the desk, laid out a few sheets of paper, and spread my crayons next to them on the desktop for easy access.

I'd seen the Axeman once in a mirror and once in trance. The sightings gave me just enough information to focus my talent. I let my breathing slow, waited, thought of next to nothing. My hand moved on its own and grabbed a crayon. I looked across the room and let my hand draw. Different colors, lots of scribbles, some straight lines, some curved lines—finally my fingers dropped the last crayon. My hand lay flat on the desk. I shook myself awake and looked at the drawing.

The picture, messy as always, showed the interior of a high-ceilinged room with an elaborate dado on the one visible wall. It might have been stucco work; it might have been fancy wallpaper. Next to a fireplace edged in matching fancywork was an open rolltop desk. A square stood on the desk beside a bright blue scribble. I'd done the square in silver, which I took as meaning "shiny." On the other side of the fireplace stood a tall cabinet. I'd put little X's on the shelves. I had no idea what they were supposed to represent. The blue and the shiny images might have added up to a computer brought illegally from Six.

"Okay, he's inside an elegant room," I said. "Now let me run a few scans on this."

Search Mode: Location placed the room fairly nearby, to the south, and slightly to the west of us, which made the Octagon House a good candidate for the building containing it. SM: Personnel put two people into the scene, a man and a woman. I knew the man was the Axeman. The only information I could glean about the woman was her emotional state.

"She's furious at him," I said. "Frothing mad about something."

"If he's threatening her," Ari said, "of course she's angry."

"He's not threatening. He's cowering."

"What? Does she have a weapon?"

"I can't see that much detail, but I suspect she doesn't. She's chewing him out. He's feeling guilty about something."

Ari and Jan both stared, shocked. I remembered something Izumi said: "They took me off the streets and gave me a home, him and his lady."

"You know," I said, "I think we may have found Ash's mother."

"Good God!" Jan muttered. "Can you clarify if we go closer to the location?"

"You bet. Let's drive down that way. Say, when you were gathering data about this place, did anyone tell you the madam's name?"

"Yes. Karina. That's all. No last name." He grinned. "Madame Karina to scum like us."

We all trotted downstairs. Ari cranked up the car while Jan sat behind the wheel and I took my place half-hidden in the back seat. With a cough it finally started, and we rattled our way out of North Beach and down to Union Street. At home, "Union Street" means a fancy district with chichi shops and expensive bars, the kind that their owners describe as "watering holes." In SanFran it's just a street, where big Victorian houses have shops on the ground floor and cheap rooms above and behind. Under the poisoned yellow sky, we passed a farmer's market, deserted on Sunday, a couple of used clothing places, and a small house that brazenly advertised itself as an opium den.

When we turned the corner onto Gough, I saw the Octagon House, painted a pale pink with white trim. A wrought iron fence surrounded its well-kept garden, which took up about a third of a city block, far more open space than it had at home. Under a maple tree two young women, dressed in girlish white dresses, sat on a wrought iron bench. Nearby on the lawn sat a beefy-looking guy openly wearing a gun in a shoulder holster, there to protect the merchandise, I assumed.

Jan drove on by and parked down at the end of the block. "Is this close enough?" he said.

"Yeah," I said, "but I've got to get out of the car."

"I'll get out first," Ari said. "You stand behind me."

We did that. When I focused my mind on the location, I received a strong impression of the Axeman, sitting at a table in a small room and playing keno with a pack of greasy cards. I transferred my thoughts to the sense of a woman I'd received earlier, and this time I added her name to my meager information. I picked up a trace; she was preoccupied with numbers and slips of paper.

"I think she's paying bills," I said. "The Axeman's in there, all right."

Ari and I returned to the car, and Jan drove on to put some distance between us and our prey. He parked around the corner, killed the engine, and turned sidewise on the seat, as did Ari, so we could confer.

"It's too bad that I'm not still a teenager," I said. "I could go in looking for work."

"People on this world level will see you as younger than you are," Jan said. "The conditions here age everyone so fast. You'd pass for barely twenty."

"I wouldn't allow it, even if you could bring it off." Ari spoke quietly, but I could sense a rumble of rage in his SPP. "As it is, you can't, because the word's spread that both of us are CBI agents. You wouldn't get very far."

"You're right." I waited until his rage quieted down again. "Well, our wolfish police guys will be human again in a week. We could ask for help then."

"The Axeman might be long gone," Ari said.

"Yeah, that's true." I thought for a moment or two. "Especially if she throws him out."

"She's that angry?" Jan said.

"I'd say so."

"Then perhaps we can persuade her to hand him over."

"Nice thought, but how? In this town she doesn't have to be afraid of being arrested, so we can't pressure her with that." I let my mind range back to the Octagon Brothel, as I'd started thinking of it. "Ari, I need to get out of the car again."

Every time you run a Search Mode, the link between you and the subject grows a little bit stronger. This time the SM:P caught Karina in a particularly vulnerable moment. I sensed tears, quickly stifled, but tears nonetheless, and movement, a flicker of the view out the window to the garden—and fear, not rage, but a fear that contrasted with her own safety. She smothered the feeling, sat down, and returned to her accounts. Working with the numbers soothed her mind. We returned to the car to include Jan in the conversation.

"She's afraid of something," I said. "Really afraid, but it's not for herself."

"Well," Ari said. "If I had a daughter, and she was off somewhere with a band of murderous terrorists, I'd be rather upset myself."

I remembered the Furies I'd seen, shrieking in the sky. All at once I understood why they'd appeared. Clytemnestra had nothing on Madame Karina.

"That's it!" I said. "Crud, I should have realized that earlier. What do you bet she's furious with the Axeman because he left their daughter back on Six?"

"A mother's love—how sweet!" Jan said. "But we can't bribe her with the daughter. Ash will have to stand trial on One—if we can even take her into custody."

"Do they have the death sentence on One?" I asked.

"No!" Jan looked sincerely shocked. "We're not barbarians, you know!"

"Okay, then prison on One would be better than being gang raped and murdered by her confederates. They're not nice guys, those terrorists. She's really beautiful."

"And who better to know the evil ways of the male heart than a madam?" Jan heaved a fake sigh.

"As for the Axeman," I said, "he's really frightened of Karina, and he damn well should be. When I ran that scan, he was ready to crawl under the table."

"She must be formidable," Ari said, "to frighten a vicious bastard like him. Look at what he did to Wagner."

"I'd rather not," Jan said. "Ugly."

"Wagner." I saw a new angle on the problem. "Speaking of being pissed off, he's sure got reason to be. I wonder if we could get him to send a message, like, he's got a lead on an orb for Six."

"Very nice," Jan said. "We'd better run that by the higher-ups. They might be able to get us a convincing-looking fake orb."

We returned to the office and the trans-world router so Jan could put that question to HQ and Spare14 as well as the liaison captain in SanFran. After a flurry of messages, we learned that no, they had none of the fake transport orbs in custody, but since the real transport orbs could no longer reach Six, we could have several of those if we'd like.

"They might as well be fake," Ari said. "They'll look convincing, better yet."

"Let's hope Wagner will agree to help," Jan said.

"He'll have to." Ari smiled his tiger's smile. "He wants

revenge, but even without that, he's been selling illegal orbs. He knows about TWIXT and the trans-world prison system. He cooperates, or we take him in. That's what we'll have on offer."

"He'll buy," Jan said. "I would if I were him."

We spent the rest of the afternoon planning our sting. We decided that since Ari and I were known, and Wagner would be minimally functional, we needed to add another person to our team. Dave Rasmussen, the TWIXT clerk temporarily stuck on One, was the logical choice. A second flurry of trans-world messages sped back and forth, and we had our arrangements made. I suggested that Ari and I could just stay in SanFran that night, but Spare14 refused to allow it.

"You're targets," his message ran, "for any gang member who wants to rise in his hierarchy by killing a government agent. Return to Four and leave the preliminaries to the rest of your team. Tell Hendriks to be careful, too. He might be recognized."

"He's quite right," Ari said. "Beyond that, we have to have some delay for the look of the thing. The Axeman knows that Wagner's incapacitated. He'll become suspicious if the orbs turn up too quickly."

I had a transport orb with me that would have gotten us home, but around sunset Danvers-Jones called Jan's office. She was down at South Park, she said, and would take us back to Four. I suspected that she wanted to talk about my father. When we joined her, she proved me right.

"I had a real interesting afternoon," Willa told me. "That gate to Six? It's stable, now that your father's there to take care of it."

"That's good news."

"Yes, sure is. The Guild authorized me to buy the house, but your Uncle Jim downright refuses to sell at any price, even a real high one. Even for cash."

"Well, it's been in his family for about a hundred and forty years."

"That's what your aunt told me. What a genuinely nice woman she is, just by the way. But anyway, your father told me that the family needs that gate for private reasons. Do you realize how irregular that is?

"Not illegal, mind," Ari put in, "but against TWIXT policy."

"Against Guild policy, buster," Willa snarled. "And that's what's important here."

Ari flinched. I made a noncommittal noise. Dad was thinking of Cam and his daughter, I supposed.

"Very irregular," Willa continued. "But Flann holds all the cards."

"He generally does, yeah. Five or six aces. At least one in his shirt pocket. Another up his sleeve."

She grinned. "He thinks he can build us another gate somewhere else that'll be permanent for Six. If he can and he does, we'll have to let him have his way. We can't go to the government and suggest they take your uncle's house by eminent domain. What would we tell them we wanted it for?"

"It might be amusing," Ari said, "to watch the Board of Supervisors arguing about trans-world gates. They've already stopped the military on Four from confiscating that portal in Golden Gate Park."

"Which is worth a laugh or two," I put in.

"Yeah, real funny." Willa rummaged in her shopping bag and brought out a blue-green focus orb. "Let's get back to Four. The gamma rays have fried your brains enough for one day."

"That's for sure," I said. "When will you be picking up Rasmussen?"

"In about twenty minutes. The lucky boy gets to stay

here tonight so Hendriks can brief him. It'll take him a while to get used to SanFran."

"It's kind of the acid test, isn't it? If he can stand Interchange, he'll know that he's got the right stuff to be a TWIXT agent."

"Right," Ari said. "And if he doesn't, he needs to get out now."

CHAPTER 15

MONDAY PASSED SLOWLY, too slowly, while we waited to return to Three. Gun in hand, Ari paced back and forth in the flat. He'd pause at the front windows, watch the street for a few minutes, then stalk down the hall to the bedroom to look for malefactors out of the back windows—back and forth, forth and back, until I was ready to scream at him. Now and then he stopped pacing to call Spare14, who repeatedly told him that he'd not yet heard from Jan. Just after noon I tried a soothing remark.

"We've got to let the sting develop," I said. "If Mitch responds too soon, the Axeman's bound to see through it."

"What makes you think I don't know that?"

"Nothing. I'm just trying to get you to stop driving me nuts. All this pacing! Where do you think you are? In a cage at the zoo?"

"It feels a bit like that. Oh, very well. I'll go downstairs and work out."

Once he was busy exhausting himself, I could catch up on paperwork. Besides the small mountain of e-mail, Lev

Flowertree's book, *Beneath the Surface: An Exploration in Pacific Myth*, arrived by snail mail. When I glanced through it, I found it better written than a lot of self-published occult writing, not that this was saying much. One of the illustrations caught my eye, a pen-and-ink diagram of the area in England around Silbury Hill. The diagram joined Avebury, Stonehenge, and Woodhenge with lines indicating the latest archaeological reconstructions of the ceremonial "ways" or roads that dated from the Bronze Age. I had to admit that the resulting pattern did look something like the front end of a big-eyed cephalopod, but I didn't share Flowertree's certainty that the builders had meant it that way.

Still, considering that the Venusian cephalopods were out to get me, I valued any and all thoughts on things squiddish. I put the book away for future study and returned to my e-mail only to have my phone ring: Maureen. She was sick and tired of sitting around Kathleen's house, she told me, unable to go off the grounds or even too close to the fence.

"I'm afraid to let the kids go outside, too, and that's the worst thing," Maureen went on. "I don't want them warped and frightened for life."

"I understand that. It's really a hard situation you're in."

"I don't want to leave town, I really don't. What if he finds out and follows us? I won't have you guys to fall back on, and things will be worse."

"Look, Mo, what if I could get you a job in a place where Chuck could never follow, but you could still be close to the family?"

"That would be perfect, sure. In our dreams."

"No, really! Do you remember Cam Douglas?"

"How could I forget him, after what happened to you? I couldn't believe it when you wouldn't marry him, I really couldn't. I mean, I know you made the right decision. I even knew it then. Don't worry about that! But I thought wow, how could you turn him down?"

"Don't tell me you had a crush on him, too!"

"Didn't everyone have a crush on Mr. Douglas? Well, all the girls. And Sean. He was so disappointed when you got pregnant, and it was obvious that Cam was straight. I bet Cam's still good-looking. Even if he's what? He must be in his thirties by now. Same as me."

"No, he's older'n you, thirty-six, I'd say. He's a widower with a couple of young kids. And he needs a housekeeper."

A long suspicious silence followed. Finally, Maureen said, "What's the catch? There's got to be a huge catch."

"There sure is. I've got a lot of things to work out about this, but I figured I'd better see if you were interested before I went ahead with it."

"Oh, yeah. I mean, it's a job, isn't it? They aren't so easy to find these days." Her voice suddenly choked on tears. "It's the kids. I am so worried sick about the kids. What if Chuck decided to shoot one of them?"

"We've got to get you out of there. Dad's involved in this, too."

We talked for maybe an hour that day. At the end of it, Maureen understood a lot more about deviant world levels and doppelgängers. Whether or not she wanted to live on another level and work for another version of the man she used to know—she hadn't made her mind up about that, and I couldn't blame her. I also filled her in on the terrorist activity. She deserved to know about it before she made up her mind.

"Well, there's a risk of that here, isn't there?" she said. "What with al-Qaeda and the Taliban."

"You've got a point. And who knows what'll happen in the Middle East?"

"Yeah. But I do know what'll happen if Chuck gets hold of me." She paused for a gulp of breath. "I'll have to figure out which looks worse."

Ari came back upstairs soaked with sweat but in a better frame of mind. While he took a shower, I kept my TWIXT communicator handy. Spare14 never called. Ari turned sullen.

"What's so wrong?" I said. "I don't get why you're so worried."

"I'm not worried. I merely want my chance to bring the Axeman in. That incident on Three, when he just walked away from us!" Ari growled and slammed his right fist into his left palm.

"Ah. You want revenge."

"Of course. Don't you?"

I considered. "Not really. I want the job done right, but that's different."

"True." Ari took a deep breath. "It's a better way of looking at it. I need to find some sort of distraction." All at once he grinned. "But one that leaves my hands free to answer the phone should it ring."

That evening the distraction arrived when Dad, Michael, and a six-pack came to our flat after dinner. They wanted to discuss the new gate that Dad was planning on building with Mike's help.

"If I can show them that I'm capable of it," Dad said. "The Guild will finance buying a building to hold the gate to Six."

"You can do this, can't you?" Ari said.

"Of course." Dad shot him a sour glance. "Or I'd never have offered, would I?"

"All right. Has Nola warned you about the terrorist group operating on Six?"

Dad's eyebrows shot up. Ari delivered the warning at some length. When he finished, Dad considered for a few minutes.

"We'll stay out of the likely target areas," Dad said. "And don't forget, Mike and I can walk fast. Tell me something. How different is San Francisco Six from here?"

"Not very," I said, "as far as I can see. Oh, and another

thing about the terrorists. The authorities there are taking steps to protect the city now. They know how real the danger is."

"True," Ari put in. "I can ask a higher-up for a report on what measures have been put in place, and what's been planned for the future."

Dad and Michael stayed for a good hour, discussing gates and possible sites. As they were leaving, I escorted them down to the front door to have a private word. I told Dad that I'd spoken with Maureen and described what I had in mind

"You know about the terrorist threat now," I said. "We'll have to take that into account before anything can happen."

"True enough, darling." Dad thought for a moment. "I wasn't going to tell you this, but I think we need to keep it in mind. When I was inside, I met a man who'd killed his wife and children for trying to leave him. He stalked them for three years before he got his chance."

"Three—oh, God!"

"Indeed. He bragged about the whole thing. Said he would have kept at it if it had taken him ten years."

"Did they eventually hang him?"

"Oh, yes, but because he killed the children. The wife? The jury called that second-degree murder because it was a crime of passion." He shook himself as if he could throw the memory off. "Safety's a relative thing. Chuck may be a worse danger than these bastards on Six. Well, I'll talk to Maureen before we make up our minds."

I locked the door behind them, then sat on the steps to call Maureen myself. I wanted to make sure she never mentioned my abortion around our father. She agreed that the effect of doing so would be spectacular—spectacularly awful, that is.

"Don't worry, I won't say a word," she said. "He's never going to change his mind about some things, and that's one of them."

"What about Sean and Al?"

"That's probably another sticking point, yeah. But I think we might have a little leeway there. Maybe."

"I'm not going to push it."

I heard footsteps above and behind me and looked over my shoulder. A glowering Ari had come halfway down the stairs.

"I've got to go," I told Maureen. "Unless you want to talk with Ari about your Unpleasant Ex?"

"I do have one quick question, now that you mention it. Can you just hand him your phone?"

I got up and did so, and the glower disappeared. I heard him say, "I think Jack's right. Daylight should be safe enough as long as you don't go out of the family compound." He gave me the phone back, but he waited on the stairs with me until I finished saying good-bye.

We returned to the living room. "Family compound?" I said.

"That's what Jack and Kathleen's property amounts to," Ari said. "A protected area. In the Middle East there'd be a concrete wall around it. Too bad there isn't one here."

"I can't imagine living inside walls like that."

Ari shrugged the comment off. "The kids want to go swimming," he said. "Staying inside even with pets to play with is hard on them. I remember the pool as being far enough from the fence for safety's sake."

"Good. You're the one who knows about guns and stuff."

"And stuff." He smiled briefly. "The thing is, Chuck has a rifle with a long range, but he won't be able to carry that openly in San Anselmo. You can't hide a long gun in broad daylight. Now, unfortunately, he has a handgun, too, but—"

"They analyzed the bullets, huh?" I interrupted him. "From the engagement party, I mean, if they know he used a handgun."

"I knew it already from the sound of the shots. At any

rate, if he tries to use the handgun over at Jack's, he won't be able to get close enough to the target for effective range."

The target. My sister. Ari put an arm around my shoulder and gave me a reassuring squeeze. It helped, but not enough. I reminded myself that Dad had taken charge of the problem. Dad takes charge every chance he gets, actually, whether you want him to or not. In this case, I was glad of it, because Ari and I had a target of our own, and we needed to return to the hunt.

It wasn't until the next day, however, that we received the signal that the hunt was on. Spare14 called around three in the afternoon. Yes, Wagner would cooperate.

"In fact," Spare 14 said, "he seems quite eager to help get the Axeman out of SanFran."

"I'm not surprised," I said.

"No more than I. Now, Rasmussen's turned out to be a good fit for the Wagner nephew role," Spare14 continued. "His cover story is that he's come from the Central Valley to help his ailing uncle."

"What about his status?" Ari said. "Can he play an active role in the sting?"

"Oh, yes. Kerenskya—you remember her, I think, the liaison captain on Three? She's got his status upgraded from clerk to agent recruit."

"Excellent! When do they bait the trap?"

"Soon. I'll let you know as soon as I hear."

Ari and I waited another hour before we heard the next installment. After Hendriks and Wagner drafted a note, Rasmussen took it over to the Octagon Brothel and delivered it with no trouble. Now that he'd introduced himself there, he'd be recognized and accepted when the Axeman or his messenger saw him behind the counter of the bookstore.

"The sting's set up for tomorrow around noon," Ari told me. "It's possible that the Axeman will send someone else to pick up the orbs. If so, we'll leave immediately for the Diana statue to stake out the gate there."

"It sounds like you've got things covered."

"Let's hope. It's entirely too easy for something to go wrong in this sort of operation." He smiled at a sudden cheerful thought. "Even if it does, the Axeman will still be trapped on Three."

I waited for some Negative Psychic Input, what used to be called a bad omen. None came, but, as I reminded myself, omens aren't the most reliable forecasting tool.

We arrived back in South Park 3.0 on Interchange early the next morning. We stood in a clump of concealing trees while I cleared a space for my mind. Once I had psychic room to operate, I ran scans—no immediate danger. When I did an SM: Location for Wagner's bookstore, I did pick up a hard-to-read threat nearby. I tried to zero in with an SM: Personnel and got a result that was clearer but not conclusive.

"Someone's watching the place," I told Ari. "I can't be sure who or why."

"It won't be anyone on our team." Ari took out his communicator. "Let me call Hendriks."

While he called, I ran scans for our present location. We were in no more danger than was usual for a place swirling with radioactive dust and crawling with criminal gangs. I'd just finished when Ari put the communicator away.

"Let's go," Ari said. "Rasmussen stayed overnight at the bookshop last night, so he's inside. Hendriks will drive down and park a few blocks uphill. I'll explain the plan as we walk up to Market. We'll take the streetcar to Turk."

Our trip over went smoothly. We got off the streetcar and walked about half a block to a narrow alley just up from Market, where we lingered behind some garbage cans. Ari stood behind me with his back to me and made calls with the communicator while I did my best imitation of a sleepy hooker waiting for her pimp to finish pissing against the wall. A couple of men passed the alley mouth but never gave us a second glance. We left the alley and started up Turk toward the bookstore. I saw a woman walking along ahead of us with a market basket over one arm and a couple of kids trailing after her. They turned at the corner and trudged uphill on the cross street. Otherwise the sidewalks were empty. SanFran's not a town for early risers.

"All in order," Ari said. "Hendriks is on his way down. Rasmussen's coming outside with a broom to start sweeping the sidewalk. Can you pinpoint the threat?"

"Yeah." I paused to let my mind roam up the street ahead of us. "Guy across the street from the store."

When we'd walked about half a block farther, I smelled cooking grease, or to be precise, my talent activated neurons and made them believe that my nose smelled cooking grease.

"Guy in a doorway next to some kind of diner," I said.

We strolled a little more slowly up to the corner. I could see Wagner's store about halfway up the next block. Rasmussen came out with a broom in hand and began sweeping the night's detritus into the gutter. He wore beat-up jeans and a torn T-shirt consistent with his role as Wagner's nephew. When I ran a quick scan, I became aware of Hendriks' presence nearby, just around the farther corner, maybe.

I brought my attention back to our location and saw a sign advertising a "Fry Shop" across the street from and a bit closer to Market than the bookstore. Next to it, a two-story building advertised "Rooms." In the sheltered entranceway, a tall guy in jeans, a gray shirt, and a Giants cap sat on the stairs drinking from a bottle wrapped in a brown paper bag. He leaned against the stair behind him and muttered now and then as if he were sloppy drunk. I didn't buy it in the least.

"That's him," I said.

"Wait here."

I found a relatively clean wall to lean against and looked hooker-ish. Ari crossed the street, strolled up the block, and whistled, one sharp note. I started running in his direction. Rasmussen dropped the broom and darted across the street. Ari grabbed the spy by the shirt, hauled him up, and slammed him so hard against the wall that he dropped the bottle. He yelped and made a feeble slap at Ari's face. Ari ducked under and punched up from below. He hit the guy on the point of the chin just as Rasmussen reached them. The kid caught the spy under the arms as he crumpled and began to fall. Ari stooped and grabbed his legs.

I ran to the bookstore and opened the door as Ari and Rasmussen carried the unconscious man across the street at a jog. We all hurried inside just as Hendriks ran down the block to join us. I shut the door and locked it while Ari and Rasmussen hauled their prey into the back room.

"Plenty of rope back there," Jan remarked. "I made sure of that last night."

"You never know when you're going to need a nice bit of rope."

Jan tilted his head and looked at me narrow-eyed.

"Never mind," I said. "A quote from a work of literature."

We made our way to the back of the store just as Ari came out of Mitch's living quarters. He stood behind the counter and rubbed his knuckles. I judged from the look on his face that they really hurt.

"Does Mitch have any of that aspirin left?" I said.

"He needs it more than I do," Ari said.

"What's going to happen," Rasmussen asked, "when the Axeman gets here and his stakeout guy is gone?"

"He'll think the worst of the stakeout guy, I assume," Ari answered. "Or he'll get the wind up and won't come in. I suspect, however, that he needs the orbs badly enough to risk it."

"I agree," Jan said. "Well, we'll find out. Now we wait."

While we did, I went into the back room. Wagner was sitting in his armchair, feet up on a carton of books for a hassock. His face had gone from red and swollen to slightly less swollen and purple, with black bruises here and there in the shape of gun barrels. He raised a feeble hand and waved. Beyond him on the floor lay the bound and gagged stakeout guy. He'd come round, and his dark eyes darted this way and that in impotent fury. I carried my shoulder bag past them both and went into the tiny bathroom.

I'd brought makeup with me and a slutty black top to wear with my tight jeans so I could pose as Rasmussen's girlfriend. During the sting I needed to be in the store itself to keep running scans, particularly of the Axeman and whoever else came with him to buy the orbs. The last time I'd disguised myself in SanFran I'd made my skin look darker. This time I used a very pale foundation, black mascara, green eye shadow, and dark red lipstick, all of which together gave me a Goth vampire look. Since the sleeveless top had a deep V-neck that meant going braless, I made sure I carried the pale foundation all the way down my neck and into the cleavage. I'd brought bubble gum with me for a final addition to the persona.

When I returned to the store counter, Rasmussen grinned at me and winked. The guy had a certain charm. When Ari glared at him, he wiped the smile off his face fast. Ari turned the glare on me.

"Well," I said to Ari, "I don't look like a government agent, do I?"

"No," Ari said. "That's certainly true." He sighed with what I considered unnecessary drama.

I popped my gum at him and wandered off to check out the heaps and stacks of books. To pass the time, I idly searched for books that authors we knew on Four had never written. The vast majority of Wagner's stock, however, had been published before the Great Disaster and thus pretty much corresponded to the literary history of Four. I did find some books of serious journalism—*Sacramento Betrayal* and *Central Valley Poverty*—by one of the most incongruous doppelgängers ever, Elinor Glyn. When I showed them to Ari, he bought them for the TWIXT archives.

I'd just washed my hands of the dust and cobwebs I'd picked up in my search when a car drove up and parked in front of the store. A real car, not a patchwork, it looked to be a vintage 1920s box on wheels, a shiny dove gray with spotless tan fenders and running boards. Ari and Jan rushed into the back room. I draped myself onto a stool behind the counter as Rasmussen trotted forward to unlock the door. I could make out a man in a gray chauffeur's uniform on the other side of the glass.

"We're closed today." Rasmussen opened the door about a foot. "Uncle's sick."

"My employer's come to pick up her magazines," the fellow said.

"Okay. Come on in." Rasmussen stepped back and opened the door wide.

Her magazines? I ran a quick scan, but the only danger I sensed was vague and tentative, the whisper that something might go wrong rather than that something had. I ran a quick SM: Location on the car. Only one person sat inside, a woman.

Out on the street another man in a gray uniform opened the back door of the magnificent car. Draped in a pale blue duster, the woman emerged and stepped from the running board onto the sidewalk. The fellow holding the car door closed it behind her and followed as she hurried into the store. Both chauffeur types entered with her, and I noticed that they both wore shoulder holsters under their jackets.

I was seeing Madame Karina herself, I figured, a tall woman for Interchange since she was about my height, 5'8", and one who must have been lovely in her youth. I pegged her at about fifty, a SanFran lifer. She'd dyed her long hair purple and wore it swept back from her face with a pair of diamond-studded combs. I knew that color—burgundy wine mixed with henna—and she'd done her eyebrows to match. She walked up to the counter, glanced at Rasmussen, and considered me with icy blue eyes.

"You are?" she said.

"My girlfriend, ma'am," Rasmussen said. "She's been cooking for me and Uncle Mitch."

"Ah." Karina considered me. "Looking for work, girl? I've got a few clients who like your type. Skinny and tough-looking. They'd enjoy taming you, if you know what I mean."

"Hey!" Rasmussen snapped.

Karina ignored him and smiled at me. "You'd have to learn how to use makeup right, but we're talking real money."

I felt like a mouse, smiled at by a snake right before the big gulp.

"No, thanks, ma'am," I said. "My dad would beat me black and blue." I jerked my thumb in Rasmussen's direction. "Well, if Dave didn't do it first."

She started to speak, but hesitated, caught by an honest grief that had nothing to do with me. She suppressed the emotion with another snake's smile. "I'm glad you've got a father who cares about his daughter," she said. "Unlike some I know. Okay. Have those orbs come in?"

"Yes, ma'am," Rasmussen said. "We found you two. But I gotta warn you. They ain't gonna work just anywhere. The guy we got'em from, he says you gotta use'em at a gate."

"Huh!" Karina snorted. "So that lousy rat was telling me the truth, was he? I'm shocked!"

I figured the lousy rat was the Axeman, who'd doubtless tried to explain why he couldn't just return to Six at her order.

"Ma'am," I said. "Do you know where a gate is?"

"That statue out in old Sutro's garden, right?"

"Right. I just wanted to make sure you knew. We want you to be happy with the stuff we sell."

She rolled her eyes heavenward but also smiled.

Under her duster Karina was wearing a matching blue dress with a sweetheart neckline. Under the dress, I assumed, she wore the mother of all corsets, because she had a small waist but the most formidable pair of breasts I'd ever seen. Double F's, maybe. Be that as it may, she reached into the architectural support and pulled out a small velvet clasp bag. She opened it and gave us a look at a wad of twenty-buck bills, then delicately reinserted the bag into her décolletage.

Rasmussen took a cardboard shoebox from the shelf under the counter. With a flourish he opened it and set it down in front of Madame Karina. I craned my neck and saw two yellow-green orbs gleaming on a bed of cotton batting. She picked one up and ran a manicured finger over the surface. She held it in front of the light from the gooseneck lamp and peered at it like a farmwife candling an egg, then did the same with the second orb.

"Nice," she said, "nice and real. I hear there are bad ones on the market now."

"You gotta be careful, yeah," Rasmussen said. "This guy wouldn't scam us. He knows what I'd do to him if he tried."

Karina grinned and looked my way. "You've got a good boyfriend there," she said. "But if you get tired of him, remember my offer." She paused, and I felt the touch of an SPP. "I bet you like being tamed."

"Yeah," I said. "But I get enough of that at home."

She returned the orb to the shoebox and closed it. The

velvet bag made a reappearance. When she counted the bills out onto the counter, Dave scooped them up and slipped them into his jeans pocket. Madame Karina handed the box to one of her escorts to carry. In procession, she and the two chauffeur-goons marched out of the store. I waited till they'd driven away, then ditched the bubble gum. My jaws were tired.

Ari and Jan strode out of the back room.

"Well done," Ari said to Rasmussen.

"Very well done," Jan chimed in. "I'll give the liaison captain a good report."

"Well, thank you, sir," Rasmussen said.

I got the impression that Jan was hoping to push the job of TWIXT observer in SanFran onto Rasmussen. From the way Ari swallowed a smile, I guessed he was thinking something similar. Dave's setup as Wagner's nephew would work, I figured, especially since Mitch was too afraid of TWIXT to refuse to cooperate.

"I know where Ash gets her talents," I said. "Her mom has at least one. It's no wonder she's the richest madam in town. One look, and she knows just what her customers want. Better than they do themselves, I bet."

Both Rasmussen and Hendriks let their faces drift into a misty-eyed distant expression, as if perhaps they were wondering how much one of her girls would cost. Ari cleared his throat. Loudly.

"Time for the next step," Ari said. "We've got to get out to the gate point, but we'll be back once it's good and dark to pick up the goon. See if you can get more ice for Wagner's face while we're gone."

"Will do, sir," Rasmussen said.

Before any of us left the store, I ditched the slutty top and put on my sensible blue-and-white blouse again. I also ran scans. No one who meant us harm lingered in the neighborhood except, of course, for the goon trussed like a turkey in the back room. Madame Karina was heading over Nob Hill toward Union Street. When Jan brought the car around, Ari and I piled in for the drive out to Sutro Heights, version 3.0. In a head-to-head race, Madame Karina's car would have beaten Jan's rattletrap by a mile, but she needed to give the orbs to the Axeman. For all we knew, he'd have some other means of reaching the statue and its nonfunctional gate.

"I hope," Ari said, "that he's planning to go through to Six today. I'm not looking forward to hiding in the underbrush overnight."

"I bet she makes him go whether he wants to or not," I said. "And he probably does want. The vibes I picked up from her? Fierce."

During the drive through the sand dunes of the Sunset district, Ari got out his communicator and made a number of calls. I found them mostly cryptic because he used the TWIXT code, a lot of numbers held together with fragments of English, statements like: "Seventy four to three one, we have a ninety-nine go." I did manage to figure out that someone would be meeting us out on Sutro Heights. When we reached the narrow dirt road that would have been the wide and well-paved Point Lobos Avenue back home, we continued past the destroyed mansion and its grounds rather than parking nearby. The car plunged downhill so sharply that I nearly shrieked. We rattled, shook, and jounced all the way down the steep, bone-rattling road to the beach and another narrow road that ran past the remains of the Sutro Baths.

Jan parked behind a straggling clump of half-grown cypress trees, bent double by the constant wind. I staggered out of the car, resisted the impulse to kiss the solid if sandy ground beneath my feet, and shivered in a cool wind that promised fog on the way. The ocean rumbled at low tide about twenty yards to the west. To the east loomed the weed-covered cliffs that led up to a stone retaining wall, as thick and high as any castle's. It held the dirt of the actual gardens in place. Some ten yards away from our impromptu parking spot a wooden door into the cliff stood open. A redhaired man I recognized stepped out and beckoned to us.

He was about four feet tall, a classic little person, as those people suffering from hereditary dwarfism prefer to be called, and come to think of it, the colony on Three probably would dislike being told they were "suffering," too. They'd worked out a halfway decent scavengers' life on the edge of San Fran, better in some ways than the so-called normal people had down in the slums. This particular guy, James Sheaffer, had helped us trap a criminal before. When we joined him, he told us that he and his commune were ready to do so again.

"Come in," he said to Ari. "The others are already here. It was awfully good of Agent Spare to bring us a load of blankets, I must say. It gets chilly out here in the winter."

"It's chilly enough now," I said.

Sheaffer laughed and agreed. We joined him in an open space cut out of the cliff side and reinforced with hunks of driftwood. Ahead, a long, rough flight of stairs led up toward the surface. I groaned. Once before I'd gone down those stairs, hard enough on my knees, but going up was going to be a lot worse.

"You're got to start working out," Ari remarked.

"Oh, shut up!"

I managed to struggle and pant my way up with only two rest breaks. The stairs debouched on the other side of the retaining wall, which sat on the lowest of several terraces. We came out onto a path between the rows of a vegetable garden. Marble fragments of statuary marked out its perimeter—a white hand by the carrots, a head of Apollo at the end of the spinach row. While I caught my breath, Ari talked into his communicator. I could just hear Spare14's familiar voice answering him.

Ari led us north by a path that skirted the retaining wall until we reached a stand of trees, all second-growth, the remains of Sutro's elegant plantings, now swallowed by underbrush and weeds. We made our way through on a narrow path that led up from terrace to terrace until we reached a small clearing. Spare14 stood waiting for us with Willa Danvers-Jones, dressed in jeans and a sweatshirt instead of her usual tatters, though she carried her shopping bag of orbs. Next to Willa stood a very tall person in dark slacks, a blue shirt, and a flak jacket; as her main fashion accessory, she carried a rifle with a sniper scope. She had steel-gray hair cut short, ice-blue eyes, and high Russian cheekbones. Jan introduced her as the liaison captain for SanFran, Anna Kerenskya.

"You are our police psychic, yes?" she said to me.

"Yes," I said. "Nola O'Grady, on loan from the Agency on Four."

"Good. We need you to scan the area. Warn of approaching vehicles."

I nearly saluted but caught myself in time. A quick scan showed me no vehicles moving in the vicinity. When I told Kerenskya this, she nodded in my direction and went to huddle with Ari, Jan, and Spare14. I turned to Willa.

"Why the crowd?" I said.

"No one's sure how many goons the Axeman will bring with him," Willa said. "I'm here to bring the perps back to One as soon as they're cuffed."

"This gate never led there, did it?"

"No, but there's one that does not all that far from here. The sooner we can hustle Axe Moore off this level, the sooner we can stop worrying about him getting away from us. HQ was furious over that last escape of his."

While she'd been waiting for the rest of us to arrive, Kerenskya had consulted with Sheaffer about the terrain around the statue. We all trooped farther uphill toward Diana and her leaping hound. Since the statue stood in the midst of open ground, positioning the gunmen presented problems. She set Spare14 off to the north in thick cover, and Jan to the south, ditto. When she turned to Ari, he spoke to her in Russian. They argued briefly, but I could tell from his shrug that she won.

"Stay alert," he said to me. "You won't have a bodyguard during the arrest." He turned and stalked off southward, gun in hand, to disappear into the trees somewhere west of Jan's position. Kerenskya strode over to Willa and me.

"Move farther downhill," Kerenskya said. "See the trees by the broken plinth?"

We looked; we saw.

"You should be safe there, out of the line of fire if something goes wrong. O'Grady, run scan now."

I did and felt the Axeman's presence, moving fast on Geary Street in our direction. I zeroed in with an SM:P.

"He's on his way," I said. "Three people with him, all men, one driving the vehicle."

"Very good. Now go. Hide." She started to walk off, then turned to look back with a smile. "Agent Nathan? His Russian is very good. Is surprising."

I smiled in answer, and she jogged off to disappear into the ruins of the old mansion, which lay among high grass and weeds uphill and eastward from the statue. Willa and I followed orders and hurried to the thicket one terrace down, which I hoped was out of the reach of a pistol shot. We made our way into the trees through a weed patch, where a tall plant with tiny purple flowers grew tangled with the feathery leaves of wild fennel, stinking of licorice. In the shade of the thicket only a few low weeds grew.

"I hope," Willa said, "that there isn't any poison oak in here."

"Me, too," I said. "But I bet the commune gets rid of it whenever they find it. I can sense children in the tunnels. They won't want them getting sick."

Still, I examined my patch of ground carefully before I knelt down. Willa did the same and settled her shopping bag beside her. By peering between the trees we could just see the Diana statue. I hoped that neither the Axeman nor his goons would look our way, though we certainly wouldn't be visible to someone glancing casually in our direction. I ran another scan: the Axeman and his crew had reached the dirt path that would have been 25th Avenue back home.

"Almost here," I murmured.

I sent my mind out and read scans of the aura field. The closer that the Axeman came, the more danger I sensed. He and his companions would be armed, maybe heavily so. Would they drop their weapons and accept arrest, or was there going to be a shoot-out? The scans could only give me possibilities, not answers. I began to gather Qi and wind it, ready for an ensorcellment if need be.

In a few minutes we heard a car rattling and coughing its way toward the site. I felt relieved that Madame Karina and her elegant vehicle had stayed away—for our sake, not hers. I suspected that she was a lot more dangerous than the Axeman. I ran an SM: Location and sensed that the car was stopping up at the eastern edge of the grounds. Three men got out. The Axeman I could recognize; he was a big bear of a man with thinning tufts of curly gray hair and a wispy beard. I'd never seen the others before. I could hear with my physical ears that the car started up again. Instead of heading back toward town, however, it drove around the edge of the grounds to Point Lobos and down. It stopped on the other side of the trees just about level with our position.

"Damn!" Willa murmured.

I nodded and readied the Qi I held. We heard no creak of a car door opening, heard no footsteps, either, but I stayed on the alert. I looked uphill toward the Diana statue and saw the Axeman and a skinny Cal-African man walking clear of the trees. Even at my distance I could sense their anger, a grim growling resentment. Behind them came a paunchy white guy with a drawn gun, herding them downhill. Him, I read as smug. The Axeman apparently was reluctant to go through the gate, and from what I knew, he had the right idea. I could guess that Madame Karina had sent a little motivation along with him. The Axeman reached into his jacket and pulled out one of the yellow-green orbs, then turned to speak to the gunman. The gunman gestured at the statue with his gun. The Axeman took two steps toward Diana and paused to argue.

Off to the side of my thicket, I heard the sound I'd been dreading. The car door opened, footsteps crunched on the road, came closer, swished through the tall weeds. I counted his footsteps, waited as he came closer, closer—I stood up and threw just as he appeared between two trees.

The sphere of Qi hit him full in the face with a flash of silver light. He made a muffled noise that amounted to about a third of a scream and went down. The gun he'd been holding dropped from his hand. Willa leaped to her feet and darted over to snatch it from the ground. The ensorcelled goon giggled and lifted a hand to waggle his forefinger in her direction as if to say "no no no." She stood staring at him.

"Get down!" I snapped and did so myself.

She dropped to her knees just as a bullet zipped in our direction.

"Oh, shit!" She sat down and clutched her bag of orbs to her chest.

I took this statement as meaning she was okay. The ensorcelled goon began humming a little tune and rocking from side to side. I turned and looked uphill. By shooting at us, the gunman had distracted himself from the real danger. The Cal-African guy pounced and knocked him down. They wrestled, yelling and swearing, but the gunman kept the pistol clutched in one hand. The Axeman hovered over them, looking for an opportunity to grab the weapon.

"Police!" Kerenskya's voice boomed out. "Drop your weapons!" She fired the rifle into the ground. "Are being under arrest!"

The TWIXT men burst out of cover, guns in hand. The Cal-African guy twisted free and scrambled up. The pistol went flying onto the ground. When the gunman dove for it, the Cal-African guy grabbed him by both arms and hurled him against the statue. The Axeman threw the orb. Yellow-green smoke billowed into a perfect sphere. For a moment the sphere stayed whole. I heard a scream, a drawn-out horrible scream of terror that seemed to live apart from the screamer. It wailed in agony, then faded as the fog wind grabbed and tore the smoke away. Without thinking, I got to my feet for a better look. The Cal-African guy and the Axeman were both standing with their hands high in the air. The TWIXT team came running to surround them. The gunman had vanished.

"He's gone," I whispered.

"Way gone," Willa said. "The orb opened something, all right. Too bad the bridge was broken, like your invisible friend told us." She shuddered. "Guess he had time to realize what was happening to him. I'll hear that scream in my nightmares for a long time."

"Me, too." My stomach clenched. "A real long time."

CHAPTER 16

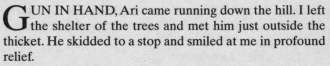

G UN IN HAND, Ari came running down the hill. I left the shelter of the trees and met him just outside the thicket. He skidded to a stop and smiled at me in profound relief.

"That shot from above missed," I said.

"But I saw a flash of light down here," he said. "Who fired at you?"

"No one." I turned and pointed into the thicket. "I never gave him the chance."

Ari took a few steps forward just as Willa emerged.

"I put the gun we took from him back down," she said to Ari. "Fingerprints, you know."

"Yes." Ari sighed with a puff of breath. "I'm glad to see I worried for nothing."

I followed Ari as he pushed weeds aside and made his way into the thicket. The ensorcelled goon was still singing and rocking. The gun lay on the ground some ten feet to the goon's right. Now that I had a moment to think, I recognized him.

"That's one of Madame Karina's bodyguards," I said. "Do we dare take him into custody?"

"Probably not. Hendriks told me that she pays the chief a lot of protection money." Ari frowned at the man at the ground. "Will he remember what happened?"

"No."

"Fine. We'll put him back into his car and leave him."

Ari picked up the gun, emptied out the bullets, and put them into his shirt pocket. "Just in case and all that. Here, let's see if I can get him to his feet."

Ari could and did with a little help from me. We walked him out to the rattletrap of a car and poured him into the front seat, where he began to punctuate his songs with car noises of the vroom-vroom kind. Ari wiped the gun clean of fingerprints on his shirt, then tossed it in after him. We returned to Willa, and the three of us walked back up the hill to the Diana statue and the TWIXT team. When I started to shiver, I looked up and saw tendrils of gray sea fog driving the yellow clouds of dust inland.

"You should have worn a jacket," Ari said.

"Gosh, gee, thanks," I said. "I never would have thought of that myself."

He ignored the remark.

The Axeman and the Cal-African guy sat, already cuffed, on the ground. Kerenskya and Spare14 were talking on their respective communicators while Jan stood guard over the prisoners. When I ran an SPP on the two perps, I found them subdued, to use the Agency's official term, though scared half to death would be more accurate. They'd heard the scream, too. When he noticed me studying him, the Cal-African guy held my gaze.

"I didn't mean to kill him," he said. "Jesus Christ, I didn't know what would happen. That scream! I mean, shit, lady! I didn't mean to do that. I thought we'd just bounce him somewhere else so we could make a run for it."

"I believe you," I said, "but I'm not the person you've got to convince. There's a judge for that. And a jury."

He nodded and stared at the ground. Like a tipped bowl of half-spilled pudding, the Axeman sat slumped half over his belly with his pudgy hands clasping one knee. The cuffs around his wrists gleamed in the uncertain sunlight. Kerenskya slipped her communicator into her slacks pocket and trotted over to the prisoners.

"We take them into custody on One," she said to me. "We have list of charges, including trans-world slave trading." She looked at the Axeman. "I suggest you cooperate with those who will question you there."

He turned his head and spat on the ground. She shrugged indifferently.

"I've got a few questions I'd like to ask him myself before you go," I said. "Unofficially, if that's possible. About his daughter."

At the word daughter, Moore looked up, his eyes glittering with rage and his mouth set in a tight line.

"Go ahead," Kerenskya said, "before I recite his legal rights."

I knelt on one knee so I could look the Axeman straight in the face, but I made sure to stay far enough away to avoid getting kicked if he tried to attack. He stared right back at me.

"Where's Ash?" I said. "We know she's on Six, but where on Six does she hang out?"

He merely stared. I could feel his SPP: rage, stubborn blind rage.

"Look," I continued, "she's running with a dangerous pack, and you're not there to protect her. She could be gangraped and murdered by these so-called Soldiers of the Risen Lord. That's what her mother's worried about, isn't it?"

"Her mother!" His voice shook with the rage, and his face turned scarlet from it. "She wouldn't listen to one fucking word I said. Oh, no, she knew best. She always thinks she knows best, goddamn her. She wouldn't have let me hide in her goddamn cat house if it wasn't for Ash."

"Well, your daughter's in danger, isn't she?"

"Hell, no! That's what I mean. Karina wouldn't listen to one goddamn word I said, and then she went and set me up."

"No, she didn't. We worked a sting to get you out here."

He considered this while his mouth twisted hard enough to make his gray clumps of beard tremble. Finally, he looked up and smiled, just a twitch of his full mouth, but a smile.

"She fell for a sting?" he said.

"She sure did," I said. "I swear it."

He leaned back and laughed, howled with laughter, while the Cal-African guy and I both watched him in something like wonder. I ran a quick SPP and realized that his rage had slackened into the generalized anger most criminals feel toward the world.

"If you tell me where Ash is," I tried again, "I'll do my best to get her safely off Six. Yeah, she'll be under arrest, but won't that be better than what those guys are going to do to her?"

"They're not going to do anything to her that she doesn't want done." He turned his head and looked at the Cal-African guy. "Curtis, am I lying?"

"Hell, no," Curtis said. "Lady, honest, he's giving you the straight dope."

I could tell from their SPPs that they both were speaking the truth as they knew it.

"What is this, she's dead already?" I said.

I could sense the Axeman's contempt for the question.

"You're sure she's safe," I said. "Why?"

"That's for you to find out, isn't it?" the Axeman said, and all his good humor vanished. "You're the fucking cop. You get back to Six and find out."

Inspiration struck. "This has something to do with the Peacock Angel, doesn't it?" I said.

All the scarlet drained from the Axeman's face. Curtis swore under his breath.

"Yeah, she's a cop, all right," Curtis said. "A good one."

"Shut up!" the Axeman said. "Okay, cop. You go back to Six and ask the goddamn Angel yourself. If you can. Yeah, if you can, and if you can find him. I'm not saying one more word. Neither is Curtis if he knows what's good for him."

And he meant that, too.

I got up and let Kerenskya and Hendriks take over. She had a long list of legal rights to tell them before she formally charged them with the crimes that would lock them into a cell on Terra One. Spare14 waited off to one side and listened to make sure she left nothing out while Jan stood guard, gun in hand. When I walked a little ways away to think, Willa stayed with Spare14, but Ari followed me.

"The Angel again," he said. "You struck gold with that."

"Yep," I said. "I was thinking of the peacock feathers we keep finding. I wonder if we're dealing with a Chaos master who calls himself the Peacock Angel."

"That's not a bad working hypothesis."

"It's the obvious one, which is why I'm suspicious of it."

"Good point."

"Your mother gave me that tip, too, about the Beni Elohim. More angels. I need to follow up on this. I really want to get home. I need to see if I can contact Bissop Keith. The more we learn about the Peacock Angel cult, the better."

I carried a transport orb for Four in my shoulder bag. Since the links between Three and Four were stable, I could use it anywhere, but Ari and I lingered for a few minutes more to help Jan load the two prisoners into his car. Kerenskya had thoughtfully brought shackles along for their ankles to keep them from trying to escape during the short trip to One. By the time they were secured, a disgusting mix of yellow dust and gray fog had crept over the entire sky. The horizon gleamed like polished steel from the lowering sun behind the soup.

"What about the goon in Wagner's bookstore?" I asked Jan.

"The captain and I will take him out of there once it's good and dark. And then send him off to One to join the others before anyone can see him disappear. We don't want the gang to know that Rasmussen's an agent."

"Or that you are, either."

He smiled in honest joy. "They already suspect. Kerenskya agrees that I need to be reassigned. If there are any gods, I thank them. The only problem left is getting the transport desk into Wagner's shop. It's quite heavy."

I could well believe it. Willa got into the front passenger seat, Jan took the wheel, and they drove off, heading for an overlap point nearby. Ari and I walked uphill through the scraggly second-growth trees to the dirt path that marked 48th Avenue.

"It's a good thing we took a cab down to South Park this morning," he said. "We can just walk home from here."

"Ari, it's a couple of miles! And don't tell me I need to work out, will you? On our world level there are buses, y'know."

He made a sour face. I took out the orb, found a fragment of pavement, and threw. We darted into the sphere of blue-green smoke and stepped out next to the flimsy little bus-stop shelter for the Number 18. Fortunately, no one was waiting, so no one saw us emerge from the middle of the air. Luck smiled upon me. The bus arrived before Ari got into full complaint mode. We made a quick trip to a stop on 46th Avenue, a few blocks from our flat.

As soon as we got off the bus, the first Venusian squid appeared, a small one, this time, floating just ahead of us as we walked down Noriega. Since they travel backward by our standards, it could fix its yellow eyes on me and wave its tentacles. I drew a Chaos ward and threw. It popped. We walked about half a block; another squid, bigger this time, manifested. I popped it, we walked, yet another, larger squid appeared—this tedious set of events repeated all the way home. By the time we climbed the stairs to our flat, I was exhausted. The last cephalopod displayed definite cuttlefish traits with a greenish roach down its back. It stretched about ten feet from beak to butt, with tentacles twice as long added on.

"You know what?" I said to Ari. "I think these ugly buggers have learned how to suck up the Qi from my wards."

"Is there anything you can do about that?"

I considered. Although the ten-foot cephalopod floated on the other side of the living room, one of its tentacles reached all the way across to the head of the stairs. I took a step forward and grabbed the tentacle in both hands. I felt the thing as slime and cold air, not as solid flesh, no, but as a presence of sorts. I began to gather Qi just as I'd do if I were preparing an ensorcellment; only this time I drained it through the tentacle. The squid twisted, flapped, pulled away, and vanished.

"Hah!" I said. "You didn't like that, did you? Then lay off, you creeps!"

Nothing appeared or answered. The palms of my hands looked perfectly ordinary, a little dirty from sitting on the ground on Three, but unmarked and free of squid slime.

"I don't suppose you saw any of them," I said to Ari. "This clutch of squid, or whatever the collective noun is."

"No. I'll take your word for it."

I saw something moving under my computer desk. A tiny cephalopod lurked in the kneehole.

"Too bad none of them are real," Ari went on. "I'm hungry enough to fry a few of them up, tref or not."

The squid swung itself around to face him. It spread its tentacles in horror.

"You know," I said. "I think it heard you. Very interesting."

"At the moment I'm more interested in dinner. I wonder what we've got in the refrigerator?"

"Moldy leftovers, probably."

"I'll order Chinese delivery."

"No. Italian."

"All right." He glanced my way. "What? You've got that look again."

"You bet. I want calamari. Calamari appetizer, the deep-fried kind. They take the live squid and slice its tentacles one cut at a time while it writhes in agony. Then they plunge them into bubbling hot oil. Oh, nom nom nom!"

The under-desk squid made a small squeaking noise and disappeared. Ari had the look of a man wondering if he should call the Psycho Squad.

"Are you serious about the calamari?" he said. "You know, I doubt if the creatures are still alive when they cut them up."

"Of course not, but they always say that the best defense is a good offense. I want a salad with that."

Ari opened his mouth, shut it again, and shrugged. "Whatever you'd like," he said eventually. "As long as you're eating, I shan't complain."

He ordered, the food arrived, and I managed to get some of the squid down. The pieces had been breaded and fried, so I could make myself think of them as onion rings. I'd started on the salad when another squid appeared, this one about four feet long, floating over the kitchen sink. I picked up a fried tentacle and chomped on it. The squid pulled its own tentacles back and retreated down the counter. I got up, strode over, and breathed the scent of cooked squid right into its ugly little face. It bubbled in terror—I heard it distinctly—and vanished.

"What in hell are you doing?" Ari looked up from his pasta dish.

"A magic ritual of squid banishment." I smiled sweetly at him and returned to my chair. "Showing my enemy its worst fear come true."

He rolled his eyes and shook his head, but no more squiddish apparitions appeared that evening, which allowed me to write my reports to the Agency in peace. I had a lot of material to send concerning the multiverse, various deviant levels, and of course the Venusian cephalopods themselves. I also tried several times to contact Bissop Keith, but no luck. I did pick up vague feeling the that he was distracted by something boring. I assumed that bissops, like bishops, had all kinds of official meetings to attend.

Although I finished and delivered the reports for the Agency that evening, I was too tired to write Y a more personal account of the problems still facing us in our hunt for the Peacock Angel cult. The squid image attack had drained enough Qi to make me go to bed early.

When we got up in the morning, I intended to write that final report, but my cell phone rang before we even left the bedroom. I'd just put on my engagement ring when Aunt Eileen called to invite Ari and me to a family lunch.

"It'll be part of the family, anyway," she told me, "Sean isn't coming, or your mother, and Jim's at work."

"Let me guess," I said. "Brian's at baseball practice."

"Yes, of course, and Sophie's off running with her friends."

"Friends" was as close as Aunt Eileen could get to saying "werewolf pack."

"At any rate," she continued, "Flann's gone to bring Maureen and the children over to my house. It's got something to do with that gate upstairs."

"We'll be there," I said. "By the way, I weighed myself this morning, and I've gained another pound."

"That's wonderful, dear! I'm so happy for you."

I probably put on another pound at the lunch she served, macaroni and cheese, salad, two kinds of pie for dessert. Every time I swallowed a mouthful, Ari and Aunt Eileen both smiled beatifically at me. It began to get on my nerves, but I did my best to ignore them. I noticed that Maureen ate very little, but out of nerves, not my kind of problem. She looked very businesslike that day, with her hair pulled back from her face and minimal makeup. She also wore a blue skirt suit with low heels—the very picture of a job interviewee.

With the meal over, we retreated to the family end of the living room. I snagged one of the comfortable armchairs, and Ari pulled up a wooden chair next to mine. Michael, bless him, lured Caitlin and Brennan upstairs to play computer games. Dad and Maureen exchanged a conspirator's smile and left for the hallway that led to the storage rooms—and the gate upstairs.

"I take it," Ari said to Aunt Eileen, "that Maureen's considering that housekeeping job."

"Oh, yes," Eileen said, "but of course, she hasn't been offered it yet. We'll have to see."

Aunt Eileen handed me a letter from my oldest brother, Dan, who was about to graduate from the Army's Officer Candidacy School. He made a few cryptic remarks about not being able to tell us his next step. I took that as meaning he'd followed my advice and applied for Army Intelligence or whatever it is that they call it. Although he's almost normal, he has enough of the family talent overlap for it to come in handy in difficult situations. He also mentioned that when he came home on leave, he'd be glad to help Ari "dispose of" Chuck Trasker or do the disposing himself. Maybe, he said, Ari could provide him with an alibi.

I had just decided to not show Ari the letter, lest he take Dan up on the idea, when I heard footsteps coming down the hall. Back already? I thought. A bad sign, if so, but Dad walked in, leading Beth by the hand. Behind them trotted the little green lizard-thing, her Chaos critter pet. Beth looked at me, grinned, and yelled, "Aunt Rose!" When I held out my arms, Beth pulled free of Dad's hand and raced across the living room to throw herself into the hug. I lifted her onto my lap, then handed Dan's letter back to the hovering Eileen.

"Donnie's a scaredy-cat," Beth announced. "I came down."

"Donnie's probably as normal as our Dan," Dad said. "Here's our O'Grady girl."

Beth turned sideways in my lap and snuggled into my arms. I realized that I'd made a few false assumptions when I'd met the Terra Six version of the Douglases. Would a doppelgänger of Donnie have been my child if I'd grown that lump of cells into a baby? Maybe, maybe not—in the genetic crapshoot across the multiverse we called family relations, there was no way of telling whom I'd have ended up with, maybe a girl like Beth, maybe someone entirely different but still recognizably part of my extended family. I glanced at Ari, who was watching the pair of us with intense eyes and a small smile.

"No," I said. "I know what you're thinking. No, nein, nyet, nope, uh-uh."

He wiped the expression away, not that I believed him. Everyone talks about maternal instincts. Well, there are paternal longings, too, even if our American culture does downgrade them. Ari, of course, came from a different culture. I'd seen it very clearly in that look.

"Aunt Maureen's going to come live with us," Beth announced. "And my new cousins are going to come, too. I know it."

"Good," I said, "then that's one thing settled."

"You believe me."

"Yep. I sure do."

"Would you like to meet Cattie and Bren, dear?" Aunt Eileen said. "I'm your new Great-aunt Eileen, by the way. They're upstairs playing a game."

Beth slid off my lap, took Eileen's hand, and trooped happily upstairs.

"Trusting child," Ari said.

"She knows us all already," I said. "Or maybe I should say, she recognizes us now that she's seen us." I glanced at my father for confirmation. "We're all connected somehow, aren't we, Dad?"

"Some of us are," Dad said. "I'm not sure how we are or why, mind, but I'm beginning to see it. And speaking of seeing to things, I've got to go back upstairs. The gate's a fair bit more stable than it was, but I'll just be keeping an eye on it."

Some twenty minutes later, Dad and Maureen returned. She looked thoughtful, a little frightened, but when I ran an SPP, I sensed that she was, above all, determined.

"Okay," she said. "I'm taking the job."

We variously clapped or cheered our approval. I made a mental note to write Dan immediately and tell him that he didn't need to risk his career by murdering Chuck Trasker, even though I had to agree that Chuck would be no loss to humanity.

Now that she'd made up her mind, Maureen moved fast. In a couple of days she and the kids had moved across to World Level Six. The Unpleasant Ex could prowl around Four all he wanted. He'd never find them.

I still had a long list of unsettled questions. For example, where was Ash Moore? And did she shelter under the Peacock Angel's wings? The biggest question, would the Agency allow me to go back to Six to try to find out, got itself answered the day after Maureen's move, when I had a much-needed trance session with Y. Eventually, after hearing my meager handful of facts and larger handful of speculations, he admitted that he would have to allow me to continue working with TWIXT.

"We're still hammering out the details of the formal liaison," Y told me. "Fortunately, I've been given some input into the process. It will allow me to protect my people here in DC."

"That's good to know," I said. "This business of the Peacock Angel really is much more an Agency problem than a TWIXT problem. They have to focus on narrow issues, like any police force does. We can take the wider view. They're lucky they've got someone like you they can rely on."

Y smiled as if to say, "Yes, I know." He actually said, "They're lucky they've got my entire team to rely on. I'll be having a conference shortly with the two Spares, Thirteen and Fourteen. They're on their way to DC. Once we have a plan of action, I'll contact you and give you a full report of the meeting."

"Great, and thank you! Huh, I wonder how clones travel together on our world level? The airline will want names for the tickets. As twins, I guess, Austin and Osman."

"Something like that, I assume." His trance-avatar radiated disinterest. "In the meantime, continue with your research."

We ended the session there.

That evening I stood in our bay window and watched the fog come streaming over the houses across the street. Ari walked up behind me and slipped his arms around my waist. I leaned into his warmth, his solid muscle and strength, and braced myself for the inevitable question.

"Why won't you even consider marrying me?" he said, right on schedule.

"Because one, I don't want to marry anyone, and two, you're a foreign national and a double agent, whereas I'm a citizen agent with loyalty to a single government."

That got him. He stayed silent for several minutes. I slithered free of his arms and turned around to watch him think things through.

"Oh," he said eventually. "I hadn't quite thought of it that way."

"Well, please do! And we agreed that we're not going to have children, married or not."

"True. I was just momentarily overcome, seeing you with Beth in your lap. It's genetic, I suppose. The sodding, pushy DNA and all that. Sorry. But it would be much too dangerous for the children to have parents in our line of work. They'd make such splendid hostages."

"Exactly. Ari, look, there's part of you that really wants kids and a normal life, isn't there?"

He shrugged, but his eyes narrowed slightly. He stepped back as if he expected me to slap him.

"Maybe," I continued, "I'm not the woman you want. If you left TWIXT and stayed with just plain old Interpol, some nice Israeli girl would love to give you a couple of babies."

"I can't deny I've thought about that. Unfortunately, it's impossible."

"Wouldn't TWIXT let you go?"

"It has nothing to do with TWIXT and everything to do with you. For God's sake, Nola!" He set his hands on his hips. "Haven't you ever believed me when I've told you I love you?"

My turn to think things through. "You know," I said eventually, "it's because of what's happened to me in the past. I guess I've been waiting for you to say it's over and leave me."

Ari took my left hand in his. "What's this?" He pointed to the engagement ring.

"Oh, okay, but—"

"There isn't any but about it. You're not getting rid of

me, whether we marry or not." He pulled me closer. "Do you want to get rid of me?"

"No! I love you. I just—"

He kissed me before I could finish the sentence. I relaxed into his embrace and kissed him again.

"I love you so much," I said. "But is that enough for you, knowing that I love you?"

"Of course," he said, and then he smiled his tiger's smile. "For now."

Agency Talents
and Acronyms

AH Audio Hallucination
ASTA Automatic survival threat awareness
CDEP Chaos diagnostic emergency procedure
CW Chaos wards
CDS Collective Data Stream
CEV Conscious evasion procedure
DEI Deliberately extruded images (visible only to psychics)
DW Dice walk
E Ensorcellment
FW Fast Walking
HC Heat conservation
IOI Image Objectification of Insight
LDRS Long distance remote sensing
MI Manifested indicators (of Chaos forces)
NPI Negative Psychic Input (aka bad omen)
PI Possibility Images
SAF Scanning the aura field
SM Search Mode
SM:P Search Mode: Personnel
SM:G Search Mode: General

SM:D Search Mode: Danger
SAWM Semi-automatic warning mechanism
SH Shield persona
SPP Subliminal psychological profile
WW World-Walking

Deviant Worlds

[The following passages are excerpted from a report Nola filed with the Agency on the contents of an entry-level exam book for TWIXT recruits. The story of how she obtained this material takes place in APOCALYPSE TO GO.]

The background material [in the cram book] covered the formation of deviant worlds and hinted at travel between them. Although the book supplied a lot of details, the basic principle was simplicity itself. Forget all those sci-fi stories about killing Hitler and changing history. Worlds split and deviated not because of human actions—or the actions of any other intelligent species—but by mathematically determined transformations inherent in the system of worlds. The multiverse turned out to be one huge fractal pattern, generating replicas and deviants of itself by its inherent nature.

The impetus or energy for this self-generation was still a mystery, according to the text. The astrophysicists on Spare14's level tended to believe that "quantum fluctuation" or "foam" lay behind the deviations. Although the process could be expressed by enormously complex mathematical formulae, the book showed none of those. I guess the authors figured that mathematical geniuses wouldn't want to join TWIXT. However, I can say that the transformations had a certain orientation in common with the evolutionary mathematics of Darcy Wentworth-Thompson, the Scots biologist on Terra Four.

A fractal pattern like the famous Mandelbrot Set only transforms along three axes: Vertical, Horizontal, and Time. In the multiverse, the transformations occur in Time and some unknown number of spatial dimensions. Like NumbersGrrl once told me, they shoot off in all directions. The process can generate splits at varying times in a level's existence. Thus two "cousin worlds" might be strikingly similar if the one had recently been generated from the other or, conversely, surprisingly different if the split lay in the distant past.

The book used an elaborate analogy to explain these principles. It postulated cars of the same brand and model parked one above the other in a multilevel car park. Although the cars were identical when they left the factory, different owners used them for different journeys. They let individual kinds of junk pile up in the trunks and glove compartments as well. In some cases an owner might even have painted a car in some eccentric way. The result would be a set of cars that had most things in common while displaying significantly distinct features. Gates between worlds would then be like elevators in the car park. No one could simply jump through the concrete floors that separated the nearly-identical cars. A person desiring to move from Car A to Car B had to walk up the spiral ramps or take the direct elevator from floor to floor. The analogy broke down at that point because in the multiverse there are no ramps, and the elevators do not stop at every floor.

With time, cousin worlds move too far apart to "continue to share information," as the cram book puts it. I took that as meaning they could no longer be reached one from the other. Therefore, a world-walker could find only recently separated and thus somewhat similar worlds. The information stopped there with a couple of cryptic notes. Recruits had to pass the exam and become sworn agents before they learned how to travel from world to world.

As I made clear in previous reports, we at the Agency already have additional information on this travel process. See my notes filed under tags "gates, orbs, overlap."

The number One is an arbitrary label and not any sort of starting point. Agent S14 had indicated that his world was chosen as One out of "normal human vanity." According to Agent JH, TWIXT scientists have found a tentative correlation between the numbers and certain factors. Worlds with an odd number contain populations who are widely aware of the existence of the multiverse. Those with even numbers do not, though some individuals may possess or postulate this knowledge. Knowledge that the multiverse exists seems in many cases to bring with it a knowledge that genetic psychic talents exist. Odd-numbered worlds are metaphorically labeled "left-handed," and the even, "right-handed."

Notes on worlds and color tags known to me follow.

Terra One—Spare14's home world, highly technologically advanced. The TWIXT headquarters are in London. Floriation point: 1919. Violet.

Terra Two—The most deviant level of all, at least as far as the solar system is concerned. An alternate wet Venus with a large single moon is the home to the psychic sapient cephalopods. A sapient race descended from leopards, the Maculates, dominate Earth. Agent S14 has hinted that the Mars of this level also contains some mystery. The floriation point must have occurred in the far distant past, but for some unknown reason, this level is part of the local cluster. Perhaps the mysterious quantum foam carried it back. Blue-violet.

Terra Three—Although the other planets in the solar system are much the same as in our world, Earth, which I called Interchange before I understood the numbering system, suffered enormous damage from a mysterious disaster in the early 1920s. Floriation point: 1919. Blue.

Terra Four—our world. TWIXT uses it as the chronological measuring stick for floriation points. Blue-green.

Terra Five—Flann O'Grady's home world, in many ways similiar to ours except for the fascist governments that dominate much of the planet, including North America. A much-reduced British Empire still exists on Earth. Floriation point: 1919. Green.

Terra Six—is linked to Four because it split off in the same floriation that produced Terra Three, i.e., floriation point is 1919, but the link between it and Interchange has been stressed to the breaking point by the defining disaster on Interchange. Some members of the World-Walkers Guild suspect human meddling may also be a factor. Yellow Green.

Terra Incognita (at the time of filing this report)—Somewhere is a deviant level where the Order-based Peacock Angel cult is the dominant religion in North America. I have spoken to a person known as Bissop Keith. I suspect he's the chief prelate in that level's San Francisco, but I cannot state this definitively at this time.

Other levels beyond these obviously exist. The O'Grady set contains sixteen orbs. How many of those lead to a deviant level that we can reach, I do not know at this time.

Katharine Kerr
The Nola O'Grady Novels

"Breakneck plotting, punning, and romance make for a mostly fast, fun read."　　—*Publishers Weekly*

"This is an entertaining investigative urban fantasy that sub-genre readers will enjoy...fans will enjoy the streets of San Francisco as seen through an otherworldly lens."
　　　　　　　　　　　　—*Midwest Book Review*

LICENSE TO ENSORCELL
978-0-7564-0656-1

WATER TO BURN
978-0-7564-0691-2

APOCALYPSE TO GO
978-0-7564-0709-4

LOVE ON THE RUN
978-0-7564-0762-9

To Order Call: 1-800-788-6262
www.dawbooks.com

DAW 180

Diana Rowland

The Kara Gillian Novels

"Rowland's hot streak continues as she gives her fans another big helping of urban fantasy goodness! The plot twists are plentiful and the action is hard-edged. Another great entry in this compelling series." —*RT Book Review*

"This is an excellent police procedural urban fantasy that like its two previous arcane forensic investigations stars a terrific lead protagonist... Kara is fabulous as the focus of the case and of relationships with the Fed and with the demon as the Bayou heats up with another magical mystery tour that will take readers away from the mundane to the enjoyable world of Diana Rowland."
—*Midwest Book Reviews*

Secrets of the Demon
978-0-7564-0652-3

Sins of the Demon
978-0-7564-0705-6

To Order Call: 1-800-788-6262
www.dawbooks.com

DAW 176

Laura Resnick

The Esther Diamond Novels

"Resnick introduces a colorful cast of gangsters and their associates as she spins a witty, fast-paced mystery around her convincingly self-absorbed chorus-girl heroine. Sexy interludes raise the tension...in a well-crafted, rollicking mystery." —*Publishers Weekly*

"Esther Diamond is the Stephanie Plum of urban fantasy! Unplug the phone and settle down for a fast and funny read!" —Mary Jo Putney

DISAPPEARING NIGHTLY
978-0-7564-0766-7

DOPPELGANGSTER
978-0-7564-0595-3

UNSYMPATHETIC MAGIC
978-0-7564-0635-6

VAMPARAZZI
978-0-7564-0687-5

To Order Call: 1-800-788-6262
www.dawbooks.com

Tanya Huff

"The Gales are an amazing family, the aunts will
strike fear into your heart, and the characters Allie
meets are both charming and terrifying."
—#1 *New York Times* bestselling author
Charlaine Harris

The Enchantment Emporium

Alysha Gale is a member of a family capable of changing
the world with the charms they cast. She is happy to escape
to Calgary when when she inherits her grandmother's junk
shop, but when Alysha learns just how much trouble is
brewing, even calling in the family to help may not be
enough to save the day.

978-0-7564-0605-9

The Wild Ways

Charlotte Gale is a Wild Power who allies herself with a
family of Selkies in a fight against offshore oil drilling. The
oil company has hired another of the Gale family's Wild
Powers, the fearsome Auntie Catherine, to steal the Selkies'
sealskins. To defeat her, Charlotte will have to learn what
born to be Wild really means in the Gale family...

978-0-7564-0686-8

To Order Call: 1-800-788-6262
www.dawbooks.com

DAW 200